Rules of the Road

K. Aten

Yellow Rose Books
by Regal Crest

ISBN 978-1-61929-366-3

First Edition 2018

9 8 7 6 5 4 3 2 1

Cover design by AcornGraphics

Published by:

Regal Crest Enterprises

Find us on the World Wide Web at
http://www.regalcrest.biz

Published in the United States of America

Acknowledgments

As always, I would like to thank Regal Crest Enterprises for giving me this chance to live out my dream as a published author. Cathy and Patty are saints with their patience and knowledge when it comes to all things publishing and a successful manuscript. I would also like to thank my editor, Mary, because of her humor and insight when it comes to churning out a good novel. I would like to thank my good friend and beta reader, Ted. You push me, you correct me, and you prop me up when I need it. This was our first project together and we quickly discovered that we work very well as a team. Thanks for the hours you've put in on this labor of love of mine. Lastly, I want to thank someone who has given me information and true stories about the dental industry. Kelsey Slammer, you are one in a million!

Note: Most of the people, places, and events are based on reality. But, as a writer often does, I've twisted or changed nearly all to suit my needs. I like to think of it as the cafeteria plan of writing. If you see yourself in this book, or see me, I apologize. Most of all, a lifetime of thanks to my closest friends who stayed with me through the journey. You know who you are.

This book is dedicated to the pets in our lives, even the naughty ones. Because without them the world would be just that much colder, and more than a little lonely.

Chapter One

KELSEY WAS IN the left lane when she drove by the poor deer that had sacrificed his life to some sleep-deprived trucker. Sure as anything, nothing exploded living flesh quite like the impact of a semi. It was 6:25 a.m. as she approached what everyone referred to as the "nexus of the universe." Brake lights lit up across all three lanes ahead of her and she glanced desperately behind, looking for a way back into the center lane. Her exit was approaching and she got caught off guard by the roadkill.

"*Verkehr verlangsamen voraus.*"

The voice was in German and she had no idea what the actual words meant, but the way she slowed to a stop in her lane explained it pretty well. She glanced at the phone hanging from the holder suction-cupped to her front window. Her side of the highway was colored red and the traffic jam indicator had popped up. "Sonofa—" She never finished the statement because a police car went flying by her left side in the margin between her lane and the concrete divider. Her car rocked back and forth with its passing and she jumped in her seat. "Shit!" All she could do was put her blinker on and pray someone would let her into the next lane so she could make her exit. She crossed her fingers, hoping she wouldn't be late for work. Then she practically crossed her legs and regretted finishing the entire bottle of water during her drive. It was going to be a long day and she really had to remember to change the voice back to English. Or learn German. She shrugged at her own thoughts and cranked up the music to block the sound of a blaring horn. The car she was driving next to didn't appreciate being cut off in traffic.

THE ICONIC LYRICS to David Bowie's "Major Tom" filled the car with nostalgic sound. Its current rendition was a cover version by Shiny Toy Guns and poor Carah Faye Charnow's voice was drown out by a harshly done amateur. Jamie's single woman car karaoke abruptly cut off with the chime of her driving app. She flicked her glance right to where her cell phone was clipped to the dashboard within easy sight. Jamie hoped it wasn't a delay of some sort because it was 6:40 a.m. and she was making good time for once.

"Obstacle on road ahead."

The male British voice that came across her sound system via Bluetooth seemed mild enough but Jamie thought he sounded a bit pretentious and snarky. She nicknamed him Nigel months before when she first started using the app. Following her own rules, she was in the middle lane of the three available and the highway was busy with morning commuters heading off to their dream jobs. Or not. She knew the "obstacle" was fast approaching but the app didn't give details like lane location. It was one of the few limiting factors in an admitted lifesaver to her morning drive. She turned down the radio to concentrate better when sudden brake lights flashed ahead, of course in her own lane. She slowed quickly but was unable to switch lanes. When she came upon the animal remains her face scrunched up in disgust. "Oh. OOO-HHHH! Is that a deer? Oh my God, that is so disgusting." She maneuvered through the minefield of exploded ungulate and tried to keep her coffee down. Once she was safely through the mess, Jamie turned up the music again and resumed her solo serenade with a new tune. Tegan and Sarah sang the hard hitting song, "Like O, Like H" and Jamie rocked out with them.

DESPITE HER WORRIES, Kelsey was neither late to work, nor did she wet herself. Dr. Davies looked up as she hustled in the back door of the dentist's office. "Spaghetti highway traffic hell?"

She nodded at his nonsensical word soup. "That and a Bambi bomb."

Her boss nodded his head knowingly and wrinkled his nose in disgust. "Eww. And speaking of eww, Mr. Sorenson is our first appointment."

Kelsey's eyes widened at the news. Frank Sorenson was a big mountain of a man from somewhere very rural. His one and only previous visit was three weeks prior and he had come in needing a crown. While Kelsey herself wasn't the dental assistant for Dr. Davies that day, the stories were still circulating about the guy who wasn't real big on oral hygiene, or any hygiene really. He also smelled strongly of cigarette smoke and kitty litter. No one was sure why because he didn't exactly look like a cat owner. "Doesn't June—"

Her boss shook his head and grimaced. "Sorry, June called and said she had car trouble this morning."

Kelsey narrowed her eyes. "She looked at the appointment

book before she left last night, didn't she?"

David Davies continued leafing through his cooking magazine and scratched at the graying brown hair near his temple. The diminutive man didn't meet her eyes as he answered. "I believe so, yes. Sorry."

She wanted to be angry but didn't really blame June. Had she herself remembered to look at the appointment book, she may have called in with car trouble as well. Kelsey shrugged and put her lunch in the fridge of the break room. "Oh well, I'm sure he wasn't that bad. June and the others exaggerate everything." As she walked out of the room she missed seeing her boss shudder and cross his chest in a prayer.

Kelsey had the forethought to spray some disinfectant into her mask before prepping Mr. Sorenson for the doctor. Dr. Davies had to do two fillings on the man's top teeth before fitting the crown on the bottom molar and she didn't want to gag during such a lengthy appointment. Something caught her eye as she was holding the small pad with composite on it. Seemingly out of nowhere, there was an ant crawling across the surface. The patient's eyes were closed and she discretely looked up and around them to see where the bug had come from but found nothing. Not wanting to cause a scene, she removed the top sheet to give him some fresh composite and stayed quiet. Other than that, the fillings were routine, as was fitting the crown. After he left, they had a half hour before the next appointment. She turned to her boss. "Did you see that ant? I was wondering where it came from."

David Davies paled at the recent memory and nodded. "I saw it, and all the rest of them."

Kelsey was cleaning the station and looked up at him in surprise. "What? Where?"

"You probably couldn't see them from where you were sitting but his beard was crawling with ants."

She blinked and looked back at him in shock. "Oh my God."

He nodded. "Oh my God, indeed."

The thought came to them both at the same time and they frantically began brushing at their clothes to make sure none had gotten on them. It was in that moment that the other dental assistant, June, walked in.

"Hey, what's going on?"

If looks could kill, Kelsey would have been up on murder charges as soon as her gaze swung to the older woman. "From this day forward, every spider I find in this office is going into your purse." She pushed through the doorway in search of her morning cocoa fix.

June looked at their boss, clearly shaken. "She's kidding, right?"

Satisfied that he did not have any little hitchhikers on his lab coat, David straightened. "Probably not." And with those ominous words, he left to get some strong coffee for himself.

JAMIE ARRIVED AT work with a little time to spare before her shift. She decided to run out to the factory floor and check on the new production line she had been setting up over the previous week. As the Production Engineer for the department, it was her job to design and implement new assembly lines and handle all the equipment orders and placement. Maintenance was supposed to install a new tester on third shift and she wanted to check on it before the day crew came in and things got busy. Before moving into the engineering role and switching to day shift, she had previously been the manager over the third shift crew. They were mostly a rowdy younger bunch and had a distinctly warped sense of humor. "Hey Jamie, are you coming back to us?" One of the end-of-line inspectors called out to her as she put her safety glasses on and left the official foot traffic aisle.

The tall and lanky blonde shook her head and smiled good-naturedly. "I've finally worked my way into an engineer position. Why would I want to go back to that thankless manager job over you lot? Besides, you've got Joe now!" Another person working on the line rolled his eyes at her words. She looked over at the new third shift manager. "So how's it going, Joe? They really are thankless, you know."

The fairly young supervisor made a face. "I figured that out pretty fast. But luckily I can handle all jobs small or large!"

"That's what she said!"

The entire crew of the line that Joe stood near cracked up laughing, and Jamie hid a smile behind a fake cough. "Some things never change I see." Joe either didn't hear the words or was completely clueless about the long running joke. She watched as he randomly picked up a duster and stood behind a large exhaust fan to dust it off. The wind blew an inconvenient amount of fuzzies and debris away from the line and into his face. "Uh, hey Joe, wouldn't it be easier to stand off to the side and clean that?"

He looked up at her and replied with an affable grin. "Nope.

I like it when it gets on my face, that's how I know I'm doing a good job!" Jamie blinked at him in response. He stared back, clueless. The line clearly didn't hear him and she thought it best to simply let the comment go.

"Hey Jamie, can you come check scrap for me while Joe is busy blowing, um, off the fan. We're about to close a box."

The box packer's pause told Jamie that she had indeed heard Joe's questionable statement, but maybe she just didn't want to pick on her new boss too soon. After all, it had only been a month since he took over their shift. "Sure, I'll be right down." Jamie turned to grin at Joe. "I'm going to go do your job now, man. Just so you know."

He raised an eyebrow at her and moved on to another fan. She tried not to snicker at the large gray fuzzy that was stuck to that raised brow. "Maybe Maria can see that I'm too important to be bothered so she's just calling down the cast-off."

The engineer laughed. "Or maybe she's calling on the professional because she wants the job done right. Later, newb!" Jamie made her way down the assembly line to sort through the bin of suspect scrap for the box packer. If there were any that were legitimately good, she would sign her initials to the back for the line operator to pack, and the rest would be sent for tear-down and disassembly. Noting that two were marked for bad circuit boards, she walked them halfway down the line to the appropriate station. You could only remove circuit boards if you were wearing a grounding strap. It was something that looked like a metal watchband connected via wire to the station. There was no one standing there and she was on the backside of the line so Jamie called out to anyone in the vicinity. "Hey, who has a strap on?" The words left her mouth before she could call them back and she immediately fumbled in an attempt to clarify her statement. "Uh, a grounding strap. Who is wearing a grounding strap, um, thingy?" She reached around to set the parts on the empty station as one of the more naïve younger guys walked up.

"That would be me. Sorry, Jamie. I ran to get a drink. Give me a second and I'll have those switched for you and sent back down for testing."

Ears red, she walked to the back of the box packing station. She muttered obscenities under her breath and hoped no one else heard her ill-fated words. When she looked up to meet Maria's gaze her heart sank. She pointed her finger at the smirking woman. "You didn't hear that. Those words never left my mouth!" It probably wouldn't have been half as funny if she were not publicly out at work. But everyone knew she was gay.

Maria pointed back at her. "*Dios mío!* That is the funniest shit you've ever said!"

Jamie grimaced, still blushing bright red as she finished signing the last few suspect parts. "Funnier than Joe's comment about the fan?"

The packer snorted. "No, that was good too."

The new engineer sighed. "Nice. Now that I've humiliated myself in front of my old crew, I'm going to go check on my new line. *Ciao, chica.*" Maria just grinned.

With so much to do in her new role, the day moved pretty fast. Before Jamie knew it the end of her shift had arrived. Per her normal routine, she clamped her phone into the holder while the Bluetooth connected to her car. She started the Drīv app and hit the button on her dash screen that would also bring up her music app. So while she had the streaming music station on the six inch touch screen of her car, her phone continuously displayed the navigation and traffic map.

Jamie loved her car, a pretty blue turbo that perfectly suited her lead foot. But her love of speed didn't mean she was a crazy driver. She actually drove very defensively and cursed out half the people she shared the highway with. And she had rules. Her friends had called her anal- retentive many times with the way she navigated her personal life by a very specific set of rules and personal standards. But it wasn't just her personal life, it carried over to her driving as well. Driving from the same place, to the same place for years had given her a pretty good handle on the route and all its quirks and troubles. The Drīv app just made it a lot easier.

As soon as she merged onto the highway and made her way into the center lane, she relaxed and checked the traffic app. The lines of the highway on both sides were rapidly changing from orange to red as the traffic slowed up for rush hour. Her gaze flicked to the left, taking note of the faster moving traffic and the too-good-to-be-true amount of space that she could merge into. She did not move though. She plodded along behind a pickup truck that belched smoke every time the driver gave it a spurt of gas. There were rules after all. Rule number one was to stay in the center lane whenever you approached a busy exit, unless you were actually exiting. More often than not the faster left hand lane would come to a complete stop for more than a few minutes right where the on-ramp began. She had no idea why, but she accepted it as law and stayed in the center lane until she passed the more urban section of highway.

Rule number two was to immediately get into the left lane as soon as she got past the slow down and merge section, then stay in the left lane until approaching another exit. She turned up the music as she watched the left lane come to a stop. She didn't make up the rules, she just followed them. Well, she did make up the rules actually, but that didn't make them less true. A chime sounded as all lanes slowed to a crawl and the traffic jam indicator popped up on her phone.

"Traffic slow-down ahead" Nigel was no captain, he was the king of obvious.

Jamie sighed and started counting colors aloud. "Black, gray, gray, tan, orange, white, tan, silver, navy, silver, and boom! Eighty percent!" She slapped her steering wheel to emphasize her statement. Another rule, or maybe just an observation, was that eighty percent of the vehicles she saw on the highway every day were black, white, gray, silver, or tan. She was convinced it was a sign of some sort of bland vehicular apocalypse. The guy next to her slowly swerved into her lane and she moved right to hug the opposite line. His eyes were staring intently at his crotch. Assuming he wasn't getting his very first erection, she laid on the horn to bring his gaze up off his cell phone. "Stupid ass!" Road rage was a very real and understandable thing.

"Object on road ahead."

Jamie gently tapped her brakes to give herself more space from the car in front of her. She scanned the highway ahead to look for the pothole that had popped up on the Drīv app. Seeing that the tire-killer was safely in the far lane and not in her own she okayed the popup on the screen. Not for the first time she wished there was some way she could let other drivers know the location of such hazards. Again, the app was limited in that it just warned of a problem, but it could not tell which of the multiple lanes the hazard obstructed. All of a sudden Jamie heard the lyrics to one of her favorite songs and cranked up the volume. "Kill Kill Kill" by The Pierces had come on and she excitedly sang along to the angry lyrics. Her favorite part was the little cat meow in the second half of the song during the hook. It served no purpose, and really didn't make any sense lyrically, but she loved it and always turned the radio up all the way just before that part in the song. Evening karaoke was in full swing. She made it home and into her designated parking spot in the garage at 4:36 p.m. exactly and she followed the same routine as always when entering her condo. The jacket was hung on a coat hook, as well as her messenger bag. Her lunch cooler was emptied and place on the shelf above the sink. It was Friday and she had plans. She was just throwing together something quick for dinner when her phone beeped and she glanced at the screen where it sat on the counter.

```
wut r you doin 2nite, plans?
```

She read the text message and seriously thought about how to answer the question. Kim was cute and hot in bed, but she was also about twelve years her junior and not the brightest "buddy" she'd had. Jamie wasn't really up for explaining the meaning of any long words that came up during her and Burke's inevitable deep conversation in the wee hours of the morning. She quickly typed back a response.

```
Burke is coming up for the weekend, hanging at Cul-
ture.
```

```
k, may b next time.
```

Culture was one of the gay clubs in St. Seren, the famously liberal city that she lived in. Robby Burke was her best friend and he lived about an hour south, so when he'd come up to club with her he'd just stay the weekend on her futon in her spare room. They had a pretty good system in place for when they went to the club. Burke would buy drinks if Jamie made omelets for breakfast in the morning. And neither one had to drive, instead they'd stumble home together from the bar that was only six blocks from her condo complex. Burke didn't mind the girls she brought home and she didn't say anything about his extreme OCD quirks. Like lining up everything in the medicine cabinet by size and color of bottle, all labels facing forward. Okay, so maybe she did say something that time because it was a little creepy to organize someone else's medicine cabinet. But otherwise they were best friends.

They were only acquaintances before Jamie broke up with her crazy ex-girlfriend years before. Maybe it was because Burke gave her a solidity and an understanding friend when her "perfect" relationship ended. She gave him something that not a lot of trans men and women have, complete and utter acceptance. But over the handful of years they had become "bros" of a sort. Best buds.

Later that night, Jamie was sitting on one of the low leather couches upstairs, chatting with a girl named Tori. Burke had taken over the pool table about twenty feet away from them. Tori abruptly drained her beer and playfully climbed into Jamie's lap. She traced the collar on the engineer's shirt and leaned close enough to be heard over the thump of the house music. "So, do you live nearby? Wanna hang out after the bar closes?" The way she leaned down pressed her breasts firmly against Jamie's chest. While Jamie didn't have much in the way of cup size, her nipples hardened painfully when Tori gave a little shimmy against her.

Jamie took a slow sip of her own beer to appear calm and collected, though in reality her heart was racing. "My friend Burke is staying with me for the weekend, but you're welcome to come over. I usually make us omelets and we put on some music. The walls of my condo are thick so my neighbors never complain." The woman in her lap smiled at her. Tori's pixie cut red hair appeared darker in the low light of the second floor, and Jamie appreciated a woman with green eyes and a sweet little dimple. "I also have more beer at my place. And if you decide that you absolutely shouldn't drive afterwards, you can always share my bed with me. I'm positive I have something that you can wear."

A dark red brow rose with the innuendo in Jamie's voice. "Oh? And just what would I be wearing?"

Jamie had played the game a lot since she split with her ex. She knew what was expected of her, she knew the things to say. She had rules, and she made sure that any "friends" understood those rules thoroughly before letting nature take its course. She lowered her voice just slightly and looked the younger woman straight in the eyes. "Me, of course. As long as you're just looking for a little fun tonight. I have a strict no dating rule. I'm kind of an asshole about it and I won't change my mind."

Tori shrugged. "I'd heard that about you already and I don't have a problem with it. You're hot and you're funny, and tonight I'm free."

Jamie was taken aback for a second, not liking the fact that her personal life was fodder for the gossip mill. "Who told you that?"

"Jenn. But don't worry, stud, she's like one of my closest friends. We tell each other everything." Suddenly feeling uncomfortable, the woman on the bottom squirmed a bit remembering Jenn. The redhead smirked at her. "And yes, she told me how you broke her heart."

"Hey, it wasn't like that! I told her from the start that things were only going to be casual. She tried to change the rules."

Tori laughed and shoved the taller woman back down with an easy hand to the chest. "Hey, calm down. She already told me that it was her own fault. She said that she fell for you despite your warnings. You're still friends, right? Coffee buddies or something?" Jamie nodded. "Then we're all good. I told her I would fuck you if I could ever get you alone, and here we are."

And there it was. At the mere mention of fucking, Jamie was ready to leave the bar. She quickly drained her beer and checked her watch. It was twenty minutes to lights up. She glanced at Burke and saw that her friend was just putting up the pool stick for the night. Jamie lightly tapped Tori's thigh indicating she should move off her lap, then called out across the second floor. "Hey Burke, dude we're ready to go. Are you?

He nodded and drained his own beer before setting it on the bar nearby. "Yeah, man. Is your friend coming back with us?"

Jamie looked at Tori. "How much have you had to drink?"

The redhead looked curiously back at her. "Two beers tonight, why?"

The engineer grinned. "She's driving us back to the condo and I'll make omelets and tater tots!"

Tori laughed and stood, then took Jamie's hand and pulled her up as well. "Shouldn't you be feeding me breakfast tomorrow morning, not tonight?"

Jamie leaned in and brought her lips close enough to Tori's ear to kiss the smaller woman's lobe. "I'm thorough. I'll feed you coming and going."

Before she could back away again Tori grabbed her by the short blonde hair and pulled her down into a hot kiss. Burke just shook his head and started for the stairs, glad he brought the headphones he could sleep in.

The next morning Jamie woke to the sound of music jangling from a nearby cell phone. She looked at her own sitting quietly on the wireless charger and figured it must be Tori's. She nudged the comatose woman. "Hey, your phone is ringing."

The redhead had her back to Jamie and the taller woman finally got a glimpse of her tattoo in the daylight. It was a giant Gemini symbol. Tori grunted. "Ungh! It'll stop soon." Just as predicted the phone stopped ringing but started again mere seconds later.

"Uh, yeah, I think someone really wants to talk to you. I'll just go grab it." Jamie hopped out of the bed completely nude to retrieve the phone that was in Tori's back pocket.

Tori blearily opened her eyes. "It's not a big deal, its either Jenn or John."

Without looking at the screen she handed it over to the still prone body and started to get dressed. Hoody and boxers were her normal Saturday morning attire. A perfect outfit for cooking breakfast. "Who's John?"

"That's my fiancé."

Jamie looked up from stuffing her feet into fuzzy gray elephant slippers. "Excuse me?"

Tori waved a casual hand at her. "Oh, it's fine! He knows I'm bi and said as long as I don't sleep with other guys, he's cool with an open relationship. We have an arrangement."

The taller woman just stared at her overnight guest. She blinked slowly and tried to make sense of the words. She wasn't happy that she took home someone who was in a relationship, because she had rules. Even understanding the circumstances as Tori explained them, she still wasn't happy. Finally she made the decision to simply shrug it off and let it go. Tori was definitely a one and done. She didn't say anything more because the younger woman started talking on the phone. Instead she went to start breakfast like a good host. When she walked out of her room and down the stairs she found Burke reclining on the couch, watching an episode of Grey's on his laptop. As soon as he saw her he paused it and popped out his ear buds. Burke usually got up early so he almost always watched something on his computer to avoid waking her with the sound of the TV. "Where's Tabby?"

"Tori."

"Where's Tori?"

Jamie shuffled her way to the kitchen to start coffee. "She's talking to her fiancé on the phone."

Burke stood up from the couch and was startled for a second. "Her *what*?"

"Fiancé." She walked into the kitchen and Burke followed.

"Dude!"

Jamie nodded. "Yes, he's a dude."

Her best friend waved his hand through the air. "No, dude! Seriously? What the fuck?"

The engineer stared into her friend's eyes and he stared back, then they both cracked up laughing. "I know, right?"

Tori suddenly popped her head around the corner of the stairs, holding the cell phone to her chest. "Do you mind if John comes over to have breakfast with us?" The other two in the kitchen just stared at her in response. "What? He's bi too so he's like cool with the whole gay and trans thing." The engaged red-head waved her hand around to encompass both Jamie and Burke in her statement of her fiancé's acceptance.

Another slow blink and finally Jamie sighed then shrugged. "Sure, why not? Invite him over, the more the merrier!"

As soon as Tori left the kitchen again Burke leaned toward his absolutely best friend in the entire world. "Dude!"

Jamie nodded and continued measuring coffee into the basket. "Yeah, I know. I'm stopping at the clinic tomorrow to get tested." You could never be too careful and, she had rules. After that, not another word was said about it. Geminis were insane.

AS KELSEY DROVE home she couldn't help but notice the little nerd car icon ahead of her on the highway. She had been using the Drīv app for nearly a year and loved a lot of the little details. She had a little rainbow car icon that other drivers could see on the map if they had that feature turned on. Kelsey left hers on because the icons were cute.

"*Hindernis voraus auf der Straße.*"

"Oh for the love of Pete!" She realized too late that she had forgotten to change the language back to something she could understand. She could see on the map there was an obstacle ahead but luckily the large pothole wasn't in her lane. There was a car with a flat not much farther down the road that had clearly fallen victim to its concrete maw. She gave a quick swipe from left to right on her screen. "Pothole, far left lane. Car with flat just ahead." She noticed at lunch that her app had updated and was delighted to see a new voice pin feature that let you record your own description fairly hands-free. It was much better than playing the cup game across three lanes of traffic, trying to guess where the obstacle was on the road.

At 4:50 p.m. Kelsey pulled into the apartment complex where she had being living for the past few months. She originally lived in the opposite direction from work but she hated the area and she had always wanted to live in St. Seren, which was a notoriously liberal city. They had a thriving music and art scene, as well as a large LGBTQ community. Not that she could give any sort of testimonial on it. She didn't know a lot of people in town and had yet to check out any of the bars since the move.

After trudging the three floors to her apartment she opened the door and found herself immediately accosted by two black and white tuxedo cats. Brothers, they were adopted from a rescue program near her dentist's office. "Hello Pierre, hello Newman. I see you haven't starved yet but you're in danger of doing so any second." She tossed her wallet on the small table by the door and dropped the keys into the dish right next to it. Once her shoes were swapped out for fuzzy socks she kept by the door, her evening had begun. "Hello my handsome boys! What should we have for dinner tonight, hmm?" The handsome boys in question meowed and twined around her legs, desperate for their small portions of canned food. "Salmon *pâté*?"

"Mrow!"

"Oh, good choice!" She scooped a third of the can into a cat dish then popped a lid on the remainder and set the can back in the fridge. The cats immediately began to gorge themselves on the wet food. Kelsey glanced from them to the full dish of dry food, then back to the fat tomcats. "You two are idiots." She made her way to the bathroom and checked herself in the full-length mirror. She stared at her image for a minute, taking in all that she was and wasn't. Her mid-length auburn hair was French braided to stay out of her way during working hours. She wore mint green scrubs that featured little tiny teeth and toothbrushes all over the pants and the top. Her eyes were a strange dark green that she inherited from her Irish mother. Her skin color and darker hair was from her dad's Hispanic side. It was a weird combination that more than one person had commented on. Beyond that, the thing that got noticed most was her curves. She had the hips and she had the tatas, and her waist came in just right between. Since her mom was a skinny little thing she assumed the curves came from the Ramirez side as well. There were many times she wished that she was a skinny girl too but her mama had always raised her to be grateful for what she had. Kelsey made a face in the mirror. Following her mama's advice wasn't the problem. She wanted someone else to be grateful for what she had.

She sighed at her own neediness and left the room. The cats were back underfoot, as if to thank her for a meal well-served. "What should we do with ourselves boys?" Newman stayed underfoot while Pierre jumped onto the kitchen counter and knocked off one of the takeout menus. When Kelsey bent down to pick it up a smile lit her face. "Good boy, Pierre! Chinese food it is! Then tonight is going to be Netflix and chill, the singles edition. Suddenly the brunette thought about the state of her nightstand. Her gaze lazily took in the stocky black and white tuxedo cats. "Do you think they'd bring me batteries with my Pad Thai?" Newman meowed. "No? You're probably right. Of course, they'd probably bring me some sort of drugs if they knew I was asking advice from my cats." Pierre sneezed and Kelsey went to check the drawer of her nightstand for batteries.

Chapter Two

HALSEY BELTED OUT the lyrics to "Gasoline" and Jamie sang along to the music while she maneuvered Monday morning's highway hell. Occasionally she would stop the serenade to berate her fellow drivers. "What the fuck, dude? Did you forget how to drive over the weekend?" She slammed on her brakes when a minivan sporting a "Jesus Saves" bumper sticker cut in front of her with no blinker. "You're making Jesus' job harder lady, stop driving like you're on your way to rapture!" She started singing again only to be interrupted by the chime of her Drīv app.

"Pothole center lane."

Jamie startled at the unfamiliar voice that came over her sound system. She reached up and slapped her dash then brought her hand back down to her lap, accidentally brushing the screen of the phone. "Holy shit, Nigel! This is what I've been talking about! Now why couldn't you tell me that, hmm? Because you're a pretentious summabitch and you don't know how to give specific instructions, that's why. The app must have updated, nice!" She glanced at the screen just as a popup box disappeared and saw a little rainbow car ahead of her on the road map, then put on her blinker and switched out of the center lane. She was coming up to a busy exit but sometimes rules had to be broken. Jamie was surprised when her app chimed again.

"Excuse me? Who is Nigel?"

The engineer had just taken a sip from her travel mug and nearly choked when someone answered her diatribe against Nigel. "Okay, now that's weird." With only half her mind on the road, she tried to figure out what she had done to answer her fellow driver. "I didn't do anything, just slapped my dash. Could it be noise activated?" She talked her way through the riddle the same way she would any problem. She saw that the rainbow car was flashing on her screen because it was the one that dropped the voice pin, so she tapped it. Nothing happened so she kept tapping the icon while the little car was still flashing and something that looked like a voice recorder popped up. "Oh! Uh, hey, sorry about that. I didn't know that the app could let us record messages and I was just talking to Nigel." She paused for a few seconds and the popup disappeared.

Kelsey snorted in her own car, ten miles ahead. "Who the hell is Nigel?" She did not record that though because it could have been considered rude. Instead she swiped down on the screen and responded, thoroughly loving the new feature. "Who is Nigel? Is he your carpool buddy?"

Loving the new app feature as well, Jamie listened to the message after the chime. She reached up to turn down the heat then brought her hand down to the gearshift, past the cell in its cradle as she thought about how to answer. "Great, James! Now complete strangers can see the crazy peeking out. She sounds cute though, I wonder if she's cute." She tried tapping the screen to respond but nothing happened. Her attention was pulled back to the road when all three lanes slowed to a standstill near the nexus of the universe, just like normal. The nexus wasn't really the center of the universe, but it was the spot where five different expressways converged and or branched off. The traffic jam indicator popped up.

"Traffic slow down ahead"

Before she could think about responding to the little rainbow car, the app chimed again.

"Yes, I'm cute. And you apparently are crazy. You never told me who Nigel was though."

"Oh, goddamnit!" Jamie swore and felt the tips of her ears start to burn. Since traffic still wasn't moving she started touching the screen in a variety of ways. Eventually she discovered the key to responding by down-swiping the screen. "Hot damn! Oh shit, er, I mean, sorry. I've been responding to the app on accident because I didn't know how it worked." She stopped speaking for a few seconds and the voice record box disappeared.

"I see. But you still didn't answer my question."

Jamie thought the woman on the other end sounded like she was holding back a laugh. She did sound cute thought, like she smiled a lot. Those were Jamie's favorite kind of people. Finally understanding the response mechanism, she swiped again. "Again, sorry for my insanity. Nigel is the nickname I gave to my app because I picked a British voice and he's kind of a dick."

"No problem. At least you can understand yours. Mine is in German."

The engineer glanced at her phone with surprise and responded. "Hey that's cool. So you speak German, huh?"

"Not one bit." Jamie laughed out loud at the other driver's response and thought maybe the other woman was crazy too. She didn't get a chance to respond though because the rainbow car sent another voice message. "Hey, sorry to run but I'm at work. Maybe we can chat again on the way home. I think you're ahead of me then. Little nerd car, right?"

Jamie nodded like an idiot then grimaced when she realized no one could see her. "Yeah, I think I am. Talk to you then, rainbow car!"

"Definitely!"

As Jamie got off on her exit she couldn't stop thinking about her morning commute. "That was fun!" For the first time in a long time she was smiling as she walked into work.

Kelsey rushed through the back door and quickly hung up her jacket, stuffing her wallet into the large pocket. Then she shoved her lunch bag in the mini fridge. Sensing a disturbance in the force, her boss spun around in his chair and set the magazine down. "You're cutting it kind of close this morning aren't you, Kelsey?"

Kelsey ran a hand through her hair then started braiding the partially damp strands. "Sorry, doc. I was finishing up a conversation in the parking lot."

Salt and pepper colored eyebrows went up. "You were talking to someone before 8 a.m. on a weekday?" Kelsey's cheeks pinked thinking about the funny nerd car driver. Seeing the blush, Dr. Davies dug for the root of that blush. "Oh ho, what is this? Did you finally meet someone in that big city you moved to? What's her name?"

Not for the first time was Kelsey glad she had such a kind and accepting boss. Of course, he was a lot like a doting aunt but he meant well. "No, you nosey nanny! The new driving app updated and it lets you drop voice pins instead of just the preselected buttons. And I found out today that you can send a personal response to someone's pin. Well, my new driving friend did." She laughed remembering the flustered ranting of the other woman's first message. "Once we both figured it out we chatted back and forth during my drive. We must live fairly close to each other because while I'm ahead of her on my drive to work, she's ahead of me on my drive home."

He nodded his head sagely. "Ah, I see." He shook his head in wonder. "What will they come up with next?"

Kelsey shrugged. "I don't know, doc." She glanced at the clock and sighed. "Okay, I'm off to prep for Mrs. Barnes's filling. See you in a few!"

David watched his assistant walk out of the breakroom with a spring to her step. Kelsey had been working for him for about eight years and he knew all the signs when her interest was piqued. The poor girl wore her heart on her sleeve and lost it more often than not. Perhaps things would be different with such an unusual first meeting with someone. He sincerely hoped so. She was a sweet girl and he thought of her as another daughter of sorts. She deserved someone who could make her happy.

Maybe because it was a Monday, or perhaps because she couldn't wait for her drive home, Kelsey's day went by exceedingly slow. With the exception of Mr. Timmer, the patients were all routine. Brad Timmer had come in for his final crown placement. Typically she would remove the temporary crown and dry seat the new one to check the fit, then do the final glue down. Unfortunately, his unglued new crown fit so well they couldn't get it back off for the final epoxy. She first called in June, then they had to call in Dr. Davies. June got the bright idea to have the man bite down on one of the jelly beans she kept in the break room. The doctor shrugged, thinking it was as good an idea as any and it would avoid damaging the new crown.

June looked at the man sitting up in the chair. "Mr. Timmer, what flavor would you like?"

The poor guy looked skeptical but to his credit, still kept an open mind. "I'll take a grape one if you have it."

June brought back the dish and Kelsey pulled out what looked like a grape one and held it over the new crown. "Here you are sir, now if you could just bite down slowly and force your teeth together as far as they will go." As soon as he started to bite down Kelsey pulled her hand out of his mouth. Not even a second had gone by and the man's eyes widened. He grunted and thrashed his head around a little with shock.

Dr. Davies eyebrow went up. "Mr. Timmer, is there a problem?"

"My mou ih tuck!" The poor man paused for a second and scrunched his face in disgust. "En ih mlack licrish!" A little black colored drool started to run out the side of his mouth and Kelsey quickly wiped it for him.

"Sir, I am so sorry!" She shot June a dirty look. "You brought me black licorice?" The older woman quickly scuttled out of the exam room and Kelsey turned back to her patient. "Try to wiggle your top and bottom jaw back and forth to loosen it up. I think it will eventually come unstuck. It's only candy after all."

The doctor quickly turned around and stifled a laugh in his fist but hiding was completely unnecessary. Despite his disgust at the jelly bean lodged in his mouth, Brad Timmer started laughing hysterically through his clenched jaw. That only increased the flow of dark drool and Kelsey could not help joining until the three of them had tears in their eyes. It finally came unstuck about five minutes later but it was one of those moments that Kelsey was sure she'd never forget. She also knew that she owed June a lot more than spiders in the purse since the older woman should have warned her that there were both grape and black licorice jelly beans in the dish.

For the first time ever, Kelsey got into her car at the end of the day and was excited for her drive home. Pushing all thoughts of work and spiders aside for the moment, she quickly clipped her phone in the holder and brought up the app. As soon as she got on the expressway she was stuck in the middle of traffic hell but she didn't even mind that. Her phone chimed as she approached exit 30 and an amused voice sounded immediately after.

"Bloated raccoon, center lane. Possibly rabid, but he looks dead."

Kelsey snorted at nerd car's humor. Yes, she was seriously loving the app.

NEARLY FOUR WEEKS had gone by since Kelsey had struck up a navigational friendship with the nerd car. They still didn't know each other's names but that only added to the novelty. Things were kept short and polite, but also fun. She had a feeling that the other driver was a bit of a joker in real life. She often wondered what the other woman looked like. Despite the initial comment about whether or not Kelsey was cute, nothing else had been discussed along those lines and she contemplated the nerd car's sexual orientation. She thought about it a lot.

"Shovel in far right lane near exit 35."

The hazard warning was from none other than her new nerd car friend. Kelsey was still crawling along just past exit 30, so not near the voice pin yet. She glanced at the screen and saw a traditional hazard symbol appear right where the rainbow car was located. "Uh oh." She selected it and replied. "Hey nerd, a shovel?" She was still a couple of miles from the pin so she waited patiently for a response.

Jamie was sitting in her car with the flashers on. She ran her hand through the top of her undercut dark blonde hair then answered rainbow car's question. She really wanted to learn the other driver's name but she was too chicken and didn't want to cross any lines. "Yes, a shovel. And it wiped out the front passenger tire on my pretty blue car."

"Hmm, that sucks. Do you have a spare?"

The engineer sighed. "Of course I have a spare. Now ask me if I've changed a tire before."

Kelsey laughed in her own car. "Have you changed a tire before?"

After a tick, the app chimed. "Nope."

She grinned at the nerd car's answer. "Oh you poor child. Do you have some strapping young lad coming to your aid then?" Kelsey mentally crossed her fingers, hoping the answer would be no. She wasn't sure why but she really wanted this stranger to be single. Oh, and gay.

Tinny laugher followed the chime. "No lads at all, strapping or otherwise. And none of my lady friends are close enough to help."

Kelsey squealed and did a little dance in her seat. "Woot, she likes the ladies!" She abruptly sobered as traffic picked up again. Deciding that it was only right that she come to her fellow driver's aid, she signaled and merged into the right-hand lane. She down-swiped. "So you have a lot of lady friends, do you? You sound like trouble." Meanwhile her internal voice was asking what she was doing and pointing out that the nerd car could be a serial killer, a mouth breather, or dumb as a rock. Kelsey had a thing for smart girls. Shaking her head to silence the annoying voice she spoke aloud to the empty car. "She's probably not dumb because I don't think she'd have picked a nerd car icon. That's one status you don't claim unless you are one."

Jamie nearly swallowed her tongue when the reply came. She ran her finger slowly down the phone screen. "Um, maybe? What about you, *rainbow* car? Do you have a lot of *lady* friends?" While she was pretty sure rainbow car must be gay, one could never be too sure.

"Oh, I've had a few here and there. And by the way, that's a cute car you have."

The driver of the cute, if broke-ish, car looked into her rearview mirror to see a little silver economy car pull up behind her and put its flashers on. Both cars were far enough off the highway that they could exit on the driver's side of their respective vehicles safely. The woman who got out of the silver vehicle was wearing a set of scrubs which did little to hide her curves, and she sported a dimple on her left cheek. But it was the stranger's smile that did Jamie in. It was a real heartbreaker. Before the rain-

her arm hard. "Ow, damn it! That was stupid, Jamie. Now get in the car, bring up the dulcet voice of Nigel, and get your ass home!" The speedy little blue turbo gunned its way into traffic without disrupting the flow whatsoever. There was something to be said for fast girls and even faster cars. Jamie thought about the way she was just shot down and came to the conclusion that Kelsey didn't seem to like either. "Damn."

THE NEXT WEEK Jamie was sitting across from her friend Jenn. It was the same Jenn who was best friends with Tori, and she spent the first three minutes of cooling coffee smirking at Jamie. The coffee shop was busy but not too noisy. The Scalded Crow was a popular place in the gay district and they served vegan cookies, which was why Jenn always wanted to meet there. Not for the first time Jamie wondered why she couldn't just settle down and get serious about someone. And if one didn't mind the strange veganism and a few other quirks, Jenn was a great catch. Beautiful chocolate-brown skin, shoulder length hair pulled back into a wrap, a great smile, and quick-witted. Jenn's eyes were so deep you could drown in them. She was a woman that can and had made Jamie whimper plenty.

Unfortunately Jamie had her rules and a relationship with Jenn broke a few of the main ones. Besides being on a severely restrictive diet, the gorgeous black woman had a ten-year-old son named Malcom. Jamie got along really well with Malcom but she had no desire to have children of her own. And they'd always been careful to limit the amount of time Jamie spent at their house, so Malcom never got attached to her as more than just his mom's friend. Besides the whole parenting thing, there was an even bigger reason why they would never have worked out. Jamie didn't want to be tied down by anyone. She had been there and done that twice and was not doing it again.

Jamie sighed as she watched her ex-lover's lips curve into a smile. Jenn certainly had confidence and curves in spades and she knew how to use them. Jamie's mind wandered to her highway savior and she had to admit that Kelsey seemed to possess both as well. "So." She was startled back to the here and now by her friend's voice.

"What?"

Jenn sipped her bubble tea. "Tori?"

Jamie leaned over to the empty side of the table and thumped her head on the wood surface a few times, mostly out of self-punishment. At least until she grew concerned that it would cause permanent damage, then she stopped. She looked up into amused dark eyes. "You could have warned me! Or at least told me she was engaged!"

Jenn laughed. "Oh, for fuck's sake! We talked about it ages ago and it's not like I thought she was going to go after you, she is engaged after all." She smirked. "But she did text me a week ago to tell me that you have a bigger dick than John's. Oh, she also said you lasted longer than him too. I agreed with her."

"Wait, what do you mean I have a bigger dick than John? And how do you know?" Jamie narrowed her eyes at her friend, suspecting a strange hidden kink that she had never discovered in their short time as friends with benefits.

The other woman snorted. "She sent me his dick pics."

Jamie shuddered. "Dudes are weird. I mean, you don't see lesbians snapping pics of their sex toys and sending them off to girls they're interested in."

"Maybe they should." Jenn gave her a saucy wink and went back to her tea. "So what else is new with you? How is the engineering job going?"

The fairly new engineer sat back in her seat and smiled. "I really like it. It is definitely different than being a manager, not to mention the perks of coming to first shift!"

Jenn raised a single eyebrow at her notoriously randy friend. "I take it that means your sex life has picked up?"

"You know it!"

"You're hopeless." While Jenn meant it in jest, both women suddenly became aware of the past between them.

Jamie rested her hand on top of Jenn's and was struck by the contrast between dark and light skin. When Jenn met her eyes, she said the first thing that came to the surface. "I'm sorry."

The other woman just shook her head and smiled fondly, if a little sadly. She pulled her hand out of Jamie's grasp and patted the top of it. "It's fine. We have talked about this both before and after our little fling. I knew what I was getting into and I'm over it. Yes, it hurt for a while but it is okay now and we're still friends. Now let's talk more about Tori."

"How about we don't and say we did?"

Jenn laughed and let her off the hook. "How is Olivia?" Olivia wasn't a person, or a pet, and certainly wasn't a fuck buddy. Olivia was Jamie's pretty blue car. The engineer wasn't just a low-level nerd, she was pretty high up on the scale. Right after she got her little turbo-charged ride she announced that the car's name was Olivia. Not only that, but she also made anyone riding in it refer to the car by name as well. Yes, Jamie was a bit of an odd duck but Jenn loved her.

Jamie made a face and described the harrowing ordeal with the shovel. "I hit a shovel one day on my way home from work and had to drive with a fecking spare for two days until the dealership got my new tire in. The metal of the spade gouged the rim just a little bit but it wasn't noticeable enough to have to replace it."

Laughter peeled out of the woman across the table, loud enough to catch a few other's attention. "Are you telling me that those prissy butch hands finally changed their first tire?" The words she said, while not a secret by any means, were definitely not something that was well known by most people. Jamie was tall and athletic with short blonde hair and a jawline for days. She occasionally got picked up on sports teams, rode her bicycle around town, and worked out whenever she had time to spare. For all practical appearances she was one hot butch. Women expected her to be dominant in bed and that's exactly how she was when playing the game. But she and Jenn had been friends for a long time and Jenn knew what few others did. Jamie was not very butch. She preferred equal partnerships in and out of the bedroom, she hated getting her hands dirty and she got manicures once a month. She wore lip gloss and eyeliner, and loathed grease in any form. She also loved receiving flowers and writing sappy poetry. She was a paradox of traits that seemed diametrically opposed to each other.

Jamie sighed at the question and a strange look came over her face. "No, luckily my new driving friend helped me out."

Another raised eyebrow. "Driving friend? Did you start carpooling with someone?"

The faux-butch shook her head. "No, you remember the traffic and navigation app, Drīv?"

Curls bobbed despite the wrap. "Yeah, but I work six blocks from my house so I never use it. Why?"

"You still know how it works and you know I use it religiously for my commute because, well, rush hour hell. Anyway, the app recently updated and you can now record your own voice as a pin drop. So you could say dead deer, and tell what lane it was in. It allows you to give more explicit detail than the standard button choices."

Jenn nodded. "That sounds like a good update. What does this have to do with changing your tire?"

"Actually, there is someone who is ahead of me every single morning, a cute little rainbow car icon. And the same car is behind me on the map every night when I'm on my way home. Anyway, I accidentally responded to her voice pin and we've been kind of chatting via the app for the past month or so. When I got my flat on the way home from work last week she saw the pin pop up and stopped to help me out." Jamie shrugged, not wanting to convey just how attractive she thought her new friend was.

"She changed your damn tire, didn't she? So is she a big ol' brawny butch for real?"

Jamie laughed. "Actually, no. She's gorgeous with auburn hair, the thickest eyelashes I've ever seen, and some kickass curves. She's ethnic but I'm not sure what, maybe Latina? I think she works in a doctor's office because she was wearing scrubs that matched her green eyes..." Her voice trailed off as she noticed her friend staring at her from across the table. "What?"

Jenn smirked at her friend. "So how long did it take you to get her number?" Jamie's lips turned down and she mumbled something under her breath. "What was that? I think you had a mouthful of failure, can you say it again?"

"I said, I didn't. I asked her to dinner as a simple show of appreciation for changing my tire."

"And she said no."

"She said no."

Jenn reached across the table and patted Jamie's cheek lightly. "You poor, poor thing! Looks like your new friend isn't one to fall for your handsome wiles, Ms. Schultz." She wanted Jamie to be happy and settle down with someone even if it wasn't her. Jenn had not lied when she told her friend that she really was beyond their sexual relationship. They didn't have enough in common to make a relationship work anyway. Jenn also knew her friend would run at the first sign of serious. She watched the blonde across the table as Jamie pushed her hand away and began rambling excuses.

Jamie laughed. "Shut up, you! And it doesn't matter anyway, I don't even know her. She's probably not even my type, probably one of those lesbians who sits home with her cats and knits on the weekends. Boring!"

Jenn's eyes twinkled at the way her friend tried to talk herself out of the attraction. It was cute. She just nodded her head and played along. "I'm sure she does."

Chapter Three

IT WAS 8 p.m. on a Friday night and Kelsey was sitting on her couch, book-ended by her two cats. Her knitting needles practically flew while she watched the newest lesbian prison show episode. Out of the corner of her eye she observed Pierre get up, stretch, and amble toward the coffee table. As soon as one paw touched the table she called out to him. "Don't even think about it, mister!" The cat paused for only a second then stepped completely onto the table. He nonchalantly walked up to the full glass of water and sat next to it. When the black and white face started to dip down, Kelsey yelled. "Pierre!"

Pierre paused. "Mrroooowwww!"

"Don't sass me and leave my water alone!" He stared at her. She stared at him. Newman watched them both. Sensing an impending disaster Kelsey pushed pause on the remote. A white tipped black paw came up to just caress the side of the glass. "Pierre." Her voice was a low warning, not that the cat cared in the least. Then faster than a cat up to mischief should be, his paw swiped the full water glass off the coffee table and onto the carpet, then he took off like a shot toward the bathroom.

"Mrroooowwww!"

Kelsey scrambled up to find a towel to soak up the mess. "You asshole!" Her phone chimed as she settled back onto the couch again a few minutes later. It was a text from her friend Tam.

Yo, Kels. You busy tomorrow night?

She quickly texted back.

No, why?

Me & Shell want to check out DeMarcos on 4th Street. You in?

Tamara and Michelle Stevens were her closest friends in the world and one of the main deciding factors in moving to St. Seren. They had only been married for a year, but had been together for just over ten. They were one of thousands of happy couples who had been waiting for the marriage laws to change. She loved them and she loved hanging out with them but sometimes she felt like a third wheel. However, she also loved Italian food.

`Sure. Time?`

`Pick you up at 7. Pool at Culture after.`

Kelsey sighed and played with the button on her pajama shirt. It wasn't that she didn't want to go out. She had actually been wanting to check out Culture since moving into the city. She'd been to the bar before, but it had been a while and certainly not since she started living less than fifteen minutes away. That made for a much nicer drive back home, or cab ride. But she was still nervous to get out and meet new people. While Kelsey Ramirez wasn't shy by any means, she had yet to find someone that really kept her interest, or that was interested in knowing the real her. She loved the clean lines and style of the butch and andro girls but she wasn't a fan of all that butch attitude. She wanted someone softer, someone different.

Her mind flashed to the cute woman stranded on the side of the road. Jamie was totally her type with her short blonde hair and crisp button down shirt. While Kelsey couldn't really get a good read on her in such a short time, she definitely picked up on the fact that the tall woman was a huge flirt. Unfortunately her ex had been the same way and turned out to be a player. Kelsey just wasn't into those kind of games. Shaking the thoughts away she grabbed the remote and pushed play. "Ooh look, Newman! Nicky is such a bad girl and she's in handcuffs, so hot! Though we like Alex better, don't we Newman? I love this show!"

NIKKI ONWUALU WAS in handcuffs, and her legs were tied spread eagle to the bed with silk rope. Her lips were slightly parted as she peered up at the tall blonde standing over her. "Now you've got me, what are you gonna do?"

Jamie took in the naked woman lying on the bed. She was built like an Amazon with short cropped hair and skin so dark it was nearly black. Nikki had beautiful brown eyes and the most delicious lips that she'd tasted in a while. The gorgeous woman had multiple piercings in her ears, a nose ring, and nipple rings. Oh, how Jamie loved a woman in jewelry. Prompted by the tied woman's question, she crawled onto the bed and rested her pelvis gently against Nikki's. With a slow roll, she rubbed the entire length of her body against the woman below her. Nikki gasped and Jamie smiled as her breathing picked up in anticipation. "I think I'm going to do whatever I want. Now," She leaned down and took a large nipple into her mouth, tugging the ring not-so gently as she pulled back again. "This is your bed and these are your toys, is there anything in that drawer that's off limits?"

Nikki gasped at the tugging and her eyes rolled back as arousal surged through her. Her accent was a delight to Jamie's ears. "N—no. I'm all yours, lover. Time to make good on all that teasing, no?"

Jamie was out of town for the weekend. She had met Nikki, an attractive and charismatic network engineer originally hailing from Nigeria, six months before at a training conference for work. The sexual chemistry was immediately felt by both and Nikki never went back to her own hotel room that night. They chatted online occasionally, striking up a casual and flirtatious friendship immediately. Neither expected anything more than just a bit of fun. When Nikki invited her down for the weekend, she said yes. Jamie smiled down at the goddess below her. "Oh, I think I can do—what the hell?" She jerked her foot as soon as she felt something tickle across the bottom. She swung her gaze around and saw a sleek black cat sitting at the end of the bed.

Nikki started laughing. "Chill baby, that's just King. I would grab him and lock him out of the room but." She rattled the cuffs and gave Jamie a smoldering look. "I'm a little tied up right now."

Jamie groaned but laughed anyway. "That was terrible!"

"Then shouldn't I be punished?"

Jamie's eyes narrowed at the innuendo and she quickly got up and moved the cat out of the room. When she got back to the bed, she reached into Nikki's bedside stand and pulled out a riding crop. She grinned wickedly at the way her friend's eyes widened. "Yes. Yes you should."

Nearly an hour later the statuesque black woman wore a satisfied smile on her face and Jamie was collapsed on the bed next to her. Licking her lips, Nikki gave her fellow engineer a lazy grin. "Even better than the hotel."

Jamie's eyes were still shut but she nodded in agreement. "Definitely better than the hotel!"

Nikki eyed the bottle of lube on the nightstand and shifted slightly. "I'm gonna be some sore tomorrow though, love."

A blonde brow went up as one of Jamie's eyes came open.

"Are you saying you want me to go home tomorrow?"

The woman still cuffed to the bed started laughing. It was a rich, velvety sound that gave the blonde goose bumps despite her level of satiation. "Fuck off with you if you think that! You Americans give up so easy, there are other holes and other toys." Both eyes came open with her friend's words. Nikki was a lot kinkier than she originally thought, though the cat-o'-nine-tails in her drawer should have been a clue. The immobilized woman rattled the cuffs again. "Now, care to unlock me? I really need to take a piss."

Jamie smiled and pulled herself out of the bed and shivered in the cool air. "Where is the key?"

Nikki nodded her head vaguely toward the nightstand. "It should be right on top, in the dish between the lamp and clock."

The blonde peered down at the stand. There was a lamp, a clock, and an alarmingly empty dish. "Hmm."

"Problem?"

Jamie looked back at her with concern. "The dish is empty."

"You're fucking with me, no?" Jamie shook her head. "God damn it, King! The cat must have taken it out of the dish."

"Are you kidding me? Has this happened before?" Jamie's face paled slightly when Nikki nodded. "Where did you find it last time?"

The cuffed woman sighed. "Little fucker knocked it onto the floor, near the heat vent."

Jamie walked around the stand and found the register set into the floor. There was no key next to it but when she got down on her hands and knees she could just make out the gleam of the key at the bottom of the duct, right before the passage took a hard right under the floor. Even if she got the register unscrewed, the key was farther down than she could reach. Her mind raced ahead with thoughts on how to solve the problem. "Do you have a metal coat hanger and a good magnet?"

Nikki looked back at her curiously. "Sure, in the closet. I've got a few hard drive magnets on the fridge. Why?"

"It's in the register."

"Fucking cat!" She looked up at Jamie with desperation. "I wasn't kidding, love. I really do need to take a piss."

Jamie patted her foot. "No worries Nik, just let me do some MacGyver shit and I'll have you out in no time." First Jamie retrieved the magnet from the fridge and was happy to see it was a heavy-duty block. It wouldn't stick to the aluminum ductwork but it should have no problem picking up a little key. Then she got the coat hanger out of the closet and the multi tool she kept in her backpack. She untwisted and straightened the coat hanger then stuck the magnet to the end. Next she used the screwdriver on her tool to remove the screws from the vent cover. The rest was easy. She lowered the hanger into the hole until it was close enough for the key to jump onto the heavy magnet. "Got it!" She quickly set her tools aside and took the key over to unlock her friend. As they both untied Nikki's feet from the ropes Jamie looked her dead in the eye. "I recommend you keep this in your drawer from now on."

Nikki laughed and kissed her thoroughly for the rescue. "My hero!" Then she was off the bed in a flash, heading for the bathroom. Jamie just shook her head and started cleaning up her tools.

THE FIRST STOP for Kelsey and her best friends after leaving the restaurant was a little gentleman's bar just off Main Street. While "On the Rocks" had classic hardwood booths and tabletops with brass fixtures, it wasn't your typical gentleman's bar. The Rocks' clientele leaned heavily toward older gay men and the jukebox was usually loaded up with show tunes at any given time of the night. Kelsey sang along to "Hello Dolly" and drank chocolate covered cherry martinis until the craziness of her week slipped away. She was excited to go to the club until Tam let it slip that their friend Jenn was meeting them there. She let the information fall away, but when they were halfway through the three block walk to Culture, Tam brought it up again. Kelsey figuratively and literally put on the brakes. "No way!"

Tam pleaded. "Oh come on, Kels! You're gonna love her! She's gorgeous, she has a great job and a great smile. Have I ever steered you wrong?"

Kelsey thought of the many times that Tam had gotten them into trouble in college with her shenanigans, and frowned. "Too many times to count, so no."

Always the voice of reason, Shell walked over to the intractable woman. "Its fine Kels, you don't have to do anything but meet her. She really is one of our friends and she was already coming out tonight. We thought you might like to know more people than just us in St. Seren. Tam didn't even tell her about you, I swear. But come hang with us, please?"

Shell's bottom lip poked out ever so slightly, whether by accident or design Kelsey wasn't certain. She sighed and pointed at the lip in question while looking toward Tam. "Seriously, how do you resist that?

The short brunette with spikey hair grinned and shook her head. "I don't."

"Fine!" Kelsey scowled. "But if this is some sort of elaborate setup I'll have both your asses!"

Knowing exactly how vindictive her best friend could be, Tam held her hands up in front of her in a gesture of surrender. "No tricks, it's all on the up-and-up, I swear! So keep any damn spiders you find to yourself, Kels!" Shell chuckled, having heard many of the stories from her wife's college years.

Culture was pretty busy, even for a Saturday night, but the trio was lucky enough to score a pool table on the second floor. Kelsey bought the first round of drinks and had to fend off some straight couple looking for a third. While the redhead with the pixie cut was cute enough, she wanted no part of the woman's fiancé. It was nothing against guys in general, but Kelsey didn't *do* dick, and she certainly wasn't looking to be in a *Ménage à trois*. She sent Tam off to the bar to buy the second round because of the looks that the strange couple continued throwing her way. Kelsey stared intently at the green felt, deliberating her shot. The thumping bass of the house music vibrated through the soles of her shoes and made her eardrums tickle.

"Jesus, woman! Are you gonna go or what?" Shell's outburst was nothing out of the ordinary. For the most part the diminutive redhead looked and acted all sweet but she had a real short fuse. And she was losing. Badly. It wasn't enough that she drew the losing straw, so to speak, and had to play Kelsey, but Kelsey was a pool shark and an obnoxious winner.

Kelsey laughed. "Pipe down over there, red! I'm lining up my shot. After you lose you can go lick your wounds on the dance floor and I'll run your wife around the table for a while."

Shell laughed. "You're such an ass!"

"Of course she is, that's why we're such good friends." Tam had returned with their drinks and an extra woman. The black woman was about Kelsey's height and had a great smile. Since Tam only had two beers in hand for her and Shell, Kelsey assumed that one of the drinks in the new woman's hands belonged to her. "Hey Kels, this is my friend Jenn. She said she's game to shoot some pool with us, if we want to play doubles."

Always the polite one, Kelsey held her hand out toward the other woman. While the woman was gorgeous as promised, she was completely not Kelsey's type. Rather than shake her hand,

Jenn pressed the beer into her palm. "It's nice to meet you, Kelsey. I believe this is yours." She smiled and shrugged her shoulders. "And I'm going to apologize ahead of time for not being a very good player."

"Hallelujah!"

Kelsey couldn't help laughing at Shell's comment. "Don't worry about it, I could take these two with one hand tied behind my back."

For the next few hours the foursome drank, shot pool, and danced. At one point Jenn leaned over and spoke directly into Kelsey's ear in order to be heard over the loud music. "I get the feeling that Tam and Shell are trying to set us up."

Kelsey laughed. "You think? No offense but I told them no before I even met you. However I am looking for friends since I'm fairly new to the city."

The return laughter that came from Jenn startled her. "I'm not offended at all. Tam and Shell mean well, I think we both know that. And you are a cutie for sure." Jenn looked the curvy Irish-Latina up and down and shook her head. "But girl, no way. I like them a little more — "

"Androgynous, butch? You're gonna get a double thumbs up from me there." Kelsey grinned in agreement with her new friend.

Jenn nodded. "Yes ma'am. Now my friend James, girl! Mmm hmm!"

Kelsey rolled her eyes. "I don't like them that butch!"

"No, no, no, James is all woman with just the right amount of butch sweetness."

Kelsey couldn't help flashing to her driving app friend. Nerd Car certainly fit that description as well. She grinned. "Good to know we're on the same page. Best friends forever?"

Jenn cracked up laughing. "Sure, why not. I'll put you on the list." The rest of the evening went pretty fast after that. They all went out to breakfast after the bar closed, where the laughter continued. Kelsey was surprised to learn that Jenn had a ten-year-old son who was spending the weekend with his dad. And Jenn was intrigued to find out that Kelsey worked forty minutes away, just past the city of Livingston. "Hey, my friend James works in Livingston!"

Kelsey rolled her eyes, thinking about the commute. "I'm sure she enjoys the drive through the nexus of the universe as much as I do then." Everyone at the table had navigated the five highway interchange and every one of them shuddered at the slow crawl of rush hour traffic that seemed to take place no matter what time of day.

Always quick to see how puzzle pieces fit together, Jenn was pulled up short by a thought that popped into her head. "Do you use the Drīv app?"

"Oh yes, religiously! I swear by that bit of programming, it's a life saver. And I have the cutest little rainbow car icon, it's ridiculous. Why? Do you use it?"

Jenn smirked as she took in the interesting bit of information and shook her head. "Nope, I don't really need it since I walk to work. But I've heard some great reviews." After that, conversation seemed to wind down naturally until the four women left to go home.

MONDAY MORNING FOUND Jamie sore in some delicate places and tired from her long drive home, but she was in a remarkably good mood. She had the music cranked up and was making good time on her commute. Jamie was singing along to "Dreamy Bruises" by Sylvan Esso when the music suddenly cut off as her navigation app chimed. Jamie was irritated to have her tunes interrupted until she recognized the voice.

"Monday drudgery ahead, all lanes."

With a single down-swipe her mood returned to its previous level despite the lack of music. "Good morning to you too, rainbow. You know, that's kind of a gay icon, right?"

"And the little white car with the taped glasses is a nerdy one. What's it to ya, nerd?"

Jamie laughed at her response. "Did you have a nice weekend? What kind of trouble did you get up to?"

Kelsey raised an eyebrow at the other woman's interest. She was paying close attention to the road even though traffic was flowing pretty well. Those were the times you had to watch closest because you could never tell when brake lights would swamp all three lanes. "I had a pretty low-key weekend, stayed in and knitted with my cats."

Back in her own car Jaime choked on her coffee. Hadn't she made nearly that exact comparison to her friend Jenn? She fished a napkin out of her door and wiped the brown liquid off her shirt before responding. "Holy shit, is that a thing? Do they have their own needles or whatever? And don't cats have a short attention span or something?"

Laughter came through first. "Not my cats, they can stare for hours. And I wasn't knitting all weekend, just Friday night. Also, cats don't knit, smartass!"

Jamie raised an eyebrow at the feisty woman. "Good to know. By the way, you owe me a shirt since your cat knitting comment made me spit coffee on myself."

"Poor baby! I'm afraid that I'm pretty busy right now but I bet if you break down on the side of the road again you might actually find someone who cares."

Kelsey was no light hand at teasing the fair sex but she had surprised even herself at her boldness when messaging her new friend. It was strange that she had gone out over the weekend and made actual real new friends, but she didn't consider Jamie any less valid. The woman in the nerd car was a bit cocky but seemed nice enough. And she was funny, really funny. Kelsey loved her some smart, funny, andro girls. She smirked and decided to just go with the flow and enjoy the low-level of flirting that she was sending the blonde's way. Her app chimed and it was followed by a particularly whiny nerd.

"Hey, that was mean! You like me and you know it. Admit it, rainbow!"

The dental assistant giggled. "I admit nothing. But, I did add you as a friend on the Drīv app. That way I can get a message box that pops up as soon as you come online."

"Stalk much, jeez? So you like me enough to make me a friend on the navigational app, but not enough to give me your number. I see how you are!"

Kelsey laughed. "I'll hazard a guess and say that you don't seem like a girl who lacks for numbers."

"Ditto, babe!"

The woman in the little silver car blushed at the term that Jamie threw out across the miles. "Careful there, nerd. You're getting awfully familiar with your terms of endearment!"

Jamie drove along in Olivia and snorted to herself. She was getting awfully familiar but that's how the game was played. Flirt, push boundaries, and see where the other woman's line was. "It wasn't a term of endearment, it was an observation. I simply call 'em like I see 'em! Oh, and thanks for the warning about the ladder across the far left lane, you jerk!"

"Sorry about that but it must have fallen off someone's truck after I went through. You didn't hit it and do damage to your pretty blue car did you?" Kelsey started laughing before the message cut off.

"No I didn't hit it! Olivia is just fine." Jamie's voice dripped scorn at the mention of doing damage to her precious baby.

"Did you just call your car Olivia? And just what makes you so confident? For all you know, you're not even my type."

Kelsey signaled and started to exit while she waited for Jamie's response. Even if Jamie wasn't into her, flirting had been really fun. The nerd car icon flashed and Jamie's voice came through, bringing more than a little blush to Kelsey's cheeks.

"I don't know if I'm your type, but you're certainly mine so I'm just gonna roll with it. And also, never talk bad about my Olivia. She's sensitive!"

Her eyebrows went up with the mention of the car's name again. The woman was for sure insane, but hilarious too. The smile that lit Kelsey's face was unexpected and slow. She slapped a palm to the steering wheel and jumped when her horn sounded. "She thinks I'm cute!" She didn't respond with that though. She went with something much more innocuous, but suggestive. "Maybe you'd get further if you didn't try so hard."

Jamie smirked at the unexpected turn in the conversation. Unfortunately she was sitting in the parking lot at work and needed to end it. "Maybe I would. Okay Kelsey, I need to get inside but I hope you have a nice day."

"Ditto. To you and Olivia."

The engineer was still laughing as she scanned her badge and walked through the security door. Unfortunately for Jamie, the week passed slowly and with more than a little frustration. Preparation for two new lines under her design suddenly went into rush mode and Jamie had to go in an hour early each day and stay an hour late to try and get everything accomplished by the projected start of production. Not only was she cranky from lack of sleep but she also found that she missed chatting with her driving buddy. By Friday morning she was sick to death of her new schedule.

At 11:30 a.m. Jamie stood in the break room of a different building than she normally worked. Her company owned an entire city block and their facilities were all scattered around the perimeter with adjoining parking lots and connecting roads in the middle. She had already been waiting an hour for validation to be complete on a tester, and the crew running the eval told her it was probably going to be another thirty minutes to finish. Not enough time to go back across the campus to her office, but too long to enjoy sitting in the break room. A person could only drink so much coffee. Two men and half a dozen women were sitting at a cafeteria-style table, clearly on their lunch. She took a seat at another table and just watched the people that came and went. The simultaneous highlight and horror of her week came when the creepy little forklift driver ran face first into the glass break room door, before backing up and pulling it open. Jamie shuddered when she noticed that he left a grease smear on the glass. He was heading toward the bank of vending machines that ran along the back wall but stopped in front of her first.

"Hey, what's yer name?"

His question caused her eyebrows to go up so far that she thought certain they were going to mingle and have babies with her scalp. "It's Jamie." She answered him, but expected some sort of stupid comment or homophobic slur in return. She could not have been more surprised if the grungy man had pissed on her foot, but she may have been less sicked out.

He made a show of looking her up and down then grinned, displaying at least one missing tooth. "My name's Bud and just so you know, I like the ladies that look all tough like." Then he winked at her and finished his walk to the Coke machine.

Her face scrunched up in disgust when the man could no longer see her and she muttered under her breath. "Oh hell no, eww! Ugh!" Jamie shuddered. "No, no, no." She continued muttering "no" as if something inside her had permanently broken, until she was interrupted by high pitched screams. She whipped her head toward the commotion just in time to see a mouse scurry across the break room floor. All the women were up on their seats in a flash. Jamie glanced around, hoping to spot a box or something to catch the little critter in. Turns out that she didn't need to bother.

The poor mouse made the unfortunate decision to run toward the vending machines where he found Bud with hands full of a sandwich and a Coke, and Bud's size 10 steel toe boot found the mouse. Bud lifted his foot to see the now flat rodent and shrugged his shoulders. Jamie watched with horrified fascination while the man crammed his sandwich into his mouth to hold it, then bent down and picked up the mouse by the tail and walked it over to the trash. After that he dusted off his hands, grabbed his sandwich back out of his mouth, and walked out the door.

"Eww!" The chorus of disgust followed him out. Appetite for anything gone, Jamie dropped her coffee into the trash and went off in search of the tester group. She'd help if it got her out of the building that much faster. She couldn't wait for the day to be over.

Later on in her own building she was irritated further by one of her fellow engineers. On her way back from the warehouse, she passed by Dave's line where he was struggling to maneuver a large piece of equipment into position. It was a sensitive camera and he was rocking it back and forth as it if didn't have fifty grand worth of sensors and lenses inside. She slowed her pace and called out to him. "Hey Dave, you want some help with that? I have a few minutes."

He glanced her way with a pissy look on his face. "I've got it, James. Isn't it feeding time for your cubemate? Best get back to the fag zoo now." He emphasized her shortened masculine name the same way he always did because he was a raging homophobe and hated her guts. Of course there was no one else around to hear him. She shrugged and refused to be baited by the jackass. Though it was made more difficult when she heard him muttering something about "fucking dykes" under his breath. She let it go because it was never worth fighting with him about it.

By the time she walked into the engineering office an hour and a half later, she was just starting to get her appetite back. She shared a large double cube with one of her coworkers who was a great guy but also a notorious garbage disposal when it came to food. Bill looked up from the stack of vending machine packages arrayed in front of him. "Hey, how did the validation go?"

Jamie threw herself into her chair. "Seriously, what is wrong with the tester group? I will be happy if I never set foot into the West 15 building again!" She shuddered remembering Bud.

"Oh, come on. It can't be that bad." Because of the layout of their cube, they sat facing adjacent corners with mostly their backs facing each other. When he mumbled something else around a mouthful of food, she kicked his chair to get him to turn around.

"I can't understand you when you're talking with your mouth full." Bill spun in his chair to face her and the moment seemed to slow to a stop for the blonde woman. In his hand he held some sort of sandwich on a bun, but it was the long tendril of something hanging from the corner of his mouth that gave her pause. She had been getting ready to tell her coworker about the incident at West 15 but those weren't the words that came out of her mouth. "Dude, what the hell are you eating?"

He held it up and smiled as he slurped the tendril back in to his mouth. "It was one of the new sandwiches in the wheel of death. It's called a mouse burger—" Jamie's face paled and the rest of his words were lost as she flashed back to the poor flattened mouse dangling from Bud's fingertips. Bill's voice filtered back in as the memory faded. "Has beef and onions, and it got its name because it's so small!"

Jamie stood abruptly from her chair and grabbed the safety glasses off her desk. "Oh, hey man, I gotta go check the line."

She was already walking toward the office exit when she heard him yell over the cube walls after her. "Are you sure you don't want a bite?" She shivered in disgust and walked faster.

Chapter Four

KELSEY'S FRIDAY WASN'T going much better than Jamie's. The second patient of the day was a regular named Joe. Joe was seventy-nine years old and a terror to every female in the office. She was certain that his picture would be in the dictionary in the dirty old man section. It was a small office with a handful of techs and just the two assistants. June suggested they play rock-paper-scissors to see who had to be the one to help the doctor. Kelsey lost. He started his shenanigans as soon as she entered the exam room. "Hiya toots!" Kelsey was pretty sure she felt an arthritic hand brush her thigh as she walked by, but when she turned around he was grinning at her innocently with hands on the arms of the chair.

Kelsey turned away from him and counted to ten under her breath just to stay in her happy place. When she turned back her professional smile was firmly in place. "Good morning, Mr. Sacks. How have you been? Anything new to report?"

"Well honey, my plate's been giving me some trouble lately."

She looked back at him curiously. "Oh? I'm sorry to hear that. Trouble how?"

He pointed to the top right side, near the place his incisor would be if he still had actual teeth on top. "I got me a sore spot right here where it's been rubbin'. I can't have me a sore spot, little lady. What if the misses wants to serve me up some lunch all down-home style?" He jogged her arm with a bony elbow and gave an exaggerated wink. "If you know what I mean!"

She stepped back slightly and gave him a slow blink, trying to deny what her ears had just heard. Without a word to him she quickly donned a pair of gloves and held her hand out. "If you could just give me your upper, I'll go see if I can find the rough spot that's causing your problem. He cackled and spat the top denture into her hand. She walked away and tried to ignore the wandering fingers. There wasn't a lot she could do to the plate without actually looking into his mouth to see where the problem was, but she wasn't going to tell him that.

She was only gone fifteen minutes when Sheila, one of the techs, came to find her in the lab room. "Um, Kelsey?"

Kelsey looked up from the plate where she was chipping off something that looked a whole lot like super glue buildup. "Yes?"

The young woman looked nervous and in turn it made Kelsey nervous. "It's about your patient, Mr. Sacks."

The dental assistant sighed partly in resignation and partly with hope. "Is he dead?"

Sheila did a double take, shaken by Kelsey's morbid comment. "Um, no. He's asleep."

"And?"

The younger woman suddenly looked flustered and the explanation came out in a rush. "He fell asleep in his chair and his zipper is open, and he's also saying lewd things in his sleep that every patient can hear as they walk by his room!" Face red with mortification, Sheila ran back out of the room while Kelsey tried to make sense of the tech's rapid word vomit.

Before she could leave to see and hear the problem for herself, June poked her head into the room. With an evil grin, she pointed at Kelsey. "Your patient's a perv and his fly is down. He's scaring the other patients coming into the clinic." She paused for a second. "You should probably go wake him and ask what's up." Then she laughed as she popped her head back out and closed the door.

Kelsey growled. "Seriously?" She gave the freshly cleaned plate one last rinse then left the room to go wake up the old menace.

She was still in a cranky mood hours later when she got into her car and headed for the highway. She merged into traffic then turned on her radio and opened her driving app. Less than a minute later the chime sounded. A huge smile took up residence on her face when she heard Jamie's voice.

"Don't get on the highway, it's a trap!"

The image of a fish-faced admiral popped into the dental assistant's head as Jamie wetly slurred the last three words, quoting an infamous sci-fi epic. "Jesus Jenny, but you are such a nerd!"

"You must have a little nerd in you too or you wouldn't have recognized that quote."

Jamie laughed and responded, happy for the first time all week. "You're crazy!"

"I think you like crazy."

Kelsey didn't dignify the other woman's response by feeding her ego. She changed the subject instead. "Where have you been all week?"

Jamie ran a hand through her hair and switched back to the center lane as she approached a busy exit. Always the center lane, unless you were near a not so busy exit, or you're already past the on ramp. Because, rules. She tried to always follow the rules. Once she had safely maneuvered Olivia into the optimal lane, she down-swiped the rainbow car that she had saved as a favorite. Two could play at Kelsey's game. "Why do you want to know, did you miss me?

"You wish!"

There was a part of the nerd in the pretty blue car that did wish. She wasn't sure why Kelsey had piqued her interest but the feisty woman with the dimple definitely had. What was weird was that she didn't even know anything about Kelsey. Maybe it was time to change that. "Hey, do you work in a doctor's office?"

"Kinda. I'm a dental assistant, why? And what about you?"

"Ah, just wondered because you were wearing some kind of scrubs when I met you. And I'm an engineer for Electro-corp." The smug voice that sounded through her Bluetooth enabled speaker system made her laugh out loud.

"When you met me? You mean the day I out-butched you and changed your tire?"

Cars started to slow across all lanes and Jamie cursed as the traffic jam indicator popped up. "Traffic slow down ahead"

Nigel's pissy voice made her flick the screen of her phone a few times, then flip it off. "Fuck off, Nigel!" Her finger must have accidentally swiped on Kelsey's car because she responded immediately.

"Still having problems with your Brit?"

Jamie smirked, starting to get a real feel for Kelsey's personality and humor after chatting with her for more than a month. "Is your navigator still set to the German voice?"

"Fuck off, Nigel!"

"Such language! And why are you talking to my nav app like that? Also, do you kiss your mother with that mouth?"

"I kiss whomever I like with this mouth! Not that you'll ever find out, nerd!"

Jamie laughed and replied. "Ahh, that's the meanness I've come to know and love!"

Kelsey blushed at the playfulness in Jamie's voice. She had really come to enjoy the other woman's voice on her daily commutes and missed her when she was not on. She cursed as traffic slowed to a stop.

"Verkehr verlangsamen voraus."

With a great sigh, she realized that in the grand scheme of things it really didn't matter how long it took her to get home because she had no plans. It was a Friday night, she was a single Irish-Latina with "a dimple to die for" according to Tam, and she was probably going to spend the evening knitting with her cats again. She switched into the left lane since it was moving faster. "So where were you all week?"

"Work has been crazy busy. I had to go in an hour early and stay an hour late every day since Monday. Luckily I wrapped things up so I could get out at my normal time today."

Kelsey swore as she went under an overpass and traffic in her lane slowed to a complete stop. It was with no small amount of irritation that she took in the traffic rocketing by her in the center lane and the traffic merging with little resistance on the far right. "What the shit is this? This is supposed to be the fast lane!" The stream of ranting profanity continued until traffic in her lane started moving again, five minutes later. She was startled by her app chime.

"Uh, you still there?"

"Shit, sorry! I got stuck in the left lane near exit 32, for five freaking minutes!"

Jamie shook her head at her driving friend's mistake. "You totally broke one of the sacred rules of the road!"

Kelsey's voice sounded incredulous as it came back via the app. "The what?"

The engineer glanced at the phone in disbelief. "The rules of the road, you know, tips for commuting every day. Always stay in the center lane when approaching a busy on-ramp, even if the other lanes look faster. Exceptions, if there are no exits around, or not much traffic. You can get into the left lane only after you pass the busy exit, but not if traffic is heavy and you need to exit soon."

"Um, you've given this a lot of thought. Are there a lot more rules in your book, nerd?"

Jamie thought for a second then answered as if she were reading from a book. "Hmm, let's see, never drive next to a phone watcher, don't get on any highway that is at a standstill, leave a gap in front of you for stopping space, drive defensively—" She didn't get to say more because the time ran out on her message pop up. Jamie still had a head full of rules but she didn't bother sending any more. That was perhaps too big of a peek into her strange and quirky skull. Nearly two minutes went by before Kelsey responded again.

"Wow, that's a lot of rules to follow. Do you have such rules for all parts of your life and do you ever break any? Come on, you can tell me!"

It was a lot of rules to follow but Jamie had her rules for a reason. Things were simpler with rules and people were less likely to get hurt. Rules were clean, rules were convenient. Finally, she responded. "Yes, I have them for everything. And I try not to break them because it never turns out well."

Kelsey listened as the other woman's message came back to her and her eyes widened slightly. "Whoa, obstacle alert, Nigel! Issues across all lanes!" While they were said aloud with astonishment, in no way was she going to send her thoughts back to Jamie. Not that she was any more level-headed since she apparently was talking to Jamie's nav app like it was her own. Clearly the other woman had been hurt, or something, to cause such a pained response. And for whatever reason, Kelsey didn't like that at all.

One thing she was known for among her closest friends was the fact that she had a protective streak a mile wide. She was a fighter when it came to the people she loved. She took care of people, she looked out for them, and it was something she had always done. It had also caused its fair share of problems for her too. Perhaps the trait came from her father, Manny Ramirez. He was about as blue-collar as a man could get. He spent his whole life working as a mechanic and fighting prejudice on every level, even from his own friends and family. While he was born in the United States, his Irish wife was not. Other than both families being rampant Catholics, there was zero overlap between the two cultures. Yet Kelsey's parents made it work somehow and they were even more in love at sixty than they were at nineteen. It was disgusting really. But her dad always told her that if she wanted something, she had to work for it. If she believed in something, she had to fight for it. And a person should always watch out for the little guy. Deciding not to poke the sleeping bear of Jamie's issues, Kelsey opted for a subject change. "So I'm guessing you must be exhausted after your schedule all week. Going to catch up on your sleep tonight?"

A snort came across the line in response. "As if! Trouble doesn't find itself you know! And you? Knitting with the kitties again?"

Kelsey flipped off the phone before swiping on the screen. "You're such an ass! And I might be knitting but there is nothing wrong with that. Everyone needs a hobby. You should try it sometime, hobbies make a person well-rounded."

"Are you knitting your kittens some mittens?" Kelsey listened as Jamie cracked up at her own joke. "And I have a hobby, I happen to enjoy eating out. Fine dining is all the rage now you know."

Kelsey's mouth dropped open at such a blatant sexual innuendo. "Seriously? Did you really just say that? You are such a pig, Jamie, uh, what is your last name anyway?"

The little blue turbo was speeding along prettily as Jamie neared the exit for her condo. "You want my last name, huh? So you are stalking me! But fine, it's Schultz. So you can find all my social networking accounts later tonight and stalk to your heart's content."

"Ass! And my last name is Ramirez, so now you can do the same."

Jamie chuckled to herself and followed the off ramp. "So have you given any more thought about having dinner with me?"

The dental assistant's smug voice came back to her. "Nope. Not in the least."

"You wound me, Kels!"

Kelsey's response was almost immediate. "Aww, that's what my friends call me. Aren't you sweet! But I'm afraid you're going to have to stay wounded because I'm not going to kiss it better for you. Nice try, nerd!"

Jamie laughed and pulled into her parking garage. "You can't blame a girl for trying. I'm home now, rainbow. I'll talk to you later. And try not to cause a disturbance with those cats this weekend, the cops might show up and mistake your knitting needles for weapons then you'll be all over the news." Before Kelsey could respond Jamie messaged again. "On second thought, get crazy cuz I want to read about that shit in the paper!"

"You're insane! And no one reads the paper anymore. Talk to you later, Jamie, and have a great weekend."

AS SOON AS Jamie walked into her condo she put away her lunch container and went to change into workout clothes. The building had a gym and she wanted to get some exercise in before starting her evening proper. Burke wasn't coming up, but her sister was coming into town to stay the next night. So her Friday was completely free. Despite what she told Kelsey, she really was exhausted from her hellish week at work, but she was also full of twitchy energy. She wanted to work it off with someone. Before heading downstairs to the gym, she shot a quick text to one of her friends. She hadn't seen Chloe in a while but they had always

been good together for a casual night of fun. Her phone buzzed
less than a minute later.

```
whats up james?
```

Jamie typed a quick reply then went to fill her water bottle.

```
You busy tonight? Want to come over?
```

The response from Chloe was swift.

```
No. Not available like that anymore.
```

Eyebrows rose in surprise. She never took Chloe for the dating type.

```
Ah, seeing someone then? Congrats!
```

Her phone buzzed again. She read the text twice as a sick
feeling came over her.

```
Not seeing anyone, just cant see you. Sry but I
knew your rules and still fell. I know you don't feel
the same way so I need some time. Need to take a break
and maybe we can be just friends after.
```

She typed back a response but her head was spinning from
Chloe's words.

```
Okay. And I'm really sorry, Chloe. For what it's
worth I think you're really great. I just can't date
anyone.
```

Jamie was a pretty happy-go-lucky soul. She believed in
working hard and playing hard. But no matter what outside per-
sona she showed everyone but a select few, Jamie was sensitive.
She didn't like hurting people. She knew that she walked a fine
line between getting her needs met, and not stepping on other
people's hearts.

That was the reason for her rules. No matter how awkward it
seemed in the middle of the conversation, she hammered home
her convictions. That was the reason she always warned about the
fact that she would never want to date before she so much as
kissed someone that she was pursuing. Because if everyone had

fair warning, it wasn't her fault if they got hurt.

But over the past six months she had been getting more and more responses like Chloe's. She had a pattern and that was meet someone she was attracted to, express interest in a causal relationship, and when the other woman became too attached she cooled things off to friendship. And while it took a little time on occasion, everyone was eventually good with just being friends. Jamie shook the negative thoughts from her head and grabbed her water bottle and key card. She warned them and it wasn't her fault if they got hurt. She was still muttering under her breath as the door to her condo clicked shut behind her. "It's not my fault."

Later that evening she found herself sharing a booth at "The Rocks" with Jenn. Malcom had begged to stay with his grandma that night which gave Jenn a rare free Friday. Jamie had been quieter than normal since they arrived and both women were sipping Mort's infamous chocolate covered cherry martinis. Mort and Walt owned the place and had been together for forty years. The bar had been open for thirty of those years and was a fixture in the LGBTQ community. "So what's got your panties in a twist?"

Jamie snorted. "I'm wearing boxers tonight, if you must know!"

Jenn waved off the taller woman's words. "It's so cute the way you pretend to be butch! And you didn't answer my question."

The blonde shrugged her shoulders. "I don't know. Just in a funk, I guess." "Hello Dolly" started playing over the juke box. It seemed to be a crowd favorite. She looked up at her friend with a hint of humor finally reaching her eyes. "Would you prefer if I started singing?" Jenn's immediate reaction was to hold a hand up in front of Jamie's face.

"Girl, just no." The beautiful woman shook her head and her hair bounced with the motion. The trademark wrap was gone for once. "Please, it's bad enough nobody has heard of the stuff you listen to but your voice is enough to scour pans!"

"I'm not that bad!"

"You are as bad as my grandmama's mountain oysters!"

Jamie pulled a face. "No way did your grandma make that. Did she?"

Jenn nodded. "Clearly effed me up for life cuz I'm a vegan now, aren't I?" The black woman leaned back to avoid Jamie's manicured finger.

"You're just weird."

Jenn pushed the blonde's finger away from her face. "Takes one to know one!"

Jamie held up both hands in protest. "Hey, you don't see me putting balls in my mouth!"

"Anymore." Jenn added the last bit slyly.

Jamie pointed at her again, deftly avoiding the swat-away. "Takes one to know one!"

Laughter erupted from the confines of the booths, turning more than a few graying heads their way. Once they calmed down again Jenn prodded her friend a little more. "You never answered my question."

Jamie hung her head and sighed, twisting a slightly damp cocktail napkin between her fingers. Then she said something that completely took her friend by surprise. "I've developed a pattern in my life and I keep hurting people."

Once she got over her momentary shock Jenn nodded, intimately aware of those very words. She was better because it had been nearly a year since their fling, but it still stung. "Yes, you do."

Jamie looked stricken. "But I don't mean to! I do everything I can to warn women that I'm not interested in more than just casual. I mean, I go out of my way to make sure they understand. I'm kind of a dick about it."

Her friend sighed. "I know you do, James. But not all women are the same as you, a lot aren't. Women are emotional, they get connected, and a lot of us are convinced that we are the one who is different and will get through."

"Is that what happened to you?"

Jenn shook her head sadly. "No. I knew I wasn't going to be the one to get through and that's why I backed off when I did. I refuse to chase someone who's not interested."

"I'm really sor—"

Jenn cut her off. "Sorry, I know. But that doesn't change what you did, or what you continue to do. Think about this. If you drive down a certain street every day and more often than not you hit someone's cat on that street, would you keep taking it? Even if you honk your horn and there are signs up that say no cat crossing, would you keep taking that street or would you go down a different one?"

Jamie sat back in the booth and looked horrified. "Oh my God, that is a terrible analogy! You are so effed in the head! And of course I'd take another street, Jesus!"

"But why? You honk your horn, there are signs up that say

no cat crossing, it's not your fault if they run out in front of you and get hit. Why change the way you're driving?"

The look on her face said clearly that Jamie thought she was insane. "Because they're cats. You can't tell a cat not to cross a street, they do what they want. It's in a cat's nature to be assholes and do their own thing."

Jenn leveled a look at her that said she better listen. It was a lot like the mom look that she gave Malcom. "Women feel, James. Most of us have hearts that behave like a cat. We can't just tell it not to love, not to stay on our side of the street. Hearts do what they want and have since the beginning of time." She reached over and touched the back of Jamie's hand. "I understand the need to protect yourself, believe me. I have two hearts to protect every day of my life, me and Malcom. But I also have a duty to look out for others too. If you really don't want to hurt anyone, you have an obligation to take another street."

Jamie stared into the martini for a minute after Jenn stopped speaking, deep in thought. Then with a mercurial change of mood, she downed her drink in two swallows. "This conversation got weird. Let's order another round!"

"James." The voice was stern, a warning that said she wasn't playing.

Jamie sighed and looked up to meet her friend's dark eyes. "I understand and I'll give it some thought." She held her hand up to catch Mort's attention and signaled for another round. "Speaking of cats, my driving friend has two of them. Apparently they knit too."

"You're such a goddamn liar, James!" They chatted for a while longer about a lot of nothing. Jenn found it interesting that Jamie spend most of the rest of their evening talking about her mysterious driving buddy. A little after midnight Jamie went home to finally catch up on her sleep. Jenn went home to friend request Kelsey, if only to see if the woman's cats really did knit. It wasn't hard for her to figure out that Jamie's driving buddy was none other than the woman Tam and Shell had introduced her to.

KELSEY WAS NOT knitting with her cats, but she was knitting for them. It was a possibility that people would think she was certifiable if they learned about the little tiny sweaters she had made for Newman and Pierre. It was possible people would scoff at the way she frequently asked Newman if he preferred Alex or Piper while they watched her show, or remarked on how

Pierre's black coloring on his upper lip made him look just like Porn-stache.

When the show was over and popcorn gone from her bowl, she gave in and set the needles down. The urge to find Jamie online was nearly hurricane force and she was only human. She searched fruitlessly for much too long then gave up and switched over to check out Tam's page. The last post had a comment on it by Jenn. Feeling a surge of excitement she clicked on her newest friend's profile and immediately sent her a friend request. It was approved less than two minutes later. Looking at the clock in the lower right hand corner of her computer, Kelsey's eyebrow went up when she saw that it was 12:30 in the morning. She smiled and sent off a quick message.

```
Most people are either out with friends or home
sleeping at this hour. What are you doing up, BFF?
```

She watched as the ellipses came up in the message box and Jenn's message came in a few seconds later.

```
I could say the same about you. So, you knit with
your cats?
```

Both dark brows went up in shock when she read the words.

```
What the hell? Who told you that?

A little bird. So is it true?

Of course it's not true!'
```

Kelsey waited a beat and wrote a little more.

```
I might knit FOR them.
```

Jenn was sitting at her house on the west side of the city, curled up in an old leather recliner that had been worn smooth with age. She had her long dead maternal grand mamma's afghan over her legs to ward off the nighttime spring chill. Jenn laughed at Kelsey's admission. The evening they all hung out the previous weekend had been a lot of fun, and she learned real fast that she couldn't pin down the other woman's sense of humor or personality. Kelsey was quick-witted and her comments kept everyone on their toes.

Oh, so you're one of THOSE? A certified crazy cat
lady? I would have never guessed that about you. LOL

Kelsey's response came in within seconds.

I've actually never been tested so I don't know if
I can claim to be certified or not.

So what are you doing now?

Jenn was curious why Kelsey was at home on a Friday night.
The woman was hot, from an objective point of view. They
weren't each other's type, after all.

Um.

Jenn's curiosity was piqued.

What? It can't be that bad!

I've been home knitting with my cats.

Water sprayed harmlessly across her living room as Kelsey's
answer came back. Luckily Jenn had turned her head at the last
second. She quickly typed back to her new friend.

Are you for real, seriously? Test passed, Kels.
Consider yourself certified!

They chatted for a little while longer until exhaustion
pleaded with Kelsey to go to bed. As she drifted off to sleep, her
original intent to find her driving buddy was completely forgotten.

Chapter Five

"GOLD GUNS GIRLS" by Metric fired up the drive first thing Monday morning. The song immediately had Jamie drumming on her steering wheel and tapping her feet on the way to work. Cruise control was a wonderful thing. It had been a little over two weeks since her sister came into town on a Saturday night. The fun had continued when they went out to breakfast at Mozart's the next morning. Despite standing for nearly an hour outside waiting for a table, Mozart's was worth it. But when Maya went home a little after noon that Sunday, Jamie sat in the silence of her condo.

Maya was actually her half-sister and lived about seven hours away in Wisconsin so she wasn't able to come into town very often. Neither one of them stayed in touch with the family much after Maya's high school graduation. No one took it well when Jamie came out. It was a big drama and Jamie became a pariah within the entire redneck Shultz clan. The only one that stuck by her was Maya, who was also blacklisted by the family. After Maya left for home Jamie remained lost in thought. She didn't feel like watching her favorite shows, she didn't want to work out, and she had no interest in talking to any of her friends. After years of living only for herself Jamie had finally reached a point where she wasn't sure she liked who she had become.

At loose ends she decided she had to do something. Forcing herself to get up and move, Jamie spent the rest of Sunday cleaning, working out, and reading two books before finally settling in to catch up on the recorded episodes of her favorite prison girls. She wondered idly if Alex ever regretted the things she did to Piper.

Over the course of the two weeks following her conversation with Jenn, and her sister's visit, she had been keeping to herself on the weekends. She was trying to change her pattern of behavior and it was hard. It was also lonely and she leaned on her friends more than ever. Jenn and Burke had become the priests of her confessional and neither minded because they both sensed a shift in their friend. Jamie also relished her morning and evening chats with Kelsey. They teased and laughed during the daily commutes and managed to cover a surprising variety of topics while driving. But neither had taken the step to connect in any other way.

For Jamie, it was because she was afraid of following those old patterns of seeking someone out then hooking up. She was trying very hard to stay away from that behavior. And Kelsey had initially tried to find Jamie but she had failed miserably. She assumed that her driving buddy had simply given her the wrong name, or perhaps was listed under a different name on social media and didn't want Kelsey to find her.

But it was a new Monday morning and, after two weeks of purging her old life, it was like the slate of her conscience was starting to come clean. Jamie was determined to make a fresh start, beginning with a fast-paced anthem that was one of her favorites. Her jam session was interrupted by Nigel, much to her disappointment.

"Object on road ahead."

"What the hell, Nigel? That's all I get from you?" She muttered to herself while scanning ahead to see which lane had the object. "Kelsey gives me way more detail than that. I wonder where she is." Jamie searched for the little rainbow car icon as soon as she logged into the app but Kelsey wasn't online. Mondays always sucked and it was just another thing that had brought her down.

She was in the left lane following all the rules, having just gone past a busy exit. But she slowed with the rest of traffic then slammed on her brakes as the car in front of her abruptly stopped. Jamie heard a sound and looked up into her rearview mirror in a panic. Unfortunately the view matched the sound as ten wheels of stuttering rubber locked up tight. The dump truck barreling up behind her had slammed on its brakes as well. She shut her eyes and braced for the impact that never came. "Oh my God oh my God oh my God—"

When she dared open them to peek out, the dump truck had veered into the space between the left lane and the concrete divider. Black marks like charcoal art trailed the truck's tires about forty feet back on the road. Jamie took in a deep breath and let out a shaky sigh, then patted Olivia's dash. "We're okay girl, and I didn't even piss my pants!" When traffic started moving again, she waited and let the truck driver pull out in front of her. "No way am I letting you follow me again, buddy!"

Work went much like her drive. It seemed like one thing after another was going wrong or breaking and Jamie was kept running all day just putting out fires. Near quitting time, someone came around with packages of crackers that they had brought back from Japan. The company was an international one and associates from Japan would rotate over for a few years to work, then go back to the parent company overseas. Even the group in Mexico would send people up to work for a while in a cross-cultural exchange of sorts. Both groups would bring strange candies, crackers, and other such delicacies from their home countries.

Jamie liked a lot of things but the food items that were passed out in the office were definitely hit or miss. Green tea flavored candy bars and chocolates made with goat's milk were just a few examples of culinary strangeness that invaded the engineering office on a regular basis. A lot of times Jamie saved hers for Burke because he liked all kinds of different foreign foods. Both Jamie and her cubemate, Bill, were given the decorative little packs of crackers. Each package had four crackers total, wrapped up in twos. Jamie immediately dropped hers into her empty lunch cooler and waited while Bill opened one of the two packs inside his. Then she watched as he took the first bite and started chewing. He made a face.

"Well?" she prompted.

He took a second bite and wavered his head back and forth a little. "Hmm, salty." He took another bite of the large cracker and made another face.

Jamie started laughing. "Dude, you don't have to eat it. Just spit it out."

Bill shrugged. "Eh, it's not that bad. You wanna try the other one?"

She suspiciously stared back at him. "It's not that bad?" He shrugged and shoved the open wrapper containing the second cracker over to Jamie's side of the cubical. She picked it up and sniffed it, then made her own face. "It smells fishy, you know I don't like fish."

She started to put it down again and Bill rushed to reassure her. "You like crab though, and that smells fishy too!"

"Hmm, you have a good point. Fine." Before she could second-guess her actions anymore she took a large bite of the cracker. She tried to give it the benefit of the doubt by thoroughly chewing the cracker mass in her mouth but eventually she gave in to disgust. Pulling the trash can out from under her desk she spat out the entire masticated glob. "Bleh! Holy nastiness, that was terrible! What is wrong with you, man?" She grabbed a napkin out of the drawer and started scraping her tongue to remove the cloying flavor.

Bill looked surprised. "You didn't like it?"

Jamie looked back at him in horror. "And you did? That

tasted like I was licking the underside of a dock, or an oceanfront area where all the fish had died. It was like a cracker version of tofu, times ten." After drinking down some water she grabbed three pieces of gum and stuffed them all into her mouth to kill the taste. She watched as Bill shrugged again and opened the other two-pack. Jamie shuddered when he shoved another cracker into his mouth and began chewing. "Dude, I feel so bad for your wife."

He looked over at her and shoved the other cracker into his maw. "Why? I eat whatever she cooks, even the burnt stuff."

Jamie made a face. "Then clearly you two were meant for each other." She looked down at her smart watch and smiled for the first time all day. "And now it is time for me to get the heck out of here! See you tomorrow!"

He nodded and gave her a little wave. "See you tomorrow, James."

It was with a great sigh of relief that Jamie hit the road after work. And it was with a huge grin that she saw the rainbow car icon pop up on her driving app. She immediately down-swiped without giving thought to how needy it seemed. "Hey, where were you this morning?"

"Good afternoon to you, Nerd. Are you stalking me?"

The nerd in question grinned. "Of course I am, now answer the question!"

"I had a doctor's appointment, so I took the morning off. Jeez nosey!"

Jamie grew immediately concerned. "Uh, is everything, um, okay?"

Laughter came through her speakers before Kelsey's voice. "Everything is fine, Jamie. It was just my annual checkup, won't have another til next year. But it's sweet that you were concerned for me."

Back in Kelsey's little economy car she had a smile that would not go away. Rather than spend the entire weekend with her cats like a shut-in, Kelsey had accepted Tam and Shell's invite to come over Saturday night for pizza and games. She loved game nights but did tend to be a little competitive. Usually her friends steered the group more toward card games that involved horribleness and laughter. Sunday she cleaned her small apartment and took the cats for a walk around the building. It too was hilarious. But much like Jamie, she had really missed her friend on her drive to work and she was glad when the other woman messaged her for the drive home. Jamie's voice sounded through the speakers of her phone so Kelsey turned down her radio a little more to hear.

"So what did you do this weekend, Kels? Knit a blanket for uh, what are your cat's names anyway?"

Kelsey snickered. "I have two handsome tuxedo cats, Newman and Pierre. And I have never knitted them a blanket!"

Jamie's voice came back with laughter. "But you have knitted them stuff, haven't you? Because there was something in your denial that just didn't ring completely true. Are you secretly a crazy cat lady?"

The crazy cat lady sighed and responded. "Maaaaybe. And Pierre and Newman might have a couple of little monogrammed sweaters. But I'm not admitting to anything else!"

"How about admitting that you want to have coffee with me?"

Without fail, Jamie asked Kelsey if she wanted to go for coffee every Monday and every Friday. Kelsey never accepted and it had become almost a game between them. She laughed at the persistent woman. "Don't you have enough women willing to have drinks, or more, with you? Besides, I don't even know you!"

A minute went by, then two, and still Jamie didn't respond. Finally, when Kelsey thought she wasn't going to get an answer from the other woman, Jamie's voice came across the little speaker of her phone. It was more serious than she'd ever heard from the driver of the pretty little blue car. "Not a lot of them have the potential to be good friends, Kels. And with all our conversations, you know me a lot better than most."

"Oh!" Kelsey glanced down at the phone, then back up at the road ahead of her. She wasn't sure how to respond but she had to admit that Jamie was right. While they had only spent fifteen minutes in each other's actual company, they had come to know a lot about the other person. And over the previous few weeks, Kelsey had also sensed a change in her friend. While the other woman continued to be flirty, she no longer seemed as serious about it. Their conversations touched on more than just bad drivers and other superficial things. Despite the fact that they were fairly limited with the app, over the past two months they had become friends. "I feel exactly the same way. Despite the fact that we don't hang out in person, and have no contact outside our daily commute, I think of you as a friend too. I don't have many since I moved to St. Seren, so it really means a lot to me."

"So, coffee?"

Kelsey cracked up laughing in her car. "You have a one track mind, Jamie Schultz! Oh, and speaking of your name, I tried to find you online. Did you give me a wrong name?"

In her own car, Jamie glanced at her phone curiously before answering. "Um, no. Oh, wait, I don't have my own picture I have a picture of Olivia."

"Of course you do! But I searched for Jamie Schultz and still couldn't find you."

Jamie thought for a minute then realized why Kelsey couldn't find her. "Oh damn, sorry Kels. I forgot that I'm listed under my nickname, so you probably just thought it was some dude's profile of their car. Everyone calls me James."

"James? You wouldn't happen to be friends with Jenn White would you?"

Jamie's eyebrows rose. "Yes, I am. How do you know Jenn?"

Kelsey thought about how to answer her nerd friend. "My friends Tam and Shell introduced me. Well, they were actually trying to set us up but neither of us were interested."

Laughter came back over her phone speaker and Jamie's voice followed. "I don't know your type at all, but I do know that you aren't Jenn's. That's pretty hilarious. And I believe I've met Tam and Shell before at a mutual friend's house party. What a small world."

"That is funny actually." Kelsey went out on a limb and said what she had been thinking for a while. "So what is your type?" There was no response for nearly five minutes and Kelsey knew that Jamie had to be nearing her exit by then. So she worried that she may never get an answer to her question. She was startled by Jamie's voice just as she switched back to the center lane. She decided to try the nerdy woman's strange rules to see if it helped her commute. So far it had been working.

It wasn't that Jamie didn't want to answer Kelsey's question. It was simply that she didn't know how to answer. She had to think long and hard about the things she liked in a woman. She was nearing her exit and didn't want to leave Kelsey hanging so she quickly answered. "I like smart women with curves who know what they want. Someone with personality and humor, but also a woman who is sensitive."

"Jeez, you're not asking much are you?" Kelsey's laughter came through the little blue car's sound system and Jamie got goose bumps.

"No, I'm not asking for much. I believe I was only asking for coffee." She left the statement open and wondered how the other woman would respond. It had become a game between them and

Jamie had actually come to enjoy it. Perhaps it was twisted the way she looked forward to Kelsey's shut downs, but she liked it.

"Hmm, why don't you ask again on Friday? You never know, I may say yes one of these times."

Jamie wondered how it was possible to be crestfallen with disappointment, yet grinning in delight. It was confusing. "Okay little miss rainbow car, I'm pulling into my parking spot now. Talk to you tomorrow morning?"

Kelsey's response was almost immediate. "Unless I stalk you tonight when I take a break from knitting."

The pretty blue car was in park before Jamie responded, but her mind continued racing ahead. "I will cherish your stalking, should you grace me with your online presence. Good day to you, madam!"

"Have a nice evening, Jamie."

DESPITE ALL THEIR talk of stalking and finding Jamie on social media, Kelsey never got the chance. She spent the evening making cake pops and brownies for her office because the next day was Dr. Davies's birthday. The two secretaries, two assistants, and the techs, all pooled their money together and bought him gourmet cooking lessons. Kelsey's Drīv app chimed less than a minute after she started it up after work. Jamie had neglected to bring up Kelsey's social media absence on their way to work but was quick rectify that oversight after.

"All talk and no stalk, huh Kels?"

Still riding a sugar high from baked goods, the dental assistant cracked up laughing then responded to her. "You know, you could friend request me. This isn't a one-way street, nerd. You have two fingers, put them to use!"

"That's what she said!"

Kelsey blushed when she realized that she did indeed say that and it could be taken in a very dirty way. And oh how she would like that good-looking woman to follow through with those words. Kelsey shook the fleeting wish away because that was never going to happen. She'd heard enough from Tam and Jenn to know that Jamie was a bit of a playgirl and wasn't going to settle down for anyone. Which was too bad really because the engineer was kind of a catch. "She did say that, now what are you going to do about it?"

The app chimed and laughter came back over the tiny speaker of her cell phone. "Ooh, you're so feisty this afternoon.

Did your whole office cut out early and go for happy hour drinks?"

"Nope. It was Dr. Davies's birthday and I stayed up last night making cake pops and brownies for the occasion. The entire staff is riding high on a massive sugar buzz right now. And that, my dear nerd, is why I wasn't whiling away my hours searching for you."

Jamie perked up in the leather seat of her little blue car. "You're a baker? Holy mother but you're my new favorite person! Feel free to stuff me with sweets for the rest of your life." Jamie's sweet tooth was well known among her friends, though she wasn't a big fan of the vegan stuff that Jenn seemed to like. Donuts, cake, pie, cookies, brownies, and ice cream, none were safe around the blonde. "On second thought, I've changed my mind about going out to coffee. I think you should invite me over and feed me your goodies!"

The laughing voice of her driving buddy rolled through the stereo system with ease. "Jamie Schultz! You can make the most innocent things sound perverted! And there aren't many treats left. I was going to go home and give them out to my neighbors."

A pout started to form on the blonde's face and she down-swiped to protest the travesty of not giving her the leftovers. "Nooo! You can't let such glorious things go to waste!"

"But they're not going to waste, my neighbors are highly appreciative."

Jamie harrumphed. "Eeent, wrong answer, Kels! If you're not putting it into my mouth you're wasting it!"

A beat, maybe two went by before Kelsey's laughing voice came back. "That's what she said!"

"Holy shit, I can't believe you just said that!"

Kelsey responded. "In all honesty, I can't either!"

"So what are you doing after work today? Any plans?"

"Nothing huge. I've got to stop for gas at my exit then I have a Krav Maga class at 7:00, then probably home to catch up on my shows. Why?"

Based on their many conversations, Jamie knew that Kelsey's exit was the one right before her own downtown one. Without over-thinking her actions, she exited one sooner than she needed. She pulled into the gas station on the corner near the exit and parked her car. She thought for a second about whether or not her actions would be crossing a line with her friend, then she decided to just roll with it and replied to the flashing little rainbow car icon. "So Kels, let's talk about a handoff." Jamie had actually left work a little late that day so was only a couple minutes ahead of Kelsey on the highway, which meant the dental assistant would be pulling into the gas station any time. Jamie grabbed the note pad from her laptop bag and wrote a large note across the top sheet of paper.

"Hold on, getting off the highway now. And what do you mean a handoff? Oh! You're here!" Rather than pull up to the pump, Kelsey parked next to where Jamie had backed Olivia into a parking space. Their driver's windows were facing each other and both women wore a goofy grin. Suddenly Jamie held her note up to the window so Kelsey could see, and Kelsey immediately started laughing. She rolled down her window and waited for the other woman to do the same. "Will buy coffee for sweets? Do you ever give up, woman?"

Jamie flashed her a wide grin. "On sweets? Never! On coffee?" She shrugged her shoulders. "I suppose that's up to you."

Kelsey laughed then peered at the other woman, who gazed innocently back. "Yes to the first one, no to the second."

Jamie's face lit up, then fell, then just looked befuddled. "Wait, no to which? I'm confused."

"Which one would disappoint you more?"

"Ooh, that is a hard one!" Jamie's face scrunched up in deep thought, and Kelsey thought she looked adorable. But instead of saying that she shot back one of the other woman's favorite lines.

She pointed at Jamie and let her have it. "That's what she said!"

The woman in the pretty blue car immediately registered shock then she slapped her steering wheel. "Goddamnit Kels! That is my line! You can't just steal my lines like that and especially not twice in one day!" The end came out almost as a whine, which only made Kelsey laugh harder.

"Poor James, whatever will you do? And it's yes to the sweets. I have some cake pops and some brownies left over. Which would you like?"

"Yes!"

Kelsey snickered. "That doesn't answer my question."

"Sure it does, yes. To everything." She comically wiggled her eyebrows.

Kelsey sighed. "Yes to the sweets, Jamie. No to coffee." Jamie pouted. She full-on stuck out her bottom lip and pouted. When Kelsey maintained her intractable gaze, she pouted even harder. Kelsey pointed at the lip. "You're ridiculous! Now come around and get your goodies, I'm not your server."

The excited woman hopped out of her car and ran around to the passenger side of the little silver economy. Kelsey unlocked it and she practically dove through the door to see what was in store for her. Kelsey opened both lids and pointed at the items inside. "This one has the cake pops and the little slip of paper tells which is which. The other has the last three caramel-filled double chocolate brownies —"

"Oh my God, gimmee gimmee gimmee!"

Kelsey laughed. "Simmer down there." She pointed at the blonde taking up her passenger doorway. "I want my containers back too!" Kelsey transferred the remaining cake pops out of her specialized carrying case into disposable plastic containers with the leftover brownies, but she still wanted them back.

Jamie put the lids back on and stacked the two containers before hastily backing out of the car and closing the door. "Yup yup, containers back. Gotcha!"

Kelsey covered her eyes for a second then watched as the other woman lovingly placed the plastic bins of baked goods onto the floor of her front passenger seat. She called out to her. "Please tell me you have friends that are going to help you eat all that!"

Jamie came back around her car and crouched in front of Kelsey's open window. She seemed proud of the answer she gave. "Nope, all me."

"James, you're gonna make yourself sick!"

"Will you come nurse me back to health if I do?"

Kelsey started laughing. "You're incorrigible! And no, I will not."

Jamie gave a dramatic sigh and grabbed her heart. "Oh, you wound me! I'm afraid coffee is the only thing that will take the pain away! Say you'll have coffee with me tonight."

The Irish-Latina wasn't sure when she had last seen such dramatic antics with the exception of her great aunt Juanita on her father's side, but she was entertained. "I already told you, I have Krav Maga tonight." She watched the attractive blonde's face light up with her smile. She really did have a great smile and there was just something about her. But Kelsey was not going to admit that to the persistent woman.

Jamie looked hopeful. "So tomorrow then?"

"No."

An indignant look came over the blonde's face. "What do you mean no?"

Kelsey laughed. "I'm going to be sore from Krav Maga. Ask me again on Wednesday." With that she rolled up her window and pulled her car over to the gas pumps.

Jamie got in and started her own car then pulled to the exit drive and stopped. When Kelsey got out of her car to pump gas Jamie took a second to check her out then called to her. "So we'll have coffee on Wednesday then?"

"I said ask again Wednesday, I didn't say I would accept." Another car pulled up behind the little blue one and honked its horn, wanting to exit. Kelsey just smiled and waved at the nerd car. "Bye James!" When Jamie left the gas station she was more determined than ever to win Kelsey's friendship. Yes, friendship was definitely the right word. And it was going to work because she had already gotten the beautiful woman to let her ask on Wednesday instead of Friday. She was wearing her down slow, but still wearing her down.

When Kelsey got home she decided on a tuna salad sandwich before her class. As soon as the can opener came out both cats were immediately and desperately underfoot. She looked at the two black and white beggars. "Really guys? I just fed you your own meal in a can. You're fatty cats!"

Newman stopped twining around her legs and looked up at his owner as if to say "who, me"? She pointed at both of them. "Yes, you! The vet says you're both overweight. What do you have to say for yourselves?" Pierre answered by jumping up on the counter and knocking her clean fork onto the floor. The cat stared at her and she squinted back at his sheer audacity. Finally she shoved him off the counter and picked up her fork. "You're an asshole, Pierre!"

As Kelsey ate her dinner of sandwich and store-bought pasta salad, she thought about her interactions with her driving friend. Jamie was certainly persistent, but it helped her case immensely that she was also sweet and funny. And Kelsey thought she could do a lot worse than to have a friend like Jamie. What didn't help was the fact that she was also attracted to her nerdy friend. Minus a few minor things, Jamie seemed totally like her dream type. But she shrugged her shoulders and cleaned up in time to leave for her class. She was sure that attraction would sort itself out in time.

Chapter Six

DESPITE HER WORDS to Kelsey, Jamie did not eat all the treats herself. She took some of them to work the next day where she had the opportunity to show Bill what good things actually tasted like. Though she wasn't completely certain the man hadn't burned his taste buds out after watching him eat microwaved mac and cheese covered in mayonnaise and taco sauce for breakfast. She pushed the container toward the dividing line where one person's desk ended and the other's territory began. "Despite the fact that these are probably really unhealthy, eat one anyway. I think your body will thank you."

Bill's eyes lit up with glee. "Oh man, score! Where did you get these? I love cake pops!"

"Seriously dude, is there anything that you don't love? One of my friends had some left over from a work birthday party and she let me have them."

The man mumbled around a bite of cake. "Oh, mmm, these are good." Luckily he swallowed before speaking again. "Is that all she made, just the cake pops?"

Jamie glanced at the bin that had eight treats remaining and flashed back to the three caramel-filled brownies she ate for dinner the night before. "Yup." She stood and grabbed the re-sealable container. "I should probably ask if anyone else wants some—"

She was stopped by a hand on her wrist and a deadly serious look from Bill. "No. You shouldn't."

Jamie slowly lowered the container back to the desktop, exactly on the line between their two spaces. "Okay, man, I'll just leave them right here." She sat down again and spun in her chair to go over the designs for a new tester. She didn't let out the laugh that was threatening but a smirk was firmly in place at Bill's behavior when introduced to Kelsey's treats.

KELSEY WAS SORE, really sore. She started taking Krav Maga classes six months previous on her father's urging. Well, he hadn't urged her into that specific discipline of self-defense. He and her mother had moved back to Texas to be near his family seven years before, but she talked to them on the phone every single week and flew down to visit once or twice a year. It hardly seemed like enough but she only made so much money as a dental assistant and student loans were a killer on her budget.

Her parents owned a garage down in San Antonio, but her dad rarely worked on the cars anymore. He had a solid staff of nephews and one niece that did all the dirty work while he and Kelsey's mother managed the place. But they were pretty tied to the business and couldn't really leave to come up and visit Kelsey either. It was during one of her weekly phone calls that her dad had practically begged her to take some sort of self-defense class. She tried to protest that she could handle herself but her dad still got his point across. In his very no-nonsense way, he elicited a promise from her. Her dad was a proud man and never begged for anything, but he had begged her then after they had spent at least twenty minutes talking about the uptick of hate crimes across the nation.

"Mi pequeño, I worry. Please say you will learn some things to protect yourself."

She tried to laugh off his words in response. "Papa, I'm thirty-two years old! I'm a little beyond classes to protect my delicate sensibilities!"

Frustration was evident in his answer. *"¡No, mi hija!* If you do not learn karate or something, I will send your cousin Lupe up to camp on your doorstep."

Kelsey shuddered at her father's words. "Has he started showering more than once a week?"

"No."

"And does he still wear his hair in a long mullet?"

"Si."

Kelsey sighed. "Fine, I'll start looking tonight."

It was actually one of their clients at the office that had helped make her choice of Krav Maga. The man was in for a routine cleaning and he mentioned how sore he was from his new class. He said it was the most hard-core thing he'd ever taken up. Out of sight, Kelsey had actually rolled her eyes because the guy had always been a bit of a douche. But out of learned and ingrained politeness, she asked him about it.

His voice was full of smug ego but she listened while he explained what Krav Maga was.

"It's considered contact-combat and it is a self-defense system developed by the Israeli Defense Forces. It combines a variety of different martial arts along with realistic fight training. It's the best self-defense system out there."

He sounded like he was parroting a manual but the more he spoke, the more she was interested in the discipline. "Wow. That is good to know. I'm actually looking for self-defense classes right now, perhaps I'll check into the Krav Maga thing."

The man turned his head toward where she was standing next to the chair and looked her up and down. "Sweetie, you don't want to do that. It's really hard. Maybe you should look into some ladies' kick boxing or something."

And that was how a very stubborn Irish-Latina decided to learn Krav Maga. Though six months in, she was kind of regretting it. Because she was incredibly sore, Kelsey was more than a little cranky on Tuesday morning. Jamie sent her a voice message as soon as the engineer hit the highway. "So, Krav Maga huh?"

Kelsey's uncharacteristic grumpiness had one of the blonde's eyebrows climbing toward her hairline as the other woman growled back at her. "It hurts to blink and I want my cocoa fix!"

"Cocoa, not coffee?"

"No."

Jamie snorted at her friend's pissiness. "I can see you're not in the mood to talk this morning. Poor Kelsey, maybe you need a massage? I've been told I have good hands."

"I'm sure you have."

Another growl had preceded the response that came across Olivia's speaker system and Jamie snickered again. In some twisted way, she was enjoying tormenting the other woman. But she also sensed that it was more than the normal level of attitude. "Are you really that sore, Kels, or is there more to your attitude this morning? Did one of your kittens lose his mittens?"

Jamie started laughing before the message ran out so Kelsey heard it loud and clear on her end. She sighed. "Besides having every part of my body hurt, I have cramps." Kelsey hated admitting to something so blatantly female and weak-seeming, but she trusted Jamie not to be a dick about it. She probably shouldn't have.

"Ooh, maybe I won't ask you out to coffee tomorrow!"

Kelsey scowled in irritation and that irritation carried through via the voice message. "Really, James? Really? We're both women here, ass!"

The blonde's reply came back seconds later. "No I didn't

mean it like that! I simply meant that it might be smart to wait a
few days to ask a woman who isn't interested in me to coffee,
when she's both PMSing and Krav Maga trained! I mean, I know
how I am when I'm PMSing."

And just like that, Jamie's words had returned Kelsey's
laughter. "You are crazy! But feel free to ask tomorrow, I won't
bust your ass." She snorted before the message cut off.

"Ooh, the lady is encouraging me to ask her out to coffee!
Does that mean you're going to say yes?"

Kelsey smirked in her silver car, as always loving their little
games and interactions. "It means you can ask tomorrow and I'll
decide then whether or not to say yes."

"Damn!"

They messaged back and forth for a little while longer until
Kelsey arrived at work. They had to be at work at the same time
but because Kelsey left earlier than Jamie, she typically had
slightly better traffic at the beginning of her drive, so she made
better time per mile. Once she started work, it quickly became
clear that Kelsey was not in the best of moods and most in the
office gave her a wide berth. They were used to her grumpiness
the day after her classes. And she only seemed to suffer from bad
cramps every few months. So it was like a rare lunar eclipse when
the two physical discomforts intersected on the same day.

Kelsey caught June crossing herself more than once and the
middle-aged woman wasn't even Catholic. That was when she
decided that she needed to chill a little and be more cheerful.
With that thought in mind, she entered the room to see their next
patient. He was a younger guy and had been coming to see the
doctor for years, since his parents started bringing him. He was
never a very calm patient, and since he was in for wisdom teeth
extraction, he was especially nervous. "Good afternoon, Mr.
Kline. How are you today?"

The twenty-year-old swallowed thickly, causing his Adam's
apple to bob up and down. "I—I'm fine, I guess." She nodded and
smiled at him, then clipped the bib around his neck. She leaned
around to look at him when he called her name. "Um, Miss
Kelsey?"

"Yes?"

The poor kid was white with fear. "Is this gonna hurt? I'm
afraid that I'm gonna pass out or something. I really don't like my
teeth worked on."

Dr. Davies walked in just in time to answer Steve's question.
"If you're that nervous, son, we can just put you to sleep. You'll

have to wait a little longer after but you won't be awake for any of the procedure."

"You can?" His face looked so hopeful that Kelsey had to turn away to hide her smile.

The doctor did smile congenially. "Sure can. Is that what you'd like to do?" Steve nodded vigorously. "Okay then. Kelsey will just need to get your signature on a few papers then we can get started."

Once everything was sorted out, the doctor sedated the man with Versed. It was a standard medication and worked quite well, but it was not without its side effects. Forgetfulness was the most innocuous of them. Not long into the procedure movement near the unconscious patient's lap caught Kelsey's attention. Dr. Davies heard her groan and glanced at his assistant. "Sup, Kels?"

She laughed at his newest attempt at slang. "It's so cute the way you keep trying to be relevant to the younger generation." She paused then added the problem. "It's the Versed."

The doctor glanced down that the patient's crotch and grimaced at the way Steven Kline was scratching at his erection. It wasn't idle scratching either, the man had a serious itch. Pruritius was one of the unfortunate side effects of the highly effective drug, that and the erection. "Sheila!" The young tech came around the corner into the room wide-eyed with panic, thinking something had happened to the patient. Dr. Davies nodded toward Steve Kline's raging hard-on that now had both hands scratching away at it. "Throw a drape over that, will you?"

Sheila's nose wrinkled with disgust. "Oh, eww!" Then she caught the look on her boss's face and rushed to comply. "Yes sir, sorry!"

Once the drape was in place the tech took off out of the room and Kelsey started laughing. She nodded toward the drape over the young man's lap, indicating the frantic movement beneath. "I don't know if that's any better, now it just looks like he's choking the chicken under there!"

The doctor glance down and went back to the extraction. "It could be worse."

Kelsey looked at him seriously. "How is that?"

"He's gonna be in the chair a while. I'd hate to think all that stimulation leads to a culmination of sorts. The poor kid will be very embarrassed."

The assistant looked at her boss, then back down at the action under the drape. The scratching had clearly picked up in intensity. "Oh, eww!"

Dave Davies chuckled because he'd seen just about everything in his near thirty years of practice. "Don't worry, thanks to the Versed he won't remember the erection or the itching. But he'll sure wonder what went on in that chair if he makes a mess in his shorts." His laughter continued as he dropped a wisdom tooth into the metal pan with a wet sounding clank.

Kelsey was in a slightly better mood that night on her way home. It brightened further when Jamie was the first one to send a message.

"For the love of feck, don't get on the highway!"

She responded, still a good half mile from the on-ramp to the expressway she usually took after work. "Why, oh wise admiral? Is it a trap?

"I'm actually being serious here, Kels. Check your app, there's some kind of freaking accident halfway between me and home and I'm stuck on a stopped highway!"

Kelsey looked down at the map on her phone and noted that the highway was a solid red line with multiple heavy traffic symbols. She replied to her friend's message. "Woo, you caught me just in time! Looks like I'm taking the back way home. I'll just hop on Grand River Drive and take that down past the accident."

"Olivia is grumbling at you right now!"

"Just Olivia?" Kelsey laughed at the way Jamie had become the cranky one, a one-eighty from that morning. A few minutes of silence went by and Kelsey assumed that Jamie was trying to navigate her way off the expressway. After ten minutes went by she gave in to the urge to check on the nerd car. "You still there, James?"

Another couple minutes of silence then it was broken by a burst of profanity that had Kelsey cracking up in her seat. "Mother-sonnofa-furkin-fecking, goddamn piece of—"

Jamie's voice cut off so Kelsey tried again. "Um, James?"

A long sigh came through the speaker of Kelsey's phone then Jamie's calmer voice followed. "The good news is that I got off the highway."

"I'm assuming that means there is bad news too."

"Nigel is pissed at me. I'm in the middle of nowhere and apparently I'm not taking any turns that bastard likes. I've taken so many wrong turns now that he just told me, 'well fuck off then!' and shut down. So now I'm flying blind here."

By that point Kelsey nearly had tears in her eyes she was laughing so hard. "He did not!"

"Well, no." Jamie conceded. "But he wanted to!"

"Jamie Schultz, you are certifiably insane!"

Jamie was in her own car grinning like a mad fool. It was very possible that she was indeed insane. Why else would she feel so happy while lost in the middle of B.F.E. with only the guidance of a pissy digital Brit? Despite their drastically different routes home, they still arrived at their respective places about the same time. Though they were each significantly later than normal. Jamie did a forty-five minute workout in the gym before grilling a boneless chicken breast and steaming some broccoli.

While the deck for her condo wasn't huge, it was big enough for a gas grill and table with two chairs. Jenn told her once that it was cozy. After dinner, the cleanup, and a shower, she decided to just chill for a while on the couch with her laptop. "Let's see who is online tonight."

Kelsey's evening was not so productive. She still hurt and felt exhausted but she managed to feed the two greedy pigs as soon as she came home. Instead of eating her own dinner right away she opted for a long hot bath. Only after her soak did she pull two tamales out of the freezer for dinner, made from her *abuela's* recipe. Meal cleanup involved throwing away the paper plate and tossing her fork and glass into the dishwasher. By 8 p.m. she was settled onto the couch with a heating pad across her abdomen and a laptop on her thighs.

First she checked e-mail and other headline news, then she checked all her regular friend's social network pages. She gave in to her desire to search for Jamie after she couldn't find anyone else she wanted to chat with online. Typing in "James Schultz" immediately brought up a profile with Jamie's pretty blue car as the picture. She clicked on it and was disappointed to see her nerdy friend's page was private. "Damn it, Newman!" She usually addressed the cats out of the blue and they were quite used to it. "How am I supposed to stalk her properly if her profile is private?"

Her obsessing was interrupted when she caught movement out of the corner of her eye. She looked over to her large aloe plant that sat in a pot on the floor. Then without missing a beat she grabbed the spray bottle from the end table and shot Pierre right in his stalking dickish face. "You stay away from Lo, you evil plant-killing bastard! I mean it, Pierre!" The cat jumped and ran out of the reach of her sprayer, then settled in to glare in her general direction.

"Mrow!"

"Sass all you want, mister. But you better not touch either

one of my plants!" She glanced up to the second plant, which sat at the very top of a six foot book shelf. That one was named Auntie after a friend of her mother's that had passed away before her parents moved to Texas. She got the pothos plant at the funeral because no one wanted to take the poor thing home. Even though he had never bothered them before, for whatever reason Pierre had become obsessed with her plants in the last few months. He would bat at the leaves, shred them with his claws, and just terrorize them unless Kelsey tossed a shoe at his head or sprayed him with the water bottle.

Lo had been looking a little sad of late, but so far Auntie was out of his reach. He was crafty though and she didn't trust him one bit. Once satisfied that he was going to leave it be, she turned back to her laptop. She scanned the page one more time and before she could talk herself out of it, she hit the friend request button. She was startled when seconds later it was accepted. Startled, but pleased. However she nearly jumped out of her skin when the message box popped up.

```
Still stalking me, I see.
```

Kelsey chuckled and typed back to her.

```
Oh, of course. Since you are so shy and all, I had
to do all the work!
```

```
Is it too soon to ask about coffee?
```

The woman surrounded by her cats giggled.

```
Yes. But you get points for persistence.
```

```
Siiiiiiiggghhhhh
```

Jamie's response brought on a wave of affection for her friend and a smile to her lips. It also elicited an eye roll from the sore woman. Curious, she typed back.

```
Shouldn't you be out gadding about or something? It
seems early for you to be settled in at home.
```

Jamie was settled in at home and actually enjoying it for once. She was also borderline giddy that Kelsey had friend requested her. She didn't really know why but thinking about her friend made her really happy.

Gadding? Who says gadding?

Kelsey's response only made her smile wider.

People. People say gadding, James! Psshh!

Jamie was shaking their head as she typed back.

Nope, nobody outside the middle ages or something. Try again.

Fine, out on the town then? Being les-b-social?

Jamie cracked up laughing as the little ellipses disappeared and Kelsey's words appeared.

Well I USED to "gad around" but I've been staying home a lot more lately.

Immediately after sending the message Jamie wondered if she wanted to confide such things to her new friend. The revelations prompted by her conversation with Jenn had been eye-opening. And the changes she had made since that day were deeply personal. She wanted to call her words back but it was too late as they placidly sat on the screen in front of her.

So why are you staying home more?

Because she was still changing, Jamie wasn't sure how to answer or if she wanted to answer. She didn't talk about deeper things to most people, but Kelsey wasn't like most. Even though they had only know each other a few months, Jamie felt as close to her as she did Burke and Jenn. She believed that sometimes you just know if you're meant to be friends with someone. Sometimes you are so drawn that you know without a doubt your life will be happier with that person in it than without. Kelsey was one of those people. Because of that, Jamie made the decision to trust her.

I've found myself in a rut the past few years and I'm not sure I like who I've become. So I've been spending a little more time with me and a little less time with others.

Kelsey's eyes widened as she read the other woman's personal message. She grew concerned about her new friend.

```
Is everything okay, James?
```

It took a few minutes for Jamie's reply to come through, the entire time Kelsey stared at the little ellipses that signaled the other person was typing.

```
I've just been through some shit, you know? Of
course everyone has, I know this. But I ended my last
serious relationship about five years ago and I was
damaged for a long time. I finally feel like I'm coming
back again.
```

Kelsey forgot all about her cramps and focused solely on the screen in front of her. "Whoa, Newman! Did you read that?" She looked down at the cat who was completely dead to the world next to her. Pierre was laying along the length of her legs with his fat head pressed against the back of her laptop screen. She thought about how to answer and realized that if they were really friends then trust had to run both ways.

```
I know exactly what you're saying. My ex cheated on
me for months before I found out. We were only together
two years but it still stung.
```

```
Yes, something similar for me too. My ex was my
first girlfriend though, together almost seven years.
And I clearly saw everything through rose-colored
glasses because I ignored the drugs and cheating as
well as the verbal and emotional abuse.
```

After a second, she sent another message.

```
What's funny is that we were the "Poster Couple"
and people were so surprised when we split up, when I
left her.
```

"Oh, James!" Kelsey covered her mouth out of sympathy for her friend. She herself suffered from insecurity for a long time just from a couple months of cheating. She could only imagine what her friend had gone through. But the more she thought about it, the more she started to understand the things she had heard about Jamie. Her friends described a woman who never dated, never got attached, had a lot of acquaintances but only had a few close friends. Jamie was the life of the party when she was there but never stayed for long. Yes, everything made sense. Before Jamie could wonder where she went, she sent back a message to her.

I'm really sorry, James. No one should have to go through that with someone, and clearly she wasn't worth your time.

She also sent along a cartoon heart with the word friends forever written in script over it.

Aww! Friends forever huh? Well I think that sounds about right.

Jamie sent the same cartoon image back. They chatted for a little while longer until Kelsey's day had thoroughly caught up to her. She finally said bye to Jamie, then said good night to the cats on her way to the bedroom. Of course, once she was actually in bed her mind refused to shut down. Her thoughts raced with everything Jamie had told her. She could completely understand why her friend had stopped dating. Though sleeping around wouldn't have been Kelsey's first choice to deal with circumstances, everyone had their own way of coping.

Of course one thought led to another and before she knew it Kelsey was imaging what Jamie would be like in bed. She sighed. "She's probably some hard-core top, all butch attitude and disposition." She then imagined shoving the attractive blonde onto her back and completely taking control and realized that was a much hotter image. Perhaps too hot. Giving in to the heat that had started from a place slightly lower than her heating pad, Kelsey fumbled to open the drawer next to her bed. She tried to rationalize aloud to herself. "They say it's good for cramps."

Chapter Seven

WEDNESDAY MORNING FOUND Jamie in a fabulous mood. Despite her heavy chat the night before she felt surprisingly free when she woke. In the past she would get panicky or irritable if she discussed her ex with either Burke or Jenn. But with Kelsey, it felt right. Jamie figured either it was the right time for her to start letting go of the hurts she suffered in the past, or Kelsey was something special. Perhaps it was a little of both. And with the new day she too felt new.

Spring had officially sprung and the day was going to be warm and sunny. Traffic sprinted along at a joyous pace for her and Olivia. And the tunes on her music app were rolling with the miles. One of her favorites was on and she mangled the lyrics to "Music Is My Hot Hot Sex", by Cansei de Ser Sexy, with abandon. The band was only listed as CSS on her music app but she had downloaded their songs a few months before because she liked the band so much. Jamie made it nearly through the song when her app chimed.

"So, how is Olivia on this beautiful morning?"

Despite the sun being in her eyes for the eastbound direction of their morning commute, it was supposed to be in the sixties with blue skies and for that Jamie was happy. She smiled and responded, glad that Kelsey seemed to be in a better mood too. "Shouldn't we be asking you that? I assume you're feeling better today?"

The other woman's laughter came through before her words. "It's called hot soak, hot pad, Motrin, and a good night's sleep. Miracle workers, all!" Before Jamie could respond Kelsey sent another message. "I'm waiting."

At first she was legitimately confused. "Waiting for what?"

Her driving buddy's voice cleared it up fast. "Really, James? It's Wednesday."

She glanced down to her app then moved her eyes back up to the road so she could switch lanes. "Oh yeah, heh." She quickly responded to give Kelsey what she asked for. Jamie was almost giddy with the fact that her friend actually wanted her to ask. "So Kels, you ready to go out for coffee with me yet?" She waited a few minutes for her friend's response.

"Is that the best you can do? Where is my innuendo? Where

is the teasing? Such a lame nerd you are." The message ended in laughter.

"Hey, that was mean! Fine, you want innuendo? Ahem! Kelsey, are you interested in seeing my favorite place to taste the bean?"

"Groan!"

Jamie tried again. "Why don't snakes drink coffee? Because it makes them viperactive!"

There was a few more minutes pause before Kelsey responded again. "No. Just no."

The woman in the pretty blue car pouted. "Aww, no to coffee or no to my jokes?"

"Yes to both."

Jamie glanced at her phone, then back at the road. Then she glanced at the phone again and back at the road again. Kelsey was confusing. "Wait, yes to coffee?"

"It was a yes to your question about 'no's. So that means no to both."

The blonde huffed in her leather seat, disappointment having brought her down to a slight whine. "But you said to ask you!"

Kelsey's rich laughter rolled through Olivia's speakers and gave Jamie goose bumps. She could listen to that laughter all day. "Maybe you're not asking the right question then."

Jamie thought hard about what the correct question could be. She always asked her to coffee and Kelsey always turned her down. The logically minded engineer tried to talk herself through the problem. "I always ask her to coffee, she always refuses. What if—" She was interrupted as another message from Kelsey sounded over her speakers.

"Have you figured it out yet?"

"Hush you! I'm thinking really hard here and I need a minute!"

More laughter. "By all means then, carry on."

Jamie tapped on her steering wheel then turned down the music so she could concentrate. "Okay, what do I know about Kelsey? She's half Irish and half Mexican-American. She bakes, she gets cranky after her Krav Maga classes and wants—that's it!" She quickly changed her question. "So Kels, would you like to go for hot cocoa with me? I know someplace that makes the best in the city." Kelsey's response came back about twenty seconds later.

"Yes."

Back in Kelsey's car, Jamie's shock came through loud and

clear and she giggled. "Yes?"

She answered with a smile on her face. "Yes, James."

"You promise the princess isn't in another castle? You're not just pissing with me?"

Kelsey snorted her laughter and responded again. "You are such a nerd! And no, I'm not pissing with you. Definitely not my kink!"

The response that came back took her completely by surprise. Jamie's voice was normal at first but quickly escalated into unintelligible screaming. "Hey, that's great! I can't wa—holy fecking summabich! Oh my God, oh my God, oh my—" Then the message cut off with the squealing of tires and horns.

Kelsey panicked when Jamie didn't send another message. A minute went by and she spent the entire time trying to talk herself down from the ledge. "I'm sure it's fine Kelsey. Just because you finally make plans to meet a cute woman for cocoa doesn't mean karma is gonna be an ass and kill her in an accident on the way to work. I mean, karma is much slower moving than that, right?" Talking to herself wasn't helping so she finally gave in and swiped the screen. "Are you okay, what happened? You're freaking me out over here, James!"

Seconds after she sent her message Jamie's much calmer voice came back to her and Kelsey could hear honking in the background. "I'm okay." A split second calming breath came through, then Jamie's voice again. "There's a goddamned cow in the middle of the highway!"

Kelsey glanced at her phone in disbelief. No way was there a cow on the eastbound lane of the expressway. Where would it have come from? She answered her friend's declaration with dubiousness. "I'm gonna call bullshit on you there. No way that a cow could be on the highway!"

"Does this sound like bullshit to you?" After Jamie stopped speaking Kelsey listened to the sharp sound of multiple horns and the mooing of one lost cow.

Disbelief turned to hilarity as Kelsey neared her exit. "So what are you going to do? Are you at least close to your exit?" She scrolled back on her map and tried to remember which exit Jamie took for her job.

"Oh, sick!" Jamie laughed. "But at least old Bessie didn't leave that in front of my car. Good luck Range Rover! Oh, and a cop is here now leading the cow off to the shoulder by her head gear harness thingy."

Kelsey snickered. "You mean halter, James?"

A beat, then Jamie replied. "Yeah, that!"

"All right, nerd, now that I'm at work and you're safely underway again I'm going to leave you to your day. I'll talk to you later, right?"

"But we didn't set a day or time for cocoa!"

Kelsey smiled at how eager her friend was to meet up. "Catch me on the ride home. We'll set something up then."

"Okay, bye Kelsey. Have a good day at work."

"You too!" Kelsey shook her head as she grabbed her lunch and went into the back door of the office. One thing about commuting nearly forty minutes one way for work, things were never dull.

JAMIE WAS ONLY a couple minutes late for work after that, but she spent the first fifteen minutes after she got there telling Bill all about the cow incident. Of course he didn't believe her so she pulled out her cell phone and showed him the video. She had the foresight to pop her phone off the holder and get a short video of the officer leading the cow to the side of the highway, then handcuffing the halter to a metal sign. She even zoomed in on the officer's face, perfectly catching the look when he realized that his job had come down to wrangling beef off the road. He also had a look about him that said it probably wasn't the first time he'd put cuffs on something other than a criminal. Or maybe Jamie was just reading into it. Either way, the video was funny and it wasn't long before the entire engineering office had seen it. Of course it helped that she was able to screen mirror her phone to the large flat screen TV hanging on the back wall. Before Jamie could get her phone back from Bill, he did a quick swipe in her photos and whistled at the picture he saw. "Hey, who is this?" He held the phone up so Jamie could see the picture of Kelsey she had saved from the other woman's online photos.

She snatched the phone from his hands. "Give me that!" She quickly stuffed the phone into her pocket and spun around to look at her computer screen, answering him over her shoulder. "It's just my friend Kelsey, the one who I chat with on the way to work." Bill didn't respond, but he gave Jamie a knowing smile behind her back.

"You mean the same friend who made those excellent cake pops?"

Jamie still didn't turn around. "Yup."

He kept prodding her to see if she'd give anything else away.

Because, sure as anything you don't save photos of your friends onto your phone unless you had more interest than just friends. "The one who works at the dentist's office?"

"Yup."

"Hmm." He waited another thirty seconds then hammered it home. "The one who you have a mad crush on?"

"Yup." Suddenly Jamie spun around in her chair and glared at him. "No! I do not have a crush on her. I don't have a crush on anyone." She scowled and pointed her finger at Bill as he struggled not to lose his shit with laughter. "Jamie Schultz doesn't do crushes!"

He nodded. "Oh, of course she doesn't."

Jamie spun back around again but he already got what he was looking for. His cubemate had a crush.

A little while later the jackass engineer, Dave, came ranting into the office. His lines were the oldest in the building and he was usually complaining about one thing or another. However, Dave was louder than normal and everyone in the office couldn't help but hear him as he disparaged his team and their family trees. "Those dipshits wouldn't be able to pick their noses if I didn't write explicit instructions and hang them in front of their faces! What a batch lot of 'tards!" His ranting didn't stop there either.

Jamie and Bill glanced at each other and then at the office door of the engineering manager. She glanced at the desk in front of Bill and noticed that he must have hit record on his phone right after Dave started his tirade. "Dave the Dick" was not a well-liked man in their office. He belittled everyone, not just Jamie. No one was ever safe from his racist, homophobic, and rude comments. Bill especially didn't like him since the time Dave had effectively thrown him under the bus. Bill was on vacation and the other engineers took turns covering his lines for him. Since Dave was least familiar with the newer lines that Bill had under his purview, their manager wasn't going to put him in the rotation. But eventually their boss gave in. Dave crashed the motors on a robot the first day and tried to say that Bill had left it programmed that way. Jamie herself went into the program and showed her boss that it hadn't been changed until after Bill left for vacation. From that moment on, Bill hated Dave, and Dave hated Jamie. It was all sunshine and roses in the engineering office.

Eventually their boss did come out of his office but only heard the last few words of Dave's angry verbal vomit. "Is there a problem, Dave?"

Dave looked up at his boss, his face still dark with anger. "No, sir. Nothing I can't handle."

Their boss scowled at the irritating man. "Then I suggest you handle it quieter. I was on a conference call and they could hear you on the other end."

"Sorry, sir." Dave acted apologetic and the engineering manager went back into his office and shut the door.

Jamie looked over at Bill and watched as he stopped the recording. "You know, he said some pretty offensive things just now. And I'm pretty sure he broke about three big rules in our code of conduct manual with that little speech. That recording will get that POS fired for sure."

Bill nodded and made a face at her. "Gee, tell me how you really feel about him, James! Seriously though, you know Sally? She's one of the older ladies that works on his line." Jamie nodded. "She sliced her hand on his new tester the other day. He tried to say that maintenance must have done something to the edge when they installed the plates."

Jamie shrugged. "It's possible. It wouldn't be the first time maintenance has screwed something up."

Her coworker shook his head and his features took on one of uncharacteristic anger. "I watched him install those plates myself. He lied and she's got five stitches."

She nodded back at him. "Do it. But don't walk it into the office or Dave will know for sure it was you. He seems like the vindictive type and it's probably better not to give yourself away. E-mail the voice file to yourself, then send it to the boss man."

Bill grimaced. "You know what this means, don't you? We'll be stuck covering the decrepit line until a replacement gets hired." Something slammed over in the vicinity of Dave's cubical, followed by another curse from the volatile man.

They both answered at the same time. "Worth it!" Fifteen minutes later they watched as the human resources director walked into their boss' office.

Jamie glanced at her cubemate. "Oooh!"

Five minutes after that their boss's voice sounded over the plant-wide intercom. "David Carson to the engineering manager's office, ASAP!"

Bill grinned and jumped up from his chair. "I'm going to go make popcorn!"

Things calmed down a bit once their former teammate was escorted out of the building. Before Jamie knew it her smart watch was chiming the end of her day. She shut down her computer then stood and stretched her back. "Finally! It's time for me to get out of here." Jamie was full of nervous excitement when she hit the road after work. She didn't see the little rainbow car when she got on the highway so she brought up the music app and cranked the tunes. 'Radio' by Sylvan Esso was playing and she belted out the song like a pro. There was a freedom that Jamie found while listening to music and driving that she didn't find many other places. She couldn't explain why it made her so happy, it just was. She didn't care that her voice could "scour pans" Jenn had told her often enough. She just loved to sing along. By the time the chorus hit she was completely into it, despite the fact that a muddy toad probably had a better voice. The song finished and Jamie sang through another before she started to grow a little concerned. Usually Jamie came online before the first song was done. Then, like Pavlov's dog ready for dinner, her app chimed and Jamie's heart started to race.

"Is it Friday yet?"

The frustration in Kelsey's voice caused Jamie to giggle. "Sorry to tell you it's not. What's got you down, Kels?"

"Some woman smuggled her frickin dog into the office. It was in her purse and she hung it on the hook across from the chair. I was in the middle of a procedure when movement caught my eye and this little ankle biter pops his head out of the purse and barks at me." The message ended and before Jamie could reply another came through. "It startled me so much I almost fell off my damn stool! I had to stop the procedure so she could take the damn dog out to her car. And it's not the first time this has happened!"

Jamie tried to stifle her laughter enough to respond sympathetically. "Wow, um, sorry? I mean, that sucks!"

"Seriously! That woman is nuts. She probably stays home and has birthday parties for that damn dog!"

"Hmm, do you think she knits little sweaters for it?"

Kelsey made a face back in her car. "You are an ass! She brought her dog into a dentist's office. I would think that should show her level of crazy!" She waited for her friend to answer. How could Jamie not understand what a kook Mrs. Ginker was? When the engineer's voice came back it sounded like she was holding back a laugh.

"And you've never done anything strange or unusual with your cats?"

Kelsey's ears grew warm when she thought about her once a

week walks around the apartment building with Newman and Pierre. "I plead the fifth!"

Jamie's exuberant laughter came over the tiny speaker of her phone. "I thought so!"

Instead of responding to the blonde's teasing, Kelsey changed the subject. "So, you mentioned a great cocoa place?"

There was a pause before the other woman responded. "You weren't just messing with me then? You really want to go have coff—, er, cocoa?"

"Of course I do! I said so didn't I? So where is this amazing place?" Kelsey watched as brake lights started flashing across all three lanes. "Dammit! This is why I hate leaving late!" She sighed and quickly switched to the center lane as her app chimed.

"Verkehr verlangsamen voraus."

Kelsey rolled her eyes and glanced down to see how long the traffic jam was supposed to last. She sighed when she realized that Pierre and Newman were probably going to shred the curtains or something during her half hour or more of lateness. They were a total pain sometimes. Her app chimed again and the little nerd car's message box popped up.

"Hey, if you want to meet tonight I'm free any time after 5:30, traffic is really moving today!"

With one last glance at her phone, Kelsey slowed to a stop and replied. "It's not moving if you left work late! I just stopped, along with all the other lanes."

"Where are you? Are you at least past the nexus of the universe yet?"

"No, just before. Damn!"

"Sorry, Kels. So if you want to meet tonight, when is a good time for you?"

The agitated woman thought about all she had to do when she got home, then answered her friend. "Tonight is fine, and how about 7:00? Is that too late for you? Or should we go someplace for dinner instead?"

"Have I won the lottery? Did a gorgeous woman just ask me out to dinner?"

Kelsey groaned at Jamie's persistence even if she sensed the other woman was no longer seriously pursuing her. It was nice to know they'd made it to solid friend stage. Now if she could only convince her libido and dreams of that fact! More often than not she used the pictures of Jamie that she had saved on her phone to fuel her fantasies at night. She was going to have to invest in another jumbo pack of batteries again. Being Jamie's friend was costing Kelsey money and sanity. "Nope, just average Kelsey. Now, do you want to have dinner or cocoa?"

"The coffee place also makes delicious sandwiches. So if you don't mind that we can just eat there. Maybe cocoa for dessert?"

Kelsey laughed. "As long as I'm not cooking it, it sounds wonderful. Just message me the address when you get home and I'll meet you there at 7:00."

Jamie did a little dance in her seat as she continued down the highway. She was extremely excited to meet her friend for dinner. Sadly, reality was a bucket of cold water and she calmed down again. "Chill James, she's just a friend and not anything more. You're turning over a new leaf now." After talking herself down a bit, she found that she was actually sad that there was no potential with her friend. On the plus side, she really needed more solid people in her life and she knew that Kelsey was one of the good ones. Her thoughts were interrupted when her app chimed.

"You didn't answer. Will you message me the address when you get home?"

The engineer shook herself out of her musings. "It's called The Scalded Crow. You should be able to just search the place online. But I can also message you the address when I get home. I'll send my phone number too, just in case you're running late." Jamie grinned at her smooth idea.

"Oh, very smooth, James! Nice job working a legit way of slipping me your number!"

"Damn, she's quick!" She laughed and replied back to her friend. "Hey, it doesn't hurt to try! All right, Kels, I need to get gas when I get off the highway so I'm going to let you go. I'll see you later."

"Yup, see you in a few hours!"

IN KELSEY'S BEDROOM, she had multiple shirts scattered around her bed, one of which was on Pierre's head. She didn't normally let them in her bedroom but had left the door open by accident when she got home. "This isn't even a date, Newman! Why am I so nervous about meeting a friend for dinner? It's just Jamie."

Newman looked back at her, all dapper in his stately black and white tuxedo markings. "Mroooow"

She glared back at her cat. "You're not much help!" Then she glanced over at Pierre, whose head had managed to poke out an armhole but was still very much wrapped in her shirt. "You're definitely no help! And I can't wear that one now even if I wanted to because it's covered in cat hair!" She untangled the cat from the shirt and tossed the garment in the hamper. Rather than consult the cats any longer, she chose a soft long-sleeve t-shirt and her favorite jeans. She paired the shirt with a lightweight zip up hoodie and called it good. She looked at the alarm clock on her nightstand and sighed. It was twenty to seven. Rather than rush out the door, she picked up all her clothes and put them back into her closet and shooed the cats from the room. Then she made one more trip to the bathroom to spray some cologne on herself.

Afterwards she took a minute to stare into the mirror. She pulled her shirt and hoodie down a little more to cover her hips then shrugged her shoulders and watched both ride back up again. She turned sideways and frowned at the way her belly was rounded out. She ignored her ass because she had accepted a long time before that the booty would never ever be flat. It just wasn't in her genetics. She lifted her hair off her shoulders and held it up folded over to see what it would look like shorter. "Hmm, maybe I should get it cut off?" Kelsey let the hair go and tucked the front part that came across her forehead behind her ear to keep it out of the way. She looked into her strange dark green eyes as an even stranger thought popped into her head. "I wonder if Jamie would like it short." Her mental musings were halted as she glanced at the little watch on her bathroom counter and saw that she was going to be late. "Well, shit!" She quickly left the bedroom and grabbed her wallet and keys. She yelled to the cats on her way out the door. "Be good boys, Mommy will be home soon!"

Jamie was having a strangely similar experience across town, minus the cats and hips. Since she wasn't meeting Kelsey until 7:00, she had plenty of time to get a quick workout in and clean up her apartment. Not that she needed to clean her apartment because no one was coming over, and no one had come over in weeks. After the gym and cleaning she painted her toenails while she watched the newest episode of her prison show. She was nervous and was trying to do anything to distract herself. But why she was nervous, she had no idea. Instead she paced around her living room, walking with her toes pointed up to avoid smudging the paint.

During her pacing, she picked up a stuffed moose that she got when her company sent her across the bridge into Canada to research a potential supplier. She named him Dudley after the cartoon from her childhood. No, it wasn't the moose's name from the show, but it was another Canadian character. The one who always did the right thing. She stopped pacing when her mind ran off onto the new tangent. Looking at the adorable little moose in her hands she asked him the questions that she couldn't ask anyone else. "Am I doing the right thing?" She did another wobbly pacing circuit on her heels. "I mean, I'm not doing anything wrong. Kelsey is my friend and I meet friends for coffee or dinner all the time. It's not like I'm trying to pick her up. I'm not trying to pick anyone up anymore." She looked down at the moose cradled in the crook of her left arm. "Jenn was right, Dudley. I needed to start taking a different street. Do you think Kelsey would approve?" She stopped abruptly and hobbled over to put the moose back on her shelf. "Kelsey would think I was insane for talking to a stuffed animal! Okay James, enough fooling around!"

She pulled the toe separators off her feet and put away the rest of the pedicure stuff, then took herself to the shower. Afterwards, she stressed for twenty minutes trying to decide what to wear. In the end, she settled on a light blue button down, jeans, a pair of buckskin colored boots that were laced halfway, and a navy puffy vest. After swinging her messenger bag back across her chest, she took one last look around the condo then let the door shut behind her. It was only Kelsey, what was she so nervous about?

Chapter Eight

KELSEY WAS LATE. It wasn't her fault, rather she couldn't find parking for the coffee shop. Mostly because it was a lot busier than she expected. At least she wasn't too late though, only five minutes. When she walked in she spotted Jamie immediately. The blonde had gotten a lucky two-top table along the wall of windows and waved at her as she entered. She had to shake herself a little as she realized her friend had a really great smile. They'd only seen each other twice in person, for maybe fifteen minutes total. Jamie wasn't exactly smiling when she was stranded on the side of the highway. Then there was the time at the gas station but Kelsey was distracted by her impending class. It was only in the coffee shop that Kelsey started to understand the stories about why the engineer was so popular with the ladies. She took a deep breath and sighed at what could never be, then walked over to her table. Jamie stood up when she arrived and before Kelsey could even register what she was doing, the other woman gave her a big hug. It felt a little too good.

As soon as Jamie pulled back she started to speak rapid-fire. "Hey, only a few minutes late I see. Did you find parking okay? They're really busy today."

Kelsey laughed lightly, realizing that Jamie was nervous. "Yes I did, but I had to park down the street. That's the reason I was a few minutes late. I would have called you but you forgot to message me your number." Taking a chance, and with more than a little twinkle in her eye, Kelsey spoke again. "So, do you come here often?"

Jamie barked out a laugh then quickly stifled it. "That was really lame, Kels. Seriously!"

"Whatever, nerd! Now lead me to the place where I can get the promised sandwiches and amazing cocoa, I'm starving!"

The blonde grinned and looped her arm through her friend's elbow before she could protest. "If you could come with me, madam, I believe you will find a fine assortment of meat and bread arrangements to meet with your hunger demands. Even if you're a," Jamie shuddered for a second. "Vegan or vegetarian. They have it all." Kelsey snickered at her words as Jamie gestured toward the hand-written board of sandwiches and wraps that was high up on the wall behind the counter.

The woman behind the counter smiled at Jamie. "Hey, James, good to see you again."

Jamie gave her a casual smile back. "Yeah, you too, Hazel." She nodded toward Kelsey. "I've got a new customer here. I'm trying to convert her to the wisdom of giving the Scalded Crow her patronage."

Kelsey giggled at her friend's antics. "All right, I'm always open to new things and I'm ready to order."

Jamie looked at her in shock. "But there's like, twenty sandwiches up there! You can't tell me you've read every single one already."

She got a shove to the arm for her teasing. "I skimmed them all but found one that I have to try." Then she turned to Hazel, who was waiting to take her order. "May I please have the Cubano and a bottle of water?"

"I thought you wanted a hot cocoa?" Jamie looked genuinely confused.

Kelsey turned to her and scoffed. "It would be cold by the time I'm done eating, I'll just come back up and order later."

Jamie nodded at the wisdom of her statement and Hazel offered a suggestion. "I can put it on your order and you can just come back up and have me make it when you're ready.

She got a big smile and thumbs up from Kelsey. "That would be perfect, thanks!"

After Kelsey paid, Jamie ordered her own sandwich. "I'll have the double BLT and a Dr. Pepper."

"Is that like a double-decker sandwich?" Kelsey looked at her friend in disbelief and wondered how she would fit a double-decker in her mouth.

"No, it just has double bacon."

Kelsey grinned at her. "Way to be healthy, James!" Jamie just nodded as they walked down to the end of the counter to wait for their sandwiches.

Once they had their food and were seated back at their table Jamie watched as Kelsey took her first bite. Her friend chewed thoughtfully and a look of wonder came over her face. "Oh damn, this is easily one of the best Cubano sandwiches I've tasted!" She looked up at Jamie. "Where do they get their meat? This pork is delicious!"

"Hazel is the daughter of the owners and she told me that all the veggies and meats come from Zingerman's Market and Deli. They also get all their bread from Brown's Bakery and like Zingerman's they are another place that gets their ingredients from local suppliers." Kelsey was listening intently while chowing away at her sandwich.

"Wow, I love supporting local places. And this is about as local as you can get, huh?" She wiped a bit of mustard she could feel on her upper lip and smiled at her friend. "I think this is also going to become my new favorite place."

Jamie smiled smugly. "I told you it was amazing." Kelsey didn't bother answering. They made short work of their sandwiches then went back up to have Hazel make their hot drinks. Coffee for Jamie and a caramel hot cocoa for Kelsey. When they were seated again, Kelsey gazed at her friend while she sipped the hot, sweet liquid. She thought it would be awkward keeping up a conversation in real life since they didn't really know much about each other. Not to mention they had really only interacted in a limited capacity via an app. But she was mistaken. She felt so comfortable with the other woman. Jamie was thinking nearly the exact same thing. Then, as with any other time, her brain switched gears and took off on a tangent when she remembered something that Kelsey had said via the app. "Hey, you said that anything was good as long as you didn't have to cook. Does that mean you don't enjoy cooking?"

Kelsey shook her head. "Nope."

Jamie cocked her head at the woman across from her. "Nope, it doesn't mean that and you do like cooking? I don't understand, you bake such yummy treats"

Kelsey laughed. "Baking is not cooking! And I don't like it or dislike it, I just can't do it." She thought for a second and shrugged. "Okay, so I don't particularly like it either."

"Really?" Jamie looked at her friend in disbelief and Kelsey nodded. The blonde seemed appalled that her friend didn't cook. "How do you survive?"

Kelsey made a face. "Frozen meals, take out, sandwich shops, cake pops, you know, like a college kid."

Jamie started shaking her head. "Oh, Kels, no. There is a world of flavor at the tip of your tongue, you merely need to taste it!"

"That's what she said!"

Jamie stopped at the beginning of what promised to be a foodie rant and a sour look came over her face. "There you go again, stealing my lines!" She pointed at her friend. "Stop it!" Kelsey laughed at the way Jamie seemed so put out, but that didn't deter the engineer. "Okay, seriously though, I can't believe that you don't cook!"

Kelsey shrugged. "It's not a big deal, it was just never some-thing that interested me. I played soccer in junior high and high school and never had a lot of free time. My *abuela* came to live with us for a while when I was ten. She taught Mama how to cook authentic Mexican food for Papa but the only thing I learned was not to sass my *abuela*." Jamie snickered. "Actually, she did teach me how to make homemade tamales."

The woman across the table did a double take. "Wait, you mean from scratch? Beef or chicken?"

"Either. I cook the meat in a crock pot."

Jamie gave her wide eyes. "Cooked in the corn husk and everything?" Kelsey nodded again. "Oh for the love of –, you can cook then!"

"Nope. I have a very specific recipe that I wrote down as my *abuela* described it to me. I have no interest in cooking any-thing else. It's just, eh, that's why I decided years ago I just needed to find a wife that liked to cook." She laughed and shrugged.

"I like to cook." Jamie blurted out the words then immedi-ately realized how they sounded and rushed to explain. "I mean, I've always liked to cook. I like food and I like to experiment with stuff."

Kelsey looked at her friend with fresh eyes. "You're not at all what I expected."

She got a slow blink from Jamie in return. "What do you mean?"

"Honestly?" Jamie nodded. "When I heard you flirting via the app, and some of the comments you've made, I assumed you were a bit of a partier. You know, clubs, women, dancing, and stuff. And I'm not going to lie that your name is out in the com-munity as a bit of a, um, lady's lady, if you know what I mean. But after all our little talks, and with every bit of new information I learn about you, I just think there is a lot that you don't show other people. You don't let people see the real you. For instance, you come across as a major extrovert but I sense something com-pletely different. Like you are only putting on a show and secretly you're very private." Kelsey stopped and sipped her cocoa and watched her friend's reaction.

Jamie sat back in her chair, completely blown away by Kelsey's serious insight that seemed to come out of nowhere. But it wasn't the fact that the other woman had changed gears with the conversation, it was that she was so frighteningly accurate.

Her mind immediately flew back years into the buried recesses of memory.

"Be more social, James. People think you're a bitch when you don't talk and just sit there like some kind of freak!"

"You're embarrassing me, try to watch what you say when you're around my friends."

"Why can't you just lighten up a bit and go with the flow?"

"Why are you so fucking weird?"

"Everyone does it, James."

"You're nothing but white trash and you'll never be anything but white trash. You'll never have it as good as you do with me!"

"Where did you go?"

Jamie was startled when Kelsey's hand touched the back of her own. "I, uh, I was just thinking about something." She looked up to meet Kelsey's interesting dark green eyes. "And you're right. I, um, taught myself to be an extrovert. I learned how to be social with people that I don't know."

Kelsey knew there was more to her friend's words and to her silence but she sensed that it was not the right time to push her for more information. But she was even surer of her initial assessment months before when she thought that Jamie had been hurt in the past. She squeezed the hand below hers. "Hey, I get it. Really. I think we've all changed, or been changed, by the people and events in our lives. We make mistakes, and if we're smart enough we learn from them." She chuckled.

Glad for the shift in mood, Jamie looked back at her curiously. More than once she had wondered why her friend was single. "And what mistakes have you made?"

Kelsey took a few seconds to decide how she wanted to answer. She could go with something generic, or she could share a little of her inner self with Jamie in response to the vulnerability she could sense in the other woman. "I learned that just because you live with someone and they tell you they love you, it doesn't mean they aren't cheating with one of your close friends."

Jamie made a pained face. "Ouch! I'm sorry Kels, that's a pretty shitty thing to go through." She looked at her friend and a thought popped into her head. "Is that why you decided to move to St. Seren?"

It was near 8:00 p.m. and her cocoa was almost gone but Kelsey didn't want their time to end. She answered honestly because it wasn't in her DNA not to. "It was part of the reason. I didn't have to move, the apartment was in my name. I stayed there another six months after I kicked her out, then decided I needed a change of scenery. The area I lived in was okay enough but it wasn't very diverse. It was also heavily conservative and I'd always wanted to live closer to St. Seren, so here I am. And even though I hate the complex I'm in right now, my lease is up at the end of December so maybe I'll find something better when it's closer to that time. I can always pay month to month after that, it's just more expensive." She shrugged. "But I really love the city. I have a few friends that live here and it seems pretty easy to make more." She gave her new friend a genuine smile.

Jamie smiled back at her, already considering Kelsey a good friend too. She shook her head and decided to change the subject back to the original one. "I still can't believe that you don't cook!"

Kelsey snorted. "Why, because I'm all femme looking and all femmes like to cook?"

The blonde gave her a strange look. "Uh, no. It's because you're always talking about how close to your family you are and you just have this protective, nurturing vibe about you. It has nothing to do with how you look. I hate stereotypes." She waves toward herself. "I mean, look at me. Everyone thinks I'm some big bad butch, a real baddass. Would you think that?"

The Irish-Latina who had hated stereotypes her entire life peered at the woman across the table. "Having gotten to know you? Not at all."

"But what if you didn't know me? What would you think?"

Kelsey smiled. "You mean like when I first saw you? At first glance I thought you were a hot andro who was probably all full of typical butch attitude, at least until I changed your tire while you discretely kept wiping dirt off your manicured fingers."

Jamie's ears turned red at having been caught by her friend. "Yeah, you got me there. I'm a total prissy pants and I hate getting my hands dirty."

"Really? But what about your job? I'm assuming you don't sit at a desk all day. You mentioned putting manufacturing lines together and setting up sensors and things. I would think you'd get dirty doing that."

The grin on Jamie's face was full of smug accomplishment. "It's called gloves. I can do anything while wearing gloves!"

Kelsey couldn't resist teasing her, and dropped her voice down into that sexy register and gave the blonde a once over with her eyes. "Anything, James?"

"Oh my God! You did not just say that to me!" Kelsey was

too busy laughing to answer her but she took pleasure in making Jamie blush. "No, seriously though, I feel a little like we are kindred spirits here. I've struggled my entire life not to be defined by my upbringing, or by how I look. I am who I am and I won't apologize for it."

To Kelsey, it almost seemed as if she left the statement open. As if the word "anymore" should have been there but was just another thing that Jamie kept inside. But she knew what the other woman was trying to say. "Yeah, I know what you mean. People expect me to act a certain way, to dress a certain way but I'm just me, you know? I mean, I came from a mixed-culture home where my very strong-willed and feisty Irish born mother wore the pants in the family. She was definitely the dominant one and strangely enough my Mexican father was just this sweet supportive guy. He wasn't all bravado and swagger like people associate with Hispanic men. And when people look at me, they expect all that Latin attitude in a femme package. I don't even speak Spanish!"

Jamie started laughing. "Even I speak Spanish, Kels! I'm surprised your dad didn't try to teach you."

"Oh, he tried and I even took it in high school. But none in college. I'm afraid the only Spanish I know now is stuff that I've picked up around my dad's shop. And most of its not fit to be repeated, if you know what I mean." She wiggled her eyebrows which only set Jamie off into laughter again.

"You're hilarious!"

Kelsey just smiled and shrugged at her. "What about you? You look butch and you like fast cars. Yet you also like to cook and you get manicures, what else? Tell me something about you that no one else knows."

She got a raised eyebrow for her demands. "I have surprisingly few secrets. Hmm, let's see, I blow my nose in the shower."

Kelsey rolled her eyes. "Doesn't everyone? Try again."

Jamie looked deep in thought then held up a finger. "I have hair on my big toe!"

"Seriously? Are you even trying here? I'm half-Irish and half-Mexican, I know about hair on the big toe."

Finally Jamie sighed in defeat. "I write poetry."

The Irish-Latina looked back at her in surprise. "Wow, now we're getting somewhere. Have you always written poetry?"

Jamie nodded. "Yeah, probably since I was ten or eleven."

"And you've kept it all, haven't you?"

"How did you know that?" Jamie's eyes were wide with how

perceptive Kelsey was.

Kelsey shrugged. "I don't know, you just seem like someone who holds onto things that matter most. And poetry, well poetry is more than just a person's thoughts. Sometimes it's their heart and soul on the page."

Jamie was continuously amazed at the depth and awareness of her new friend. "You sound like someone who has written a little poetry."

"Eh, I went through a phase in high school. Right about the time I realized I was gay and came out to my parents." Kelsey made a face and Jamie returned it with a look of sympathy.

"Ooh, that sounds like a rough kinda phase. I'm assuming it all turned out okay, right? You're still close with your parents, from all that you've told me."

Kelsey's lone dimple was obvious with her big grin. It told clearly of the level of love she felt for her parents. "They were great actually. My family had always been pretty liberal and open-minded. They just said that they kind of suspected it and told me that it didn't matter to them as long as I was happy. And while my extended family in Texas is a little more typical, I have a few gay cousins so we've all just been kind of accepted for who we are."

Jamie reached over and gave her hand a squeeze where it rested next to the empty cocoa mug. "That's really great, Kels. It's wonderful that you have that kind of love and support."

Kelsey looked back at her curiously. "What about you? Was your coming out hard? How old were you?"

"You could say that, and I was twenty-four."

"You were twenty-four when you finally came out? Whoa!" She sat back in her seat, more than shocked at her friend's age. But the shock was nothing compared to what she felt with Jamie's next words.

"I was twenty-four when I realized I was gay. I had been married for five years at that point."

Kelsey's jaw dropped open. "Holy shit!"

Jamie nodded. "Holy shit."

"Oh my God."

Jamie snickered. "Yeah, I said that too. It kind of threw me for a loop when I realized that I liked women. It also clicked on the light bulb above my head and everything in my life until that point suddenly made sense. It was an eye-opener, let me tell you."

Poor Kelsey still looked a bit shell-shocked. "What did you do?"

"In order?" Kelsey nodded yes so Jamie ticked the items off on her fingers. "I got a divorce, said goodbye to my pets, went to college, then quit my job and moved two hours away to a more liberal city."

The other woman held up her hands. "Whoa, whoa, whoa, slow down there, nerd. You said goodbye to your pets? Why?"

Sadness washed over Jamie's face. "When I left my ex, he kept the house and I moved into an apartment where I couldn't have pets. The cats were happy at the house and I knew he'd take good care of them."

"Did you miss them?"

Jamie smirked. "A hell of a lot more than I missed my ex."

Kelsey nodded with understanding. "And that was what?" She did the math in her head, remembering the age Jamie had told her. "Ten years ago? You live in a condo now, why haven't you ever gotten another cat or something?" Kelsey grew alarmed as the blonde shut down right in front of her eyes. "What's the matter? Did I say something wrong?"

Jamie shook her head and took a few seconds to speak. "No, sorry. I had two cats with my ex after him, my first girlfriend. She kept them when I left." She glanced down at her smart watch and saw that it was already after 8:30. "Listen Kelsey, it's getting close to their closing time and I have a few more things to do at home. We should probably head out." She stood and started to clean up her dishes but was stopped by a firm hand on her wrist. When Jamie looked up she was caught in the understanding gaze of her friend.

"Hey, it's okay. We don't have to talk about that if you don't want. We all have those sensitive subjects, I get it. But don't shut me out, just tell me you can't talk about something if it comes up. Okay?"

After close to ten seconds of them staring into the other's eyes, Jamie nodded. "I won't shut you out, I promise. But we really should get going."

Kelsey checked the time on her cell phone and made a face. "Oh jeez, I didn't realize it was so late. Yeah, Newman and Pierre will be all discombobulated that I haven't spent time with them tonight."

"Are they worried that you'll get behind on your knitting schedule?" Jamie laughed and Kelsey swatted her on the arm.

"You're a regular comedian, aren't you?"

Jamie grinned. "I try."

"Yeah, well try harder." Both women cracked up laughing

but managed to get everything cleaned up and dumped in the right bins in only a few minutes. After donning their jackets, they made their way out the front door of the coffee shop. But before Kelsey could walk away, Jamie pulled her to a stop and held out her right hand palm up. She suddenly remembered that she'd never messaged her phone number to Kelsey before their meetup.

"Give me your cell phone."

She got a raised eyebrow from Kelsey but the other woman lifted her hoodie and slid the cell out of her back pocket. Jamie made an obvious show of appreciating the view and Kelsey just rolled her eyes as she set the phone in Jamie's hand. The engineer went into Kelsey's contacts and programmed her own number into the phone, then handed it back. "There you go, now you can talk to me whenever you like."

Kelsey snorted. "Does that actually work for you?"

Jamie nodded. "All the time. Or at least it used to."

"Used to?"

Jamie shrugged and her response was more than a little cryptic. "I've changed my street and I haven't been giving out my phone number lately." When Kelsey shot her a confused look she elaborated. "I find myself wanting to be a better me." Then before Kelsey could ask any more questions Jamie gave her a wink and pulled her into another hug. "Thanks for meeting and for the good conversation. I'll talk to you tomorrow morning, right?"

When they pulled apart, Kelsey smiled at her showing that lone dimple clearly in the streetlight. "Absolutely." Then she turned and headed down the street toward her car.

Jamie loved dimples and she knew that she was totally infatuated with her new friend. As she turned to head for her own car her thoughts whirled a mile a minute. But one word tumbled toward the front more than all the rest. "Damn."

That evening in her apartment, Kelsey sat on the couch in her pajamas, knitting and talking to her cats. "I really like her, Newman. She's funny, she's gorgeous, and she seems like good people. But damn, someone sure did a number on her! I thought my ex was bad, Jamie's must have been a psycho bitch from hell!" Newman chirruped at her as Pierre tumbled off the couch with her skein of yarn. "You little asshole!" She quickly grabbed the water bottle to chase him away, then leaned over and snatched the yarn off the floor before he could come back and grab it again. She grimaced at its slightly damp feel. She called out to the bathroom where she saw him run. "You're such a dick, Pierre!" Needles started going again and she addressed the better behaved cat. "And can you believe that she's been married?"

"Mrow."

The cat was simply answering to her tone and inflection, not because he actually understood what she was saying. He was only a cat after all. She shook her head. "I just don't see it. She's so, so, gay!" She paused as another thought came to mind, then made a face. "I suppose that means she's not a gold star either. Not that it matters to me." She stopped her knitting then. After that she stopped her words and consciously stopped her train of thought. "It doesn't matter because Jamie is my friend, nothing more! You hear that brain? That handsome andro girl is completely off limits!" The problem wasn't totally with her brain though, at least half of it was her libido. Kelsey sighed, remembering that she never did replace her dead batteries.

Looking at the clock on the wall, she decided to call it a night and packed everything back into its basket. She stood to set it under the end table when Pierre came tearing through the living room, knocking the video game remote off the coffee table. She snatched the remote off the floor and went to yell at the rambunctious cat but stopped before a single word could come out. She flipped the remote over and read the words on the battery cover. "Two AA batteries. Hmm, that sounds perfect. She quickly removed the batteries and shut off the living room lamp, then made her way down the hall toward her bedroom. She called out to the naughty cat as she was walking into the bedroom. "Good boy, Pierre! Mama loves you!"

Chapter Nine

JAMIE AND KELSEY'S friendship really started to deepen after meeting in the coffee shop. Over the next month they met every Wednesday for drinks and sandwiches at The Scalded Crow, each one learning more about the other. They continued to chat during their morning commute. They also texted and teased each other mercilessly. After four weeks of such meetings and conversations they both felt pretty confident that they had made a great friend. On a sunny Thursday morning the highway rolled clear for the little blue car. Thursdays usually weren't too busy in the morning and Fridays were a dream. In the morning at least. Friday after work was a nightmare on a good day, let alone if weather was bad.

Jamie had her stereo cranked up and sang along to the chorus of The Pierces song "How Can I Love You More." She loved the tune and couldn't resist belting it out every time it came on. She was surprised that Kelsey wasn't logged into the app when she hit the road since the other woman usually left fifteen minutes earlier. The last time Kelsey didn't show up online was the morning after their first coffee house meeting. At the time she thought that Kelsey may have been put off to find out that Jamie had been married. Some women were like that. Then she remembered that Kelsey wasn't interested in anything other than friendship, just like Jamie. It turned out that Kelsey had simply forgotten to set her alarm the night before.

The engineer signaled and got back into the middle lane as traffic started to pick up near the nexus of the universe. She still hadn't heard anything from her car buddy by the time she pulled into the parking lot and seriously started to think that Kelsey had overslept or had car trouble. About a half hour after she began work her cell phone vibrated from where it sat on its wireless charger. She picked it up and smiled when she saw who the text was from.

Hey there, sorry I missed you this morning!

She texted back.

Alarm?

The phone vibrated in her hand.

Yeah. Forgot to set alarm last night & overslept. Again. <grumble>

Jamie looked at the message curiously then typed back.

Didn't ask last time but I don't understand how you can forget to set your alarm. Don't you use your cell?

Um, no. Does that work better?

The engineer read the text and immediately thumped her forehead onto the heel of her hand. Then she brought up her alarm app and took a screen shot and sent it to her friend.

The app lets you customize individual days and times, as well as snooze functions, alarm sound and volume. You should look into it.

I'm always afraid my phone will die overnight if I forget to plug it in.

Jamie made a face and wrote back.

You don't have a wireless charger?

Um, no. Is that a thing? Sounds like magic.

The engineer started laughing, which brought Bill's head up away from the breakfast burrito he was busy scarfing. "What's so funny?"

She held up her phone. "Kelsey is hilarious."

He nodded. "Oh, is that your new girlfriend?"

"She's not my girlfriend!"

Bill amended his statement. "I'm sorry. I meant to say, your 'friend who's just a friend.'" He made air quotes for the second half of his sentence.

Jamie narrowed her eyes at him. "What's that supposed to mean?"

Bill shrugged. "I dunno, you don't normally text someone at work unless you're trying to score and you've been texting Kelsey a lot lately." He held up his hands at his coworker's dark look. "Hey, I'm not judging you, James."

She wanted to be angry and deny his words but Jamie stopped to think for a second. She did text a lot after meeting someone new, usually just playing the flirt game until she reeled someone in who was interested in a no-strings-attached arrangement. But she didn't do that anymore and wasn't doing that with Kelsey. She sighed and watched Bill take another big bite. "I know what I used to do, but I don't do that anymore." He raised an eyebrow at her while chewing. "I just needed to make some changes, you know? And Kelsey is good people, she's a good friend. And," She paused, unsure how to say the thing that had been slowly growing inside her.

"What?"

She leaned back in her ergonomic chair and looked at the office tile on the ceiling. "I really like her and I guess it's just nice not to always be on the make. I like being friends and not having certain expectations placed on me."

Bill swallowed his food and smiled at her. "You know what it sounds like to me?" She shook her head. "Sounds like you've got a crush!" She scowled at him. "Or you're finally growing up."

"Whatever, dude." She rolled her eyes just as her phone vibrated again.

You never answered about the magic so I'll assume you're a wizard. Also, hitting the road now, chat after work?

Jamie quickly texted back.

Yes and I'll explain cell alarms then. Drive safe!

You too.

Jamie read the text with a confused look on her face until the next one came in.

Uh, not you too. I'm an idiot because you're not driving, duh! Have a great day James.

Wearing a stupid grin, Jamie did have a great day.

KELSEY WAS NOT having a great day. Because she was late for work she caught a lot of grief from June right off the bat. Then the receptionist asked her to cover the front counter so she could "take care of her oatmeal problem." Kelsey didn't ask, she merely stood by the front desk in case someone came in. Unfortunately someone came in. The bell on the door jingled as a woman of middling years walked through it. She came right up to the counter saying she had a question and Kelsey smiled at her, eager to help. Her excitement lasted until the woman put a tooth, root and all, onto the counter and began spinning it around with her index finger. Jamie struggled to hide her disgust. With much effort, she wrenched her gaze away from the spinning tooth and looked at the woman. "Can I help you?"

The woman nodded with a quick jerk of her head. "Yeah. My husband's tooth fell off. Can this be put back in his mouth?"

Kelsey blinked at her. The woman stared seriously back. Finally the dental assistant pulled herself from her disbelief and shook her head slowly. "I'm sorry, ma'am, but that is just not possible." The woman didn't quite believe her so she had to explain in detail why they would be unable to do such a thing. Afterwards the woman picked up the tooth and walked back out of the office. When the receptionist returned Kelsey was busy spraying CaviCide all over the counter and wiping it down. She had already cleaned both the door handles, door window, and everything else the woman touched.

"I already cleaned that first thing this morning."

Kelsey made a face. "Some woman came in and played spin the bottle with her husband's tooth on the counter. She left when I told her we couldn't put it back in for him. I thought you'd appreciate another wipe down."

The receptionist made a face. "Eww!"

Kelsey nodded. "Yeah, exactly."

"Speaking of eww, don't go in the bathroom."

"Seriously?" Kelsey looked at the petite older woman and could not for the life of her figure out how such a small thing could blow up their work bathroom on a regular basis. She continued to grumble under her breath as she walked to the back, avoiding the hallway where the employee bathroom was located.

Her reprieve didn't last long. A little after lunch time they had a client come in who said she'd lost a veneer. Even though they didn't specialize in cosmetic dentistry the woman had been adamant that she make an appointment at their office. When Kelsey walked into the room she was taken aback by the patient. Ms. Donovan was sitting in the chair in yoga pants, a housecoat, and slippers. Trying to maintain professional decorum, Kelsey pasted a smile on her face and addressed the woman. "Good afternoon, Ms. Donovan. What seems to be the problem today?"

She looked down at the chart. "It says here you lost a veneer? I believe the receptionist told you that we don't do cosmetic dentistry here—"

"I know what she said. I just need me some of that good glue you doctors got."

Kelsey tried again. "Ma'am, I'm not a doctor." She stopped talking when the woman held up something between her fingertips. "What is that?"

"I didn't want to spend all that money for the doc's fancy fake teeth so I been buyin' these press on nails and supergluing them to my teeth. They look real nice and don't cost much. But I'm getting tired of gluing them on so much. Don't the doc have some of that special permanent glue?"

The shocked dental assistant leaned closer to the woman to better see her mouth because they actually did look real nice from a few feet away. "Can I see the spot where that one came off?" Ms. Donovan opened her mouth and pointed to a right front incisor that was crusted with layers of old glue. They were a rotting disaster. She backed away slowly. "I'm sorry ma'am, but we cannot put anything into your mouth that is not approved by law for such a purpose. But you do have a lot of glue built up, as well as food and plaque. It would be in the best interest for your teeth if you let us clean them off properly." Kelsey backed away even farther when the crazy house-coated woman's face turned red with anger.

"You leaches are all the same, you're only in it for the money! I can't believe you won't help out a poor mother. I've got four kids at home and I can't afford to pay your fancy doctor bills!" She ripped off the bib and leaped from the chair, then stormed out the door, down the hall, and out of the office. Hopefully for good. Kelsey didn't move from the doorway, but rather craned her neck in order to follow the woman's progress out of the office.

"Is there a problem, Kels?" The assistant was startled by Dr. Davies's voice as he walked up from the opposite direction.

She gave him a slightly wide-eyed look. "Not any more. Ms. Donovan wanted us to use our "doctor glue" to re-stick her fake fingernail homemade veneer back onto her tooth. A tooth, which was covered in old glue, rot, plaque and food. I told her that by law we were not allowed to use anything in the mouth that was not made for such a purpose and suggested that she let us clean the rest of her teeth. You probably heard the rest."

He nodded. "But how did they look?"

Kelsey conceded. "Pretty good actually, from afar and without smelling her breath."

Dr. Davies shrugged. "I'll give her points for ingenuity then. All right, I'm headed to room three. June is busy prepping Doug Blivens for his three fillings." Kelsey shivered when she remembered who Doug Blivens was and thought that her day might actually be looking up.

The afternoon drive was significantly better than her morning one after Kelsey merged onto the highway at her normal time. She was in a great mood, especially after she heard that Mr. Blivens vomited down the front of June's scrub shirt shortly after Kelsey's encounter with the crazy woman in the house coat. After that she decided to give the older woman a break and take a week off from depositing spiders in her purse. About fifteen minutes after she logged into the Drīv app, Jamie popped online. She down-swiped on the nerd car icon. "Hey stranger, long time no speed!"

"How did you know I was speeding? I'm a perfectly upstanding, law-abiding citizen!"

Kelsey laughed and replied. "Who also drives a slick little turbo and admitted to me that she doesn't like to go slow."

Jamie's voice was indignant when it came back over the speaker of Kelsey's cell phone. "No, Olivia doesn't like to go slow and I don't like to disappoint my girl."

"Too bad you can't say that about the rest." Kelsey left the statement open, clearly teasing the other woman about her reputation.

The response that came back was nearly a squawk. "Hey! I'll have you know that I've never had any complaints from the ladies, so there!"

Kelsey snorted and replied. "So much talk and bravado. I hope for your ladies' sake you put your money where your mouth is when it counts."

"Darlin' I leave my mouth right where it's at when it counts. Though sometimes I swap out with my fingers—" Jamie dissolved into laughter on the other end.

"And such a dirty mouth it is, too! I can't believe you use those lips on friends and family!"

More laughter came through the app. "I'll have you know my lips are a treasure!"

Kelsey couldn't resist. "That's what she said?"

Jamie shrugged in her own car, unseen by no one but the nosepicker in the lane next to hers. "That *is* actually what she said. It's also for only a select few to find out!" She was seriously enjoying the playful banter between her and her driving buddy. They often teased each other back and forth and despite their deeper than normal discussion from the month before, Jamie was relieved that nothing had changed with their friendship. She felt a little more emotionally exposed to Kelsey, but also freer.

"Select few? Funny, that's not what I heard!"

Jamie laughed, able to see the humor in her own past. "Kels, Kels, Kels, get with the program chica! That was last quarter's issue, I'm a new woman now!"

The disbelief was obvious as Kelsey's voice came back over Olivia's speaker system. "Ohhh reeeeeaaaally? But you've got the same old cover on that tired magazine." Some of her disbelief was due to the fact that Jamie had not told anyone she had stopped sleeping around. She simply quit and changed some of her old patterns to avoid temptation.

"Hey, there's nothing wrong with my cover, thank you very much! But yes, the content has totally changed." Jamie did the mental calculations as she drove along. "It's been seventy-four days since I turned over my new leaf." She was quite proud of herself for that. It had been hard but she had started liking herself more when she stopped picking up women at the bar or going home with any of her old fuck buddies. Jamie had turned into a saint. Practically.

"Wow! I'm impressed, James. Well I'll have you know it's been, hmm, exactly one day for me!"

Something strange happened in Jamie's stomach at her friend's words. It was a feeling she didn't like as she wondered aloud at Kelsey's words. "What the hell? Is she seeing someone?" She gripped the steering wheel tighter and tried to figure out why she didn't like that idea very much at all, and Kelsey's voice came back through the app.

"We are counting ourselves in this, right? I mean, I was at least. Or is that TMI?"

Jamie realized what she meant and started laughing and answered. "Oh my God!"

"TMI?"

"No, you're just cracking my shit up over here. And if we're counting ourselves I'm going to have to seriously change my number of days without an incident!"

Kelsey's ears practically perked up in her little silver car as she responded to Jamie's statement. "Oh yeah? What is your new number then?" She waited a minute for Jamie's voice to come back and her ears turned red when it did.

"Hmm, about eleven hours now."

"James! Seriously?"

"What? TMI? You started it, perv! Now stop distracting me, I don't want to miss my exit. I'm not very good at remembering to get off on the right one when I take a different way after work."

Kelsey shook her head and moved into the center lane as she approached a busy exit. Though she would never admit it, Jamie's crazy rules of the road totally worked. She found her drive to be just a little less frustrating if she followed the anal-retentive engineer's driving system. She sent another voice message back to that engineer. "You're right, I totally did. Now I'm changing the subject before I end up driving distracted as well. And why are you taking a different exit?"

"Hair appointment. I've got to get my trim on."

Kelsey looked down at her phone momentarily, as if that would clear up her confusion. Finally she broke down and asked. "Didn't you just get your hair cut a few weeks ago?"

"Every four weeks, Kels! I have short hair and if I don't get it cut every four weeks I start to get scruffy. I have to stay on fleek you know."

Perhaps the large gulp of water was a bad idea when Jamie answered her because Kelsey started laughing and choking at the same time. She responded to Jamie's message. "You are seriously such a dork! Do you even know what that means?"

After a minute's hesitation Jamie's voice came back over her little cell speaker. "You mean the exact definition? Um, no. Do you?"

Kelsey answered. "Psshhh, yeah! I may not speak German but I do speak millennial."

Jamie gave her phone a look of consternation as she moved over to exit the highway. She finally messaged her friend and tormentor back. "Are you going to tell me?" Her hairdresser was just off the highway and she turned into the parking lot as she waited for Kelsey to answer.

"Nope!"

Olivia glided smoothly into a parking space. "You're such an ass! Fine, I'll just ask my hairdresser then."

"Man or woman?"

Jamie's brows furrowed and she replied. "Man, why?"

"He's gonna laugh at you if you ask."

"And if it was a woman?"

"She'd laugh too." And laughter followed Kelsey's statement

down the line, eliciting goose bumps on Jamie's arms as it sounded through the car's audio system.

Jamie grumbled. "Whatever! I gotta go or I'll be late for my appointment. Drive safe, Kels!"

"Will do!"

Just as Kelsey predicted, Richard did laugh when she asked. "Oh my God, girl! You've got a smart phone don't you? Look that stuff up! You can't be walking around not in the know." He shook his head and "tsked" her as he checked her hair over. "Ooh, what have we here?"

Jamie, who was busy searching for the meaning of "on fleek" on her phone, looked up and met his eyes in the mirror. "What do you mean?"

He unflinchingly peered back. "Grays, James. You've got 'em. Good thing you color every four weeks."

She made a face, hating the fact that she was going gray. "I'm only thirty-four! That hardly seems fair!"

He trimmed up the sides a little and spoke without looking at her in the mirror. "What hardly seems fair is the fact that you won't let me color your hair anything but this shade of blonde. At least let me go with a nice purple or something!"

"No way! You know I can't do anything like that with my job."

Richard snorted. "Conservative bitches! Well then how about going back to your natural color? You've been dying it blonde for what, nine years now?"

Jamie scowled. "No, just the blonde like normal."

"But sweetie, you look great in dark hair! So handsome and broody."

She laughed as he pouted. "Is broody even a word?"

He framed her face from behind and stared at her from over her head. "Girl, you make broody a word! So, natural?"

Jamie just shook her head. "No."

Richard sighed. "Fine! So tell me what's new with you. Still catting around on the weekends, and weeknights? Any more broken hearts? How's your new friend, Kelli is it?"

"Kelsey. And she's great!" Unbeknownst to her, Jamie's face lit up at the mention of her new friend and Richard watched it all through the mirror as he mixed her color. "And for your information, I don't sleep around anymore."

One perfectly waxed eyebrow went up. "Oh? And when did this start?"

"Um, about two and a half months ago?"

"What? And you're just now telling me?" Richard had stopped mixing and walked around in front of her to level the full power of his disapproving gaze. "I cannot believe that you've kept such news from me!" He put a dramatic hand to his chest. "Me, your priest and confidant. Me, who is the keeper of all your secrets! My heart bleeds at your calloused indifference to my feelings!"

Jamie snorted. "Still taking those acting classes?"

He nodded and smiled. "Yes, ma'am! But I'm still hurt you didn't tell me. What's going on, James?"

She shrugged. "I don't know, maybe I gave it up for Lent or something."

"Sweetie, you're not Catholic."

Jamie grinned at him. "Didn't you just say you were my priest? Are you judging my confession, Father?"

He rolled his eyes and started applying the dye to her hair. "As if I were old enough to be your father! But if I was I'd totally tan your hide for keeping secrets." He paused with the brush in hand and looked at her honestly in the mirror. "So why are you on the lady wagon, hmm?"

Jamie sighed as he started applying the paste again. "I don't know, I'm just in a rut and my friend Jenn pointed out that even though I mean well, people still get hurt when I'm playing around. And I guess I'm tired of hurting people."

"Hmm."

She looked at him curiously as he finished applying around her ears and started the delicate task of bleaching her eyebrows. "Hmm, what?"

He smiled because he'd known Jamie a long time, ever since she moved to St. Seren at the tender age of twenty-five. "I think this is a good change for you. It sounds like you're finally moving on." Richard knew more about Jamie's ex than most people. He also knew what the woman had done to his good friend and client.

Jamie scoffed. "Please! I moved on a long time ago."

"No, honey, you closed off. There is a big difference between the two, believe me. And this is the much healthier way to go, so stick with it!" He sighed. "I know, I've been there."

Her voice was quiet in a moment of vulnerability. "Did you get lonely?"

He nodded, heart breaking just a little for his friend. "At first. But then I started surrounding myself with better people. And I met a guy who had no expectations of me other than to be the person that I was. We just *clicked* and there was no going back."

"Do you ever miss the excitement of meeting new people? Of just hooking up with no strings?"

He thought for a few seconds and nodded slowly. "I think everyone has that moment where they want to escape when shit gets tough, you know?" She nodded. "But while hooking up with people might be exciting in the moment, it doesn't take away the loneliness. You know what I mean?"

Jamie looked down because she did know. "Yeah, I get it."

He patted her shoulder. "All right sweetie, I'm gonna have you switch chairs while your color sets so I can give my next client a trim."

She moved over to a seat in the waiting area and pulled out her cell phone. Smiling, she texted Kelsey. The dental assistant would have arrived home by then and had probably just finished feeding her cats.

I'll have you know that I'm halfway to being on fleek! I looked it up

The reply came back seconds later.

Such a nerd! You know the original meaning referred to eyebrows, right?

Jamie texted back.

Well those were done too. But Merriam-Webster says it basically means perfectly done, so there! <sticking tongue out at you>

She snorted at her friend's response.

Best put that away before you trip yourself. Loose tongues will get a girl into trouble!

Hey! My tongue is tight!

Oh reeeeaaaalllly? Do tell? LOL

Jamie's phone vibrated again.

Or don't tell. I don't really want to know your kinky stories!

She smiled and responded.

Actually, I have some really hilarious ones. You
should ask about them next time we meet at the Crow.

Maybe I will. One more day til the weekend, got
plans?

Jamie didn't look forward to the weekends as much since she
started changing her old ways. She could still have fun when she
was out, but most of her crowd knew she had a reputation. People she just wanted to hang out with as friends turned her down,
assuming she wanted more. Or they agreed to meet up, thinking
that Jamie was interested in a casual night of sex. No matter what
she did she felt like she was letting people down. Burke had been
in town a few weeks before but they pretty much shot pool then
waxed philosophical into the night. He had started dating someone so was laying low lately which left Jamie at loose ends. She
wasn't about to tell Kelsey all that and admit to how pathetic her
life had gotten, so she texted something simple back.

Nothing set in stone. You?

Friend of some friends surprise bday Saturday. Was
talked into going.

You could always skip and hang out with me instead.

Already promised them, sorry James. Maybe Scalded
Crow Sunday?

Her weekend brightened immeasurably at the thought of
meeting Kelsey for drinks and coversation.

Ooh, and break out of our normal routine? Sure,
sounds great! Um, 2 okay?

2 is perfect!

Ok, see you then. Gotta go, Richard is ready to
rinse. Bye Kels!

Bye James

The days flew by for Jamie, but not well. She attempted to go
out for a little pool and dancing on Friday night and the evening
ended in a bit of a disaster. A couple of drunk hetero guys started
a fight and she caught a random swing to the lip while she was on

the dance floor. And to add insult on top of literal injury, when she left the bar at 1:00 a.m., she found a big dent in Olivia's passenger door. She went to bed angry and woke up not much better. Because her mood was "piss poor" as her mom would have called it, she probably should not have started making Bloody Marys at noon, but she did anyway. She drank all afternoon and watched the Food Network while yelling random comments to the blonde troll doll on the screen. Around three she texted Jenn.

```
heeeyy, want to come over for bloody maryss? got
nuthn doin tonight an im bored.
```

Jenn's message came back a few minutes later.

```
What the hell, James? Are you drunk?
```

Jamie giggled.

```
Noppe. Prolyl should've ate something for lunch
tho. And showered.
```

```
God bless America! Malcom's dad doesn't pick him up
until 5 so you know I can't come over there and prop yo
carcass up! Eat some food, dammit! And when you're
done, go wash your stank ass.
```

The blonde pouted where she was slouched down on her couch.

```
don't wanna cook.
```

```
So order a pizza, fool! But get some food in you and
I'll check back in a while. Okay?
```

She frowned and texted back.

```
k
```

Jamie was tipsy, not wasted, and she successfully ordered a sub from the local place down the street. Following Jenn's advice, she ate, showered, and made herself a drink. Maybe it wasn't all per her friend's advice, but it's what she felt like doing. She was holding that drink when she answered her door at quarter after five. "Hey, Jenn! You here to hang with me tonight? Let me fix you a drink. Vodka cran, right?"

Jenn stepped through the door and snagged Jamie's sleeve as she started to walk away. "Nooope! Come back here you! I've got plans tonight, James. I'm already an hour late because I had to wait for my ex to pick up Malcom. I just stopped in to make sure you're taking care of yourself." She looked at her tipsy friend, taking in the slight sway and split lip. "You okay, hon? What happened to your lip?"

"Couple a' straight guys fighting at the bar last night, one clipped me in the lip when I was dancing. And Olivia got her door dinged in the parking lot! Was a shitty night."

Jenn looked back at her. "Is that why you started drinking at?"

"Noon."

"Noon today?"

Jamie shrugged. "Kinda. This new street is hard." She finished her drink then went to the kitchen to rinse her glass and Jenn followed.

When the blonde turned around again Jenn had a confused look on her face. "New street? What in the world are you talking about?"

She hadn't told her friend about becoming the new Jamie. She hinted at it with Kelsey but only Richard knew the whole story. She tried to explain to Jenn as best she could. "You know, when you told me not to kill so many cats, and that I'd have to drive a different way. So I've been driving a different way."

Jenn blinked at her and Jamie swayed a little. "Oh." Then she blinked again in realization when her brain finally translated the blonde's confusing words. "Ohhhh! You've stopped cattin' around?" Jamie nodded. "Uh, when did that start?"

Jamie set glass in the sink and thought about it, doing the math in her head. Then she gave up on the math. "Right after you talked to me."

She got a swat on her shoulder. "James! That was more than two months ago! And you're just now telling me this?" The other woman shrugged and looked a little lost. Jenn knew that her friend had seemed down lately but she had no idea what was going on with her. Jamie tended to hold things pretty close to the vest. The black woman was torn. She had to go to her friend's surprise party but she didn't want to leave another friend alone who was clearly in need of emotional support. Finally making a decision, she pointed at Jamie. "Go fix yourself up, you're coming with me to Sal's birthday party. You remember Sal, right?"

Jamie nodded and went into the bathroom to put some product in her hair. Even tipsy she still managed to style it to perfection. When she came out again she grabbed her messenger bag off the coat rack by the door. "Is she the one who was the Ass Quarters champion last year?"

Jenn snorted and held the door for her friend. "Yup, same one. She's turning forty and Brandi is having a surprise party for her."

"Hey, Kelsey is going to a surprise party tonight too!"

Seatbelts were clicked into place and Jenn started her car. "Yeah? The same Kelsey that you met through your driving app and whom you talk about constantly?"

Jamie's face took on a dreamy look. "Yeah. I really like Kelsey."

Jenn looked at her curiously, more than a little taken aback at how open and honest Jamie was being with her. "Wow, she sounds like a good friend then."

"She's amaaaaazing!"

The blonde would probably be appalled that she was spilling the beans but Jenn was thoroughly enjoying it. And she thought it was about time that someone actually snagged Jamie's attention. "Well then, maybe it's the same party and we'll see her there."

Jamie smiled for the first time since she woke that morning. "Maybe we will."

Chapter Ten

THE PARTY WAS all right, but Kelsey was a little bored. She had only met the birthday girl once or twice before. And the only ones at the party that she really knew were Tam and Shell. She grabbed one of her cake pops off the tray and wondered what Jamie was up to. A random dark-haired woman walked into the kitchen and made a beeline for the center island where most of the food was located. She picked up one of Kelsey's treats by the stick and took a large bite. "Hot damn, these are amazing! This is like, my fourth one." She wandered back into the living room, and Kelsey just shook her head. At least she had contributed to the party. She felt bad just showing up empty-handed so she made two dozen of her specialty to bring along. Someone cranked up the music in the other room and she cringed at the twangy sound of country so she decided to go through the dining room slider and check out the back yard. Her face lit up when she saw that Sal had a genuine hammock. "Oh, I've gotta try that!" Fifteen minutes later she had a grass stain on her elbow and sticks in her hair so she gave it up as a lost cause. After that she wandered over to the koi pond and pondered what it must be like to be as well off as Sal.

Inside Jenn and Jamie had arrived and Jenn immediately led her friend to the kitchen with explicit instructions to drink some water and sober up. When Jenn walked back out of the kitchen Jamie spied the cake pops on the counter. "Oh my God, cake pops!" She immediately snagged two and started eating one. Then she paused and looked around. "I wonder if Kelsey is here. I know these are Kelsey's cake pops!" Before she could wander out an older brunette came into the kitchen and went straight for the dessert.

"Seriously! I can't freaking stop myself, these are so good!"

Jamie nodded. "I know, right?"

The other woman looked up, startled. "You're not the woman that was in here before! Sorry about that, my name is Beth." She held out her hand, the one not holding the cake pop.

"Uh, I'm not? Who was in here before? Was her name Kelsey?" Then as an afterthought, Jamie dropped her first empty cake pop stick into the nearby trash and reached out to shake her hand.

Beth shrugged. "I don't know. She was close to your height, curvy, and I think Hispanic. Does that sound like her?"

"Yeah, she made these!" Jamie held up the remaining treat like it was a torch in the Olympics. Before either woman could say another word a particularly annoying song came thumping through the kitchen door.

The brunette's face brightened noticeably. "Ooh, I gotta go! That's my jam!" Then she scampered back though the door into the living room where the main party was located. Before Jamie could fully appreciate that the older woman thought "Insane in the Membrane" by Cypress Hill was her jam, someone else came pushing through the door. She had just taken a bite of her second treat when a familiar voice nearly made her choke.

"Who do we have here? It's been a while, lover."

Jamie paled. "T—Tori?"

The redhead winked at her. "You remember my name, that's a good sign. Too bad you didn't remember to return my texts from a few weeks ago when I was out looking for a repeat." Tori stepped close, right into Jamie's personal space. "But that's all right, you can definitely make it up to me tonight since we're both here and all." Jamie started to move back away from the other woman, but Tori's hand was faster as she pulled Jamie's head down for a kiss.

It was in that exact moment that Kelsey came through the back slider and saw her close friend, and unacknowledged crush, locked in a kiss with the annoying woman from Club Culture. "James?"

Tori released Jamie abruptly and stepped away from her before running a finger across her own bottom lip seductively. "Yum, you taste sweet! Just like old times, huh?"

Jamie covered her throbbing lip, which had been split the night before, with the hand not holding a cake pop. "Ow, god-damn it! What did you do that for?" She took a stumbling step back. "And it wasn't old times, it was one freaking time!"

The redhead pouted. "Aww, you didn't like it?"

"Jamie?" Kelsey's voice finally registered in Jamie's alcohol-fogged and pain filled brain. Her face lit up when she saw her friend standing by the door.

"Hey Kels! I was just getting ready to look for you!"

Kelsey looked from Jamie to the skinny little redhead, then back at Jamie. "Yeah, it sure looks like it." Before the blonde could make her shocked mouth work Kelsey pushed between them and walked out into the living room. Jamie grabbed her hair and cursed for a minute straight when she realized what had just happened.

Tori's voice broke through her ranting. "What was that all about?"

Jamie shook her head. She was sick to her stomach with anxiety and exhausted from drinking all day. "Please just leave me alone okay, Tori? I'm sorry but I'm not interested in anything more."

The redhead looked from Jamie to the doorway where Kelsey had disappeared. "Clearly you're interested in something right now, James. But no worries, we're all good here." She turned to make her way back into the main room and stopped before pushing the door open and turned back to Jamie. "For what it's worth, I hope you find what you're looking for." Then she was gone.

The door swung open again and Jamie threw her hands into the air. "What is this, Grand Central freaking Station?"

"Why, is there an asshole train departing?"

"Jenn? What's that supposed to mean?" Jamie was upset and she was already considering calling a cab to take her home.

Jenn scowled at her. "I'm talking about you! What the hell did you do to Kelsey? She came barreling out of the kitchen looking like she was going to cry then walked straight out the front door. What the fuck, James?"

Jamie pointed at her. "Hey, keep your judgmental bullshit to yourself! I didn't do anything wrong this time. Your friend Tori came in here and kissed me. It's not like I wanted her to. Then Kelsey walked in and saw it."

"And what were you doing before that to prompt such an action?"

Jamie grew angry. She tossed the last bit of her dessert into the trash. "I was eating a cake pop, Jesus! I don't even like her like that anymore, I like—" She stopped speaking abruptly and grew still. Jenn watched as a strange look came over her friend's face.

"You like what, James? Kelsey?"

Jamie sighed and didn't answer the question. "It doesn't matter. She probably hates me now, and even if she didn't I'd never have a chance because all she knows of me is a reputation that is built of exactly what she walked in on." She ran her hand through what remained of her meticulously styled hair, sending it into further disarray.

"Your lip is bleeding." Jenn walked over and grabbed some paper towels then folded them up and wet them with cold water.

She reached out and gently placed the compress against Jamie's split lip. "Hold this to your lip. I don't think it needs stitches, but let's get the bleeding stopped then we'll go see if Kelsey is still here, okay?" She watched as Jamie nodded her head and politely ignored the way her friend's eyes were wet with emotion. Jamie never cried and she certainly wasn't crying now.

Fifteen minutes later they were on a manhunt for the missing cake pop maker. When they didn't find her Jenn hunted down Tam and Shell. "Hey, have you two seen Kelsey? Did she ride with you or drive herself?"

It was Tam who answered. "Yeah, Kels said she had a head-ache and that she was gonna go home. She asked us to grab her dessert container when we left. And she met us here. Why, what's up?" She looked at Jamie and narrowed her eyes at the other woman's disheveled look and split lip. "Why, what happened? And I know you! Weren't you the one who dated Lindy about a year ago?"

Jamie shook her head. "Uh, no. Lindy and I never dated. We hung out for a while, that was all."

Tam scoffed. "She told everyone you were dating. She also mentioned that you broke her heart when you dumped her and were out with someone else the following weekend."

"Knock it off, Tam!" Jenn stepped close to her overprotective friend. "Clearly Lindy was lying because I was there the night Jamie told her that she only wanted to be friends, that she wasn't interested in dating anyone."

"But—" She was interrupted by the soft voice of her wife.

"Tam." All three of them turned to Shell and she shook her head at Tam. "Let it go. You know Kelsey has been going through some stuff lately and you also know she can fight her own bat-tles." She glanced at Jamie. "Jamie here is good people." She held up a hand to forestall Tam's protest otherwise. "No, you have always listened to too many rumors. Jenn says she's one of her best friends and Jenn is one of mine. Let it go."

Tam looked at Jamie, then back at her wife and wisely let it go. "Sorry, Jamie, I shouldn't have judged you based on gossip."

Jamie shrugged. "Its fine, everyone does." Then she turned and headed for the front door herself, gently shoving her way through the crowd.

Jenn hung her head for a second and let out a big sigh, then she looked up at her friends. "Looks like I have to go. I'll come back if I can."

She turned to leave but was stopped by a hand on her arm.

Shell looked at her in concern. "Will you text later and let me know what's going on?"

The black woman grimaced. "As much as I can. I mean, it's not really my business. But my friend is hurting and I also happen to be her ride so, eh. We'll see."

Shell nodded. "Fair enough. Drive safe, Jenn." Tam just nodded.

Jenn found Jamie sitting in the passenger seat of her car. She got in, put on her seatbelt, and noticed that the other woman was already wearing hers. Making a quick decision, she grabbed her cell phone out of her purse and sent off a quick text message. Jamie glanced over at her when it rang a minute later. Jenn didn't say anything about the incoming text, she simply started the car and backed out of the driveway. "I'm taking you home."

Jamie looked at her smart watch. It was a little after seven. "Are you mad at me?"

With a quick glance at her passenger, Jenn turned her eyes back to the road. "I'm not mad at all. I just think you need to get some rest and maybe put some ice on that lip. I'm going to drop you off and that's what you're gonna do, doctor's orders, all right?"

She got a sad look in return. "You're not even going to come up with me? You are mad. I'm sorry I made you leave the party, Jenn, sorry for embarrassing you."

Jenn nearly rear-ended the car in front of her when she heard Jamie's words and cut a sharp look to the other woman. "Now where in the world did you get that idea? I'm not embarrassed at all. And I'm not mad at you, freak! I'm going over to hang out with Kelsey for a while."

"What?" Jamie's head whipped around. "How do you know where Kelsey lives?"

Jenn chuckled and shrugged as she pulled up in front of Jamie's condo. "I'm friends with her too, you know. And she's been teaching me to knit!"

Jamie snorted. "With her cats?"

"They certainly don't help us. The one is a real demon!"

"So you're choosing her over me?"

Jenn socked her in the shoulder. "You're so dense sometimes! No, I'm going over there because I think she could use a friend right now that she can talk with objectively. And I will be sure to let her know that while you act like you've been dropped on your head a few too many times as a baby, that you're really good people. Okay?" The blonde nodded and unclasped her seatbelt. "Get some rest, James."

Jamie nodded and opened the door. She leveled a serious gaze at Jenn. "Text me tomorrow, okay?"

Jenn smiled at her. "Of course!"

KELSEY'S APARTMENT WAS less than ten minutes away, even after making a quick stop at the grocery store. Jenn arrived at her door with a plastic bag in one hand and a six-pack of bottles in the other. Kelsey took in the groceries and the woman outside her door. "What's this? I thought you said you were bringing dinner."

"So I did." Jenn smiled at her and walked in, careful to avoid stepping on nosy felines as she made her way to the dining room table. It was a small apartment, so the kitchen overlooked the tiny dining room space, which overlooked the living room. Typical setup for an apartment complex dwelling. There was a short hallway that led to the bathroom and bedroom.

The Irish-Latina peeked in the bag. "I don't think beer goes with ice cream, Jenn."

Jenn smirked. "I'm positive it doesn't. Look again."

Kelsey pulled out a bottle and started laughing at the pale colored liquid. "Cream soda! I haven't had that in years! I love cream soda. What else do you have?" She started rifling through Jenn's grocery bag while the other woman took off her shoes and left them by the door. "Gummy bears and microwave popcorn! Ooh, and its dark chocolate and cherry ice cream!" She looked up at her friend. "Are we having a girls' night?"

Jenn nodded. "We are definitely having a girls' night!"

"Squee!"

The black woman raised an eyebrow at her. "Did you just 'squee'?"

"Maybe."

She got laughter in return. "You're a hard duck to pin down, Kels. I can't seem to put you in a box, you know?"

Kelsey shrugged and grabbed a couple of spoons out of the kitchen drawer. She found two bottle cozies and popped the caps off a cream soda for each of them, then led the way into the living room. "I don't really like to be put into a box. That's not who I am. I'm not a label and I hate when people try to define me!"

Jenn held up her hands. "Hey, I get it. And nobody is trying to define you here. I was just making an observation. You're not the only person I know who feels that way." Kelsey held up a movie and Jenn gave her a thumbs up, so she put it in the DVD player. The black woman laughed. "Anticiiiiiiipation! The movie never goes out of style! You ever see it live?"

Kelsey shook her head no. "What do you mean live? Like a musical?"

"Oh, girl, no! Seriously Kels? You've never seen it at the theater with a live cast?" She got another shake of the head. "Wow. You have to go. There is a theater about forty-five minutes away that plays the movie once a month and has a live cast to accompany it. My cousin and I go a few times a year. We should get a group of people together. It would be a blast!"

"Sounds like fun." She put the movie in and they both settled onto the couch with spoons and their pints of ice cream. Kelsey took a bite then pointed her spoon at her friend. "This is not even remotely healthy!"

"A little ice cream is not gonna kill you. Live a little, Kels!"

Kelsey laughed. "Some doctor you are!"

Jenn started laughing too. "Hey, I'm a pediatrician, what do you expect from me?"

"Oh, I don't know, the bedside manner of something other than a cranky iguana?"

The pediatrician snorted. "If you're a ten-year-old I have a great bedside manner. Now where the hell did you come up with that? Can iguanas even be cranky?"

Kelsey shrugged. "Who knows? I have cats for a reason." She took another bite of ice cream, slowly sucking it from the spoon as a pair of giant lips and teeth took up her TV screen. "So who else doesn't like to be put into a box?"

"Huh?"

"You said I wasn't the only one you knew who didn't like labels. Who else do you know like that? Because I feel like most people seem content with this label or that. It drives me nuts."

Jenn gave her a look, measuring the impact of her next few words, then decided to just go with it. "Me, for one. But the person I was really talking about was James. She hates labels and to be fair she does seem to defy them. She's another one that's hard to pin down."

"I don't want to talk about Jamie."

Jenn gazed at her honesty, ice cream momentarily forgotten and slowly melting in the container. "Why not?"

"You know why!"

The pushy woman shrugged. "Actually, I don't know why. I know you stormed out of the party, and she was really upset. Did she say something to you?"

Kelsey sighed. "No, she didn't say anything to upset me."

"Did she do anything?"

The other woman didn't answer because she wasn't sure how to answer. She knew she had been having feelings for her driving app buddy, but she also knew that there was no hope of a relationship with the other woman. Jamie was just Jamie, and Kelsey was looking for someone she could settle down with, not a playmate. She shrugged. "I just saw something that bothered me. It's no big deal."

Jenn arched an eyebrow her way. "Really?"

"I think it bothers me more that I was even upset about it."

"You're going to have to elaborate because I'm kinda in the dark here." Jenn took another bite of her melting ice cream and waited.

"I was in the back yard when you both got to the party. When I walked back into the house I saw Jamie kissing some redhead named Cory."

"Tori." Kelsey gave her a look and she elaborated. "She's an old friend of mine from college and has had the hots for Jamie for years. But go on." She waved for her friend to continue.

"Anyway, from the way they were talking I gather that Tori is someone that she's been sleeping with. And Jamie has mentioned more than once how she hasn't slept with anyone in months. I just don't like to be lied to, or mislead."

Jenn looked at her knowingly. "You're not the only one, my dear. What if I told you that Jamie didn't lie to you? If I said she hasn't played around for nearly three months? How do you feel about the two of them kissing? Does it still bother you?"

Kelsey thought about the scene that played out in her head. The exact point when all she saw was Jamie's lips on those of another. She was forced to give the real and honest reason for why she was so upset. "It still bothers me."

"Why does it bother you, if y'all are just friends?"

Kelsey scowled. "You know why!"

Movement out of the corner of her eye prompted Jenn to grab the spray bottle and hose down Pierre before he could get any closer to her cream soda bottle. "Ah ha! I got you, little asshole!"

That cut a little of the serious mood and Kelsey chuckled. "Nice shot."

Jenn blew on the barrel of the spray bottle and set it back on the end table. "Thanks! Now answer the question."

Kelsey grumbled at her. "Jesus, woman, you're so pushy!"

"You know it!"

Kelsey stared into the ice cream container, as if the collection of cherry pieces and dark chocolate chunks held the answer to all her woes. "Fine! It's because I like her, okay? But you don't have to worry, I know the score with her and I'm happy to just be her friend."

Jenn's gaze was gentle as she put a hand on Kelsey's knee. "If it were anyone else, I'd agree with them. But since it's you, I'm going to say you're wrong."

Dark green eyes stared back in confusion. "What do you mean? Jamie is Jamie. You and I both know how she is. She's told me the stories herself!"

"Kels, Jamie has only told you stories of who she used to be, not of who she is becoming."

Kelsey blew out a frustrated breath. "But what does that even mean?"

Jenn shrugged. "Truthfully? I'm not completely sure. I know that someone from her past hurt her, and she's never really moved on from it. But that's only what I've put together myself. I've never actually heard her say that though because she refuses to talk about that part of her life with anyone. I know that she's been unhappy for a while and has started making changes over the past few months to be a better person."

"She told me a little about her past. The person who hurt her was her first girlfriend, I believe. And she may be changing and turning over a new leaf as she calls it, but you and I know that Jamie isn't dateable."

Jenn shook her head. "The old Jamie wasn't dateable. I know she has her scars, but I truly believe that she's changing and finally moving forward. I also believe that if a woman were patient, they would see that Jamie is someone worth waiting for."

Kelsey placed the half empty pint on the coffee table and took a drink of her cream soda before answering. "The problem is, I have my own scars. And they're the reason I can't take a chance on someone like Jamie. She's one of the sweetest and funniest people I've ever met, and she's been a great friend, but that's all it's ever going to be between us. Okay?"

Jenn watched her to gauge the other woman for resoluteness. She found exactly what she expected to see staring back at her with resigned green eyes. "Okay." Then she set her ice cream on the table next to Kelsey's and stood up. "Now, if you'll please turn up the music, my song is gonna come on and we need space to dance to the Time Warp!"

AFTER JENN DROPPED her off, Jamie did exactly as promised. She went upstairs and drank down two glasses of water, peed, then came back to pour another glass. Then she made an ice pack with a Ziploc baggie full of crushed ice from her fridge. She took the water and icepack into the living room and settled into her recliner to chill, literally. She didn't even put the television on, because she was just too tired to watch. Her thoughts raced with newly realized feelings for her friend.

In all their conversations and teasing, Kelsey had never once told Jamie if she found her attractive. She had never once mentioned any kind of interest in her at all. Clearly she wasn't interested in that way, and it made Jamie's chest ache to think about it. She couldn't help wondering why Kelsey was so angry then. She thought through the puzzle logically, or at least as much as her brain could handle. She thought back to the scene in the kitchen and pictured what Kelsey had walked in on. If Kelsey wasn't jealous, then what prompted her anger and hurt? Especially since Jamie had told her that she hadn't slept with anyone in months. Tori's words came back to haunt her.

"Yum, you taste sweet! Just like old times, huh?"

The redhead's words made it obvious that the two had slept together and Kelsey would have no idea when that occurred. "She thought I lied to her!" Jamie winced as her split lip protested her declaration. She realized then that Kelsey was not interested in her and that she probably would never be after the scene in the kitchen. Exhaustion rolled over her all at once and eventually she reclined all the way back in the chair and fell asleep.

Chapter Eleven

JAMIE WOKE CHILLED. The collar of her shirt was damp where the forgotten ice pack had rested all night. She had a kink in her neck and the sun was cutting a swath through the French doors, right across her eyes. Other than a faint headache, she seemed no worse for wear from her Bloody Mary binge the day before. Clearly all the excess water she drank the previous night did the trick. It also meant her bladder was screaming at her. She picked up her cell phone and made a face at the early hour. "Too early, going back to bed." She set the Ziploc bag of water in the sink and hung the towel to dry, poured herself some fresh water, then went upstairs to pee and catch a few more hours of sleep from the comfort of her bed. Before drifting off again she checked for messages from Jenn or Kelsey and was disappointed to see nothing. She woke almost three hours later feeling significantly better. The swelling had gone down in her lip but it was still tender. She checked her phone again and saw she had a message from Jenn. Relief washed through her at her friend's words.

She's not mad at you. She thought you were lying when you said you hadn't been sleeping with anyone.

Jamie grinned ruefully and messaged back.

Figured that out on my own.

Well aren't you just the genius. Too bad that brain didn't kick in before you decided to drink all afternoon.

A couple of seconds later another text came in.

How's the head?

She rolled her eyes.

My head is fine. Followed the doc's orders and drank lots of water. Neck hurts from sleeping in the recliner most of the night though

```
James. *sigh*
```

```
What?
```

```
I love ya, but sometimes you're a real idiot. <3
```

Jamie snorted aloud but knew her friend was right.

```
Yeah, I know. Thanks for taking care of me last
night.
```

She thought for a second then sent another text.

```
How did you know I was drunk yesterday before you
showed up?
```

```
Your spelling & grammar were terrible and you were
lacking some serious punctuation. And you are a freak
about those things.
```

She scowled as she stood in front of her armoire deciding what to wear after her shower. She didn't feel like working out. She just wanted to be clean. Finally she texted back.

```
Whatever! You are just as bad!
```

She set the phone on top while she opened the cabinet and dug out a sports bra and brief set, soft white ankle socks, a pair of running shorts and a soft t-shirt. Her phone vibrated and she smiled as she read the incoming text.

```
Not like you tho
```

It vibrated again as she was getting ready to go shower.

```
Gotta go J. Heading for yoga to work off last
night. We'll talk later.
```

```
Bye, and have fun!
```

Jamie wanted to know what Jenn did the night before that she felt she needed to work it off. She looked at her reflection in the bathroom mirror. Was she drinking? Not getting an answer from her reflection, and knowing that Jenn wouldn't tell her, she shrugged and jumped into the shower. Clean and dressed, Jamie finally broke down and texted Kelsey.

Hey, sorry if I was an ass last night. Still want to
meet at the coffee shop?

She didn't want to hover over her phone while waiting for a
response, and she wasn't quite ready for food yet so Jamie went
back downstairs. At loose ends, she poured a glass of orange juice
and settled in to watch a few back episodes of her favorite super-
hero show. The phone vibrated halfway through the second episode and her face lit up when she saw it was from Kelsey.

Hey James, sorry for last night. Coffee shop is
good, unless you'd like to meet earlier. I'm starving!

Jamie lightly bit her thumbnail, thinking hard, then
answered.

If you've forgiven me for being a drunk mess last
night I have a suggestion.

Nothing to forgive. Suggestion?

Come to my place and I'll make us both lunch.
Haven't eaten yet either.

She waited as heartbeats went by, hoping Kelsey would say
yes and afraid she'd say no. Her phone vibrated.

Oh YES! What's for lunch?

Jamie thought about what she had in her fridge and freezer.

Dill Havarti grilled cheese on sourdough and homemade tomato bisque soup.

She jumped when her phone actually rang, not expecting it
after the texts. Smiling at the caller, she answered. "Yeeeeesss?"
"Give me your address right meow!"
Jamie laughed. "Did you just say meow?"
"Address dammit!"
Still grinning, Jamie persisted. "But, meow?"
Kelsey sighed over the phone. "James?"
"Yeah?"
"I worked out for an hour and a half this morning fueled only
by a banana."
Jamie giggled. "Yeeeaaaahh?"

"You have just promised me food, real food. Not out of a box or frozen food. Now tell me where this food is so I can come eat it!"

She couldn't stop herself from cracking up at the way Kelsey's voice got louder and louder over the phone. "Oh my God, you are absolutely insane right now. You're crazy, Kels!"

"Nope, just hungry. Though I've been told they look the same from the outside. Address please."

Jamie learned new things about her friend nearly every day. Her newest bit of info was that apparently Kelsey got hangry after working out and that she showed dogged determination when it came to getting what she wanted. The whispered words slipped out before she was aware they had been a thought. "Too bad she doesn't want me."

"What was that?"

Jamie jumped, forgetting she was actually talking on the phone. "I said I live in the condos on River Street. I'll text you the address."

"Okay, sounds good. See you in a few!"

Jamie ended the call and quickly texted her address then set the phone down in her lap and sighed. She was glad that Kelsey didn't want to talk about her actions the night before. She was going to have to do better about hiding her feelings if she didn't want to lose Kelsey's friendship, especially since her feelings never led to anything good. Before she could dwell on the subject of Kelsey any longer, her brain switched gears again to lunch. "Oh shit, the soup!" Homemade soup was in the freezer and still needed to be thawed, so she rushed off to the kitchen to begin lunch preparation.

When Kelsey arrived she parked in the lot across the street from the massive brick structure. She'd seen the Novak building plenty of times since moving to St. Seren because it was just down the street from Riverside Park. But she never knew that it housed condos. Kelsey sat in her car for a minute thinking about seeing Jamie after her admission to Jenn the night before. She really hoped that Jamie wouldn't bring it up again because she had already decided that they could only ever be friends. And she was going to try her hardest to ignore her attraction to the other woman. With that line of thought settled in her mind, she got out and locked her car doors.

Once inside she walked right past the geriatric guard and made a beeline straight for the elevators at the end of the hallway. No way was she taking the stairs after her workout. Off the elevator and down a hall, then left and down another hall until she got to 315. The faint sound of music carried through the door but either Jamie had it turned down or the doors were really thick. She knocked on the big steel-looking door and it was pulled open about ten seconds later.

"Hey! Any problems getting past the door guy?"

Kelsey narrowed her eyes. "No, he was sleeping at the desk. Why?

Jamie started laughing and pulled the door open wider so Kelsey could enter. "I was just curious. He's supposed to stop everyone that comes in and if you're not on the list he has to call up to the person they're visiting." She shook her head. "I'm glad to see he's taking the job seriously."

"James, he's like, ninety! Shouldn't he be retired or something?"

Jamie nodded. "He actually turned eighty-two this year. We had a birthday party for him. And he is retired, kind of. He lives here and the association pays for him to watch the door during the day. At night you have to have a key card to get in the front door." She shrugged. "He keeps the lobby and entertainment rooms clean and directs delivery boys up to the right place so he's good in my book."

Kelsey looked around at the open loft style condo. The living room was two stories. Straight back from the door was an outside wall made of pale brick and the tall wall to the right of the door was done in a bold maroon. The kitchen to the left was housed underneath the second floor and was done in a nice cream. Kitchen and downstairs bathroom were located on the other outside wall with a metal staircase that led to the second floor. Jamie had mentioned during one of their coffee meetups that the upstairs of her condo had two bedrooms and a smallish bathroom. Kelsey poked her head in the downstairs bathroom and ducked back out again, impressed by the Jacuzzi tub and double sinks. She was charmed and immediately loved the industrial vibe to the place.

While she was gazing around, Jamie walked over to the kitchen area to check the soup. "I know you're hungry but the soup was in the freezer. When it looks like it starting to warm, and not just sitting there as a block of ice in the pan, I'll start the sandwiches." Jamie's long expanse of leg shown by the running shorts was not lost on Kelsey, and she resolved to keep her eyes above the waist for the duration of the visit. She was startled from her internal chastisement when Jamie spoke again. "Let me give this another stir then I'll show you around."

Kelsey waved a casual hand through the air. "It's fine, you're feeding me so that's my priority right now. Take your time with the—" She sniffed then smiled. "Delicious smelling soup!" Her stomach growled loudly and she grabbed it. Unfortunately Jamie had paused the music right after she let Kelsey in so the noise was easily heard by both occupants of the condo. "Oh jeez!"

Jamie looked down as if she were addressing Kelsey's stomach directly. "Settle down over there, I'm cooking as fast as I can!" They both laughed.

Satisfied that most of the ice was melted, Jamie turned down the burner and set the large spoon on the drip catcher. "All right, now I can give you the grand tour. She gestured out to her sides. "This here is the kitchen, obviously." She walked them through to the living room, where a set of French doors led out to the deck. The doors opened inward to save space outside. Kelsey liked the cozy little area. She noted the small gas grill and two chair bistro table, as well as a few potted plants. She walked over and saw they were tomatoes.

"These are adorable!"

Jamie nodded. "And delicious, I love them on my salads." She led the way back in and showed her guest the large downstairs bathroom with the deep tub that she had peeked at a few minutes earlier. It featured two large doors as well as cupboards and other storage space.

Kelsey pointed at the doors. "What's in there?"

"Washer and dryer."

Kelsey sighed. When Jamie looked at her she explained. "I'm insanely jealous right now. I have to haul my laundry down to the communal machines in my building and then pray that there is no gum or other nastiness left behind by another tenant."

The blonde nodded. "Yeah, I had an apartment that was the same way, years ago when I first moved to St. Seren. My building had some guy that kept turning down his heat when he'd go out of town and apparently the pipes would rattle through the building. It sounded like a generator in the freaking hallway! I hated that place because the apartments were total shit."

"Yeah, I feel the same way about mine, though I don't have rattling pipes. But it was available and I wanted to move so, eh. I'm hoping to find something else when my lease is up at the end of the year." She shrugged.

Jamie led her back out of the bathroom and checked the soup, then waived her toward the stairs. "Come on up and see the bedrooms."

Kelsey snickered. "Does that line usually work for you?"

Jamie smirked and started up the stairs while Kelsey checked out her ass. She was immediately caught out when the other woman turned around to ask her a question. "So what complex to you liv — hey! Are you checking out my ass?"

Ears turned red and Kelsey tried to deny it. "No! I was looking at your shorts. They look comfortable with the built in spandex underneath. Where did you get them?"

They were both stopped halfway up the stairs and Jamie leveled an "I smell your bullshit a mile away" look at the woman who stood below her. "Uh huh." She turned and started to climb again. "I got them at Target and they are extremely comfortable for any kind of exercise. I'm sure they still have plenty of them in stock, but unfortunately for you my ass is no longer available."

Kelsey raised an eyebrow at her when they got to the top. "Oh reeeeaaaally?"

"Yup. It's off the shelf for recall. Apparently it causes uncontrollable blushing."

She got her arm punched for the joke when they reached the landing. "Oh ha-ha, you're a riot. Now show me the rest." The stairs ended facing the brick wall and immediately to the right there was a pocket door leading into the small bathroom. It had a toilet, single sink, small closet, and a standup shower. Because it was corner condo, both upstairs and downstairs bathrooms were flanked on two sides where the outer walls met. On the other side of the landing there was a hallway of sorts the full depth of the upstairs. An iron railing ran along the landing to prevent people from falling into the stairwell from the bedroom side. There were also two more pocket doors. The master bedroom was on the outside wall and featured two tall windows directly across from the king bed. The bed had a night stand on each side, a closet to the left of the bed, and an armoire just inside the door. The spare room was pretty small and Jamie used it as more of an office. There were a few book shelves, a futon, and a desk and chair. When they were heading back down the stairs Kelsey gushed about the place. "I seriously love everything about your condo! It has a great vibe to it."

Jamie walked into the kitchen and stirred the soup then began pulling stuff out of the fridge for the grilled cheese sandwiches. She got a large square griddle out of the cupboard and put it on a burner to heat. "Truthfully, I got it for a steal because I bought in when the building was just being converted to condos.

I had to do a lot of work myself, with Burke's help."

Kelsey was standing close enough to touch as she peered at the ingredients. "What work? And can I help with anything?" Kelsey subtly inhaled the smell of the food on the stove, and even more subtly took in the fresh clean scent that was all Jamie.

"You can find yourself something to drink in the fridge and have a seat at the island. I've got this." Just having Kelsey stand so near was causing all kinds of fluttering in her belly and other places but her breath caught ever so slightly when Kelsey gave her a dimpled grin. Jamie had no choice but to ignore her attraction and continue the explanation of the work that was done on the condo. "For example, the plastered walls were finished but they all had to be painted. I had to put appliances in the kitchen, hardware and fixtures everywhere, and install the hardwood floors. It was a lot of work but I really felt like the place was mine when I got done, you know?" She glanced at Kelsey over her shoulder as she finished speaking and gave her a big smile. Then she turned back to finish buttering the bread and arranging the slices and cheese on the pan to cook.

Kelsey was stuck by how much more open and relaxed her friend appeared in her own living space. Truthfully though, she had noticed the change happening over the past few months, both while chatting and in person since they'd begun meeting. Jamie seemed calmer, more settled. Jenn had mentioned that the blonde was making some changes in her life and they seemed to be good for her. Kelsey was lost in thought as she stared at her water bottle and completely missed Jamie finishing her prep and coming to stand next to her.

"What are you thinking so hard about?"

Kelsey nearly tipped over on her stool and grabbed her chest. "Jesus Jiminy Christmas! Don't scare me like that!" Jamie laughed delightedly and Kelsey pointed at her. "It's not funny, nerd! I think you just gave me a gray hair, or ten!"

"Oh come on, it's not that bad! You're as much of a drama queen as my hairdresser."

Kelsey pouted. "Oh, like you would know the struggle, blondie!"

The blonde cocked her head as if debating something internally, then shook her head. "Kels, I've got a lot of gray hair."

The seated woman reached up and caressed the back of Jamie's hair where it and the sides were nearly shaved. "Ooh, it's so soft, like a Shar-Pei! And it's not like you can see it with hair this color. Now dark auburn, I can see every one of my grays!"

Jamie shivered at the feel of Kelsey's hand running through the back of her hair. It was a highly erotic place for her and she struggled to keep her breathing normal. Especially when the other woman used her nails lightly. "My hair isn't blonde." Perhaps it was because she was so disconcerted, but the words came out before Jamie could sensor them. And her heart raced a little to admit something that was so very personal to her.

Kelsey dropped her hand away, confused. "What?" She was distracted because she liked running her fingers across Jamie's hair a little too much.

The blonde took a deep breath then walked over to flip the sandwiches and stir the soup. The cheese was starting to melt nicely and the cooked side of the sandwiches were a perfect golden brown. She spoke while her back was to Kelsey because she didn't like to admit to things that would prompt more questions. "I color it every four weeks, when I go in for a cut."

Kelsey was flabbergasted. She had never once thought that Jamie was anything other than a blonde. Jenn never mentioned it and Jamie clearly had a face that could carry any color. When the other woman turned around to face her she tried to see the signs. "Come here for a second." Her voice was a little quieter than normal because Jamie looked unsettled. She stood and placed a hand on each side of the Jamie's face, lightly cupping her cheeks. "What is your natural hair color? I'd always thought you had the thickest most gorgeous lashes I'd ever seen, and I'm half Latina. But your eyebrows match your hair!"

Jamie had stopped breathing the minute Kelsey touched her face, but she had to start again in order to answer. "I uh, Richard colors both. The man is seriously talented. And my hair is very dark brown, nearly black."

"Oh!" Kelsey dropped her hands and immediately pictured her friend with such dark hair. Then she wanted to fan herself at the image. Jamie was tall, lean, and had that angular jaw, which put her strictly into the androgynous category. Picturing her with dark hair was nearly a sin. "Oh my God! Why do you color it? I bet you look amazing with dark hair!"

Jamie didn't really want to talk about her reasons so she tried to lighten the mood instead, grasping onto the one really encouraging thing that Kelsey had said. "You don't think I look amazing now?" She grinned when she saw her friend's ears turn pink.

Kelsey snorted. "You look fine, stop fishing!"

A blonde eyebrow rose. "Just fine? You're going to hurt my feelings, Kels."

Kelsey shoved her away. "Go check the sandwiches, I'm still starving here! And I refuse to stroke your ego for you. You have a mirror and know full well how you look!"

Jamie winked at her and walked away to do as bid, but not before a parting shot. "You may not want to stroke my ego but you sure can't stop staring at my ass! Friends don't look at their friends' asses like that."

Startled, she hadn't expected Jamie to call her out, but she got even. "They do if said friend has toilet paper sticking out the back of their shorts."

Jamie spun around with spatula in hand, then twisted in place trying to see the back of her shorts. "Hey, I do not! You're such a liar!"

Kelsey cracked up laughing. "I never said that you had toilet paper. I was just giving you an example of when staring would be acceptable."

"Just for that, no soup for you!"

The starving woman held up her hands in surrender just as her stomach gave another loud growl. "Please don't do that. I'd eat anything right now but that soup smells amazing! And you can't have grilled cheese without tomato soup. It's against nature!"

Jamie smirked. "Anything, hmm?"

Kelsey rolled her eyes. "You are such a perv!" Then she clapped her hands together twice. "Now James, I believe you promised lunch. Hop to it!"

"Oh yes, ma'am, right away, ma'am!" The newly minted butler corner cut one of the sandwiches into four adorable little triangles and placed them on a small plate, then ladled up the soup into an oversize soup cup covered in scenes from the most epic sci-fi movie series ever. She walked right by Kelsey and placed them on the small dining room table. Then she turned back to her and nodded toward the food. "Come on Kels, you can't eat at my island. Get over here." Kelsey laughed and took a seat, then Jamie went over to plate up her own food.

"Oh my freaking word, this is amazing!" Jamie took a seat and started dunking her own sandwich corner. Kelsey looked up at her between bites. "Where do you get your soup? This is nothing like the canned stuff!"

"I made it."

Kelsey paused, sandwich halfway to her mouth and dripping creamy pink soup back into the cup. "No way!" Jamie just nodded. "Wow." She ate another bite, savoring the flavors of the homemade tomato bisque, the tang of the sourdough bread, and the richness of the dill Havarti cheese. "Have you always liked to cook? What got you into it?"

Jamie shrugged. "I don't know. I guess I started cooking when I was young and just stuck with it. I like food so I'm always up for trying new stuff and experimenting."

"Did your mom teach you to cook?"

The blonde started laughing. "Uh, no. It was my aunt actually. My mom was a terrible cook. She'd over-season, over-cook, or just cook way too much and we'd end up eating it for days on end. The only thing worse than eating terrible food, is eating the same terrible food for lunch and dinner for a week straight!"

Kelsey shot Jamie her dimpled grin. "Yeah, I didn't have that problem at all. Probably the opposite, actually. My mom was a great cook and could make just about anything. When my *abuela* stayed with us she even complimented Mama on how fast she picked up the knack of making authentic Mexican food. I think that's why I never learned because it's not something that interested me and I didn't have to cook for self-preservation." Kelsey finished the first half of her sandwich and took a break for water. "So did you grow up around here?" Jamie shook her head. "Does your family live nearby? It seems weird that I've told you all about my family over the past few months but I know nothing about yours."

Jamie set her sandwich down and wiped her mouth with a paper towel. "There's nothing to tell. My mom lives a few hours north and I haven't seen her in a long time. She didn't take it well when I got a divorce, and she wrote me off completely when I came out to her."

Kelsey's hand covered Jamie's. "Oh, James, I'm really sorry. We don't have to talk about it."

Jamie shook her head. "It's okay, it was years ago now. The only family member I have contact with now is my half-sister in Wisconsin. I moved to St. Seren to start new. I wanted to live somewhere a lot more liberal than the little town I was raised in, up north." She shrugged. "So here I am." She grabbed another grilled cheese corner to take a bite but froze when Kelsey brought up the subject of her hair again.

"So you never did say why you color it. Jenn has never once mentioned that you had dark hair either."

"Jenn doesn't know."

Kelsey dropped the last bit of sandwich into her soup. "Seriously?"

Jamie nodded. "Yeah. I'm guessing not many people remember me from before I started coloring my hair. I wasn't living down here very long when I began going to Richard."

"So why did you start coloring it?"

The blonde shrugged and looked down at her soup. "I don't know."

"James." Kelsey's voice was low and quiet and Jamie's eyes were drawn back up to her. "We may not have known each other very long, but I consider you a close friend. Now there will be moments when one of us doesn't want to talk about something and we will respect that because friendship is about trust and we both deserve our privacy. But I don't ever want lies and bullshit between us."

Jamie's emotions rose within her and she closed her eyes to swallow them back down. When she finally had control again, she looked up into the dark green irises in front of her and nodded. "You're right, and I'm sorry. The decision involves my ex and I'm not ready to talk about it yet."

Kelsey smiled and gave her hand another squeeze, then changed the subject in an effort to lighten the mood. "So you mentioned once that you had some hilarious stories?" The other woman looked confused so Kelsey elaborated. "We were messaging a while back and I told you I didn't want to hear your kinky stories but you said you had some funny ones."

"Oh! Yeah, I do have some funny ones. But you realize if I share you have to share too." Kelsey thought about it, then nodded. She figured it could be fun to get a little glimpse into the lighter, naughtier side of Jamie.

The blonde deliberated which story to tell before settling on a recent one. "Okay, so I was down visiting a friend in Indiana for a weekend, and she had this damn cat that got into everything."

"Hey, watch how you talk about our feline friends!"

Jamie held up her hands. "No, seriously, he was a demon. He would steal her toothbrushes out of the holder and leave them in the litter box. The first night I stayed there I didn't know about his thieving ways and sure enough, that's where we found my missing toothbrush the next morning."

Kelsey laughed. "Eww! That sounds just like something Pierre would do, which is why I keep my toothbrush in the medicine cabinet."

"Yeah, well did Pierre ever steal the handcuff key and lose it down the heat register?"

The other woman had just fished the last bite of sandwich out of her soup with the spoon and dropped it again when she heard Jamie's words. "Did you just say handcuffs?"

Jamie grinned. "Yup. Nikki was a wild one."

A little tiny bit of unexpected jealousy took up residence in Kelsey's gut and she did her best to ignore it. "So who was in the cuffs, you or your friend?"

"Nikki, of course." Jamie gave her a look that said the answer should be obvious.

"No, not of course."

Now Jamie just looked confused. "What do you mean?"

"What do you mean, what do I mean? I suppose you're one of those big bad butches who's never on the bottom." Kelsey scoffed at the notion of all big bad butches refusing bottom status.

The blonde made a face at Kelsey's assumption. "No actually, but I'm usually expected to be the top. I'm typically the more dominant one so, eh." She shrugged then looked at Kelsey and Kelsey looked back at her curiously.

"You don't seem too happy about it."

Jamie looked away and sighed. "Eh, it is what it is I guess. I just go with what's expected of me. It's all fun, right? And what about you?"

Kelsey smirked. "What about me what?"

Jamie shook her head. "You're such an ass! I mean, are you a top or a bottom?"

"Neither."

The blonde's eyebrows rose in disbelief. "What?"

"You heard me, I'm neither. I like both but I guess my problem is similar to yours in that the women I'm attracted to usually expect me to be certain way. You asked me once why I was single and I think that's one of the main reasons why. I guess I just haven't found someone I really clicked with on multiple levels." She leveled a playful glare at Jamie. "See, I'd like to be the girl in the handcuffs, then I'd want to be the girl with the key."

Jamie got warm envisioning that very same scenario. No one had ever put her in handcuffs before, or even suggested it. But she'd always had a fantasy about someone topping her. While she liked some butch and androgynous girls, she was still too dominant for most of them and she had a hard time giving up control. But if she could find the right woman, mmhmm.

"Where did you go? Because your face just got all pink!" Kelsey pointed at the other woman's warm cheeks and grinned wickedly.

Jamie slapped her finger away then scrubbed her own face.

"Seriously, Kels? You shouldn't pick on me over here, I'm practically a nun!"

Kelsey rolled her eyes. "Practically!" She grinned, showing off that pesky dimple and Jamie knew her crush had gone full-blown. "You know, if you can't handle the conversation you can always tap out."

The blonde gave her a perplexed look. "Tap out?"

Kelsey nodded. "Yeah, like with tag team wrestling or sex."

Jamie had taken a swig from her water bottle and spit the entire mouthful halfway across the living room. "Oh my God, you did not just say that! And what does it even mean?"

"You know, when one guy gets tired of beating up his opponent he can go over to the side and—" She never got to finish because Jamie made a time out motion with her hands.

"No, no, no, I'm talking about the sex reference! What does tap out mean?"

Kelsey giggled at her friend's antics. "It's when someone is uh, not doing such a good job, and you just kind of reach down and tap them on the shoulder. Like, come up here and let's do this for a while..." Her voice faded out but the implied meaning was there.

Jamie cracked up laughing and pointed across the table. "No, you have not done that!"

"Yeah, yes I have."

A look of disbelief washed across Jamie's face. "But only like, once or twice, right?"

Kelsey blushed and idly scratched at her temple. "Eh, I'm kind of a hard sell. So, more than once or twice. Why are we even talking about this again? We should totally change the subject."

Jamie grinned. "No, this is great! I'm learning so much about you! But apparently now that the shoe is on the other foot you want to tap out of the conversation." She thought for a second then lobbed another question at Kelsey since her friend seemed so open to sharing. "What was the weirdest encounter you've ever had with a woman?"

"Oh jeez!" Kelsey thought for a minute. "Ah, it was totally my friend Tam's fault. We were roommates back in college and for whatever reason Tam has always taken it upon herself to look out for me. So a few years ago, after I split with the girlfriend I had at the time, they invited me into town for the weekend because they were having their annual costume party. That year's theme was prom. Anyway, what she neglected to tell me was that they had another friend who was staying at the house. And because Becky had admitted to liking girls, they thought she could use a friend. Well, we were all drunk that night and Becky was all over me every time I found myself in a room alone. One thing led to another and we ended up sleeping together. I wasn't ready to date anyone yet and the woman said she was totally all right with just the casual one-time thing."

Jamie nodded when Kelsey paused to get a drink. "Okay, sounds all right in theory but something went wrong huh?"

Kelsey nodded. "When I told Tam what happened she was surprised because her friend was newly divorced and had only expressed interest in women before. But she reassured me that Becky wasn't interested in dating and would be cool about it. Then Becky started calling and texting, asking when we could hang out again. I told Tam and Shell about what she was doing the next time I came into town and they didn't believe me."

Dregs of her soup forgotten, Jamie leaned over her bowl intently listening. "What did you do?"

"Becky happened to call when I was sitting at Tam and Shell's kitchen table. Tam told me to give her the phone and she answered it for me. She asked Becky what she was doing then spent about five minutes on the phone with the other woman before eliciting a promise from her to leave me alone."

"Did she say what was up with Becky?"

Kelsey nodded. "Yeah, apparently our night together had pushed her right off the queer cliff. The best part about the entire experience is that Tam bought me a toaster oven for my birthday that month. She thought it was a joke but I loved it. That thing is hella useful!"

Jamie laughed. "That's awesome!"

She stood and began gathering the dirty dishes but Kelsey stood too and stopped her. "You cooked, I'll clean up." Then she nodded at Jamie. "What about you? What is your weirdest moment?"

"Let's see, well I have this, uh, I really like jewelry."

Kelsey gave her a strange look. "Really?"

Then Jamie elaborated by making vertical circles in the air in front of her chest. "You know, rings and studs."

"Ohhh! Go on." She gave Jamie a funny little smile but waved her on.

"So, I was with this cute baby butch and she had both nipples pierced, which was totally amazeballs! Well as I moved further down I discovered that her clit was pierced as well. Which was a new one for me but still pretty cool. So anyways, I'm totally loving the lower post and she can tell. Then while I'm down there she proceeds to inform me that she did it herself with a needle and some ice. Totally blew my mind. I mean my tongue was still going but my head was all like 'what the fuck!' and well, anyways, that was a definite one and done. She too got a little weird after."

"Holy shit!"

Jamie nodded. "Yeah."

Kelsey shook her head. "No, I mean holy shit I slept with her too! She told me the same thing."

Jamie gave her a look of surprise. "Really? That's weird. Are you sure? Short, cropped blonde hair and pixie-like face? Her name was —"

"Bailey. Yeah, I'm sure. And yeah, that poor girl had some real issues. We actually went out a few times before we slept together and she seemed cool and all, but after?" Kelsey shuddered. "Yeah, issues."

In that moment, the strangeness of coincidence hit them both and they started laughing while Kelsey rinsed the dishes in the sink. They talked for a little while longer then Kelsey had to leave to go do her laundry and Jamie went back to her couch. She was confused and a little sad. Kelsey had officially reached further inside than few other friends before. She intrigued Jamie, and attracted her more than any of the women the engineer had slept with in the past. But she wasn't sleeping with Kelsey. She couldn't sleep with her and maintain their friendship. The problem was, she wasn't like any of Jamie's other friends either. She was just more, and Jamie was in a little bit of trouble.

Chapter Twelve

JAMIE'S DAY WAS not going well. Not only was she in the middle of a major revamp of one of her own lines, but it was also her day to cover the old line because they still hadn't hired an engineer to take "Dave the Dick's" place. The line was one of the very first ones in her building, and being older than Methuselah it ran poorly on a good day. The supervisor had called Jamie for an issue with one of the big in-line coaters. Unlike the other departments though, the two openings for the machine were on opposite ends of the line from each other. So if there was an alarm, you had to run from one end to the other to shut it off, then run back and see what was causing the alarm. Jamie was tired of running. About forty-five minutes before quitting time she was ready to be done. Her own line had called her with a tester issue so she called Bill to see if he was available to look at it.

"Sure, James. I'm smooth sailing 'til the end of the day since my lines had to go home early."

She grabbed him before he could hang up. "Hey, if you get that figured out can you come help me with the dinosaur?"

"Yeah, let me just go check your tester and I'll come over."

The worst part about the layout of the dinosaur line was the fact that you had to exit the door at one end and immediately duck under an eight inch diameter steel pipe in order to get to the alarm controller. There were strips of plastic sheeting hanging down across the doorway so you didn't see the pipe unless you were all the way out.

Jamie had just made an adjustment and went back into the plastic enclosed clean room to cycle a tray through. There were two line operators in the room with her, Jill and Sue. When the alarm blared again she spun in place, dodged around Jill, and ducked down to plow through the plastic door, anticipating the pipe. Unfortunately she misjudged the height of it and plowed headfirst into the steel like a charging bull. The loud "bong" sound drew Jill and Sue out of the room to see what happened as Jamie staggered and reeled from the blow. Jill caught her as she nearly fell and Jamie clapped a hand to the top of her head. "Holy shit, Jamie! Are you all right?"

Jamie righted herself and gingerly reached around the controller to shut off the alarm. "I just literally saw stars. Like real blinking, twinkling lights swirling around my head just like a freaking cartoon." She moved her hand from the top of her head down to rub the back of her neck. Both were killing her. Her other hand stayed clutching the controller.

Jill watched her for a second. "I think you should sit down for a minute, that rung your bell. Do you feel dizzy at all? How is your neck?" Jamie looked at her curiously and Jill shrugged. "My daughter is a paramedic and I was always helping her study at night when she was in school."

Before they could go anywhere, Bill walked up. "Hey, what's going on, James?"

Sue chimed in. "She just plowed into the coater pipe headfirst like a bull! She probably concussed herself."

Jamie shook her head slowly. "I'm sure it's not that bad. I'm just going to have a headache for a while."

Her fellow engineer looked at her. "Seriously, dude? How often have you ducked through that door? You're such a klutz!"

"Bill, we're just going to help Jamie into the office over there so she can sit down. Can you take a look at the dinosaur for us? It's saying the coater value is off, just like last time. I think the sensor is probably bad again. You know maintenance never changes them when they're supposed to." Jill had worked on the line a long time and knew nearly as much about the coaters as the engineers did.

He nodded. "Yeah, you're probably right. Let me run a couple test sheets and check the log book."

Jamie looked relieved. "Thanks, man." The two line operators helped Jamie into a nearby office so she could sit down. Then Sue called the nurse over from the main building. Thirty minutes later she was sitting in the nurse's office sporting a massive headache and stiff neck.

"Do you have someone you can ride home with? I'm not saying you need to go to the doctor because your pupils look fine and you have a full range of motion, even if you're sore. But I don't think you should drive right now, and it would be good if someone could stay with you overnight to monitor you. Do you have someone you can call?"

The blonde grimaced. "No, I live a half hour away. There is no—wait, I might have someone." It had been more than two weeks since the unfortunate birthday party and her friendship with Kelsey was solid. She was pretty sure the other woman would help her out. It was about ten minutes before she and Kelsey normally finished their day so she took a chance and called her friend. It was answered on the second ring.

"Hey, what's up?"

"Hi, Kels. I have a big favor to ask and I'll understand if you want to say no—"

"Of course I'm not going to say no. Go on."

Jamie smiled at the way Kelsey was always ready to help. "So I kinda rung my bell here at work and the nurse doesn't think I should drive. Do you think you could give me a ride home and back to work tomorrow?"

Worry for her friend immediately flooded through Kelsey. "Oh no! Are you okay? Are you sure you don't need to go to the doctor?" Her boss walked into the back room and raised his eyebrows at her side of the conversation.

Jamie's voice sounded through the phone with more than a little humor. "No, I'm going to be okay. The nurse just says I shouldn't drive and that I should have someone monitor me over night. I was going to see if I could stay with Jenn."

Kelsey's eyebrows went up. "Why would you do that when you've got a friend with no kids to worry about? How about I just stay with you tonight since I need to give you a ride back to work tomorrow anyway? It makes perfect sense."

"Oh, I can't ask you to do that! What about your cats?"

The marginally crazy cat owner laughed. "James, they're cats. As long as they have food and water they are fine to be left overnight, or even a few nights. They'll live. My boss just said I can cut out a few minutes early so text your work address to me and I'll head out now."

Dr. Davies just nodded at her and gave her a thumbs up. He also whispered to her. "If you need to come in a little late tomorrow, let me know."

Kelsey covered the receiver. "We should be fine. She starts at the same time I do, so I'll just drop her off a little early."

She stopped talking when Jamie came back over the line. "All right, you win. I'll see you in a few minutes. But takeout is on me tonight!"

"Perfect! See you soon." Kelsey put Jamie's work address into her Drīv app and it only took her twelve minutes. She parked next to Olivia since the sporty blue car was a standout in the large employee parking lot and texted the engineer when she got there. The lean blonde walked out a few minutes later with her messenger bag slung across her chest and carrying her lunch box in her right hand. When Jamie got close to her car, Kelsey rolled down the window and called out to her in a terrible Bronx accent.

"Yeah, I gotta car here for Schultz?"

Jamie smiled but Kelsey could see the little pain lines etched between her brows. "Cute, Kels." She stopped and stared back at her own car, then frowned. "I don't like leaving her overnight."

"Seriously? You've just nearly concussed yourself and your biggest worry is whether your car will get lonely?"

Jamie made a face at her. "Jeez, when you put it like that it sounds ridiculous!"

Kelsey laughed. "Because it is ridiculous! What other option do you have?"

"We could take my car?"

The woman in the little gray economy car shook her head slowly. "I'm pretty sure I'm here for a reason, because you can't drive home."

Jamie grinned at her. "No, but you can! How would you like to get your hands on my girl? She practically purrs while you put her through the paces."

"Uh." Kelsey's ears turned pink. It had been a little bit since she'd had her hands on anyone, let alone put a girl through her paces. The last one had actually been the pierced chick with the issues. "I can't drive a stick shift, so probably best to just leave your precious baby here for the night."

The blonde disregarded Kelsey's words and walked over to Olivia's driver's door and hit the button to unlock. Then she opened it and turned back to Kelsey, gesturing for the other woman to get in. "It's not a stick so you're out of excuses. Come on, Kels, it'll be fun!"

Kelsey could see that she wasn't going to win in a battle of stubborn determination. Well, she probably would win at that, but driving Jamie's car home wasn't worth a battle. Besides, Jamie was hurt and it was best to just humor her. And maybe she wanted to drive Olivia, just a little. She rolled up her window and shut her car off before grabbing her own stuff. She got out and locked the doors then turned back to Jamie. "My car is okay here, right? I don't need a pass or anything?"

"It's fine, now get in."

Kelsey put her lunch bag and other things in the back hatch and Jamie did the same with her own lunch box, taking her messenger bag into the front seat with her. Once the dental assistant was seated in the molded leather bucket seat she was immediately impressed with the difference between Oliva and her own car. It had black leather interior, a large in-dash LCD screen, and had a max speedometer reading of 160, just for starters. She didn't have to move the seat because she was only about an inch or so shorter than Jamie, but she did have to adjust the mirrors. "Where's the key?"

Jamie patted her bag and smiled. "I've got the fob in here. As long as it's within a foot or two of the dash the car will start just fine."

Kelsey looked around the dash to the steering column and didn't see a spot for a key. Then she saw a large button directly in front of the shifter knob. The word "Start" was written in bold lettering. "Ooh, neat!" She pushed it and the only thing that happened was the radio came on.

The other woman snickered in the passenger seat. "You have to hold the brake pedal and push the button for it to start. Otherwise it's just like turning the key one or two clicks." She clamped her phone in the holder that was low on the center of the dash, slightly to the right and above Kelsey's knee. She brought up the Drīv app and turned on Bluetooth so it could synch automatically to Olivia. Then she used her LCD touch screen in the dash to bring up the music app on the phone.

"Ah, gotcha! Seriously, James, this is like some kind of James Bond car. Very cool!" When she backed out she got another surprise. "Holy shit, a backup camera! I could definitely use something like this in my car. Our parking lot at work is so tight, it's hard to get in and out of my little space."

"That's what she said!"

Kelsey turned her head and narrowed her eyes at Jamie. "Really?"

Jamie nodded. "Oh, absolutely!"

"It's not like you would know!"

The blonde smirked. "Maybe I've heard stories."

Kelsey cracked up laughing. "Now I know that's not true!"

Jamie raised an eyebrow at her, thoroughly enjoying the fact that with Kelsey driving. She was a captive audience for Jamie's questions. "You're telling me that you haven't slept with anyone in St. Seren except for Bailey?"

"I didn't say that." Kelsey focused on the drive

"Ooh, do tell!"

Kelsey glanced at her. "Are you going to tell me the girls you've slept with?"

Jamie blushed. "Um, I see your point. Never mind, don't tell. A girl likes a little mystery anyway."

The brand new driver of the little blue sports car snorted. "That's what I thought!" When they got back to St. Seren, Kelsey drove to her apartment first to take care of the cats and grab a change of clothes. She parked in her spot and turned to Jamie. "Do you want to come up or just sit here? I won't be long." Jamie had stayed pretty quiet for most of the ride after the initial conversation. She could tell the other woman wasn't feeling the greatest.

"Actually, do you have some Motrin or something? My head and neck are killing me. I'm such an idiot sometimes."

Kelsey nodded. "I do, actually. Come on." When she opened the door her cats were immediately underfoot, meowing as if they hadn't been fed in a week despite the fact that they had dry food sitting in their dishes. They went a little skittish at first when Jamie walked in behind her, then they came right over to check her out. Kelsey set her wallet on the stand and put her keys in the dish just like normal, but then gestured for Jamie to follow. "Why don't you lie down for a minute? I'll get you a bottle of water and some pain reliever." She led her friend back to her very spartan bedroom and instructed her to lie down on the bed. Then Kelsey went to get the water and pills.

Jamie complied with a little too much joy. "So is this where the magic happens?" She leaned back on the bed and snuggled into the pillows, turning her head discretely to capture the scent of them.

Kelsey rolled her eyes as she reentered the room and handed the items to the prone woman. "Shouldn't you be resting or something? I don't think talking is good for your headache."

"On the contrary, the nurse said I had to stay awake." She patted the bed next to her. "You could come keep me company and make sure I don't fall asleep."

The other woman made a face. "Seriously, James? You're incorrigible! I'm going to take out my trash and check the mail, then take care of the cats. I'll be back to pack an overnight bag after." Jamie heard her leave the apartment and less than ten seconds later she had two curious felines join her on the bed. Even though her head was killing her, she delighted in the soft fur beneath her fingertips. It was soothing. One settled in next to her while the other started chewing on the button of her shirt. She pushed him away and he came up to lie down by her head. And that was how Kelsey found them five minutes later when she returned. She stood in the doorway and took in the scene. Newman was snuggled into Jamie's side and Pierre was lying down near the pillow, cleaning her hair. She giggled and Jamie cracked an eye open at her. "You can just push him away you know."

"You know your cat is weird, right? Does he always do this?"

Kelsey shook her head and gave Jamie a dimpled smile. "That one is Pierre and yes I know he's weird. He likes to do that to me when I get out of the shower. But you're not any better than he is if you just let him do it." She sat down on the bed next to the other cat and started scratching around his ears. "This here is my sweet boy, Newman. He's not half the asshole his brother is." She didn't sit for long before standing again. "All right, come on boys. Let's leave Jamie alone and I'll get you some canned food."

They clearly knew what she was talking about because as soon as she left the room they barreled out after her. Jamie just grinned at the friendly cats. "Fickle."

It wasn't long before they were back at Jamie's condo trying to decide what to order for dinner. "Why don't you go put your stuff up in the spare room and I'll bring up some restaurants on my laptop."

Kelsey smirked at her. "What, you're not going to offer your own bed?"

"Oh, please!" Jamie scoffed. "Even with a lump on my head you couldn't handle the Schultz!"

"The Shultz huh? That sounds dirty."

Jamie winked at her. "Maybe it is." She called out to Kelsey as she walked up the stairs and winced at the sound of her own voice. "We have a variety within delivery distance. Mexican, Chinese, Thai, sandwiches, pizza, and a few more local spots. What do you feel like?"

Kelsey called from the top of the stairs. "Do you have a heating pad?"

"Yes I do, but I don't think that would taste too good."

"Such a smart ass! For your neck, genius!"

Jamie made a face and felt stupid. "In the downstairs bathroom closet."

Kelsey came skipping back down the stairs and walked around the corner into the bathroom, emerging less than a minute later with the heating pad in hand. She walked over to Jamie with a victorious smile on her face. "Do you have a plug around here anywhere?" The couch was toward the middle of the room, facing the wall that divided her condo and the condo next door. She had lamps but the cords ran under the couch.

The blonde nodded then rubbed her neck in discomfort. "There are plugs set into the floor beneath the couch."

Rather than rush to plug in the heating pad, Kelsey instead sat it down on the end table and came around the couch. "I'm going to loosen up your neck for you first, okay? If you move down to the floor I can sit on the couch and give you a neck massage."

Jamie sighed and immediately slipped off the couch to the floor. "That would be heaven right now!"

Kelsey moved to sit behind her and gently began massaging the corded muscle. The neck had obviously stiffened up and it was no wonder the other woman was so sore. Jamie moaned and leaned her head down to give Kelsey better access. Despite the pain in her neck and head, she had a hard time ignoring the feel of Kelsey's legs against each side, or the warmth of Kelsey's hands across the skin of her neck. She had a very sure and firm touch and the blonde couldn't help picturing those hands everywhere. Kelsey wasn't having any easier of a time. As she massaged the length of her friend's neck, her hands would wander up into the soft shorn hair then back down to the soft skin below. She tried to distract herself at the same time she attempted to loosen the steel-like cords below her fingertips. "So did you decide what you want for dinner?"

The blonde shrugged. "I'll eat anything."

"I heard that about you."

Jamie's eyes widened and she turned her entire upper body around to look at the woman behind her. "You soooo did not just say that!"

Kelsey giggled. "I soooo did say that! What are you going to do about it, stiffy mcstifferson?" Before Kelsey could register what was happening Jamie was off the floor and had her pinned to the couch, fingers digging into her sides. She was laughing uncontrollably as Jamie tickled her without mercy. "Dammit, stop! I'm gonna pee, James!"

The blonde was also laughing and turned to look at her. "Oh, ow! Damn, damn, damn." She collapsed on top of the woman below her at the sudden wrenching in her neck.

"That's what you get for being so mean." Kelsey was laughing but took pity on her anyway. Jamie wasn't heavy so she started massaging her neck again. It took mere seconds for both women to fully realize the intimacy of their position.

Jamie slowly raised her head, disregarding the discomfort in her neck. She licked her lips and gazed into Kelsey's dark green eyes. "I, uh, we should order our dinner." She swallowed and looked away as she carefully got up off her good friend. Her *friends only* friend.

Kelsey nodded as the blonde's weight came off her and she

shivered when the heat left with the other woman. "Yeah, true. We haven't even decided what to eat yet." Internally she cringed. Her crush on Jamie was getting way out of control.

"Oh, I've decided." Jamie's voice was a mumble but Kelsey still made it out.

"What was that?" She too stood from the couch and looked at her friend. "What did you decide on?"

Jamie raised an eyebrow at her. "I'm suddenly in the mood for Mexican."

Then she wiggled both eyebrows and Kelsey rolled her own. "You're kind of an idiot, but fine. But this better not be some weak-ass Mexican food. I have some high standards." Through supreme effort of denial and with much humor, both women had successfully ignored the sexual tension from moments before. Neither liked the direction their friendship was taking, but for different reasons. Kelsey thought that Jamie's attraction was simply her nature and she wasn't interested in being just another notch in her friend's bed post. And for Jamie, she knew that Kelsey needed someone special and the blonde had learned the hard way that she had nothing to offer in the way of a serious relationship. She especially didn't trust her own judgment where relationships were concerned. Kelsey had come to mean more to her than most others and it would devastate Jamie to lose her friendship.

Hours passed and dinner was ordered, eaten, and the detritus cleared away. Kelsey got Jamie set up on the couch again with the heating pad at her neck and the remote control in her hand. "You can watch whatever you want, James. I brought a book to entertain myself."

"I am kind of addicted to this prison show that's on Netflix."

Kelsey's face lit up. "No way, so am I! I haven't seen the newest episode. Are you caught up?"

"Neither have I, shall we?" Kelsey nodded and smiled as Jamie turned on the flat screen that was mounted on the wall. They watched that show then found a comedy special but it was still pretty early when that was finished. Kelsey glanced over and noticed the way Jamie was still rubbing at her neck. "Do you think it would help if you submerged yourself in the Jacuzzi for a while?"

Jamie thought about it for a second and nodded carefully. "Yeah, maybe. You can use the shower upstairs if you want, or watch TV for a while. Sorry I'm such a terrible hostess."

"Hush! I'm here because you're hurting, plain and simple.

I'm fully capable of entertaining myself.

"Even without batteries?" Despite the headache that would knock down a rhino at forty yards, the blonde was still slinging zingers at her friend.

Kelsey just narrowed her eyes at her. "That is not something you need to know! Now go run your water, James." Jamie laughed quietly as she walked upstairs to grab a t-shirt and lounge pants to change into when she got out of the tub. Kelsey turned off the television and followed her up. She couldn't help watching the sway of Jamie's backside as she walked up the stairs.

"Stop staring at my ass, Kels!" Jamie called down behind her.

Kelsey startled but immediately denied what she had been doing. "I'm not staring at your ass, nerd. Friends don't stare at friends' asses, remember?"

Jamie arrived at the top of the stairs and looked down at the ascending woman. "They do if they have toilet paper."

Kelsey cracked up. "Lucky you that you're such a fastidious wiper!" Laughter echoed through the condo as they went their separate ways to wind down the evening.

THE NEXT MORNING they went through their routines in separate bathrooms. Jamie grumbled a little at getting up slightly earlier but she was feeling a lot better in the light of a new day. Kelsey was happy to see that the little wrinkle of pain between Jamie's brows was absent. "How's your head?"

Jamie smiled as she fixed eggs, ham, and toast for breakfast. She turned carefully from where she was buttering the last piece of toast. "The headache is gone; I've just got some lingering stiffness in my neck. But I'll alternate heat and ice on it tonight just like you told me and I'm sure I'll be good as new in a few days." She paused and looked at her friend seriously. "Thanks again for taking care of me. It really means a lot."

Kelsey smiled back at her and melted the blonde just a little with that pesky dimple. "It's no problem at all. I'm always happy to help out a friend. And you've become one of my best." She turned her attention to the plate of food that Jamie set in front of her and moaned at the first bite. "I usually eat cold cereal for breakfast. A girl could definitely get used to this!"

"Perhaps you should sleep over more often!"

Kelsey started laughing and had to cover her mouth with a paper towel to keep from spraying egg all over the table. "That sounds like a line if I ever heard one!"

Jamie shook her head carefully as she looked at her with affection. "No, it sounds like an open invitation for my friend to come over and visit because I like her company." Kelsey didn't answer because she didn't know how. But she smiled back at Jamie anyway and continued eating her breakfast. She liked Jamie's company too, nearly craved it.

Chapter Thirteen

FOURTEEN DAYS AFTER Jamie played the part of a raging bull at work, she received a text message from her friend Burke

We're still on for this weekend, right? I'll be at your place Saturday around 3.

Jamie had a lot on her mind over the previous weeks and she completely forgot that she was hosting a bunch of people for Burke's birthday. She texted back.

Yeah, can't wait. Going to buy stuff for appetizers, you bringing fondue set?

Burke decided that for his birthday he wanted a wine and fondue party. And because most of his friends lived in St. Seren, he volunteered Jamie's condo for the event. She didn't mind because they were bros, but she also knew she'd end up doing most of the cooking.

Yes. Bringing half a dozen bottles of wine and asked everyone else to b.y.o.w. and an appetizer to pass.

Jamie groaned. With everyone bringing wine it was sure to be a shit show, but Burke was determined to have a fancy wine and fondue party so he was going to get it. She didn't say any of that to him though.

Sounds good.

She set her phone back on the wireless charger and it vibrated again a few minutes later. Jamie jumped when a piece of crumpled up paper hit the back of her head. She spun around to look at Bill. "Dude! What the hell?"

His dark hair was freshly shorn. She was never sure if he cut it himself or if he actually went to a barbershop for the look. "It's only Thursday, James. You gotta girl blowing your phone up over there?"

"It's Burke, he's coming into town this weekend for his birthday. And why are you so nosey anyway?" She grabbed her phone to check the text.

Did you invite Kelsey?

"Did you invite your friend Kelsey?"

Jamie startled at the way both Burke and Bill just asked her the same question. She answered the text first.

Not yet.

Then she turned to Bill. "For your information, I totally zoned out about the birthday party and forgot. So I haven't asked yet but I will tonight."

He nodded. "Good. It was pretty cool of her to drive you home from work and back again the week before last. She sounds like a real keeper."

Jamie scowled. "She's my friend, not a *keeper*. We're just friends."

Bill rolled his eyes. "So you keep saying."

"It's true! She doesn't see me like that."

"Mmm hmm, you are so busted! You just said she didn't see you like that, not that you didn't think of her that way."

She sighed and spun around in her chair then stopped when she started to feel queasy. "It doesn't matter how I see her, we are just friends and that is how we'll stay. Can we drop that subject now please? Let's talk about something else, like the fact that your wife suddenly wants to have a baby."

It was his turn to groan. "How about we don't? I'm thirty-eight years old; I shouldn't be starting a family."

"And how old is Holly?"

He sighed. "She's thirty-six."

Jamie shook her head at him. "Ooh, she's right at the edge of safe zone. If she really wants a baby, man, she kind of has to do it now. But you're not that old, what's the problem?"

"James, I'll be thirty-nine before any possible baby is born! That means I'll be fifty-seven when that kid graduates high school and near retirement when they graduate college. Hell, I could have a heart attack and die like my old man when I'm fifty-five! And then what? Holly will be a widow and my kid will be fatherless!" He finished his diatribe breathing hard and red in the face.

She leaned back in her chair and held up her hands with

palms facing him. "Whoa. Slow down, man, or you're going to
give yourself a heart attack right now. Clearly this is something
you've thought a lot about. Have you talked with Holly about
this?" He shook his head. "I think that is your first step. Seriously
sit down with her and explain all your fears. It's risky for her too,
but if it's something you really want then make it work."

He sighed and ran a hand over his buzz cut. "Yeah, you're
probably right." He turned back around in his chair, ending their
little tête-à-tête.

She thought about her own words and decided to text Kelsey
and invite her to Saturday's party instead of waiting until the
drive home.

```
Are you doing anything Saturday afternoon/night?
```

She didn't expect her to answer immediately since they were
at work, so she set the phone back onto the charger and went back
to work. A little while later the phone vibrated.

```
Knitting with my cats, why?
```

Jamie snickered.

```
Totally forgot that Burke is throwing his own wine
& fondue birthday party at my condo. I'm officially
inviting you.
```

```
I see. Are you inviting me or my cake pops?
```

The engineer laughed at how well Kelsey seemed to know
her.

```
Yes.
```

Kelsey sat at the desk in back and giggled at the other
woman's non-specific response.

```
What is Burke's favorite flavor?
```

```
Chocolate.
```

The dental assistant made a face and sent another message.

```
Isn't that yours?
```

A text came back almost immediately.

Um...

Then another followed.

We actually both like chocolate but Burke likes cherry too.

Okay, perfect. I'll be sure to bring the birthday cake pops and my own bottle of wine. I like the sweet stuff.

Another minute passed and Jamie's next message came in.

Me too. But fair warning, I get handsy when I'm drinking the wine.

Kelsey burst out laughing then quickly covered her mouth and looked around. Smirking a little, she found a picture in her phone and sent that back to Jamie along with a text.

I don't do well on the wine either. Shell took this the last time I got drunk on it at their place.

Jamie received the message while sitting at her desk still and her ears turned pink. She hunched over her phone just in case Bill got nosey again, then texted back.

Uh, Kels? Why were you taking your clothes off?

Apparently I wouldn't stand still enough to get my picture taken so they told me to pose like I was in a magazine. Don't know what magazine I was thinking of for sure, but I can guess. They stopped me at the button just above my navel.

"Oh my God!" The words were quiet and only slipped out on accident, but Bill spun around in his chair.

"What's up, James—hey, why's your face all red? You all right?"

Jamie shook her head slowly. "She's trying to kill me. Seriously, I'm going to spontaneously combust!"

Bill shoved his chair across the floor and peeked at the picture on her phone before she could stop him. "Holy shit, I thought you said you two were just friends?"

She whimpered. "We are! She was just explaining how she gets when she's drunk."

"Does she know how you feel?"

Jamie gave her coworker a wide-eyed look. "Hell no!"

He shrugged and gave her a knowing smile. "What was that you just told me earlier? Seriously sit down with her and explain all your fears, or something to that effect. So you should probably take your own advice, huh?" Jamie looked around then discretely flipped him off. Her phone vibrated again in her hand, making her jump.

    Sorry, was that TMI?

Jamie quickly texted back.

    No it's fine. Was just discussing something with my
    coworker. But in anticipation of the amount of wine
    that will be flowing on Saturday, maybe you should wear
    a lot of layers. LOL

    Ha-ha, you're so funny! What time should I be there
    and is there anything else I need to bring?

The blonde smiled.

    Starts at five but you can come early if you want.
    Just bring an overnight bag because you're not driving
    home after. Or you can call a cab, your choice.

    Okay, will do! Gotta run now, work calls. Talk to
    you later, James!

BURKE ARRIVED SATURDAY around three to help set everything up. Jamie was busy making two different sauces on the stove when someone knocked on her door an hour later. Burke was in the middle of putting the extra leafs into the dining room table. The music was going but not loud. "Hey Burke, can you get that? I'm kinda busy here."

He set the second leaf on top of the table. "Got it!" Jamie was standing at the stove so she had her back to the door and couldn't see which guest arrived early but she quickly figured it out. "Hey, Kels! Welcome to the party!"

Jamie turned both burners down to low and spun around excitedly. "Hey, you're here early!" Kelsey looked comfortable in a lightweight button down shirt with the sleeves rolled up and a pair of chinos. Her auburn hair was loose for once, which was a change of pace from the braid that Jamie was used to seeing. Kelsey looked really good.

The Irish-Latina smiled and walked over to set the cake pop container on the island next to where Burke had already set up his chocolate fountain. Where he got such a ridiculous thing, no one knew. She was still wearing a backpack but once her hands were empty she turned to hug Burke. "Happy birthday!" Then she accepted a close hug from Jamie, relishing the warmth and solidity of her. "And you said I could come early."

"That's what she said!"

Kelsey looked at Burke, slightly confused. "That is what she said."

"Oh my God."

Kelsey glanced over at Jamie's pink cheeks and Burke's words dawned on her. Why she didn't get it initially, she wasn't sure. It wasn't like Jamie didn't say the phrase all the time. She rolled her eyes at both of them. "You two are nothing but a couple of juveniles! Now where can I put my bag? I'm assuming Burke is staying too so do I have the couch tonight?"

Jamie smiled at her. "I have lots of floor space, plus two extra tall blowup mattresses, so there is plenty of room depending on who wants to stay. But you can put your stuff in my room for now." When she saw Kelsey's raised eyebrow she rolled her eyes. "Oh please, settle down stripper Sally! Your virtue is safe with me. Besides, I'm only having you put it there because my room will be completely off limits for the party. So no one will mess with your stuff."

Burke snorted. "Virtue!"

Kelsey pointed at him. "Pipe down over there, birthday boy! I'm as pure as the driven snow—"

Jamie interrupted with a cough and mumbled word. "In Detroit."

The Irish-Latina was full of piss and play and she whirled on her good friend next. "Keep it up, handsy-pandsy, and I'll open a can of whoop ass on you so hard you'll have to call Campbell's for the barcode if you want to report it to the cops!"

"Ooh, yes James, keep it up because I want to see this!"

Jamie flipped them both off and turned to go back to the stove, calling over her shoulder on the way. "I have to check my sauce!"

"That's what she said." Two voices in unison made the

blonde roll her eyes. They were stealing all her lines!

Jenn had also arrived slightly early and between the four of them they had the place all set up in time for the party to begin. By five-thirty, quite a few of the guests had arrived. Kelsey was two glasses of wine in and her cheeks glowed with praise as people raved about the chocolate covered cherry cake pops. The carrier featured a base and a plastic lid that went over it. The difference was that the inside was actually a set of tiers that the treats rested on, smallest diameter trays on top to the largest on the bottom. The center of the lid had a hole where she could screw a handle down into the post that held the tiers to the bottom tray. That flat spot on the top of the post was where she put the block style birthday candle. Burke was delighted at both the dessert and her thoughtfulness. Jamie was just delighted by Kelsey.

Music played over Jamie's sound system, a general mix of styles and songs. People had started various games around the room. One group was at the coffee table, another at the folding table that had been set up, and a final group at the large dining room table that had been expanded out to seat ten people. As part of her condo association fees, Jamie had a small storage closet on her floor, which was where she kept the extra dining room chairs, as well as the folding table and chairs.

Later in the evening Jamie went out on her balcony to catch a break from all the people and get a little fresh air. She was feeling quite tipsy and had struggled throughout the night to not spend a lot of time in Kelsey's sole company. Her friend was just too much of a lure and being on her fifth glass of wine, Jamie had definitely passed into the handsy stage. Jamie was leaning on the railing with her eyes closed when she heard one of the French doors open behind her. The music got momentarily louder then softened to a muffle again when the door shut. She assumed it was Burke coming to find her until an arm snaked around her waist and she smelled Kelsey's cologne. Jamie turned to smile at her and was rewarded with that heartbreaking dimpled grin.

Kelsey's voice was quiet. "Hey, what are you doing out here all alone?"

The blonde shrugged. "Just came out to think, see some stars, and get some fresh air."

"Yeah, it is hot in there. Why don't you open the French doors?"

Jamie made a face. "And let bugs into my condo? No way!"

Kelsey laughed. "Then why don't you turn up the AC?" She

got a wry smile for her suggestion.

"Hmm, good point!" They both laughed but neither moved. Kelsey's arm was still wrapped around Jamie's waist as they stared across the river, toward the lights of the city. Jamie wasn't sure how much longer she could ignore her friend's smile, or the way she felt in her arms when they hugged hello or goodbye. It was impossible to pretend that the smell of Kelsey's cologne in the mall didn't trigger some sort of Pavlovian response, because it did. Her friend was warm against her side, comfortable in a way she had not felt in a long, long time. It was frightening and exhilarating all at once. She heard Kelsey's breath catch and turned to look at her with a question on her lips. But the question never came out as their eyes met less than six inches from each other and their mouths breathed in the same air.

At nearly the same height, their position was intimate and much too close together, and Kelsey knew she was going to kiss her. She looked from Jamie's brown eyes down to her friend's full lips. Just as they both leaned forward to close the space between them the French doors opened again to a wash of guitar riff and rollicking piano. They startled apart as Burke walked up. He paused, suddenly realized that he'd just interrupted something interesting and then continued with his original thought. "Hey, we're just getting ready to play Left Right Center and we need your quarters so people can buy in. Are you both playing?"

They hesitated for just a second then both stepped back at the same time. Kelsey spoke first and Jamie used the time to recover. "What's Left Right Center?"

Jamie looked at her in surprise. "Are you kidding me?" She looped her arm through Kelsey's elbow and steered her toward the door. "Let's go inside. You're about to have a good time!"

Feeling daring with her wine consumption she whispered in Jamie's ear. "I thought I was about to have a good time outside." The blonde stumbled slightly as they came through the door and Kelsey locked her arm to help keep her upright.

Once inside Jamie disengaged herself from Kelsey's arm and pointed at her. "You are evil!"

Kelsey laughed and winked at her. "Maybe you should go turn up the AC when you're looking for quarters, your face is getting warm there, nerd." Jamie grumbled and scrubbed her warm face with a hand before going off to adjust the thermostat. Burke swooped in and took Jamie's place on Kelsey's arm and led her to the large table that was rapidly filling with people.

"Come on, trouble. I saved you and James some seats." Once

Kelsey was seated, Burke took the seat to her left side, leaving the right hand chair open for Jamie. Burke then looked into the eyes of the woman that Jamie had finally admitted to having a major crush on. "How much wine have you had, Kels?"

The tipsy woman pulled her hair up off her sweaty neck. "Ugh, probably too many. It's hot in here!" She started French braiding her hair to get it off her neck and unbuttoned another button on her shirt.

Burke smiled to think about what James was going to do when faced with such a dangerous amount of cleavage. Perhaps it would be the impetus to finally push the two *just friends* into deeper water. He knew why Jamie was so freaked out about dating because he knew Jamie's ex, Gayle. He first met them when they were a couple. The woman had emotionally scarred his best friend; there was just no other way to put it. But it was time for Jamie to move on, to be happy. And he considered it his sacred duty to help things along. Jamie sat back down with a plastic container full of quarters and Burke called out to start. "All right everyone, if you want to play you will need four quarters to start. If all you have is cash, James here will be glad to sell you some from the bank."

"What's the interest?" Stella called out from the end of the table as she leered at Jamie. She had been wanting in the blonde's pants for a long time but Jamie had never been interested, preferring not to sleep with anyone in her immediate circle of friends.

Her words had double meaning and everyone around the table laughed. "No interest at all, Stel! Just pass your dollars down and I'll give you the correct amount of change."

Someone else called down the table. "Blah, blah, blah, let's get it going already!"

Jenn was seated right across the table from Kelsey and watched the way Kelsey stared at the side of Jamie's face. Jenn thought it best if she interrupted her friend's not so discreet ogling session. "So you've never played this before, Kels?"

Kelsey pulled her gaze away reluctantly and took another sip of wine before answering Jenn. She smirked at the black woman across the table. "Nuh uh, I guess I'm a virgin. Is it a gambling game?"

Before Jenn could answer Jamie threw her arm around the shoulders of their Left Right Center virgin. "Don't worry, Kels, we'll work you in slow then it'll only hurt for a second when you lose both your virginity and your quarters at the end!" Other people laughed at her words, including Kelsey.

"All right then, nerd, give me the rules to your little game so I can pop this cherry!"

Jamie's ears turned pink, as the bowl of quarters and dollar bills came back around the table. They were on the honor system to only take the amount of quarters they paid for. "Rules are simple. You start with four quarters in front of you. You have four dice. You get one roll every time the dice come around to you, one die for each quarter."

Burke took over the explanation when Jamie paused to hiccup. He reached around Kelsey and punched his friend in the arm. "Dude, grab some water and I'll finish explaining." He grabbed the dice and rolled the four to demonstrate game play. "If you roll a one, two, or three, it doesn't mean anything. But for every six you roll, you pass a quarter to the person on your right. For every five you roll, you pass a quarter to the person on your left. And for every four you roll, you put a quarter in the center. Whoever is holding the last quarter at the end is the winner of the pot in the center. Got it?" Kelsey gave her a thumbs up as Jamie re-took her seat, sans hiccups.

"It's Burke's birthday so he should go first!" Burke just shrugged and rolled the dice. They ended up playing the game for over an hour. Kelsey actually won twice and bragged that she had laundry money for a month. About quarter to ten Jenn stood and said her goodbyes. Jamie pouted that her friend was leaving. "No, stay!"

Jenn just laughed. "I've only got a sitter until ten so I have to take off or pay double if I'm late." She turned to Burke and gave him a big hug. "I'm glad I was able to make it though, happy birthday, buddy!" She also gave Jamie a big hug, then turned and did the same to Kelsey. Except she raised up a little and whispered in Kelsey's ear. "She really likes you, I can tell. Tread lightly, okay?" Kelsey blushed and gave her that grin that Jenn knew would be Jamie's downfall.

Quietly, Kelsey whispered back into Jenn's ear. "We're just friends!"

Jenn shook her head. "Honey, y'all have been eye fucking each other all night. Just be careful with her, okay?" Despite her own history with the blonde, she wasn't jealous that Jamie seemed so taken by Kelsey Ramirez. She just hoped that Kelsey fully understood the gift that Jamie was offering before either one got hurt. As if Jenn's leaving was a signal, many others decided to go at the same time. Some headed out to the bar, others just headed home. Once the dust cleared there were only five of them left, Jamie, Burke, Kelsey, Gonzo, and Heather. Over the next hour the five of them played more games and continued to drink the wine. The food had been put away earlier, and Jamie figured she'd do the remaining cleanup the next day. She was much too drunk to do anything so productive that night.

Heather was the one who suggested the move to the living room and play Truth or Dare. Jamie groaned. "Please, no!"

Kelsey looked at her curiously. "What's the matter, James, are you tired already? If your stamina isn't up for such a late night you can always toddle off to bed and let the big girls continue to play."

The blonde flipped her off and took a seat on the couch. "I'll have you know, my stamina is legendary!"

"In your head maybe—" Burke was sitting to her immediate left and she punched him in the arm. "Ow, don't hit me, it's my birthday!" Kelsey sat down on the loveseat with Heather and Gonzo took the recliner.

Kelsey called out to them both. "Come on children, try to get along."

Heather snickered and took a drink of her wine and Gonzo clapped twice. "All right, since Burke just whined that it's his birthday, he can go first!"

The birthday boy's face lit up with an evil grin as he turned his gaze to Jamie. She sunk down in her seat and took another healthy gulp of her wine. But luckily his gaze slid past her and moved around to the loveseat. "So, Kelsey, truth or dare?"

Her eyes widened and she looked like a deer caught in the headlights. "Well shit. Um, truth?"

"When's the last time you had sex?"

Kelsey blushed. "You're seriously going to lead with that?" He nodded and she flipped him the bird. "You're such an asshole. Let's see." She counted out on her fingers. "It's been about four and a half months. Next!"

Everyone laughed but Gonzo laughed hardest and pointed at Jamie. "Good thing he didn't ask James. She'd probably have to count in hours instead of months!" All five of them laughed at that though it was a bit forced for both Jamie and Kelsey. Jamie was busy wondering if Kelsey's last lover was the pierced crazy chick or someone else when Heather took her turn.

"Why don't we ask her to confirm. Jamie, truth or dare?"

Jamie took a sip of her wine then looked up at Kelsey as she answered. "Truth."

Heather smirked. "How long has it been since you've had

sex? You can break it down into hours if that's easier for you."

Burke and Gonzo snickered but Kelsey unconsciously leaned forward to hear the answer. Jamie's voice was quiet when she spoke. "Exactly three months today."

"Bullshit!" Heather's voice barked out and Jamie shrugged.

"It's true. Nicole Onwualu, April ninth, Indiana. That was the last time I had sex." She smiled at the other four and called out. "Next!"

Kelsey had sensed a shift with her friend months before and for the first time she was starting to believe Jenn when the black woman said that Jamie was legitimately trying to change. She could see the blonde was a little uncomfortable that Heather and Gonzo were making such a big deal about her admission, so she decided to go ahead with her own turn. Kelsey turned to the woman sitting in the recliner. "Gonzo, truth or dare?"

The stocky woman with long blonde hair answered right away. "Truth! No way am I doing a dare with this group."

They all laughed and Kelsey asked her question. "How did you get the name Gonzo?" Gonzo launched into an epic story about a white elephant Christmas party eight years previous. It involved three women named Sarah, a lot of shots, and a large sex toy that was shaped like a certain Muppet's nose. Kelsey cocked her head at the teller of the strange yet funny story. "But why did you keep the name Gonzo?"

"Because we already have two women named Sarah in my group of friends and acquaintances so it was just easier to go by Gonzo."

Heather chimed in. "That's right, stripper Sara and Sarah Small!" She turned to Kelsey. "There were pictures of the event that Michelle put up for the next year's party. I wonder what happened to those pictures."

"She deleted them." Gonzo made a face. "I had to let her use my downtown parking pass for a month but she finally showed me that she deleted them all." The game continued around and around until eventually someone got brave enough to choose dare. Brave probably wasn't the correct word, Kelsey was definitely past tipsy when she answered Gonzo's question. "Dare!"

"Holy shit!" While not quite as drunk as the others, Burke was still feeling no pain. "Nobody ever dares Gonzo!"

Kelsey glanced at Jamie and she had a worried look on her face, then she glanced over at the woman seated in the recliner. Sure enough, Gonzo had a particularly evil gleam in her eye. "Hey, I'll be nice. I'll give you a choice. You can either do a full shot of tequila and a full shot of hot sauce in whatever order you want, *or* you can show us a tattoo or piercing that wouldn't be visible while wearing a bikini."

Heather spoke up. "But what if she doesn't have any tattoos or piercings, besides her ears?"

Gonzo shrugged. "Then she can just say that and she gets off lucky."

All eyes swung to Kelsey and she smirked back at them. "Who wants to set up my shots?"

"Oh my God!" Jamie's mind had gone off in a decidedly dirty direction and she suddenly and most desperately wanted to know what Kelsey was hiding.

Burke shook his head. "I'll do it since I'm libel to hold up the best if she punches me in the arm afterwards." He looked around to see if anyone would argue. No one did. Burke spent a lot of time working out and had the arms to prove it.

Everyone got up and walked into the kitchen to watch Kelsey perform the dare. "What's the tequila? Is it any good?"

Heather shook her head violently. "Hell no! You're going to lose time if you drink that shit, and Gonzo knows it."

Kelsey gave Jamie a scowl. "Thanks for the warning, James!"

Jamie came over to her and wrapped an arm around her waist. "Aww, I'm sorry Kels! I promise to make it up to you later. Cross my heart." She nodded solemnly, stumbled slightly even though she wasn't walking anywhere, and grabbed onto Kelsey even tighter.

"You're drunk!"

Jamie looked back at her and nodded. "You're drunk too!"

Kelsey just shrugged her shoulders and smiled without contesting her statement. The other three just watched the two with much interest. Kelsey continued staring at her friend until Burke set two shot glasses in front of her. He apologized. "Despite the fact that the hot sauce is going to burn your balls off, you might want to drink that second."

"Is the tequila that bad?" Burke shuddered and nodded. "And what's the hot sauce?"

Jamie answered. "It's Tabasco."

Kelsey rolled her eyes. "Weak! All right, let's do this."

"Hey, Kels, it's your last chance to change your mind and show us the goods instead."

She looked at where James was busy leering down her shirt and whistled loudly to get her attention. "Hey, eyes on your own paper, Schultz!" Jamie abruptly jerked her eyes upward and blushed, then stepped back to let Kelsey do her shots. But she did grab onto the counter just in case. Then without any sort of preamble, Kelsey picked up the tequila and downed it in one swallow, then picked up the hot sauce and did the same. She licked her lips as she set down the second glass. "Not bad. Not bad at all!"

Burke looked at her with wariness. "How do you feel? That can't all go well with the wine you've been drinking all night."

Kelsey shrugged. "Eh, it's fine. You should have seen my college years with my friend Tam. I've done a whole lot worse!"

After refilling their wine glasses, they all went back to the living room to keep playing. Jamie's turn was next. "Kelsey, truth or dare?"

"Hey, not fair! I just went."

Jamie laughed wickedly. "Now you're gonna go again. What's it gonna be, hot stuff?"

Kelsey smiled at how adorable the blonde was while drunk. "Fine, truth then."

"How many people in this room are you attracted to?"

Heather made a face and Gonzo started laughing. "Ooh!"

Kelsey looked across to her good friend and gave her a dimpled smile. "Just one." Then she gave Jamie a challenging look and called out for the next person. "Next!"

"Kelsey, truth or dare?" Burke rubbed his hands together in anticipation.

"Oh, come on! Pick on someone else, Jesus Jenny!"

Heather yelled out while laughing. "Nope, rules is rules!"

Kelsey sighed but she trusted Burke a lot more than she trusted Gonzo. "Fine, dare then."

Burke looked at her then looked around the room. When his gaze stopped on Jamie she got a bad feeling in the pit of her stomach. She started to subtly shake her head and Burke grinned as he turned to look back at Kelsey. "I dare you to make out with the one person you are attracted to in this room, for exactly sixty seconds." She shouldn't have trusted Burke.

"Hot damn!" Gonzo sat forward in her chair and chugged a few swallows of wine then looked over at Kelsey.

The Irish-Latina woman lifted her chin at Burke in response to the challenge. "Oh, is that all?" Jamie swallowed as butterflies flitted around in her stomach. She flashed back to the picture her friend had sent a few days prior and felt her ears heat up. Kelsey stood and slowly walked over to where Jamie was slouched down on the couch. Everyone watched the sway of her hips as she came closer and closer.

Jamie swallowed and wiped her hands on her jeans to get rid of the sweat. Then before she could register what the other woman was doing, Kelsey straddled her lap on the couch and gave a little wiggle. "Oh God."

"Relax, James. I promise to be gentle." Snickering sounded behind her but all either woman could focus on was the lips that came ever nearer to each other. Before they could make contact, Kelsey called out to the other occupant of the couch. "Get that timer ready, Burke, because you dared for a minute and a minute is all she's going to get."

With the first touch of lips to her own, Jamie moaned and grabbed onto Kelsey's hips. The woman above her tasted sweet and spicy, and had a lingering flavor of tequila. When Kelsey's tongue requested entrance into her mouth she willingly allowed her in.

Kelsey's heart started to race as Jamie grabbed onto her hips and she ground down ever so slightly into the blonde beneath her. Nothing had prepared her for the amount of heat she felt flare between them. Nothing. All too soon they were interrupted by Burke's voice. "Time!" Rather than wrench abruptly away, Kelsey slowly eased back out of the kiss, leaving the gift of a slight lick to Jamie's bottom lip as she pulled away. Jamie whimpered. Then Kelsey stood on lightly shaking legs and walked back over to the loveseat.

Heather playfully fanned herself. "And I thought the Tabasco trick was hot! Whew!" Kelsey just smirked and Jamie looked gobsmacked.

Not long after that the alcohol started to catch up with them all and the mini-party of five wound down. Heather and Gonzo had rode together to the party and decided to just cab back to Heather's house. Burke saw them out and gave them both hugs for coming to his party. After he shut the door and locked it he looked around to see if anything else needed to be taken care of before bed. Most had already been picked up earlier. "All right ladies, I'm going to head up. Have a good night!" Jamie and Kelsey watched him walk up the stairs. Then they listened as Burke brushed his teeth and retired back into the guest room. The distinctive click as the pocket door locked was loud in the quiet condo.

Chapter Fourteen

JAMIE TURNED TO her friend that was just a friend. The very woman whose kiss would have driven her to her knees had Jamie been standing. "I'm going to finish my glass of wine before I go up." She looked at the table next to where Kelsey had been sitting throughout the game and saw that she still had more than half a glass as well. "Want to sit with me?"

"Sure." Even though she said the word, she was anything but. While she tried to play it cool, Kelsey still felt the aftereffects of the panty-melting kiss she shared with Jamie. Instead of saying all that, she walked over and grabbed her wine glass off the table then came back to sit next to her on the couch. They were so close their thighs touched and Jamie squirmed a little.

"So, Kels."

Green eyes turned her way and they held more than what she'd seen before from her good friend. "Where was that tattoo or piercing that you refused to show in your dare?" She froze with the sound of Kelsey's laughter.

"You know curiosity killed the cat, right?"

Jamie grinned at her, feeling playful and still more than a little turned on. "But satisfaction brought him back. So what's it going to be? Are you going to satisfy me?"

Kelsey poked her in the ribs, nearly making the blonde spill her wine. "Incorrigible! But fine, which do you want to see? Tattoo or piercing?" Kelsey was dying to know what the blonde would pick, especially since learning that Jamie had an extreme love of piercings. The blush washed over Jamie's face fast as every possible tattoo and piercing location flashed through her head at once. She downed her wine in three swallows and Kelsey did the same, then raised her eyebrow at Jamie's stall tactic. "Well?"

Jamie's eyes widened with panic. "Do I have to answer right now? I'm really kind of tired." She did a big fake yawn and Kelsey started laughing.

"Chicken shit! But fine, you can ask again some other time. I just need to run upstairs and grab my backpack before you go to bed."

"Um," Jamie stood from the couch and began gathering glasses that had been left around the living room. "I have a king size bed. We can just share if you want. It will be a lot more comfortable than the couch, trust me!" She hesitantly met Kelsey's eyes and despite her level of inebriation, Jamie's gaze was serious and sincere.

Kelsey smiled at her. "That sounds fine, thanks for sharing." Jamie stumbled slightly after the lights were shut off and Kelsey wasn't much better. "Damn, I really need to brush my teeth." She followed Jamie up the stairs, thoroughly enjoying the view.

"Me too. Stop staring at my ass, Kels."

Kelsey snickered. "I'm not staring at your ass. I'm staring at the back of your head."

"Really? Why?" Jamie reached the landing and dropped her voice down into a whisper to avoid disturbing Burke.

Kelsey had also made it to the top of the stairs and stood well within the blonde's personal space. She reached out to caress the super short hair at the back of Jamie's head. "Because I love the way it feels, that's why." Jamie shivered at the feel of Kelsey's fingers but was powerless to step away. Finally Kelsey walked around her and into the master bedroom. "I call dibs on first shot at the bathroom." She came back out and walked into the bathroom, shutting the pocket door less than two feet from Jamie's motionless body.

Jamie snorted as Kelsey disappeared from sight. "Of course she does." She walked into her bedroom to find something lightweight to sleep in and contemplated spending the night on her own couch. "She's going to kill me. Just, poof, and I'll burn up into ashes!"

"Who are you talking to?" Kelsey's quiet voice startled her from the doorway.

Jamie jumped and whirled around. "Uh, no one. I'm just gonna uh—" She pointed toward the bathroom and took off with her makeshift pajamas. Five minutes later she returned to see Kelsey sitting on the edge of the bed wearing a soft pair of boxers and thin camisole. "Nice PJs." She glanced down at her own boxer and tank top combo.

Kelsey shrugged. "They're not what I normally wear, but nude is kind of hard to pull off in a sleepover." She grinned at the way Jamie's face turned pink.

The blonde scratched at her neck and mumbled. "Uh, same here." She was going to die. She was almost certainly completely positive of the fact that sleeping next to Kelsey would surely kill her. So she set her cell phone on the wireless charger and got into the bed anyway. "I usually sleep on the side closest to the door. I hope you don't mind." Laughter followed her as she slid under the covers.

"It's fine, James. I'm comfortable either way." Kelsey found a plug on the other side of the bed and plugged in her own phone before sliding under the covers. She turned onto her side and gazed curiously at Jamie's nightstand. "What did you just set your phone on?"

"That's a wireless charger. I have Qi charging capability in my phone so that it can charge wirelessly with the correct base."

"Holy cow, that's wizard shit right there!"

Jamie shook her head and giggled, nervous to have Kelsey so close. "Not at all. It uses uh, resonant inductive coupling between the charging station and the phone." Kelsey gave her a blank look so she tried to put it into words she might understand. "Have you seen a generator? Better yet, your dad's a mechanic so you probably know what the alternator is, right?" Kelsey nodded. "Do you know how it works?"

"Hmm, pretty much, I think. The belt turns the metal thing inside a coil of wires. And that creates electricity by forcing uh, electrons or something around the wires and steel thing?"

Jamie nodded. "Yeah, pretty much. Now think of a more electronic version instead of mechanical. So just like the alternator, the two coils don't actually have to physically touch to generate electricity. Does that make sense or have I completely lost you with my terrible explanation?"

Kelsey nodded, rubbing her cheek against the pillow. While she wasn't sober by any means, she was also quite aware of what had happened between them during Truth or Dare. Something had shifted between her and Jamie and she wasn't sure if it was good or bad. She just knew that there was a deep part of her that seemed to crave the blonde. She knew she should shut it down but it was the drunk Kelsey that wanted to play. "So James, have you decided which you want to see yet?"

The other woman's eyes widened with surprise. She was in no way, shape, or form, strong enough to deny her attraction to the woman in her bed. The fact that Kelsey was in her bed at all set off all sorts of alarm bells, as well as a good amount of tingling. "I uh, um."

"Is that a no?"

Jamie turned onto her side to look at her fully. "No, definitely not a no. Let me think for a second."

Kelsey's eyes narrowed mischievously. "Do you really need to think about it?"

The blonde's voice was a whisper as she slowly shook her head back and forth. "No."

Rather than show the other woman what she wanted to see, Kelsey did something even more daring. "Give me your hand."

"Why?" Jamie was immediately wary.

"Do you trust me, James?" Jamie stretched out her hand and placed it within Kelsey's grasp. She nearly came undone as Kelsey pulled it over to rest on her own breast. Jamie's breathing picked up when Kelsey took her fingers and circled them around the nipple below the camisole, perfectly tracing the ring that pierced the rapidly hardening flesh. Jamie couldn't help pinching a little and whimpered when Kelsey gasped at her actions. Kelsey hissed at the feeling. "Oh fuck, Jamie."

Jamie wanted to slip off Kelsey's camisole and take the little ring between her teeth. She wanted to tug it even more just to keep hearing mewling whimpers but she knew she was already crossing a line that should never be crossed. Her close friendships were built on rules and she had to follow those rules or risk losing it all. But before she could let common sense pull her hand away, Kelsey's hand stopped guiding Jamie's fingers in circles. Instead, it moved up to scratch lightly across the back of the blonde's head. Jamie moaned at the sensation. "Kels." That was all the incentive Kelsey needed to pull them together. Lips met in a desperate crush as Jamie worked that lone nipple to aching hardness. Things escalated quickly when a single thigh made its way between Kelsey's and she ground down against it. Jamie could feel the other woman's wetness even through Kelsey's boxers and she knew it matched her own. Jamie broke free from the kiss and moved her lips down to the side of Kelsey's neck and started kissing and nibbling the sensitive skin there. At the same time she had unconsciously moved her body further over, easing Kelsey onto her back.

Kelsey continued to arch her body up against Jamie's. She had never been so turned on, nor turned on as fast as she was in that moment. Even though Jamie was just barely touching her she could already feel her orgasm building. It was rare for her to feel so much the first time with someone. It had pretty much never happened before. She had to let her know, she couldn't let Jamie stop. "Oh, please, you feel so good. Don't stop, please."

The blonde didn't stop. Instead she moved her hand from where it was tugging on the delightful nipple ring, down the length of Kelsey's body and cupped that place that was wettest against her leg. Her hand remained outside the shorts but that didn't seem to make a difference to Kelsey. Her undulating hips increased their pace as Jamie helped her along with a very talented hand. Jamie's own clit twitched at how hard Kelsey had gotten beneath her fingertips. Kelsey's eyes were closed but Jamie drank in every single expression and feature on her face. She wanted to memorize the moment that she had been dreaming about for months. "Kelsey, I've wanted you for so long." As much as she needed to reach inside those shorts and feel Kelsey's slick heat flesh to flesh, something held her back. Maybe it was her friend's inebriation, or maybe it was her own, but she kept her hand outside. In less than a minute Kelsey's moans got noticeably louder and Jamie leaned down to steal them with a kiss. She clenched hard when her friend and now lover stiffened beneath her and cried out into her mouth. Kelsey rode the orgasm for a surprising amount of time and Jamie was entranced by her. She didn't stop moving her hand until Kelsey mewled and weakly tried to push it away. Then Jamie rolled to the side and pulled Kelsey into her arms as she continued to shake and twitch. "Shh, I've got you Kels. I've got you."

Kelsey's eyes were shut as she continued to take in the overwhelming orgasm that had raced through her with the force of a hurricane. It had never been like that. Until that moment, orgasm had never been so strong. She tried to tell Jamie, to explain how she felt, but she was so tired. "That was am…amazing. I've wanted you for a long time too. Never cum so hard before."

Jamie looked at the beautiful woman who was falling asleep on her shoulder. She adored Kelsey and that scared her. "Shh, it's okay sweetheart. I wanted you to feel good, you deserve to feel good."

"I'm so tired, James. I don't want to leave you hanging."

"It's okay, just get some sleep." Despite the uncomfortable throbbing between her own legs, Jamie knew she'd survive. She didn't want to miss a chance of having Kelsey on her arm. Her wishes were dashed when Kelsey mumbled sleepily.

"I can't sleep like this. I need to turn over." Kelsey didn't cuddle. More than one girlfriend had complained about it but she just couldn't get to sleep unless she was situated a certain way.

Jamie gave her a quick one-armed hug then withdrew the arm. "It's okay, just get comfortable and I'll be here when you wake." Jamie noted the smile on Kelsey's face as she drifted off to sleep. Regardless of her earlier thoughts and words to her friend, the call to touch herself was insistent. She throbbed with unspent passion and she knew she'd never get to sleep herself unless it was taken care of. Wanting something quick and easy, she quietly reached into the drawer by the bed and withdrew a whisper-silent egg. It was set to a lower vibrating frequency and sure to do the trick. A little more than a minute later she was smothering her own cries with her pillow and trying not to shake the bed with the force of her body falling over the precipice of desire. When she was spent, she returned the toy and turned off the light, then turned onto her side to watch Kelsey as she slept. As Jamie's eyes slid shut she realized that she had completely fallen for her friend.

KELSEY WAS SLOW to wake the next morning. She spent the first five minutes or so just getting her bearings. Sensations started to trickle in. She was warm and comfortable. Then obser-vations slowly followed. Her head was pounding like a drum and she wasn't in her own bed. She also wasn't alone. She cracked an eye open and shut it immediately with regret. But she didn't need sight in order to know who she was wrapped around. She didn't move away though. Instead she listened to Jamie as the blonde continued to breathe the slow rhythm of slumber. While Kelsey was indeed drunk the night before, she remembered everything. But lying there pressed tight against the woman who had domi-nated her dreams for nearly three months, she had a hard time regretting any of her actions the night before. The truth of what they did would probably be harder to face in the light of day though.

She thought about what it meant to cross that line, not just to her but to Jamie as well. Her friend had been trying so hard to change her ways and she wondered if the night before was some-thing as basic as falling off the wagon for her. Or was it some-thing more? Kelsey tried to look at it as logically as was possible with a raging hangover. How much more could it even mean to a woman who seemed incapable of forming a serious emotional attachment to any of her romantic partners? Looking deep inside herself, Kelsey liked Jamie too much for such accidents to hap-pen. She liked her too much to stay unattached in the kind of arrangement the blonde usually favored. And Kelsey knew they couldn't cross the line again. Her best bet was to just gloss it over and move on. To chalk it up to one of those one-time drunken things that friends sometimes do. With that decision made, she let her mind empty out again and drifted back to sleep.

By the time Jamie woke the sun was well up. Her blinds were

closed but there was a hazardous amount of light shining around the edges. She cracked open an eye and immediately shut it again. The coming day was not going to be pretty. She needed water, then ibuprofen, then something good and greasy for breakfast. The blonde thought that maybe a chili cheese omelet would fit the bill. But in that very moment, despite her pain and slightly sick stomach, Jamie did not want to move. She had shifted in the night and woke pressed tightly against Kelsey's back, playing big spoon to her friend's little. Many things had been said about the blonde in the past. She was a friendly and affectionate lover. She was passionate and playful to the women she slept with, and she was always focused on their pleasure. But once the night was over, she retreated into her friendly but reserved shell. That was her comfort zone; that was the place that discouraged her friends and buddies from wanting more. It kept them from wanting some sort of attachment or relationship. But she didn't want that with Kelsey. She wanted to turn her over and wake her with kisses. Just thinking about Kelsey's dimpled grin had Jamie unconsciously squeezing the woman in her arms. Kelsey let out an adorable sort of whimper-squeak so Jamie did it again.

"James." A very sleepy voice came from the blankets in front of her.

Jamie smiled. "Yes?"

Kelsey turned her head to look back at the woman snuggled up behind her and she couldn't deny that she enjoyed the feeling. But she also had to pee. "If you squeeze me one more time I'm going to wet your bed!"

The blonde looked chagrined. "Oh, sorry. How's your head?"

Kelsey groaned quietly. "I'm hung."

A sigh tickled the hairs on the back of Kelsey's neck, making her shiver. "Yeah, me too." They lay there in silence for a few minutes before Jamie softly spoke again. "We should probably get up."

"Nooo!" Kelsey's voice was a quiet whine.

"But I thought you had to pee?"

She whined again. "I dooo!"

Jamie's laughter was quiet to spare both their heads but the affection behind it was very real. "All right, I'll let you up. What do you want for breakfast? Anything?" She pulled away and propped herself up on an elbow to await an answer.

Before getting out of bed, Kelsey pushed the covers off her and rolled onto her back to stretch. The motion caused her camisole to ride up and show a delicious amount of creamy tan skin.

Jamie's eyes were immediately drawn to the navel ring with its twinkling blue stone. She also noticed a few stretch marks low on Kelsey's belly but nothing at all that detracted from the beauty of the woman in her bed. Kelsey was a woman and some women had stretch marks and curves. Not everyone was skinny. When Jamie jerked her gaze away from the bare skin, she met a pair of amused green eyes. "See something of interest?"

"I, uh, you have another one." She pointed down at the belly ring.

Kelsey smirked. "You're very observant for someone with a hangover."

The blonde swallowed hard as her thoughts tumbled over each other. Things were going to change the minute they walked out of her room. Her face was too serious when she spoke. "Should we talk?"

The smile disappeared from Kelsey's lips. "We probably should." Jamie didn't speak so Kelsey took the lead. "Listen, I know you've been trying to change your, uh, ways. And I'll understand if last night was just one of those things that simply got out of control between us. I guess what I'm trying to say is that you're one of my best friends and that is what's most important to me." What Kelsey didn't say was that she wanted a commitment that she was afraid Jamie couldn't, or wouldn't, give.

What Jamie heard was that Kelsey only wanted to be friends. "Oh. Um, yeah. Yeah, your friendship means the world to me too. I'd be lost without you, Kels." Kelsey gave her a smile for her words, though it was uncharacteristically sad. Then Jamie poked her arm. "Now go pee."

Kelsey held out her arms. "Can I have a hug first?"

Jamie glanced down the body that was still showing too much skin and shook her head. "I don't think that's a good idea."

"What if I just wrap you in my arms and corporeally cuddle you?"

The blonde looked both shocked and intrigued. "Oh God, is that a thing? Tell me that's not a thing!"

Kelsey grinned back wickedly. "It can be!"

"I will tickle you until you pee if you try it!"

The woman with the piercings just shrugged and laughed at her. "Go ahead, it's not my bed."

Jamie groaned and rolled away, then clutched her head as she sat upright. "Oh hell. I need coffee, and pills, and food."

"While you're up, I'll take all of those things, minus the coffee."

The blonde made a face. "Only creatures of darkness refuse to drink coffee!"

Kelsey finally sat up and pulled her camisole down. "On the contrary, only creatures of darkness drink the vile stuff. How else do they stay up all night to create chaos in the world?"

"You are certifiable!" Jamie threw a pillow at her then walked over to grab a hoodie out of her armoire. It was extra-large, fleecy, and comfortable in the AC chilled condo. She grabbed another that she'd gotten in Chicago. "You want one too?"

Kelsey nodded as she pulled on her other footie sock. "Yes, please! Why is it so cold in here?"

"I clearly turned the temperature down last night when you made the suggestion and never set it back to normal before we went to bed." Jamie shrugged and gave her a wry grin. "Someone distracted me." She went downstairs after making sure Kelsey was all set with everything.

By the time Kelsey found her way downstairs, Jamie had already started coffee, put ready-made biscuits in the oven, and was in the process of making chili cheese omelets. Burke sat on the couch in a tank top and jeans, watching a chick flick. She looked from the buff guy to the TV screen, then back again. It was anomalous but she shrugged and walked over to see what Jamie was cooking. When she got a good look in the pan, she clamped a hand over her mouth and backed away slow. "What the hell is that?"

Jamie glanced over her shoulder. "It's a chili cheese omelet!"

"It looks like vomit."

A blonde eyebrow went up. "Vomit omelet?"

Kelsey moved her hand down to her stomach instead and shook her head back and forth. "No, James. Just no. I think I'll just have toast."

"Hey?" Kelsey looked up at the softness in Jamie's voice. The cook had cut a bit of the first omelet and held out the fork for Kelsey to try. "Have I ever steered you wrong?"

The reluctant woman shook her head and stepped forward again. Then she gently grabbed Jamie's wrist and guided the fork into her mouth. The first thing to hit her taste buds was ooey-gooey melted cheese, the second was the savory flavor of the chili. Kelsey swallowed and licked her lips, then nodded in appreciation. "Okay, you were right. I want one."

Jamie grinned in triumph. "Told you so." She held out the fork. "You can have the first one and the biscuits should be done any second." Just as predicted the timer went off about ten seconds later and she pulled the pan out of the oven. She sprinkled a liberal helping of cheese on the second pan of eggs, spooned on the chili, and added some chopped cilantro, then folded it up. Rather than take her plate over to the table to eat, Kelsey stood nearby watching her work. "Aren't you going to eat?"

"I can wait for you guys."

Jamie nodded. "All right, how about you set the table then and maybe get something to drink?"

She nodded and Jamie watched her walk over to the dining room table with her plate and snickered. Kelsey called out behind her. "Friends don't check out their friends' asses, James!"

Jamie cracked up laughing. "They do if there is toilet paper hanging out."

Kelsey rolled her eyes. "Except there is no toilet paper!"

"Uh, actually, there is."

"Oh goddammit!" Kelsey had twisted around and noticed the couple squares of toilet paper stuck in the waistband of her boxers. She stalked off to the downstairs bathroom, flipping Jamie the bird as she went.

Breakfast was pretty quiet with all three people nursing hangovers. After the first few minutes of silence Burke casually started conversation. "So, I heard you guys giggling when you got upstairs last night, but surprisingly little after that. Did you sleep well?"

"Like a baby!"

"Like a rock!"

Both Jamie and Kelsey answered at the same time, then they looked at each other and blushed. "I see." It took a lot of effort but Burke stifled his urge to laugh. He turned to Kelsey. "So, any plans today, Kels?"

She finished chewing her bite of food and sighed. "Hmm, it's Sunday so I have to put my quarters that I won to good use and get my laundry done."

Jamie grinned. "I'm going to lounge around in my boxers all day, eat leftovers, and binge watch the first ridiculously cheesy sci-fi series I can find."

Kelsey narrowed her eyes at her friend. "You suck!"

"And swirl. I'm a perfectionist."

Burke started choking on his orange juice as Kelsey flushed a dark pink. Jamie's teasing words had prompted a flashback of the night before. She was reminded of just how fast and hard she came apart at the blonde's touch. "Cute. You're an ass, James.

Plain and simple."

"You could always stay and keep me company. Burke's going home after breakfast and I'm going to be all alone." She pouted.

Kelsey's look went from teasing to sad. "No, I have to get home." When she saw Jamie's face fall she tried to lighten the mood again. "The laundry isn't going to do itself. And the last time the cats tried it they shrunk all my scrubs."

Jamie gave her a hopeful smile. "Maybe next time?" She could see that Kelsey was trying to pull away and it wasn't a good feeling. For the first time she was getting a sense of what she herself had put others through time and time again.

"Sure thing!" The words sounded a little false to both women's ears. Burke was blatantly ignoring that part of the conversation.

Once breakfast was finished the three of them made short work of the remaining cleanup. Furniture was put back into the storage closet and Kelsey found herself at the front door saying goodbye. She hugged Burke then turned to Jamie. The blonde held on longer than she wanted, yet still not long enough. Kelsey pulled back and tried to focus on something other than her memories. She shouldered her backpack and picked up the cake pop carrier, then turned to Burke. "All right buddy, drive safe on your way back home."

He smiled at her. "Will do, Kels."

She turned to Jamie. "And I'm sure I'll chat with you tomorrow morning, hmm?"

Jamie nodded. "Count on it. Bye, Kelsey." Then Kelsey was gone.

As soon as the door closed, Burke turned to his best friend. "Dude, you slept together, didn't you?

Jamie nodded. "Yeah."

"Do you regret it?"

Her gaze jerked back into focus as she looked away from the door and toward her good friend. "No! Not even a little bit. She's all I think about and—" She looked down and finished her sentence. "I think I'm in a little over my head with her, and falling fast."

He could see how out of her element Jamie was and he truly felt for his friend. She had been operating in a bubble for much too long and the sensations of love and deeper emotion had become foreign to her. It was no wonder she had fallen so hard. She had starved herself for years. "Does she regret it?"

Jamie looked up again and she was as close to tears as he'd

ever seen her. "I think she does."

He cocked his head at her. "But you don't know for sure?" Jamie shook her head. "Are you going to ask her?"

"Nope."

Chapter Fifteen

MONDAY MORNING WAS a strange one for Jamie. It wasn't that her routine was different so much as she just felt different. She was in an especially contemplative place on her drive and it was one of those days that all the music just seemed to match her mood. She sang along like normal but she felt as though it had more meaning. It's what made "Sick Muse" by Metric so perfect. The lyrics drove little thorns of feeling into her heart. She had logged into the Drīv app and sent a message to Kelsey first thing but her friend had yet to respond. Her stomach hurt with worry from it. They texted like normal the day before and even chatted a little online before Jamie went to bed. But she was worried that Kelsey may be having trouble dealing with what happened on Saturday night. She was halfway through her drive when the app chimed and Kelsey's voice came through.

"Good morning, nerd!"

Jamie smiled in her car and switched back to the center lane as the cramping lessened in her stomach. The happiness in her voice was evident as she down-swiped the rainbow car icon to respond. "Good morning! Are you running late again, even after I got you to download the awesome alarm app?"

"No, I was on the phone with my papa."

The blonde had gotten to know Kelsey quite well over the months, including her vocal inflections and tone since much of their conversation was not face-to-face. She could tell that Kelsey was pretty rattled simply by the way her voice sounded over the phone. Puzzled, Jamie questioned the call. "Isn't it pretty early in Texas for a phone conversation?"

Driving along in her little silver car, Kelsey was definitely rattled. "Yeah, but he was letting me know that my *abuela* was admitted into the hospital late last night. She's had some health problems the last few years and, I don't know, I guess they're just catching up with her." Kelsey was sick with worry. She loved her *abuela* very much and had formed a special bond with her grandmother when the old woman had come to live with them for a few years when Kelsey was growing up. That was actually the reason her parents had moved back to Texas, so her abuela could live with them. "She's in critical condition right now and if it doesn't look like she's going to get any better I'll have to see if Dr. Davies will give me a few days off to fly down there."

"I'm really sorry, Kelsey. If there is anything at all I can do, just let me know. Okay?"

Kelsey smiled at the other woman's words. Despite the weirdness of Sunday morning she was secure in the knowledge that their friendship was solid. Jamie was there for her, just as she would be there for Jamie. "Thanks, James, I really appreciate it. I may need you to take care of my cats if I have to fly out."

"Anything. You can count on me."

As she maneuvered her little silver car into the ridiculously cramped employee lot behind the dentist office, she felt a prick of tears come to her eyes at Jamie's words. "I know I can and it means the world to me. Okay, I'm at work now so I should probably go in and you know, do my job or something."

A few seconds went by and the app chimed again. "Call me if you need anything or just want to talk, okay?"

"I will, and thanks." Kelsey smiled, feeling just a little bit better as she walked into work.

"HEY ROB, LET'S say hypothetically that I wanted to take two to five days off with short notice. Would that be possible?"

Jamie's boss looked up from his desk to stare at her in the doorway. "You've got the vacation time since you've only used two days out of your three weeks this year. Are you planning a vacation?" He waved her in to take a seat, then got up to shut his door. "What's up, Jamie?"

She sat down and rested her elbows on her knees. "I'm not taking a vacation or anything, but a friend of mine has a sick grandma in Texas and I was going to offer to go with her. I know its last minute, and I'm really sorry."

Rob brought up the attendance calendar on his computer. "Looks like no one else is off for at least another two weeks. And we've got someone covering Dave the Di—er, Dave's line now, so it shouldn't be a problem to get yours covered. Just let me know what you decide."

She grinned when her boss almost used Dave's nickname. "All right, I will. And thanks again." A few hours after lunch Jamie's phone vibrated on her charger. She picked it up and frowned at the message.

My mama called and said I should probably come down and say my goodbyes.

Jamie didn't even hesitate. Rather than text she just called her back. When Kelsey answered, her voice was subdued. "Hey."

"Hey, Kels. Are you okay?"

Kelsey was sitting in the back office, eyes wet with tears. She wasn't all right but she didn't want to start crying again so she tried to shrug it off. "Yeah, I'm fine."

"You're not fine, I can tell. What do you need me to do?"

Kelsey smiled. She was surprised by Jamie's intuition. "You're right, I'm not now but I will be. I just need to get down there and say goodbye, you know? Do you think you could take care of my cats for me?"

"No, but I bet Jenn would." Kelsey's stomach dropped a little at Jamie's words. Had she misjudged the blonde, thinking their friendship was more than it really was? She wondered if Jamie was pulling away from her now that they'd slept together. She was shocked into silence for about twenty seconds then Jamie spoke again. "I suggested Jenn because she has her own cat, so she knows the ins and outs of their care. And I—I thought you might like someone to go with you."

Not for the first time, Kelsey was amazed at how sweet her friend was. "James, I can't ask you to do that."

Jamie's voice was determined as it came through Kelsey's phone. "You're not asking me, I'm offering. And I would never offer if it was something I couldn't or didn't want to do."

"But your job—"

Jamie interrupted her. "I have more vacation time than I can ever use since I rarely travel. And I've already cleared it with my boss. So if you want company on your trip, you've got it."

She tried to protest one more time, convinced that Jamie was simply offering out of guilt. "But I'm going to see my family that you don't even know or care about, and you'll probably be bored."

"Kels, I may not know your family but you're my best friend and I care about you. You shouldn't have to go through this by yourself. I would like to be there for you."

Kelsey didn't know what to say. "I, um, thank you. It's just a lot to take in you know? And I'm worried. I still have to find tickets and pack for probably a week."

Jamie gave a single spin around in her chair and quickly reassured her. "Let me take care of the tickets. I can book them through our work system and just pay with my credit card. Then you can pay me back whenever. Where should I fly us to? And do you want to fly out tonight, or first thing in the morning?" She nervously waited for Kelsey to respond. She hadn't actually agreed to let Jamie come along but Jamie knew she had to go. There was something pulling her, telling her that Kelsey was going to need a friend. Every second of silence on the other end of the phone seemed to linger in the air like a heavy cloud.

"If you think that would be easiest, then sure. See if you can get two tickets to San Antonio first thing in the morning. I'm going to text Jenn after we hang up and I'll probably have to drop the key off to her on my way home from work."

Jamie made a face. "Actually, tonight is Jenn's late night at the clinic, so she won't be home until after 7:00. I have a suggestion though."

"What's that?"

"Why don't you just stay with me tonight so I don't have to leave earlier to pick you up in the morning? Your apartment is in the opposite direction from the airport. That way you can leave your car in a secure covered parking spot while we're gone. Just go home and pack after work and drop your keys off to Jenn on your way over. I'll even put fresh sheets on the futon for you."

If there was one thing she got from both her mama and papa, it was stubbornness. Kelsey had a hard time accepting help. She had an even harder time leaning on someone emotionally, and Jamie was offering both. Could she do it? Kelsey frowned as she thought about going alone, about the likelihood that she was going to Texas to say goodbye to her grandmother. She could do it alone, but she really didn't want to. Jamie just had a way about her that simply made Kelsey feel safe. "Okay. I'll be over around eight." Now she had to get through the rest of the day.

"WAIT, JAMIE IS going with you?" Jenn had immediately agreed to check on Kelsey's cats each day while she was gone. She was surprised by Kelsey's answer when she asked why Jamie wasn't asked to do it.

Kelsey looked at her curiously. "Yes, why? What's the big deal?"

Jenn shook her head. "Other than her sister, Maya, Jamie isn't close to any of her family so she tends to avoid other people's families as well. And she never travels anywhere." She paused at the look on Kelsey's face. "Oh, don't get me wrong, she's as good a friend as you could ask for, but she just never really gets involved in other people's personal lives. She's always been pretty hands off, maybe because her own family has made her so leery. It's just uncharacteristic, that's all."

Kelsey sighed and thought about how much she should tell Jenn. She knew from Jamie herself that the two women had spent a few months sleeping together until Jenn started to fall for her, then Jamie cut it off. Jenn had also told her about it when she came over for ice cream and girl talk the night of the surprise birthday party. Jenn said she had moved on but Kelsey was afraid she'd be hurt to know what happened on Saturday night. Jenn narrowed her eyes across the kitchen table. "What is it? Your face looks like you have something to say, so just say it. You know I'm not going to judge you."

There was no reason not to speak candidly with her friend. Jenn's son Malcolm was at his dad's house where he spent every Monday and Thursday night. It was just easiest when Jenn and her ex got a divorce. They had fifty-fifty custody and those were Jenn's two late nights at the clinic. Kelsey decided to just say it. "We slept together."

Anger washed across the black woman's face. "Seriously?" At first Kelsey thought Jenn was mad because she still had feelings for the blonde, at least until she spoke again. "I thought she was trying to change her goddamn ways!"

Kelsey raised an eyebrow at her friend's uncharacteristic swearing. "It wasn't exactly intended by either of us! And I sort of started it. I mean, we both agreed that it was a mistake the next morning." Kelsey was frustrated and still didn't know how to deal with that added complication in her friendship with Jamie.

Jenn cocked her head, perhaps sensing something that Kelsey was leaving unsaid. "What did she say after? I suppose she was all sweet but reserved the next day."

Kelsey looked at her in surprise. "Um, no. She actually cuddled with me the next morning until I had to pee. Then she made me and Burke breakfast and invited me to hang out afterward."

"She did?" Jenn was truly shocked because that was not the Jamie she knew. Perhaps she had changed. "And did you?"

"No. I felt weird and a little awkward. I told her I had to do my laundry and I really did, so I left." Kelsey rubbed her hand across her forehead, looking for all the world like she had a headache coming on. "Truthfully, I don't know what to think now. The next morning I told her that I could understand if it was just one of those things and that she was one of my best friends. I told her that our friendship was the most important thing to me and she agreed. I mean, it seemed resolved at the time."

"Oh."

Kelsey looked worried. "Oh, what?"

"So she didn't actually tell you anything, just agreed with you?"

Kelsey tried to remember exactly what Jamie had said. "She told me that my friendship meant the world to her too, and that she'd be lost without me."

Jenn looked at her curiously. "And how do you feel about her?"

"I feel the same way, of course. We've gotten very close and I care for her a lot. Why?"

The other woman gave her a knowing smile. "You mean you're not attracted to her at all?"

Kelsey rolled her eyes. "Of course I'm attracted to her! That's partly how Saturday night happened. Five of us were left at the end playing Truth or Dare, all drunk off our asses on wine. They started ganging up on me. Jamie asked how many people I was attracted to in the room and I said just one, thinking things would move on after that. Then Burke thought he'd be cute and pick me again. I chose dare so I wouldn't have to answer any more hard questions."

Jenn laughed. "And I'm guessing that's when things took a turn. Burke is an incurable romantic and a known matchmaker. I'm not surprised he had a hand in things."

"Yeah, well he dared me to make out with the person I was attracted to for sixty seconds. And that just kind of opened the floodgates so to speak."

The other woman snickered. "Both figuratively and literally huh?"

Kelsey huffed. "Oh yeah."

While Jamie was always pretty reserved emotionally, Jenn had gotten good at reading her in the years since they became friends. "I tried to warn you that she liked you before I left Saturday."

"Yeah, I remember that. But I already knew that Jamie was attracted to me. She'd done everything but come right out and say it on many occasions."

Jenn shook her head. "No, Kelsey. I think she *really* likes you. And I also think that it's been a long time since she's felt like this and maybe she's not sure how to deal with it."

"Oh."

"Yeah."

Kelsey looked panicked. "But I can't like her like that!"

Jenn raised an eyebrow in question. "Can't?"

"Don't. Won't! You and I have discussed this and we both know she's not dateable." Kelsey was adamant.

"No, I only know that she's not dateable for me, and most of the women in her past. But I think with the right woman she would be. And I also know that Jamie is a very determined woman when it comes to getting what she wants."

Kelsey snorted. "Yeah well we've already slept together so she should be all set."

Jenn rolled her eyes at how stubborn her friend could be. "She doesn't want to sleep with you, Kels. I think she wants a lot more. Is that such a bad thing?"

"From almost anyone but her? No. But I'm not going to lose a friend, or my heart, to another Romeo who thinks she wants to settle down. It's just better if we stay friends."

"But—" Jenn looked a little upset but Kelsey waved off her words.

"No, that's just the way it has to be. I don't want to lose her but I also can't pretend that she hasn't been sleeping her way through half the St. Seren lesbian population, breaking hearts when she inevitably moves on."

Jenn was irritated that Kelsey would just shut something so rare down. She had never seen Jamie fall for someone and she knew that first crack in the blonde's emotional armor was precious and that she'd be very vulnerable to hurt. "You're judging her."

Kelsey shook her head sadly. "No, I'm simply a realist. She's told me many times how women always want more but she just wasn't interested. I'm not going to be one of those women." She looked at the time on her cell phone and made a face. "Shit, I told James that I'd be there by eight and I'm going to be late." Jenn stood up and Kelsey hugged her. "Thank you so much for taking care of my boys while I'm gone. I'll text you and keep you updated on what's going on, okay?"

Jenn nodded. "It's no problem. I'm just really sad for you with all that's going on with your grandmamma. I hope she gets better."

"I do too, but I'm trying not to get my hopes up." Kelsey shrugged.

"If the worst does happen, lean on Jamie. That's why she's there, okay?"

That familiar feeling of safety washed over Kelsey and she smiled at Jenn's words. "I will."

"STOP FIDGETING!"

"I'm not fidgeting!"

Kelsey raised an eyebrow at her. "Yes, James, you are." She put a hand on the jumpy knee and it stilled instantly. She looked at the blonde curiously. "What's the matter, are you afraid to fly?"

Unwanted memory crashed down on the nervous woman. The same voice continuously sounded in varying tones of disparagement in Jamie's mind. The litany of comments was always the same. No matter where they were, no matter who was with them. For years it went on.

"I'm going on vacation James, and I can either go with you or go without you. Maybe it's better if you do stay home, you're always such a downer lately."

"James, you can't seriously be afraid to fly. You're not a child, try not to embarrass me in front of my —"

"Milk, really? You're so stupid, I don't know why we even bother going out to a nice dinner."

"Why would you enter that contest? You're just going to humiliate yourself, and me with you!"

"Jamie!"

A finger snapped in front of her face and Kelsey's worried green eyes swam back into focus Jamie shivered and felt a little nauseous, the same way she felt every time she remembered her ex-girlfriend. Gayle was older by five years, her first female lover, and her first love. The relationship was toxic from the beginning but Jamie was blinded to it all by being head over heels in love with the woman.

Then the verbal and emotional abuse began to wear on her. Jamie started catching her ex in a multitude of lies, catching her with hard drugs, and eventually finding out about the affair. Just the last one of what was apparently a long line that spanned their entire relationship. Drunken ranting seemed to be the norm.

"You've never been anything, you'll never amount to anything. You're just trash like everyone else in your poor-ass family! Good luck finding something as good as what you have here. You're not even good in bed, my ex was better —"

On and on it went. Even after Jamie finally left, the stalking and the calls started. She was in a pretty bad place for years because of that relationship.

Jamie jerked away when she felt a soft palm on her cheek. "Hey, what's wrong?"

The blonde blinked, sinking back to reality in an instant. "Nothing. You're right, I'm just not a fan of flying."

"Bullshit." Jamie looked up into tight green eyes and Kelsey spoke again. "You look like you're going to cry and it's not the first time you've just disappeared on me." Kelsey remembered something that Jamie had said to her months before. "Is this something you don't want to talk about? Is this about your ex?" They were interrupted when the steward came around asking if they needed anything. They shook their heads and the man continued on. It was a small plane so it was just the two of them in their row. Kelsey softly placed her hand on Jamie's arm. "You don't have to talk about it, just know that I'm here okay?"

Jamie nodded and closed her eyes as the captain announced that they had reached cruising altitude. She was quiet for about five minutes and Kelsey thought perhaps she just needed some space. She was startled when Jamie finally began to speak. "I met my ex right after I filed for divorce. I started driving down to St. Seren, just trying to meet new people who were like me, gay people. It was a completely different world than what I was used to. I was different." Jamie laughed at the person she was when she first came out. "You should have seen me, Kels. You would have never recognized me in a million years!"

"Oh, really?" Kelsey raised an eyebrow but she wasn't going to risk saying anything more than just mild comments. In the past, Jamie always shut down completely when the subject of her ex was brought up. The blonde was finally opening up to her and she wasn't going to do anything but support her. "Was it because you had dark hair?"

Jamie shook her head. "No, it was because I had long dark hair and glasses. And Flannel, oh, and a major love of hiking boots."

"No freaking way, you're kidding me!"

Jamie laughed. "Nope."

"And you didn't know you were gay until what, twenty-five?"

"Twenty-four! And I'll have you know that it's happened as late as sixty for some women!" She shrugged when Kelsey giggled at her. "So anyway, I met my ex after only driving down to St. Seren for about three months. I'd come down on Fridays and Saturdays and go to the bar to make new friends. Within two months of meeting Gayle I had gotten corrective eye surgery, a haircut, and blonde dye job. I fell hard and I just wanted to please her, you know?" She shook her head and looked down. "But I never could please her."

"James." Kelsey waited until she had her friend's attention. "You don't have to talk about it. It's okay."

Jamie looked resolutely back at her. "No, I want to, I'm ready to th—that is, if you don't mind?"

Kelsey grabbed her hand and squeezed it tight. "I'm always here for you. Always!" And for the next hour Jamie did talk. By the time Jamie was done, Kelsey was surprised that Jamie hadn't spent the past five years curled into a fetal ball. Kelsey herself knew the pain of being cheated on, but she had no frame of reference to understand what Jamie had gone through. Years of verbal and emotional abuse, years of constantly being told that you were worth nothing because of where you came from or how much money you made. The blonde had to deal with not only that, but a lover who was also controlling to the point that it threatened Jamie's career.

And because all of those things weren't bad enough, she had to deal with her ex's drinking and drug problem that spiraled out of control over the last two years they were together. Then to find out that the entire time they were together, her ex had been having affairs in secret? It was awful to hear, let alone to live through. Kelsey hurt for Jamie and had gained an understanding for her motivations and relationship fears. Jenn was right and now Kelsey felt bad for having judged her friend.

Jamie laughed nervously when Kelsey remained silent, trying to process everything she had been told. "I guess I'm pretty fucked up, huh?"

That snapped Kelsey out of her haze and she quickly raised the arm between the seats and pulled Jamie into a bone-crushing hug. "No, you're not. I'd say you were just broken for a while."

The blonde sighed and enjoyed the feel of Kelsey's arms around her. Kelsey was soft and warm, and she had the most intriguing cologne. "What are you wearing?"

Kelsey pulled back, looked down at herself, then back up at Jamie. "Uh, a state hoodie. Why?"

Jamie smacked her leg. "No smartass, I meant your cologne."

"Courage."

"Oh, isn't that a men's fragrance?"

Kelsey gave her a look. "And your point is?" She cocked her head to the side and smiled. "What, you don't like it?"

"I love it!" Jamie's eye's widened. "I mean, uh, er, it's really nice."

Kelsey started laughing. "Wow, James. You're so suave with the ladies!"

She got a swat to the arm for her teasing. "Whatever! It's not like you're a lady."

"No? Well what am I then?"

"You're one of the best friends I could ever ask for." Jamie gave Kelsey such an earnest smile it nearly melted her into a puddle. She couldn't help thinking that the flight was much too long to sit pressed up against Jamie with the armrest up.

At some point in the flight Kelsey got bored and decided to get some entertainment out of her backpack. She pulled out the two items she had brought for the trip. Contemplating both she weighed them in her hand. "What to do, what to do—"

"What the hell did you bring, the biggest books from the public library?"

Kelsey made a face at her. "No. One is a hardcover book and one is a giant book of crosswords. I wanted to make sure I had enough to do in case there was a lot of waiting." Kelsey didn't bother telling her that the book was a loaner from one of the girls she worked with. Knowing it would be plenty, she left her e-reader at home. She glanced at her friend who had been merely sitting there reclined in her seat for an hour. "I can't just sit there doing nothing like you. I get bored!"

Jamie looked confused. "Doing nothing?" She reached up to the ear that was on the opposite side as Kelsey and removed a small rubber bud. "I've been listening to music."

Kelsey scoffed. "What music? In your head? You don't even have a music player, James." Realizing Kelsey's confusion, Jamie started laughing and reached up to her neck. Then much to Kelsey's surprise, her friend removed a black plastic torque necklace thing from where it draped there. It had been hiding just below the collar of her shirt. She looked closer at it, perplexed, noting the buttons on the strange looking necklace. The rubber buds were attached to the ends of the torque. "I don't get it, how do you listen. Do you put the whole thing over your head like a headband? And where is your cord?"

"Oh my dear, sweet, behind-the-times Kelsey. This is a wireless headset."

She carefully pulled on a rubber bud and Kelsey was amazed to discover that it was connected to the set via a retractable wire. When it was all the way extended, you could get it to retract

again by just giving it a little tug. It was genius. But there was
still something missing. "How do you plug it in?"

Jamie rolled her eyes at how electronically challenged Kelsey
was. She quickly put it around Kelsey's neck and pulled the cell
phone out of her hoodie pocket. "Go ahead and pull a bud out
and put it in your ear." She waited while Kelsey complied.
"Okay, now look. Wireless means Bluetooth enabled, the same
way my phone connects to my car. Got it?" Kelsey nodded and
Jamie pressed play again on the music app.

Kelsey's eyes widened for a second then after a minute her
head started bobbing along. "Hey, this is pretty good! I've never
heard the song before, who is the band?" Jamie told her and after
another minute Kelsey took the bud out and retracted it back into
the device. Then she took the headphones off and handed them
back to Jamie. "I suppose you have something equally as nerdy in
lieu of a book?"

The blonde snorted. "You have a smart phone, you know you
can download the kindle app there."

"I don't like reading on such a small screen." She shrugged
and Jamie reached into her messenger bag and pulled out something that was larger than a cell phone but smaller than a note-
pad. It was slim and black with a gray screen. "That looks like an
etch-a-sketch minus the knobs."

"Oh my *God*, woman, haven't you ever seen an eBook reader?
What decade do you even live in?"

"Look at you, all high and mighty with your tech. So what
does it do, turn the pages for you? Big whoop!" Jamie counted to
ten in Spanish and Kelsey punched her in the arm. "Stop showing
off!"

Jamie rubbed the sore arm. "I'm not showing off, I'm trying
to keep my patience with such a techno-dweeb!" Kelsey looked
affronted and Jamie poked at her. "Yeah, I said it! How many
books do you have with you, dweeb?"

Kelsey rolled her eyes. "You just saw both my books, duh!"

"Yeah? Well I've got over five hundred right here! So suck
it!"

"That's what she said!"

Kelsey's comeback took Jamie by surprise and she cracked up
laughing. "Oh, that is definitely what she said, over and over and
over again!"

"You are such a perv!" While she didn't own any Bluetooth
enabled gadgets, Kelsey wasn't quite as clueless as she pretended
to be. But she really liked screwing with her and it made her

friend smile so that had to count for something. She knew that having Jamie open up emotionally was a huge deal and she felt very privileged that her friend felt safe with her. But it also made her think more about what Jenn had said. Did Jamie have feelings beyond that of friendship? She didn't know and she was scared to find out.

Chapter Sixteen

"OKAY, DON'T BE nervous. It's just my parents."

Jamie snorted. "That's easy for you to say!" She looked sideways at Kelsey. They were sitting in the rental car on the street outside Kelsey's parents' stucco house. It featured the distinctive Spanish tile roof and large front porch. It was an older neighborhood but it still looked kept up. "This is a really nice place."

Kelsey nodded. "Yeah, the house has been in our family for a few generations and Papa started really putting a lot of work into it when they moved down here seven years ago. One of my uncles is a contractor and he did a lot of work in exchange for Papa servicing his trucks. Plus Mama and Papa were the only ones who really wanted *mi abuela* to live with them, out of all my papa's siblings."

Jamie understood that not a lot of people would want to have a mother or mother-in-law live with them. "So are we going to say hi and drop off the bags, then go up to the hospital?"

Kelsey shrugged. Their purpose for visiting suddenly hit home. "Yeah, I guess. I wish Papa would have answered the phone so I would know if I should have gone straight there." She swallowed and looked at Jamie with such sad green eyes that Jamie thought her heart would break. "I just want to be able to say goodbye, you know?"

Jamie took her hand and gave it a little squeeze. "I know, Kels. For now we should probably get in there. I keep seeing a little face peer out the window at us."

"It's probably one of my cousins. My guess is there will be a lot of people in town to say their last goodbyes."

Less than a minute later they were standing on the covered porch. July heat in San Antonio was oppressive and Jamie began to sweat almost immediately. Kelsey knocked on the door and they waited. Even though it was her parents' house, she herself had never lived there and it would have felt strange to just walk in. The door was pulled open and a small Hispanic boy greeted them. "Kelthey!" Before Jamie could even understand what had happened, the little boy threw himself into Kelsey's arms and she spun him around.

"Carlos! I've missed you, little man! How is your papa and mama?"

Carlos grinned and proudly showed off his two missing front teeth. "Mama'th in the pool with Papa, Rotha, and the couthins.

Tía thays that yer gonna be thad and that I thould bring you out to the veranda when you get here." He suddenly noticed Jamie standing off to the side and stepped back. "Who'th that? Ith that yer girlfriend?"

Kelsey took Jamie's hand and drew her forward. "This is Jamie, she's not my girlfriend. She's just a good friend who came with me because she knew I'd be sad about our *abuela*."

"Oh! Thad, right! *Mi tío* thaid to come back right away cuth you would be muy thad." He pulled Kelsey's free hand and she in turn pulled Jamie. Kelsey felt nauseous, sure that she had missed her opportunity to say goodbye. Jamie felt a little sick herself, nervous to meet Kelsey's family.

They wandered through the sprawling two story house until they came out in a large open kitchen. From there they went through a set of French doors that led out onto a covered veranda. There were a couple older people seated at the far end of the tiled space but there were more than a dozen adults and children playing in an in-ground pool. An older redhead stood out among the sea of dark hair and sun-burnished skin in the backyard. She spun around when they came through the door and put her hand over her mouth. "*Alannah!* I am so sorry."

Kelsey teared up and gripped Jamie's hand tightly within her own. "Oh, Mama, is it too late then?"

Her mother dropped her hand and looked perplexed. Despite the fact that Kelsey and her mother were so very different, Jamie immediately recognized the expression the older woman wore. She smiled inwardly recalling that same head tilt with crinkled brow on her best friend. "Too late?"

Sure enough, Kelsey gave her the same look in return. "Are we too late, is *mi abuela* gone? Carlos said I would be sad when he answered the door so I thought she had died before we got here."

"Dead? *Aon!* Of course she is not dead. I merely thought you'd be sad to find out you came down here for nothing. Mama is feisty and ready to come home. They've no clue why she had such a dramatic turnaround, but we are all giving thanks for it." Kelsey breathed a sigh of relief and Jamie started to sweat. The blonde abruptly realized that without the purpose of Kelsey's grandmother's impending death, there was nothing to prevent the focus from going on to the one person who was not part of the family. She became acutely aware of their joined hands as Kelsey's mother turned bright green eyes on her. "And who is this? You made no mention of a girlfriend, Kelsey. And d'ya always greet your mam so cold?"

Kelsey immediately dropped Jamie's hand and threw her arms around her mother. Then she went over and did the same to what Jamie assumed was her father. He had stood up during the initial exchange between the confused women. Then she turned back to Jamie and pulled her forward. "Mama, Papa, this is my friend Jamie. She came down to keep me company because I thought I was going to have to say goodbye to *mi abuela*."

Jamie had no experience with meeting someone's parents so she just stuck out her hand toward Kelsey's mom. "Hello, Mrs. Ramirez, it's very nice to meet you. I can see where Kelsey gets her beauty and spirit from."

Kelsey's mother took Jamie's hand into both of her own and leaned back a bit. "Oh now, let me take a gander at ye."

"Mama, don't gawk!"

The older woman smiled. "You can call me Kaitlyn, and that handsome man over there is Manny. Not that yer not a fine thing yourself!"

Kelsey sighed and close her eyes. "Mama, please!"

The redhead turned toward her daughter. "What? I'm just making an observation. What's the matter?" Jamie's head was bouncing back and forth between mother and daughter and Kaitlyn had yet to remove her grip. While maintaining that grip the redhead leaned over and whispered to her daughter. It was not a quiet whisper because she had to speak loud enough to be heard over the kids and adults playing in the pool. "Why's she not yer *mot* then? She doesn't look the *moran* or *manky*. She a cute *hoor*?"

Jamie startled. "What?"

"Mama, no! And she can hear you and what you're saying sounds really bad in American English!"

Kaitlyn looked decidedly unapologetic. "Then she shouldn't be *earwigging*!" Jamie's face turned red and she attempted to extricate herself from the redhead's grip but Kaitlyn was pretty strong for an older woman.

"Kait, you're coming on too strong, *mi amor*. Let Kelsey's girlfriend go. The poor thing's losing feeling in her hand." Kelsey had talked about her parents a lot, but hearing Manuel Ramirez speak in person was unexpected. While he wasn't very tall, he wore laugh lines well on what was still a very handsome face. But his voice was startling and unexpectedly deep. Of course Kelsey's mother surprised her even more, but she didn't have time to dwell on it because Manny was pulling her into a hug as soon as

Kaitlyn let go of her hand. "Thank you for coming down with our Kels. I'm glad she has someone special in her life up there." When he was done hugging Jamie he turned to his daughter. "Why don't we all sit down for a bit and you can tell me about what you've been doing lately and how you and Jamie met. She is the engineer, yes?"

Kelsey made one more attempt to set the record straight about her and Jamie. "Yes, Papa, but Jamie and I are —"

He practically glowed as he interrupted her. "I'm so glad it all worked out and you're no longer alone! Now come and sit with us. I'll send Carlos for tea or lemonade if you prefer. You can introduce Jamie to all your cousins later."

Jamie tried to keep up, she really did. She didn't understand half of what Kelsey's mother was saying but she certainly understood that Kelsey's dad was under the impression that she and Kelsey were dating. And Jamie was not at all opposed to the idea. She glanced over at her friend and Kelsey's face was a little pinker than normal. Jamie turned to Kaitlyn and Manny Ramirez and gave them a hundred watt grin. "I wouldn't mind sitting for a bit. It's quite a lot hotter here than back home." The truth was that all families scared the bejeezus out of her, especially her own. But Jamie was determined that she would win Kelsey over, one relative at a time if that was what it took.

She shocked herself as thoughts of a future with her beautiful friend rolled through her head. She knew that what she felt for Kelsey was much deeper than anything she'd felt in a very long time. But it wasn't until their time on the plane that Jamie realized how far Kelsey had gotten inside. She was addicted to the stubborn Irish-Latina woman and she wanted more of everything from her. Jamie knew the sexual attraction was there. It was obvious with every heavy glance and long pause between them. She just had to hope that Kelsey felt something deeper too.

Before long they were seated in the shade of the veranda. Kelsey and Jamie both had iced lemonades and Kelsey's parents had sweet tea. Manny's deep voice cut through the heat like thunder. "So Kelsey has told us that you met through a telephone application. How does that work exactly?"

Kaitlyn rolled her expressive eyes. "Oh love, when will ye get with the times? It's a smart phone app, all the kids have them!" She looked at Jamie. "So which dating app was it? Knowing my darling Kelsey, it was something funny. This one time she showed me some 'Farm Gurls 4 U' app and let me tell ye, I was glad te be married and straight!"

"Jeez, Mama! Enough already! We didn't meet on a dating app, we met through a driving app. It was one where you could leave a voice message for your fellow drivers to warn them of road hazards."

Jamie tried not to laugh. Kelsey's mother was hilariously embarrassing and she enjoyed seeing her friend's face so red. She decided to cast the poor woman a line since it looked like she was drowning under her mother's love. "She's right. We started chatting via the app. Then one day I got a flat on the side of the highway and Kelsey just pulled up behind me and changed my tire."

Manny gave her a strange look. "You don't know how to change a tire?"

"Um." Jamie looked at Kelsey for help. Kelsey whispered the word "prissy" under her breath. "I technically know how to change a tire, sir, but—"

"No, no, no, do not call me sir. You can call me Manny, or even Papa when you're ready." He finished his interruption with a wink and Jamie swallowed hard.

"Okay, um, Manny. You see I know how to change a tire. I've just never actually done it before. And when Kelsey stopped to help me out she just kind of took over. There was nothing left for me to do but hand her the tools."

Kaitlyn and Manny both nodded but it was her father that answered. "*Si*, she is like that. I think she gets it from her mama."

Kelsey's mama swatted him on the arm. "Oh you! You just say the sweetest things!" Jamie looked back and forth between them, thinking that Kelsey's parents were not at all what she expected. Kelsey slumped down in her chair just a little and wished she had some vodka for her lemonade.

In an effort to get to know Kelsey's parents a little better and try to understand how two very different people ended up married, Jamie asked the obligatory question. "So how did you two meet?"

The redhead looked solemn for a second. "My daughter probably would not have told you but I've been disowned by my side of the family, the O'Brian's. It was because I decided to stay in the United States and get married to my Manny. But when I met him, it was love at first sight." She shrugged and gave Manny an affectionate look then turned back to Jamie. "The only one who stayed in contact was my aunt Kelcie and she died a few years ago, rest her soul."

Kelsey's papa took over the tale then, giving his own background. "I was living in Michigan at the time, having served my hitch in the army and learning my trade. When our time was up, Charlie and I opened up our own auto shop in his uncle's old garage. Kait and I only moved back to Texas when mama's health took a turn for the worse and she needed someone to care for her. That's when I sold my stake and moved down here where I started the garage I have now." He paused to take a sip of his tea then a soft smile came over his face. "So anyway, Kaitlyn came into this little bar near the shop, all alone mind you. And immediately said 'it's fuckin' freezin' out' and that she'd 'murder a fuckin' pint'. I was shocked, of course. I mean, here was this beautiful woman swearing like the guys I served with in the army. She was nothing like *mi madre*."

Jamie snickered a little at his description of Kelsey's mama. Within her first few minutes in the older woman's company she could tell that Kaitlyn Ramirez was probably a lot to handle. Kaitlyn herself laughed loudly at her husband's imitation of her. "After graduating university, I had my heart set on traveling around the US. I went to school with an American lass and there were so many things I wanted to see. My parents were completely against it but I had been working and saving money on the sly while I went to school. I was very close to my aunt Kelcie and she was the one who helped put the trip together. The hotel I was staying in was a complete kip and I decided to go out for a dram of fresh air. I was a bit of a chancer back then and I found myself alone in a bar near the airport." Jamie raised her eyebrow at the "back then" comment but otherwise remained silent. "Anyway, I went in to use the toilet and maybe bum a fag and when I looked around this dark and handsome man was at my elbow. While not very tall he was certainly a fine thing! He asked if I was lost or needed a ride in that deep voice of his. I asked him how far he was willing to take me." She paused and looked at Jamie with a smirk. "D'ye know?"

Jamie swallowed and Kelsey chuckled at the look on her face. "Yeah, Mama, I think Jamie knows."

The blonde nodded. "Yes, so I'm assuming that was the love at first sight part?" Both Kelsey's mama and papa nodded and graced each other with the sweetest smile and Jamie hoped that she'd get a similar look from her friend someday soon. "Thank you for telling me your story Kaitlyn. That was very, er, sweet."

Just as a lull hit their conversation, Kaitlyn suddenly sat up straight and slapped the arm of her chair. "You know what we need? We need to have a party to celebrate Mama's homecoming!"

Manny looked at his wife as if she'd gone nuts. "But Kait, we are already having a welcome home party tomorrow, after I go pick her up from the hospital!"

"No, *tu madre* is not allowed to have alcohol so we will have to keep it hidden tomorrow so she doesn't get into the cups. But tonight we could have a real party to welcome the girls proper!"

Kelsey's papa rubbed his forehead, looking very much like he was getting a headache. His voice was soft. "*Aye yai yai*, you are too much sometimes."

"Please, *mo shíorghrá*? We can hang those new rainbow lanterns to show the girls how much pride we have, and you can cook on the grill." She turned to her daughter. "Maybe for tomorrow you could make some of your *abuela's* tamales." Jamie thought she called him *mo sheeorgruh* with a rolled r at the end. She assumed it was Gaelic but didn't speak the language so she continued to follow along as best she could.

Kelsey scowled. "You know I don't like to cook, Mama."

"I'll help her. I love to cook!" Jamie jumped in and offered without a second thought. She had multiple reasons for it. First and foremost she didn't want to wander too far from Kelsey's side and be stuck on her own with her friend's family. She also just wanted to be by Kelsey's side because she felt a physical pull to be near her. Lastly, she really wanted to learn how to make authentic tamales.

The scowling face turned from Kaitlyn to Jamie. "I really don't want to cook."

Jamie smiled. "Perfect! I'll do the cooking and you can just tell me what to do."

Both Kaitlyn and Manny started laughing and her mother's heavy brogue rolled out with the laughter. "My daughter, it looks as though you've finally met your match!"

"*Si*, she does seem perfect for you, *pequeño*." Manny's deep voice held nothing but humor and affection for his daughter.

Jamie leaned toward Kelsey and whispered into her ear. "Your dad calls you little one? You're taller than he is!" Kelsey just shrugged her shoulders. She didn't want to admit that she had no idea what her father had called her for as long as she could remember. She knew what "*No hablo español*" meant and she considered that pretty good. Jamie looked at the quiet woman and narrowed her eyes. "Really, Kels? I cannot believe you are half Hispanic and you speak no Spanish!"

Kelsey blushed. "Hey, I took Spanish in high school! Two years! Plus, I'm half Irish and I speak no Gaelic so, eh, two years of Spanish is pretty good." Jamie snickered as Kelsey held up two fingers, knowing her friend probably had no clue how to say two in Spanish.

Kaitlyn shook her head back and forth with a sad look. *"Para lo que han servido esos dos años"* Jamie cracked up laughing at Kelsey's befuddled look and received a punch to the arm.

Manny's face lit up with a delighted grin. "You speak Spanish, Jamie?"

She nodded. *"Si, senor.* Not great but I can still follow along if I have to."

Kelsey's gaze moved back and forth between her parents and thought they were half besotted with Jamie themselves. She sighed, clearly aware that she had been beat. "Fine, Jamie and I will make tamales tomorrow. Do we have everything we need for both parties?"

The older woman thought for a second. "Actually, the press is fair empty. Would ya like te do some shoppin' with me?"

The younger Ramirez made a face. "I'd rather eat gravel, Mama, you know that. Actually, can we put our stuff in the spare rooms? I thought maybe I could introduce Jamie to the cousins."

"Um, actually." Her father's deep voice brought everyone's head around again. "We've got your aunt Roselyn and uncle Tuck staying in the big spare and little Carlos and Rosa are going to be on the pullout in the den. So you and Jamie will have to be in the small spare. We didn't realize you'd have company. I hope that's okay." Kelsey could feel her breathing start to increase ever so slightly. The small spare only had a twin bed. Not only would both their feet hang over the end but she would have to sleep pressed tightly against her best friend. She flashed back to the night of Burke's birthday party.

Her own mother interrupted her lascivious thoughts. "No worries though lass. There's a good sturdy lock on that door so the cousins won't be bothering you and Jamie!"

Kelsey shook her head slowly back and forth. "What about *mi abuela's* bed tonight and maybe we can just stay at the hotel just down the road the rest of the time."

"Mama has a hospital bed now. Neither of you can sleep in there. Please, Kels, I would like to have my daughter near me for a few nights. I have missed you!" Kelsey could never could say no to her mother. The woman was surely full of leprechaun magic.

Jamie didn't understand what the big deal was. A room was a room. Before she could ask, her bladder had finally gotten its fill of lemonade. She leaned over and whispered into Kelsey's ear for the second time since they'd arrived. "Kels, where is the bathroom?"

Kaitlyn gushed. "Oh, Manny, look how cute they are! Do you remember when I was that cute?"

"*Si*, but you are no longer that cute." Before Kaitlyn's fiery temper could make itself known he continued. "You are beautiful now and I much prefer beautiful, *mi amor*."

Kaitlyn blushed and Kelsey was sure she gacked a little inside, even though she was used to such displays from her parents. She stood and without a thought about how it may look to her family she held out her hand to Jamie. "Come on, I'll show you to the bathroom and we can put our stuff in the spare room upstairs." She was rattled about the prospect of sleeping so close to the woman who had dominated her dreams, but she didn't want show it in front of her parents or Jamie. The last thing she needed was to make them worry more after what they had been through with her *abuela*. They wandered through the sprawling house until they came to a bathroom near the back on the opposite side from the veranda. "Here you go. I'll just grab the bags out of the trunk —"

"Hey." Jamie grabbed her wrist and before she could respond the blonde pulled her into the bathroom. "What's wrong?"

Kelsey sighed and wouldn't meet the eyes that were so close to hers. Actually, everything was too close, Jamie was too close. "It's nothing."

"Bullshit! We promised no lies to each other." Jamie tilted her friend's chin up so she could stare into her green eyes. They seemed more watery than normal. "Hey, whatever it is will be okay. Is this about your *abuela*?"

Kelsey sniffed and nodded because some of it was about her *abuela*. She had come to Texas expecting to say goodbye and was relieved to find that was not the case. But because of all that worry and pent up anxiety her emotions were running higher than she liked. It also meant she didn't know how to stay so close to Jamie for the next few days while feeling like she did. When Jamie pulled her into an embrace, the first tear fell. "It's some of it. I guess finding out that she's going to be okay has just made me overly emotional."

Jamie nodded and continued to rub Kelsey's back. "And why did the whole thing with the room bother you so much? We're two adults here. I'm sure we can share a room with no problems." Kelsey stepped back and looked at her, trying to find any hidden meaning in her friend's words. Their gaze met and stuck, acknowledging and absorbing the full weight of their attraction for each other. Kelsey looked away first and Jamie spoke again. "I'm not going to lie and pretend that I'm not attracted to you because I very much am. But you're my best friend, Kels, and I'd never want to jeopardize that." Kelsey turned back to her and for a split second, Jamie saw it. Though it was just a flicker, it was like an echo of how she herself felt deep inside. She wondered briefly if Kelsey's feelings truly matched her own.

"Really, James?" Kelsey purposely and stubbornly shut down those deeper feelings, knowing she wouldn't make it through their stay otherwise. But much to her dismay, that only allowed space for all the heat and chemistry rise up between them full force. They stood very close in the bathroom and Kelsey couldn't help glancing at Jamie's full bottom lip. "They've put us in the small spare room. The room that has a twin bed and no floor space to speak of. You still think it's a good idea?"

"I uh—" She watched the way Kelsey was staring at her and she licked her lips in anticipation, of what she didn't know.

But Kelsey did know. She could no longer fight the attraction to Jamie and pulled the blonde toward her, into something that started slow and tender. But the fire was not to be denied and the kiss quickly flamed hard and hot. Many times she had wondered how the other woman kissed while sober and she had finally found out. It was amazing, languid one second and fierce the next. Rather than pull away like common sense dictated, she pushed Jamie against the bathroom sink and stepped between her legs. Hands clutched sides as their bodies pressed tightly together. Jamie stiffened and whimpered into her mouth. Kelsey thought it was hot so she ground their pelvises even harder.

Jamie wrenched her mouth away and pushed on Kelsey's chest. Kelsey felt rejected for just a second until her friend responded through clenched teeth. "Bladder. I told you I had to pee."

"Oh." Kelsey stepped back and gave Jamie a dimpled smile. "Sorry. I should just, um." She stepped toward the door and opened it. "I'll just go get our bags and meet you back here."

Kelsey left and Jamie shut the door right behind her. Rather than rushing to use the toilet she leaned against the door to catch her breath. Her heart hammered in response to Kelsey's kisses and she was no longer sure she would survive the visit. Kelsey had made it quite clear that she just wanted to be friends with Jamie and Jamie could live with that. But what she couldn't live with was if Kelsey wanted to become friends with benefits. She couldn't bear it if her best friend and woman she had totally fallen for wasn't interested in anything but sex. The irony of life wasn't lost on Jamie, but she could not change the way she felt. She left the bathroom a few minutes later and went off to find Kelsey and the spare bedroom they'd be staying in. When she walked around a corner near the front of the house she nearly bowled over Kelsey's mother. The redhead put a hand to her chest as her eyes got wide. "Jaysis, you put the heart crossway in me. I didn't see you there at all!"

"Oh, sorry Mrs—"

Kaitlyn held up a hand to stop her. "You can call me mama, just like our Kelsey. You're part of the family now."

Jamie's eyebrow went up but she held her tongue. Far be it for her to rain on Kaitlyn's parade. "Yes, ma'am." She searched the older woman's face to see if her response was allowed and found that apparently it was. "I was just looking for the spare bedroom. Kelsey said she'd take our bags up."

"Come along then, I was just getting ready to go to the store." Kaitlyn walked Jamie right up to the door of the room. When she opened it and stepped inside, she turned back to look at the redhead. Kaitlyn gave her a dimpled smile that was just like her daughter's and Jamie smiled back then shut and locked the door. She leaned against it and let out a sigh of relief then looked around. Kelsey was standing near an old-fashioned sewing machine, hanging clothes in a tiny closet. The room was stuffed full of furniture with the twin bed, an armchair, and a cedar chest. There was barely enough room to walk, let alone sleep on the floor. Kelsey finished with her shirts as Jamie approached to hang her own things. They made to scoot by each other but never quite achieved the switch in places. They stopped front to front and Kelsey carefully and deliberately took the shirt from Jamie's hand and tossed it onto the armchair. Then she ran a finger down the button placard of Jamie's shirt. They both watched the finger's progression as their breathing increased.

"This is probably a bad idea."

Jamie nodded. "The worst." She swallowed hard when Kelsey's other hand joined the first. "What are you doing, Kels?"

Kelsey parted her lips and stared into Jamie's brown eyes. Her gaze moved down to the blonde's lips and then took in the line of her jaw. "I don't know. I can't stop thinking about that night. I know we were both drunk but I keep remembering how you felt, how I felt." She stepped closer to Jamie and began unbuttoning her shirt.

"But, your family —"

Kelsey put a single finger across her lips. "Shh. Mama was going to the store and the rest won't bother us." She slowly worked her way down the buttons. "Tell me you don't want this and I'll stop. I'll stop and never bring it up again." She made it down to mid chest and paused before she lifted her green eyes to meet Jamie's gaze. "Do you want me to stop, James?"

Jamie took stock of her emotions and desires. She had never met someone she wanted so much. But it was more than just sex and she didn't know how to tell Kelsey that. Instead of trying to speak the words that never managed to work past her lips she decided to show her. "No, I don't." Her voice was a whisper but that was all Kelsey needed. She finished unbuttoning Jamie's shirt and pushed it down off her arms to the floor below. Before Jamie could lift her hands in response, Kelsey pushed the blonde down onto her back on the bed. Then she removed her own shirt and knelt onto the small space between Jamie's knees.

Jamie was in khakis and her bra while Kelsey was dressed similar in a pair of Capri pants. As she leaned over Jamie's body her hands drew a line up both sides of her. Though she was barely being touched, Jamie was so turned on it was almost painful. In her experience, not a lot of women took charge the way that Kelsey did. The woman just had a way about her. There was something so very raw and intoxicating about Kelsey's touch that it spiraled her out of control. Jamie reached up to pull Kelsey to her and her hands were pushed down and held tight against the bed on either side of her head.

"Nuh uh, you got to touch me that night but I never got to touch you. It's my turn now." And she did touch her. First it was with her lips. She kissed her way up Jamie's stomach, white and flat and so very different from her own. Her lips grazed the edges of Jamie's bra and worked even higher to the prone woman's neck. Eventually she was forced to let go of Jamie's hands and settle her weight onto Jamie's hips. With palms cupping each side of Jamie's face, she traced the blonde's lips with her thumbs then moved down to replace those thumbs with her own lips.

Meanwhile Jamie was left clutching at Kelsey's hips as the kiss went deeper and their bodies moved together in a sinus rhythm. Before Jamie could register that Kelsey's hands had moved, she felt one of those hands snake around behind her as her bra was undone. She pulled her lips away from Kelsey's with a smile. "Impressive!" She assisted by lifting slightly when Kelsey removed her bra, then she did the same in return. At the first touch of their bare chests both women moaned into their kiss. Jamie arched her back when Kelsey's hands came up and rolled her nipples between forefinger and thumb. She also could not help thrusting her hips upward into the woman seated on her pelvis. Kelsey released her lips and slowly moved down Jamie's body, first taking her time with one breast, then moving on to the other. Jamie thought she was going to explode. She needed more. She whispered urgently. "Kelsey, please!"

Kelsey continued to work her way south, eventually pushing the blonde's legs apart and kneeling between them. She unbuttoned Jamie's pants and moved to the side long enough to completely undress her. Then she stared down at her friend's body, taking in the line of dark hair between her legs, her small breasts, and heaving chest. She met Jamie's eyes and gave the blonde a dimpled grin. "I've dreamed of this."

Though she was already more turned on than she'd ever been, the dimple threatened to push her over the edge and she couldn't wait any more. "Please, Kelsey. I need you."

"You need someone to touch you?" Kelsey smirked and played with her just a little, not expecting the response Jamie gave her.

Jamie met her eyes. "No, I need you. Only you." Kelsey's heart skipped a little beat at her friend's words but she didn't let it deter her from her goal. The first touch of Kelsey's mouth was overwhelming for Jamie. The blonde cried out quietly and quickly muffled her voice with a nearby pillow. Her free hand clutched the bedspread below her as Kelsey ran her tongue the entire length of Jamie's hot flesh.

The woman below her was so wet that Kelsey just couldn't get enough. She wanted to take her time and go slow but she could tell that Jamie was set to go off like a rocket at any time. Kelsey introduced one finger and then another, pumping into her slowly at first, then gradually picking up the pace as she lapped at the flesh offered to her. Jamie gave her wild eyes and started moaning into the pillow. Sensing she wanted more, Kelsey inserted another finger and curled them upward while keeping her thrusts steady. She knew that Jamie had reached the end when a muffled keening came from beneath the pillow and the blonde tightened around her fingers. She changed her technique from a long and wide lick to something that swirled around Jamie's hard clit. When Jamie arched her back off the bed and screamed, having completely gone over the edge, Kelsey pushed her higher by sucking while she swirled her tongue around the little nub. Jamie screamed again into the pillow and suddenly went limp. Kelsey waited a few seconds and called out to her with trepidation. "James? Are you going to make it?" Even though Jamie's chest was heaving, she was completely unresponsive under the pillow so Kelsey moved up her friend's body and tossed the pillow off her. She patted Jamie's cheek until the other woman started to come around. "Hey, come on sweetie, open those eyes for me."

"Kelsey? Oh God, that was—" She couldn't finish her statement because an aftershock rolled through her. When she could open her eyes again she saw Kelsey smirking above her. It was in that moment that everything clicked into place. She had the words and she was ready to use them. "Kelsey, I lo—" She was interrupted by a knock at the door.

"Kelthey? Jamie? *Tía* thays to wake you from your nap and tell you to come down sthtairs. Thee altho thaid to tell you that if you break her bed while yer nappin' that you'd hafta buy a new bed." Another knock. "Are you guyth awake?"

Kelsey wondered what Jamie had been about to say but her curiosity took a back seat to the way she was throbbing with unspent energy. It was just cruel fate that left her wanting so much with Jamie's hot and satiated body below hers. She called out to Carlos. "We're awake. Tell Mama that we'll be down in a few minutes." When she was certain that her little cousin had left the upstairs, she turned back to Jamie. "I'm so turned on that I don't think I can walk yet."

"I'm certainly not going to leave you that way." Jamie quickly flipped them around and sat above Kelsey much the same way she had been doing to Jamie earlier.

Kelsey put a hand out to stop the ones that were unbuttoning her Capris. "James, it'll never happen. I'm sorry."

Jamie gave her a decidedly naughty smile. "You've mentioned before that it is really hard to get you off. However, I have not found that to be the case." She quickly removed Kelsey's pants and got right down to business. Before Kelsey could stop her and insist that it wasn't necessary, she could feel herself tightening to the blonde's ministrations. She lifted her hips in time with Jamie's thrusting as the blonde's tongue took her higher and higher. Two minutes later she was completely spent. It was ridiculously fast and she almost felt embarrassed for it. Looking at things objectively, Kelsey had to admit that it was the fastest she'd ever gotten off, even just by herself. A few minutes later they pulled themselves from the bed, got cleaned up, and

202 *Rules of the Road*

redressed. Before walking out the door of the bedroom, Jamie brushed the sweetest kiss across Kelsey's lips. Not for the first time, Kelsey wondered why she always had such a strong response with Jamie.

As the evening wore on, Jamie was introduced to all the cousins as well as Manny's brothers and only sister. It was his youngest sister Rosalyn and her family that was staying at the house with them. Rosalyn was the baby of the Ramirez siblings which was why her own kids, Carlos and Rosa, were the youngest of all the grandkids. And Kelsey was happy to introduce Jamie to all the other grandkids too, her cousins, except for one.

Kelsey's cousin Veronica arrived late, per her usual. She was the one female cousin who worked at her dad's shop. Breaking all the stereotypes, she was also one of the best mechanics that he had. She was cocky, openly gay, and not too picky about who she hit on. Every summer Kelsey would go down to Texas for a month when she was a kid, to spend some time with her grandparents and cousins. Maybe it was because they were both girls and near the same age, but there had always been a major rivalry between the two women. Staring across the small bit of watered lawn, Kelsey felt a little ball of jealousy grow out of control as she watched Veevee's eyes roam all across Jamie's body and finally settle on her face. "So this is the friend that *tía* Kait says came down with you." She made no secret of her interest in the attractive blonde.

Kelsey looked at Jamie and waved her hand vaguely toward her younger cousin. "James, this is my cousin Veronica, or Veevee as we call her." She turned back to Veevee and looped her arm through Jamie's. "And Veevee, this is my –" She paused and took one last glance at her cousin's leering gaze before finishing her introduction. "My girlfriend, Jamie."

Jamie's startled eyes met hers seconds before Veevee came around her and looped onto her other arm. "Oh, well done, Kels. This one is *muy caliente!*" Jamie had no idea what had just happened but she had a feeling it was going to be trouble before the night was through.

Chapter Seventeen

JAMIE FOLLOWED KELSEY around the party and Veevee was never far behind. Drinks were pressed into Jamie's hand at regular intervals, most of which were glasses of some punch that Kelsey's aunt Rosalyn had concocted. It was tasty but deceptively strong. After a vicious round of croquet, Veevee suggested they do shots. Jamie didn't really want to do the shots but she also didn't want to be a drag for what had turned into a reunion of sorts between Kelsey and her family. As a lot of the older cousins made their way into the house to find the tequila, Kelsey held back and pulled Jamie to a stop. "You don't have to do the shot if you don't want to."

Jamie shrugged. "It's okay, one shot of nasty tequila won't kill me."

"Plus it's the good stuff and won't make you lose time!" They both laughed remembering Jamie's tequila at home. Then their eyes met and Jamie's mouth opened to ask about the girlfriend declaration only to be interrupted by Veevee.

"There you two are! I went ahead and poured you both shots. Come over to the veranda with us." Of course, Veevee wasn't going to let Jamie out of her sight. She had a feeling that the more the blonde drank, the easier it would be to have some fun with her.

Of all Kelsey's Texas cousins, the only ones joining them for shots were the ones without kids or a lot of responsibility. And of course, were of age to drink because Kelsey's mama would not tolerate breaking the law. The group on the veranda with Kelsey and Jamie were all male with the exception of Veevee, and covered a wide range of looks and body types. The oldest was Antonio, Veevee's brother. He was nearly forty and still a bachelor, much to his mama and papa's displeasure. Tall and strapping, with his uncle Manny's deep voice, he never lacked for female attention, which was why he refused to settle down. The four guys ranged in age from thirty-nine down to twenty-five. Appropriately, Kelsey's dad was the middle child of five, and Kelsey was near the middle in age of all her cousins, if you didn't count Rosalyn's little ones who were significantly younger than the rest.

While there were more that weren't doing shots, and some

that were not in attendance at all, the little group on the back porch was the usual crowd of misfits that raided uncle Manny's tequila cupboard during family gatherings. Besides Antonio and Veevee, there was Manuel, Jose, and Alex. Preferring the shortened name to his full name of Alejandro, Alex was only twenty-five and worked at the hotel. He was young, suave, and very gay. Jamie found it funny that three of the Ramirez cousins turned out to be gay, but was happy for Kelsey too. It was hard to disown one when there were so many in your family tree, and clearly her family had come to accept it. Jamie wished that had been the case with her own family, but it was not. Rather than dwell on her childhood, she shook free of the memories and raised a shot glass with the rest of the group. Antonio led the toast. "Here's to those who've seen us at our best and seen us at our worst and can't tell the difference!" Everyone threw back the shots and slammed the glasses down on the tile tabletop.

Veevee immediately started pouring out more shots and Kelsey held her hands up. "No more for me, thanks." She actually didn't care if she did another shot but she knew that Jamie didn't like tequila so was trying to get them both out of it without putting all the pressure on her friend.

Antonio quirked a perfect eyebrow at her and gave them both an evil grin. "*Mi querido primo,* have you gone soft while living up north? Can you no longer keep up with the family?"

Jamie knew that Kelsey liked tequila and knew that she had turned down more shots for her sake. She also found it cute the way her friend scowled and growled a little under her breath with Antonio's teasing. She put a hand on Kelsey's arm and leaned close to whisper in her ear. "It's fine, really. We're not driving anywhere so what's the harm?"

"Speaking of driving." Kelsey looked up at the group in general. "How are you idiots getting home?"

Alex grinned. He knew his cousin was going to cave to Antonio's teasing. She was too competitive and always caved. "Mateo is driving us all. He's going to drop Antonio, Manuel, and Jose at 'Tonio's house, and he'll drop me and Veevee off at the club. I can ride home with friends. See, we will all be safe. Live a little, *chica!* Show your girlfriend that you know how to have fun!" Mateo was their nineteen-year-old cousin and because he was under the legal drinking age, he was not allowed to drink at family gatherings.

Kelsey sighed and rolled her eyes. "Fine, line them up. But you delinquents are going to pay if we have a hangover at *abuela's* party tomorrow!"

"*Bueno!* All right, I think Jamie should be the one to give the next toast." Veevee turned her dark gaze onto the blonde at her side and Kelsey could see the calculation in her cousin's look. She didn't like it at all.

Jamie shrugged. "Okay, let me think for a second, let's see, all right." She thought of a toast and raised her glass. She was mimicked by the other six adults on the veranda. "Here's to the nights we'll never remember with the friends we'll never forget!"

A rousing mass response was said by the Ramirez cousins. "*Salud!*"

Jamie had been feeling pretty good with all the punch she drank earlier but two shots of tequila in a row left her feeling decidedly unsteady. She sat down abruptly and watched Kelsey and her cousin Alex, joking with each other. After a few minutes, Kelsey called her name. "James, Alex is going to show me his new car. You want to come?" She understood Jamie's look and answered her unspoken question. "He drove here but will just leave his car overnight. He'll be back for the party tomorrow so it's no big deal."

"Oh, okay. I think I'm just gonna sit right here for a bit."

Kelsey grinned down at her, taking in Jamie's lazy grin and heavy sleepy eyes. "You're wasted aren't you?"

A wobbly nod. "Oh yeaaah. I think the tequila just hit me, Kels. What is that stuff?"

"El Luchador. It's one hundred and ten proof, so if you're not used to it I'm not surprised it has you on your ass." She looked down at Jamie one more time and decided her friend should probably sober up a bit or she'd really regret the next day. "I'll be right back, okay?" Sure enough, Kelsey returned a minute later with a glass of ice water. "Here, drink this while I go look at Alex's car."

Jamie looked at Kelsey and gave her full puppy dog eyes. "Don't leave me, Kels! What if an, uh, armadillo or something eats me out here?"

Kelsey couldn't resist giggling at the blonde and running her hand through Jamie's hair. Jamie leaned into the hand and Kelsey knew they'd have to talk soon. "The yard is walled in and we don't have any armadillos back here. I think you'll be completely safe. Now I'll be back shortly, all right?"

"Fine, just leave me then! The only soul I know." She sighed dramatically. Kelsey started to laugh but it was abruptly turned to a frown as Veevee walked up.

She sat in the chair right next to Jamie and put her arm around the drunk woman's shoulders. "Hey, you know me!" She turned to look up at Kelsey with a decided smirk. "Don't worry Kelsey, I'll keep her company. Aunt Kaitlyn was telling me all about your friend here and how she came down to keep you company. I won't leave her alone for a second, I promise!"

It was in that moment that Kelsey knew Veevee had found out that Jamie was not actually her girlfriend. "Fine." She ground the words out through gritted teeth and spun around to go with Alex. She couldn't help mumbling under her breath as she walked away. "That's what I'm afraid of!"

Alex glanced sideways at her. "What was that, cuz?"

"Nothing. Let's go see that car. Brand new, you said?"

Jamie missed Kelsey as soon as she was out of sight. But she didn't have time to reflect on the emotion because she was quickly distracted by Veevee. "So how long have you and Kelsey been friends?"

She turned her head to focus on the person who only bore the slightest of resemblance to the woman who had been dominating her thoughts. She wanted to correct Veevee and tell her that they were girlfriends, but she didn't know if that was the right thing to do. Kelsey had not actually talked about anything with her. She always seemed to avoid any serious discussion about the night they slept together and now they'd done it again. Jamie wasn't sure what it all meant. "Um."

"Hey, want to do another shot?"

Jamie shook her head and felt it spin a little. "I don't really like tequila."

Veevee looked shocked. "What? How can you not like tequila? It's the favorite drink of all the Ramirez cousins, including our Kelsey! You don't want her to think you can't keep up, do you?" Jamie just shook her head again. She didn't want Kelsey to think that at all. "Okay then!" Veevee leaned over and poured two more shot glasses. When they picked them up, Veevee's grin had turned decidedly predatory. "Cheers to the Ramirez women and their friends!"

They downed the shot and Jamie barely noticed the flavor. She giggled and mumbled to herself. "Third time's a charm!"

Veevee leaned closer to her. "So Jamie, are you seeing anyone back home?"

Jamie looked up at her, wide-eyed. "Kelsey said—"

The less than honorable Ramirez cousin interrupted her. "I know what Kelsey said. She only said it to keep me away from you. We've had a rivalry for a long time. Besides, Aunt Kait said that Kelsey told her you weren't the dating type. So I know she was lying about you guys being girlfriends."

Pain lanced through Jamie's chest at the younger woman's words. "*What?*" Kelsey had to feel the same way she did, she had too!

Veevee didn't see the other woman's pain. She saw an opportunity. If her cousin didn't want the attractive blonde, then she had no problem with scooping her up. "What's the big deal anyway? Clearly you two were just pretending, and I can attest that this Ramirez cousin is a lot more fun." She kept leaning closer while speaking until the last few words were spoken right in Jamie's ear. And when Jamie didn't move away, Veevee let her tongue run up the curve of the blonde's ear.

It was in that exact moment that Kelsey had walked through the gate into the backyard. The gate was right behind where they were sitting so she had no problem at all hearing her cousin's words, nor seeing her actions. Her temper flared immediately with a flashback to a surprise party all those months ago, then it burned itself out just as fast with what Jamie did in response. The blonde pulled back from Veevee's too-near face. "No!" She abruptly stood, then had to grab the table to keep from falling back down again. "I don't want you. I only want Kelsey!" She swayed and grabbed the table tighter again. "I—I don't care if she lied. I still only want her." Tears had started to fall down the very drunk woman's cheeks.

Kelsey watched for only a second and could not stop the whispered words. "Oh, James." She quickly rushed to her friend's side when it looked like Jamie was going to fall over. "Hey, what are you doing over here? I got you. Just put your arms around my neck."

"I'm—sorry, Kels. Got s—so drunk. Dunno how. It hurts though." Veevee looked on with interest.

"How did you get this drunk? You weren't like this when I left."

Jamie held up two fingers. "We did a nuther sh—shot." Then she held up three fingers. "Was only one more, Kels! Don't be mad."

At only an inch shorter, Kelsey barely had to look up to meet Jamie's eyes. Her best friend was completely hammered. She whipped her head around to glare at Veevee. "What the hell were you thinking? How could you give her another shot?"

Veevee shrugged. "She seemed fine. And she's a grown

woman who is very single. She can make her own decisions."

There was steel in Kelsey's voice as her innate overprotec-
tiveness kicked in. "You are a grown woman as well who damn
well should have known better. That was completely irresponsi-
ble of you to give someone so drunk even more shots. You've
completely crossed the line."

The seated cousin raised an eyebrow at her. "So? What are
you going to do? It's not like you two are going anywhere. I
didn't think anyone would get hurt." Kelsey glanced at Jamie's
face as the blonde clung to her in an attempt to stay upright. She
understood her cousin's double meaning. Truthfully, Kelsey
really didn't know where she and Jamie were going but that
didn't excuse her cousin's behavior. She coldly looked down at
the woman who had made Jamie cry. Family or no, she had to
leave. "That's the problem with you, Veronica. You never think
about how your actions affect other people. You're selfish."

"Hey, what's going on?" Alex had come back in with Antonio.

Antonio also took in the scene of a very drunk Jamie, Veevee's smirking grin, and furious gaze of Kelsey. "What's up,
Kels?" Then he moved his gaze back to Veevee. "What did you do
this time, *bruja*?"

Anger finally replaced the sneer on Veevee's face. "Just like
always, *hermano*. You take her side!"

"I grew up with you, Vee, and I know exactly how you work!
Let's go, we're leaving." She started to protest and he held up a
hand. "Mateo is in the car already. That's what we came in to tell
you. You can go to your bar and get laid like everyone else. Leave
Kelsey and Jamie alone." Veevee's face took on a stubborn look
but her older brother was having none of it. "*Vamanos!* Or I will
tell Mama why you really missed her birthday party last month.
"*Entiendes?*"

Veevee snarled and shoved by him through the gate. "*Si*, I
understand just fine!"

Antonio sighed and ran a hand through his thick black hair.
He looked at Alex, and the youngest of their group gave a nod of
his head to the older man. "I'll be there in just a minute. I'm going
to help her take Jamie up." The blonde was only standing because
she had a lot of help from Kelsey. He took one side of the inebri-
ated woman and Kelsey took the other. Everyone else had gone to
bed hours before so they had to be quiet going up the stairs. Once
Jamie was situated on the bed, Alex turned to his favorite relative. "You okay, cuz?" Kelsey rubbed her forehead, looking very

much like her papa in the moment. Then she gazed down at Jamie's sleeping form and shook her head. "You want to talk about it."

She looked up at him. "Yes and no. But I know you have to go, so maybe tomorrow." She looked back at Jamie again and her features softened with affection. "I just didn't know."

"Does she know how you feel?"

Kelsey wrenched her eyes away from the blonde and looked back at him. "She's my best friend."

He gave her a soft smile. "But does she know how you feel?" She shook her head but stayed silent. Alex gave her a little chuck to the shoulder and took a single step to the door of the room. "Maybe it's time you told her because it's pretty clear that she's already fallen for the Ramirez charms."

That finally elicited a smile from the Irish-Latina. "Maybe it's my O'Brian charms. Everyone says my mama is half leprechaun."

He smiled tenderly. "Or maybe it's just Kelsey's charms, eh? I'll see you tomorrow, cuz." Then he was gone.

That left her to put on some light pajamas and get into bed with her best friend. Jamie was facing the far wall and because of the size of the bed, Kelsey was forced to spoon her from behind. She both cursed and reveled in their position and let out another sigh that rustled the hairs on the crown of Jamie's head. Her voice was quiet as she spoke the question into the midnight hour. "Oh Jamie, what am I going to do with you?" She was only slightly startled when Jamie pulled her hand up close to her chest and sleepily mumbled a response. The words were so quiet Kelsey nearly didn't make them out.

"Please love me." Kelsey shivered in the air-conditioned room and drew the blonde closer.

SUNLIGHT SHONE THROUGH the tiny window that was situated on the wall opposite the door to their room. Something tickled Kelsey's awareness, both a sound and a vibration. She became aware that the woman in her arms was moaning softly as she swam upwards from the depths of sleep. "James, you okay?"

Jamie moaned a little louder but managed to whisper a word at the end. "Sick."

"Oh damn." Kelsey quickly moved away from her and rushed to grab the small trash can that was sitting under the sewing machine. She made it back to the side of the bed just as Jamie was leaning over. The smell threatened Kelsey's own resolve but she held her breath as best she could to avoid joining her friend. Kelsey didn't like vomit but she'd actually smelled and seen worse while working.

When Jamie finally stopped heaving she hung over the bed, curled around her pillow. Her face was scrunched up in pain. "Gonna die."

Kelsey looked from her friend to the can of sick, then back to Jamie again. "You're not going to die, James. You're just hung. I'm going to get you some water and ibuprofen. I'll be back in a minute." She quickly rushed to dump the trash can into the toilet and rinsed it thoroughly before leaving it upside down in the shower to dry. Then she ran downstairs to grab a glass of water. Her mother entered the kitchen a minute later.

"D'ya know why my trash can is in the shower, Kels?"

Kelsey went to get a glass out of the cupboard, then changed her mind and opened the fridge to see if they had any bottled water instead. "That's my fault, Mama. Jamie got sick and that was the nearest thing at hand. I'm just down to grab her some water and ibuprofen."

"Ah, she's wrecked then?" At Kelsey's nod she went on. "You kids weren't giving her that tequila, were you?" Kelsey nodded sheepishly. "Nothing but demons, all of ye Ramirezes! Ye don't stop til you're all half ossified." She shook her head at her only child sternly. "And speakin' of Jamie, I'd like to talk to ye. You keep sayin' yer friends but friends don't look at each other the way you two have been goin' on."

Kelsey sighed. "Please, Mama, can you just let it go?"

The redhead nodded. "I will, yea. Now go take care of yer *friend*." Kaitlyn emphasized the word friend, her words lilting with a fine Irish brogue. Kelsey narrowed her eyes at the older woman. Her mama always said "I will, yea" when she actually meant the opposite. But at least she had bought herself the morning without any heavy discussion. She turned and rushed upstairs to deliver the water and pills to Jamie.

Later that afternoon, Kelsey was off playing another intense round of croquet with her papa, aunt, and uncle. She and Jamie had made the meat for the tamales in a crock pot the night before, but she put them all together after breakfast, without Jamie's help. Now that it was later in the afternoon Jamie was at least up, though barely. The blonde was sprawled in a chair on the veranda, wearing a pair of borrowed aviator sunglasses. She was nursing a water and trying to keep the piece of dry toast down that she'd eaten for breakfast. She glanced up as Kelsey's mama and *abuela* came out of the house through the French doors. Kaitlyn's hands were busy helping the elderly woman keep her balance as she tottered along with her walker. There was a portable oxygen tank in the little basket attached to the front with the hose running up the front of her shirt to wrap around her ears and come back across her cheeks under her nose. Other than the oxygen, she looked in good health, certainly better than Jamie herself felt. She scrambled to pull out a chair and winced when her stomach threatened to rebel. Again. "Here, let me help you ladies." She situated the chair for the old woman and helped to settle her then went back to her own seat. Kaitlyn went back inside.

"Young Jamie." She gestured to the yard full of bickering adults and spoke with a heavy accent. "Why aren't you playing with the other kids?"

Jamie had been introduced to the feisty old woman when Manny brought her home from the hospital a little before noon. She had immediately poked at Jamie stomach and declared that Kelsey had caught a fresh one. Jamie's sore stomach severely disagreed with the old woman's treatment, but she appreciated the acceptance from someone of her generation. It was refreshing. Jamie shook her head slowly and pushed her glasses up a little higher to try and block out the midafternoon sun. "I'm not feeling the best, *Abuela*. I told Kelsey I wanted to sit this one out."

Isabel Ramirez, the matriarch of the Ramirez clan, nodded her head with understanding. "*Si*, you do not know how to hold the liquor. No?"

Kaitlyn returned just in time to hear the old woman's question. "Nay, Mama. Twas all the kids last night, they were acting the *maggot*. Poor Jamie was already locked, unused to that foul tequila they all liked. Veronica was actin' the floozie per usual and gave her one more shot. I'm afraid that's what has Jamie feelin' like she's got a bad dose."

Isabel scowled, adding even more wrinkles to her already well-mapped and sun burnished face. "*Ai yai yai*! Of all my grandchildren, that girl will be the death of me."

Kaitlyn snorted and tossed her mane of red hair like a wild horse. At least that was the way it looked to Jamie's eyes. "Then you ought to be talkin' with Jose then. That's her papa after all. You'd think with him being the eldest that his kids would be most settled. But no. Antonio and Veronica, hmm." She made a noise of disdain. "Delinquents both!" The old woman didn't respond to a truth she was already aware of. She just worried her hands together.

Manny walked up a few minutes later and sat a cup with a lid and straw down in front of his mother. "Here you are, Mama. I put some lemonade in your cup."

The old woman squinted up at her son. "Did you put some vodka in it?"

He shook his head. "No, Mama, the doctor says no alcohol, remember?"

She scowled. "I suppose I shall have to drink it like a sick person then, like *mi nueva nieta.*"

Jamie shook her head in denial. *"Abuela,* I have no problems treating you like my own grandmother out of respect but I don't want you to be confused. Surely they told you by now that Kelsey and I are just friends."

The old woman chuckled. "Ah, that is what their lips say but not what my eyes see." She tapped her cheek, just below the right eye. *"Abuela* knows everything, *querida.* My granddaughter is very taken with you." Jamie's heart stuttered in her chest and she only wished the old woman's words were true.

Manny could see that his daughter's friend was suffering on a few different levels. His wife had explained the situation earlier in the day and not for the first time he regretted that their only child had inherited his stubbornness. He turned to his wife and gestured toward Jamie. "Did your remedy not work for her?"

Kaitlyn looked up at him in surprise. "I did not give it to the lass."

"Why not?"

She shrugged. "Truthfully, I did not think of it."

He threw his hands in the air. "Jaysis, you!" Even hung over, Jamie couldn't help smiling at the exclamation that Manny had clearly picked up from his Irish wife.

"Manuel Diego Jose Ramirez! Language!"

Manny's eyes widened at the way his mother had just reprimanded him. He, a fifty-seven year old man, got scolded by his elderly mother. He pointed at his wife. "What, Mama? She says it all the time and you don't have a problem with her talk."

"Mi hijo, you are not her. She has her own custom and language, no? So she is allowed. But you are my *bebé,* and you will respect my customs. *Bueno?"*

Jamie snickered as Kelsey's papa rolled his eyes and he answered her in the only way that was allowed. *"Si,* Mama."

Kaitlyn also smirked at the familiar reprimand from her mother-in-law. She stood and turned to Jamie. "If you trust me, I will make something that will calm your stomach and sooth your head. Okay?"

The blonde groaned. "Yes, please! Anything!"

Manny mumbled under his breath. "You may regret that."

As Kaitlyn started for the French doors, Jamie called out to her. "Wait, what's in it?"

"Oh, 'tis a secret. Just a few things from the press that I put together. I'll be back in a jiff!" She returned less than five minutes later and placed a mug in front of Jamie. The blonde noticed that Kelsey's mother had left the French doors open but didn't want to be rude and call her on it. She stared hard into the cup. Whatever glob was inside looked dark and sludgy. The three older people at the table unconsciously leaned forward and watched her study it.

Jamie sat back and pointed at the colorful mug with the unknown remedy inside. "Are you sure this is safe?"

Kaitlyn nodded enthusiastically. "Oh, absolutely! Now remember, just drink it straight down and don't be stoppin'!"

"I know I'm going to regret this." Jamie mumbled the words under her breath and picked up the mug with some trepidation. Her stomach gave another roll and she knew she had to do something. Quickly tipping it up, she drank down the half mug of unknown substance then set it back on the table and stared straight ahead. She wobbled a little in her seat and her eyes glazed over. It was foul and her tongue felt like it was going to fall out of her mouth. Then the mystery glop hit her stomach and she found herself up and out of the chair, making a beeline for the nearest bathroom, through the conveniently open French doors. Kaitlyn smiled at her departing back and Manny winked at his wife.

"Hey, where did she go?" Kelsey walked up just in time to see her friend bolt through the open doors into the house. She looked back at Jamie's empty seat and spied the mug on the table. That only prompted her to sigh and rub the worry line between her eyes. "Oh, Mama, you didn't!"

Kaitlyn snickered at the way her only child looked just like her papa when she worried at something. "*Alannah*, she was miserable! I had te do something. Besides, it was your papa's idea."

"Oh no, do not bring me into this, *mi amor*!" Kelsey's parents decided to play it safe and not be there when Jamie returned. They wandered off into the backyard farther to join in the next game. Kelsey sat down at the table to talk with her *abuela* while she waited for her friend to come back.

"*Mi nieta*." When she had Kelsey's attention, the old woman began to speak in a quiet and serious tone. "Do you remember when you were still *adolescente* and I came to live with you up north?"

"*Si, Abuela.*"

"Do you remember the day I taught you to make tamales?"

Kelsey nodded her head. "*Si.*"

Isabel spoke gently to her granddaughter. "I told you that many people thought the secret to good cooking was in using the best ingredients. I also told you that they were wrong. No ingredient will ever be perfect. Sometimes the tomatoes are bruised, sometimes the peppers are not as sweet. The real secret is in finding the ingredients that work best together."

Kelsey looked at her seriously, not really sure why the old woman was repeating advice from long ago. "*Si, Abuela.* I remember."

Isabel nodded, pleased. "What I did not tell you that day, because you were too young still, was that you should use the same philosophy when it comes to love."

The younger woman cocked her head in confusion. "*Qué?*"

The old woman leaned across the table and gently took Kelsey's hands into her old and frail ones. "Granddaughter, you have been searching for the perfect ingredient but you yourself are flawed." Seeing her granddaughter's half-Irish temper start to flare she gave a little shake to her hand. "No, we are all flawed. What I am trying to tell you is that you have already found your best match. You should not discount her so easily because she is not perfect."

Kelsey sighed. "*Abuela*, there is a lot you don't know about both of us. As much as I don't want to admit it, she has a past and I'm—"

"You fear. *Si*, we all have a past but we don't live there. You do both of you a disservice by not giving her a chance to offer her future." She smiled and patted Kelsey's hand. "Your ingredients would mix well, I think."

There was a part of Kelsey, deep within her heart, that agreed with her grandmother and that made her scowl. "You know I hate cooking." Her face lightened again when Jamie reappeared through the door.

There was a twinkle in Isabel's eyes when she saw Kelsey's smile. "Ah, but with the right person it can be fun, no?"

Jamie came around the table and threw herself into the chair she had previously occupied. She looked directly at Kelsey. "Your mama is the devil incarnate."

Kelsey laughed rich and full. "But do you feel better?"

The blonde sighed and straightened the collar of her short sleeved shirt. Her reply was begrudging at best. "Yes."

Chapter Eighteen

KELSEY AND JAMIE ended up staying four nights total with Kelsey's parents in San Antonio. The last two days Kelsey took her best friend around the city to see the sights. They walked along the river downtown, took a sightseeing boat, visited the Alamo, and even the San Antonio Zoo. Jamie was enamored most by the way the river meandered its way through the buildings and streets of the downtown area, shaded by tall hanging trees. There were footbridges that crossed every so often throughout the city. Though she'd never been to Venice, San Antonio seemed to be the Americanized version of the way she'd always pictured the ancient Italian city in her head. It was incredibly romantic yet there was still no acknowledged romance between them. She knew that it wasn't a very good time to talk while they were staying at Kelsey's parents. They had been good for the remaining nights, though it was a more than a little torturous. It was for that very same reason she dreaded going home.

If Kelsey didn't bring up the growing thing between them, then she was going to have to. There were a lot of hugs and tears when they left early Saturday morning. It felt nice to be accepted by Kelsey's family, something Jamie had never really experienced for herself. She liked them all, save for Veronica. She even liked Kelsey's *abuela*, though the old woman was just a little crazy. When they were leaving, Isabel Ramirez whispered something into her ear and she still had no idea what it meant. Jamie just assumed it was cooking advice since she admitted to the old woman that she loved to cook.

Their plane touched down at the Detroit airport just before noon and Kelsey was nothing but nerves. Despite the previous two days of sightseeing and all the fun they'd had, she knew that a conversation was coming. It was necessary, it was essential, and Kelsey was afraid. Jamie pulled into one of her two allotted spots and shut down the engine. The other was taken up by Kelsey's little silver car. She looked at her best friend and gave her a little smile. "Would you like to come up?"

Kelsey nodded. "Sure. When I texted Jenn at the airport she said that the cats were taken care of this morning so I don't have to rush home or anything."

"If there's no rush why don't you bring your bag up and I can throw all our clothes into the washer together. That will save you a little laundry at least." Kelsey gave her a grateful smile and they trudged into the building and up the stairs. Jamie sighed when they got to the top and Kelsey cocked her head at her. The blonde answered the unspoken question. "I think I ate too many of your tamales while we were in Texas." Both women laughed as they made their way down the hall and into Jamie's apartment. They worked efficiently together to unpack the bags and load the washer.

"Hey, that's the same detergent I use!"

Jamie grinned. "Isn't that convenient!"

Eventually they found their way into the living room and collapsed onto the couch. Jamie started laughing out of the blue and Kelsey gave her a strange look. The blonde scrubbed her hand over her face tiredly. "Your mother." She shook her head and chuckled again.

Kelsey frowned. "What about my mama?"

Jamie grinned back at her, meaning no disrespect at all. "It's just that she's so, so, Irish!" She burst out laughing again and Kelsey joined her.

"Yes, she certainly is. And embarrassing, you totally forgot to mention embarrassing." Kelsey grimaced.

"Oh, Kels, she's not that bad." Her face softened wistfully. "You can tell she loves you a lot."

They got quiet for a little bit, exhaustion finally making itself known. The early start to the day and all the traveling caught up with them at once. They fell asleep leaning against each other with a soft fleece throw blanket over Kelsey. Jamie woke first about an hour later and found that Kelsey had slid down and was lying with her head in Jamie's lap. Without waking the other woman, she gently ran her hand through Kelsey's thick auburn hair. Her pulse raced as the silky strands slid between her fingertips. After only a few minutes her hand started to wander. She traced Kelsey's temples and forehead, then the shell of her ear. She thought her beautiful friend was still asleep until her fingertips ran down Kelsey's neck and the woman in her lap giggled. Kelsey's voice was sleep-thick as she nuzzled Jamie's hand. "That tickles." When her green eyes opened the first thing she saw was Jamie's mischievous gaze and she knew she was in trouble. "Don't even think about it, James!"

"Think about what? That you would complain about a single little finger tickling you?" She held her hand up menacingly. "What would you do if it was an entire hand, hmm?"

"Don't you dare!"

Jamie's hand came closer. "Or what?"

Kelsey tried her best mean face but the cute little dimple made a serious mean face impossible. "I have my ways!" The hand came a little closer. "Don't make me go all Krav Maga on your ass, Schultz!"

The blonde pretended to consider her options but in all actuality, having Kelsey go "Krav Maga" on her sounded kind of hot. With one last smirk she looked straight into Kelsey's eyes. "Bring it." Jamie's hand was in motion and Kelsey immediately started squirming.

"James! Jaaaammeesss! Stop!" Kelsey wiggled around on the couch, trying to get up, but Jamie just followed her with those strong fingers of hers. "Oh my God, seriously, stop!" Both were panting hard and eventually Kelsey got the upper hand. Using her weight and martial arts training, she flipped Jamie onto her back on the couch, then quickly pinned her to the cushions below. She looked triumphantly down at her winded friend. "Do you surrender?"

Jamie looked up into those green eyes then moved her gaze down to Kelsey's lone dimple and knew she was totally and inescapably lost. Her voice was quiet when she answered. "Always. I will always surrender to you." She paused then decided to throw it all into the wind. "I love you, Kels."

The woman on top released her hands and let out a sigh. "James."

Using Kelsey's words back at her, Jamie reached up to cup her cheek. "Tell me you don't want this and I'll stop. I'll stop and never bring it up again."

Kelsey's eyes welled up with tears but she covered Jamie's hand with her own and pushed both against her face. "I'm scared, Jamie." Jamie's face fell for a second, then Kelsey's words continued into a declaration that was all-encompassing. "I want this with you. I know there is more between us than just sex and I want to discover it all. And I'm sorry I doubted you."

Jamie's smile, her true smile, was like a long lost friend. "So, you want to uh, do this?"

Kelsey snickered. "I think we've already done it a few times."

"No, I mean do you want to date?" Kelsey nodded at her. "Exclusively?" Kelsey smiled and nodded again and Jamie felt a lightness inside that she had never felt before. Yes, she had loved and been in love, but it had never been a love that was good. Before Kelsey it had not been based on truth or respect. And it was not returned with the openness that she witnessed looking back at her with those deep green eyes. She pulled Kelsey down into a kiss that nearly melted her into the couch. A tongue begged entrance between her lips and she was hard pressed to deny Kelsey anything. Minutes went by as the kisses got hotter. Hands wandered outside their clothes until eventually Kelsey's slid beneath the soft cotton t-shirt that Jamie wore. That lone hand started a metaphorical fire and Jamie was about to suggest they go up to her bed when a knock sounded at her door. It took a second for the sound to register but eventually Kelsey pulled back and sat upright. Jamie scowled. "Who the hell could that be? No one even knows I'm back! And how did they get past the security guard?"

Kelsey snorted and crawled off Jamie's body and subsequently off the couch. "Really, James? Your security guard is two naps from a nursing home!" Another knock sounded and suddenly Kelsey remembered who it could be. She looked sheepish as she held her hand out to help Jamie up from the couch. "Um, actually, one person knows we're back."

Jamie looked at her curiously then the answer dawned on her. "That's right, you texted Jenn when we were waiting for our bags." Jamie groaned. "Dammit, I don't want to have company. I want to keep kissing you!"

"I know you're in there. I can hear you talking. Let me in, I think your security guard is after me and he'll be catching up with me any week now!"

Jamie ran a hand through her hair and straightened her clothes while Kelsey snickered and walked over to let their friend in. Jamie called out to Kelsey as she headed for the downstairs bathroom. "I'm just going to go switch the laundry real quick."

As soon as Kelsey opened the door Jenn stepped inside and pulled her into a big hug. "Hey, Kels! I'm so glad that your grand mama's okay." Jenn pulled back and looked around. "Where's James? You did bring her back from the airport with you, right?"

Kelsey cracked up laughing out of the blue and Jenn raised an eyebrow. Kelsey shook her head and finally got control of herself. "Sorry, I just had an image of James riding the luggage carousel around and around, riding someone's suitcase like a bronco."

Jenn chuckled and shook her head too. "You are absolutely insane."

"You didn't figure that out when she admitted to knitting for her cats?" Jamie came around the corner just in time to hear

Jenn's comment.

Kelsey swatted her arm. "Shut up you, like you don't have your own quirks and peculiarities."

Jamie's face was one of shock. "What? What in the world are you talking about?"

"Hello? Olivia? You named your car, and you talk to her like she's a person!"

Jenn's manicured finger poked Jamie in the arm. "She's got you there, James! So anyways, how was the trip? Besides the family drama, of which Jamie managed to survive, did you both have fun?"

Jamie remembered one particular bit of fun and blushed bright red. Kelsey just gave her a genuine smile. "We did actually. Well, the first two days were all family stuff and Jamie was sick, but the last two days we did a lot of sightseeing. I've always loved the Riverwalk there."

"Sick?" Jenn looked over at Jamie, who was still sporting a pink tinge to her cheeks. "Was it a virus? How do you feel now?" Noting the flushed face she felt Jamie's forehead for a fever.

The blonde batted the hand away and shook her head, then swallowed thickly. The memory of both the hangover, and Mama Kaitlyn's remedy would stick with her forever. She was never drinking tequila again. Kelsey came to her rescue, somewhat. "No, she tried to keep up with the Ramirez cousins and failed miserably. So she paid for it the next day. Of course my mama's cure is almost worse than the disease."

Jenn looked at her curiously. "What's in it?"

"No, I do not want to know that!" Jamie had raised her hands to protest and narrowed eyes at Kelsey. "Never ever, ever, tell me."

Kelsey snickered. "Actually, I can't tell you because I don't know. I've only had it once and I will say that I learned to hold my alcohol after that." She looked back at Jenn. "It tastes like sweet bog mud and Jameson with a hint of pepper and it smells like death."

"Holy shit, that sounds awful!" Jenn looked a little horrified at the description but Jamie shook her head and made a face so the black woman questioned it. "What? You're saying it's not awful?"

The blonde made a face. "No, I'm saying that's not the worst part. As soon as it hits your stomach, you have about sixty seconds before you begin purging all the sickness from your body." Jenn looked at her with questioning eyes and Jamie elaborated.

"As in, you better have two receptacles ready!"

"Damn!"

Kelsey nodded. "Exactly!"

"I wouldn't have been so bad the next morning but Kelsey's cousin, Veronica, gave me one more shot at the end of the night that totally pushed me over the edge."

"*Puta!*" Kelsey growled out the word.

Both Jenn and Jamie spun their heads around to look at Kelsey in surprise. Jamie said what they were both thinking. "I thought you didn't know any Spanish!"

The Irish-Latina laughed. "I don't, not really. But my cousins made sure I knew all the important words. She reached down to grab her crotch and leered at both of them. "*Chupa mi verga!*"

"What was that? I know some Spanish but I don't know that. Suck my what?"

Jenn may have looked confused but Jamie immediately cracked up laughing again. "You did not just say that to us!" Then she turned to Jenn and translated. "The word you didn't know is dick. She just told us to suck her dick."

"Our sweet little Kelsey?" Jenn pretended shock.

Jamie shook her head and snorted. "You don't know the half of it!"

Jenn looked back and forth between the two women and gave them both a secret little smile. "Oh, I think I know quite a lot actually. Like what you two were doing before you answered the door."

"We were sleeping!"

"Watching Netflix!"

Both answered at the same time and Jenn smirked. "Uh huh, try again ladies. For one thing, I know what a woman's hair looks like when someone's been running their hands through it. Both of you were in disarray when you answered the door, and your lips are still red and kiss-swollen." She looked back and forth between them. "Is there something you need to tell Auntie Jenn?"

Kelsey looked from Jenn to Jamie and back again. She had no problem telling their friend that they were a couple now, but she didn't know how much Jamie wanted to say. She didn't have to wonder about it more than two seconds because that was all it took for Jamie to respond. "I love her!" She blurted it out like she was two years old and those were the first three words she'd ever learned. Just saying them aloud made Jamie feel new again and strangely whole. She looked at both Jenn and Kelsey who stared back at her in shock. "What? Did you think I'd be all stoic and quiet about my feelings?" She gave Kelsey a look that was both serious and tender. "I'd tell the world if I could."

Jenn broke into a huge grin and she pointed back and forth between the other two women. "Have you told Burke yet?" Jamie shook her head no. "Hot damn, that boy owes me twenty dollars!"

"What?" Kelsey's voice came out a little louder than she intended.

Jamie narrowed her eyes at her friend. "Yeah, what do you mean by that?"

Jenn shrugged. "Burke and I talked about it a bit the night of his birthday party. I told him it would happen before the benefit show. He thought it was going to happen after."

"Happen?" Jamie looked at her curiously.

"You know, you and her getting together serious-like." Jenn grinned again. "I won!"

Kelsey held up a hand. "Wait, what benefit show?"

Jenn looked at Jamie. "You didn't tell her?"

Jamie looked back at her. "When was I supposed to tell her? Things have been a little crazy lately!"

"Tell me what?"

Both heads snapped around to look at Kelsey and Jamie rushed to explain. "Every August the McMillian Center hosts a drag show fundraiser. All the proceeds go toward free and subsidized treatment and drugs. That's how I originally met Jenn. She's friends with the director of the AIDS clinic. Anyway, I've been doing the show for about five years and this year's is almost exactly a month from now. It's on a Friday night, August 12th at 9 p.m." She shrugged. "It's no big deal really. Years ago after I split with Gayle I wanted to do something to help out and one of my friends suggested the drag show." Jenn's eyebrow went up at Jamie's unexpected mention of her ex-girlfriend. The blonde really had changed.

Kelsey looked at them curiously. "So how does it raise money?"

Jenn took over the explanation. "You have to buy tickets to get in. They're twenty dollars a person. The bar donates all their profits for the night to the charity, and the drag kings and queens donate all their tips. It is one of the biggest LGBTQ fundraisers in the city every single year. We even have drag champions that come from out of state to perform, simply because it's for such a good cause."

"Oh! Well count me in then, and I'm going to talk Tam and

Shell into coming too!" She looked at Jamie. "Does Burke perform?"

The blonde shook her head. "No, he says it would be weird for him. He's trans and identifies completely as a man. Whereas with drag, it's all about dressing as the opposite gender. He told me once in no uncertain terms that there was no way a dress would ever cover his body, unless a hot woman was wearing it." They all laughed at something that sounded so incredibly Burke.

When they stopped laughing Jenn watched as her two friends locked eyes. Their look was heavy and hot and she suddenly remembered what she had interrupted with her arrival. "Oh hey, look at the time!" She held up her wrist and looked down at her non-existent watch, then reached into her pants pocket to pull out Kelsey's apartment key. "I just stopped by to drop this off and let you know that I gave your cats some catnip this morning. So, if they burn the place down, it's probably my fault."

"You gave drugs to my babies?"

Jenn gave her a look. "Kels, it is just catnip. All the hip cats are doing it nowadays. They'll be fine."

Kelsey scowled. "I can't believe you got my cats high. It's a gateway drug you know. Before long they'll be out hookin' for Friskies or Pounce or something!"

Jamie snorted. "Do you really believe that?"

"Well, no. But still, I don't do drugs myself so I've never given it to my cats. And before you ask, I'm not opposed to my friends smoking a little weed. It's just not at all for me." She turned to Jamie. "What about you?"

"I've never done any drugs, and I don't want to be with someone who does them even casually." There was a look that crossed her face and Kelsey knew exactly where the look came from. During their conversation on the plane Jamie admitted that drugs, hard and soft, were another one of her ex's wonderful vices. She didn't blame her.

Then another part of Jamie's declaration hit her. "Wait, you've never done anything? Not even a puff on a 'puff-puff-pass'?"

The blonde shook her head. "No, never. And I've never wanted to either, not even when Gayle—" She stopped mid-sentence and shrugged.

Kelsey nodded in understanding. "I tried it twice in college. It was enough to know that I never wanted to do it again. I can't even stand the way it smells." They both turned to Jenn and the black woman laughed.

"James knows I'm not opposed to a little gange on the rare occasion." She raised an eyebrow at Kelsey's shocked face. "What? You think just because I'm a doctor that I'm against it? On the contrary, there have been many studies on its medical effectiveness in treating a variety of symptoms."

"Oh, are you sick?" Kelsey was genuinely curious.

Jenn laughed again. "Hell no! I just like to get high every other full moon!"

Kelsey just shook her head. "And you called me crazy!" After a round of hugs, Jenn left with the promise to save three tickets for Kelsey and her friends. Jenn's personality was a little larger than life sometimes and when she left the condo seemed strangely empty. Kelsey looked up from where her finger was tracing lines in the marbled surface of the island top. The motion that had caught her eye was of Jamie slowly approaching, one step at a time. The blonde's look was heated and she decided to tease a little. "So, what would you like to do now? If you're busy I could probably go home and check on Newman and Pierre."

Jamie came to a stop right in front of Kelsey and reached down to cover her new girlfriend's hand. "Is that what you want to do? Check your cats?"

Kelsey took the bait and stepped even closer, pressing the front of their bodies together from thigh to breast. "Do you have a better suggestion?"

"Hmm." Jamie pretended to consider her options as her breathing increased and her gaze remained fixed on the dark green of Kelsey's irises. "I got some new sheets I could show you."

"Just the sheets, hmm?" Kelsey leaned in, nearly breathing the same air.

Jamie swallowed hard as her gaze moved down to Kelsey's lips. "Um, I also have really spacious drawers in my nightstand."

Kelsey smirked. "And what is so special about your night-stand?"

A hand came up and snaked around behind Kelsey's neck, then fingers threaded through her hair. With only a slight tug, Jamie pulled their faces even closer together. Impossibly close without actually touching lips to one another. Her voice was a husky whisper. "It's where I keep all my favorite toys."

"Oh." Kelsey blinked and smile slowly spread across her lips, perfectly placing that dimple within kissing range. "I love toys."

Jamie leaned a little closer and kissed the dimple, then moved to the side of Kelsey's face and whispered directly into her ear. "I know."

Kelsey shivered then abruptly brought her hands up to grip Jamie tightly by the hair. With one fierce look at the blonde, she crushed their mouths together into a kiss that was nothing but passionate heat. When things threatened the stability of their legs, Kelsey pulled back. "I want to see those sheets now, I want to see your drawer, and most of all I want to see you!" Then without further ado, she grabbed Jamie's hand and started pulling the delighted woman toward the stairs.

Once inside the bedroom, they didn't waste time slowly removing their clothes. Everything came off in a rush then they fell onto the bed in a tangle. Jamie's hand reached down to caress the entire front of Kelsey. The other woman moaned as her nipple rings were twisted and tugged. Jamie was delighted to find two for her to play with. She had only known about the one until the day they had sex at Kelsey's parent's house. But she didn't have time then to play like she wanted, not like that very moment. When her hand started to wander down to caress Kelsey's belly, the woman below her abruptly stopped it. "Don't."

Jamie looked up into an embarrassed face. "Kels? What's wrong?"

Kelsey was self-conscious as she lay there below Jamie. "I just don't like my belly and I don't like people looking at it or touching it."

"Hey." When Kelsey looked up and met Jamie's eyes, the blonde smiled. "I love you, every single part. But I also think every single part of you is beautiful!" She leaned down and kissed Kelsey's belly and trailed her tongue away as she pulled up.

The curvy woman shut her eyes and shivered at Jamie's touch then opened them again and graced her lover with the sweetest dimpled smile. "Thank you. And I love you too."

Jamie froze. She knew that Kelsey cared for her, but she never dared hope that all her feelings were returned. Stupidly she responded to the declaration. "You do?"

"Come here." Kelsey pulled her up and they both rolled onto their sides so they could look each other in the eyes. "I know I tried to fight it, but this has been here for a while now." She brought a hand up to brush away the tear that had started down Jamie's left cheek. "I am utterly and hopelessly gone for you."

"You're in love with me?"

Kelsey nodded. "Completely. You're all I've thought about for months."

She couldn't speak so instead Jamie pulled them into the longest and most tender hug she had inside her. Her voice was muffled against Kelsey's shoulder. "I was so afraid you wouldn't feel the same way."

When Jamie pulled her head back, Kelsey rubbed her cheek with the same thumb that had wiped away the tear. "You don't have to worry any more. I want an equal partnership with you. I want a lover and a best friend. Is that what you want?"

Jamie nodded, understanding Kelsey's double meaning. Knowing that Jamie did worry about her own past with her abusive ex. "That's all I've ever wanted."

"I know, baby. And I'll give you everything I can, and hope that it's all you need."

Jamie smiled. "It will be."

"You know what else I want to give you?" Jamie shook her head and Kelsey abruptly pushed her onto her back and quickly pinned the blonde's hands while straddling her hips. "I want to give you whatever I find inside your drawer. Are you interested?"

Jamie swallowed and her face turned pink with the thoughts that raced through her head. "Oh, God yes!"

"Whatever I want, James?"

The blonde thought about all the things in her drawer and a lazy smirk graced her lips. "Whatever you want. After all, your pleasure is my pleasure."

Kelsey looked down at her with warmth, her eyes filled with heat that was more than just sexual. "I love you so much and I'm glad you're my best friend."

Jamie smiled back at her, enamored by every look and touch. "Meeting you was the best day of my life."

"Well then, let's see if we can one-up that, shall we?" Kelsey abruptly released her and rolled across the bed to open the top drawer of the nightstand. "Oh my!" She glanced back at Jamie. "And you're sure I can pick anything I find in here?" Jamie nodded and Kelsey got a particularly naughty look on her face. Her hand reached into the grab bag of orgasmic things and slowly withdrew a harness. Jamie's breath caught in her throat as she tried to process the fact that one of her greatest fantasies was about to come true. When Kelsey glanced back at the frozen woman, she looked concerned. "Is this not okay? I mean, I love being the giver and receiver, but if you're not comfortable."

She made to put it back but Jamie's hand grabbed her wrist. It took a second to make her words work since her brain was threatening to short circuit. "I'm very comfortable, but I've only ever been the giver."

Kelsey pulled it all the way out of the drawer and held it out to the blonde lying prone on the bed. "Do you want to, um?"

Jamie stopped the hand and a truly wicked smile came over her face. "Eventually. But ladies first. I insist!" Kelsey started laughing, realizing only then how much Jamie really wanted to be topped. She was delighted because she rarely found a woman who was comfortable going both ways. It was something she'd always searched for in a lover. It was perfect. The rest of their afternoon and evening continued the same way. Then again the next day. Parting on Sunday was hard, but both women knew they'd talk first thing in the morning on the way to work. They always did. They also knew their words would have a lot more meaning than before.

THE FOLLOWING WEEK flew by and Kelsey felt busier than normal after four days off. It was Friday morning and she was happy that she was coming up to another weekend. She had met Jamie on Wednesday for drinks like normal, but sadly they went home to their separate places afterward. On her drive to work she waited patiently for Jamie to log into the app so she could say good morning. Even though they could text all they wanted, or even call in the mornings, it just felt right to use the app since that was what brought them together.

"*Hazard voraus auf der Straße.*"

Kelsey glanced at the cell phone in the holder to see the blinking indicator on the road ahead, then pumped her fist. "Woohoo! It's a hazard, I finally understood that one!"

"Good morning, beautiful!"

A quirky dimpled grin formed on Kelsey's face as she down-swiped to answer. "Good morning, nerd! So what are your plans for the night?"

The little blue car sped along in the center lane, not having any problems with the early morning traffic yet. But things were bound to pick up closer to the nexus of the universe. Jamie sighed and thought about her girlfriend's question. Her girlfriend. She still wasn't used to that term, and her heart raced every time she thought the words in her head. It wasn't in a bad way. It was very good actually. Jamie had never met anyone who challenged her like Kelsey did. She was funny and cute, cranky and adorable. Even though they had spent a lot of time together over the previous six months, and she had fallen hopelessly in love with Kelsey, there was still much that they had yet to learn. They'd never even had a proper date. Suddenly Jamie slapped Olivia's steering wheel. "Holy shit, Olivia! We've never even taken our girl out on a real date. Coffee doesn't count. Do I even know how to have a real date?"

"Um, hello? Are you still with me, James?"

Jamie swore. "Oh, yeah. Sorry. Plans, right, I have them!"

Kelsey glanced at her phone in shock and switched out of the center lane. Even though she was in a busy section of highway, she was approaching a long line of slow-moving semis in the middle lane. Sometimes you just had to break the rules. Like when she broke her "no sleeping with friends" rule with Jamie. It all worked out in the end. Thinking about Jamie only brought her back to the burning question in the forefront of her mind. "What plans do you have?"

"I think I'm going on a date."

Kelsey's stomach flipped at her girlfriend's words. At least she hoped Jamie was still her girlfriend. "What do you mean date? Number one, how would you not know for sure? Second, who are you taking out, Jamie Alexa Schultz?"

"I don't know because I haven't asked her yet. I mean, she's kind of hot and I don't want to get shot down." There was a pause and Jamie's voice came across the little speaker of Kelsey's phone again. "She has the cutest dimple on her left cheek and she does this thing with her tongue that simply drives me wild."

The woman in the little silver car successfully navigated around the line of semis and switched back into the center lane. She smirked at Jamie's words and felt her face go hot when the blonde started to talk about one of her favorite tricks during sex. Kelsey willed the heat to go away and responded. "If she's that cute and amazing you better ask her before someone else does. What if she has plans?"

"Oh, no. I have it on good authority that Fridays are reserved for knitting with her cats."

"And you think she's going to give up on all that fun to go have dinner and play arcade games at Harvey's with some scruffy engineer?"

Thirty seconds went by then Jamie's voice came back over the app with a screech. "Scruffy! Woman, I am fly! Wait, did you just ask me out to Highscore Harvey's?"

Kelsey snickered. "Wow, you're awfully slow for a smart girl." She signaled and exited the highway. "So, you'll pick me up at seven tonight?"

Another long pause filled the car with nothing but the sounds of road noise, then Jamie's happy, if shocked, voice came back to her. "Uh, yeah. I mean, yes I will!"

Kelsey went inside the dentist's office just as Jamie was pulling into her parking spot at her own company. She sat in Olivia for a minute just trying to process everything that had just happened. The she grinned as she realized that her tentative half-assed plans were now fully-assed thanks to Kelsey. She snorted. "Oh, she's good!"

Later that afternoon Jamie's boss called her into the office. She poked her head in and saw that he had another man in the guest chair. "Hey there, Jamie, I was getting ready to interview Sam Toomie here for one of the lines on south side. Are you interested in sitting in on the interview with me?"

She looked from her boss to the earnest, if nervous, looking twenty-something man. Her boss routinely grabbed other engineers to sit in on interviews. He thought it brought new insight to the process and gave them a little glimpse at what the managers went through to fill empty rolls. Because of that she had a printout of standard interview questions handy at her desk. "Sure. Do you have a room booked already?"

He nodded. "One-nineteen."

Once they were in the room they took turns asking him a series of questions about his past experience and skills. Sam did well on the questions but seemed very nervous and kept glancing at his watch. At the end, Bob told him that he'd have to report to the nurse for a drug screen. Sam seemed even more distressed at the news. He glanced at his watch again and asked if it would take long. Jamie looked at her boss, and he returned the look for a second, then turned his irritated gaze on the young man. "Is there a problem? Are we keeping you from something, Mr. Toomie?" Jamie's jaw dropped at his response.

"No, but my wife is in labor and I dropped her off at the hospital on my way to the interview."

Bob stared at Sam in shock. "Why didn't you call and reschedule?"

Sam shrugged. "Because I really need this job."

Jamie chimed in. "And how does your wife feel about this?"

The man blushed and smiled. "Oh, Peggy's the reason I'm here. She said that it was her second child so she'd be fine. She told me that it was more important for our family that I go to this interview." After that Bob rushed him out of the office and

directed the man to get to the hospital. He told Sam that they'd
schedule the drug screen in a couple days but that he was hired.

Jamie shook her head in amazement as she walked back to
her cubicle. "Talk about dedication!"

Chapter Nineteen

JAMIE CHECKED HER smart watch as she bent down to give her slim-legged pants a single cuff. She had on her favorite and most broken-in chocolate brown work boots. They were only tied part way, leaving the ankles themselves unlaced. She had a short sleeve button down shirt tucked in with a navy blue bow tie and navy blue suspenders. When she straightened again and looked at herself in the mirror she smirked and said aloud to an empty room. "She invited a nerd to dinner, she's gonna get a nerd." She gave one last straighten of her tie and grabbed her messenger bag off the coat hook by the door.

Back in her apartment Kelsey was going through similar preparations. Only she had two intently curious felines to listen to her rambling. She was in her bathroom with one cat on the back of the toilet and the other sitting on the edge of the tub. Cats loved to have the highest vantage point available to best look down on humans. It was a proven fact. Newman, the significantly less troublesome one of the duo was watching her from the commode. Her hair was pretty easy, not a lot to do there. Kelsey also wasn't big on a lot of makeup so after brushing her teeth she applied a little eyeliner and some gloss and called it good. She looked at her reflection then glanced over at Newman. "This is a big day, Nooms. Jamie and I are going on a real date! You like her, right?"

"Mrow mrrrooooww."

She looked at the sweet black and white cat as he tilted his head at her. She had no idea what he was saying because she wasn't a cat, but her imagination filled it in anyway. "Well yeah, we have slept together already, a few times. But this is different. She said she loves me!"

Newman chirruped at her and put a paw up on the counter. "Mrow."

"Of course I said I loved her back! I'm not that foolish!" Pierre chittered from the tub, as if he were laughing at her. Then he knocked over the shampoo and conditioner bottles before bolting from the bathroom. "Pierre! You're an asshole!" He sassed her from the other room and she went over to replace the bottles on the edge of the tub. Before she could get any more relationship advice from her cats, there was a knock at the door. She gave one last look in the mirror to check her appearance, wondering if Jamie would like the outfit. The blinding white V-neck t-shirt looked great against her tan skin. She wore jeans that hugged her ass perfectly, a black vest, and a pair of black and white casual tennis shoes. Just before walking out of the bathroom, she snatched her sterling silver Celtic knot necklace off the medicine cabinet handle and fastened it around her neck. When she opened the apartment door she expected to see Jamie waiting on the other side. She did not expect her date to be holding out a plastic canister of cat treats.

Jamie smiled sheepishly. "I know it's not very romantic, but I also know that a lot of flowers are poisonous to cats so I brought these instead." When the cats heard the shake of the container they bum-rushed Jamie and she tossed the can to Kelsey to keep them from rubbing all over her dark pants and leaving another cat's worth of hair.

The owner of the cats just laughed. "You scored points with all three of us. But you forgot something."

Jamie became instantly alarmed. "What? What did I forget?" Kelsey reached up and tapped on her full bottom lip, then gave her girlfriend a smile. "Oh, heh." Not needing further invitation, Jamie stepped closer and leaned in for a sweet kiss. When she pulled her head back again they both opened their eyes and smiled. Jamie was first to say it, maybe because it had been so much time since she had truly felt the emotion. She was overfull. "I love you, Kelsey Ramirez."

Hearing Jamie say the words aloud caused a flutter of butterflies in Kelsey's stomach. She knew that the blonde loved her but it always seemed surreal after so many months of longing. But when she said the words, when her lips formed them with such a tender look on her face, Kelsey felt like she was going to melt into a happy little puddle of mush. Her romantic musings were cut short by Jamie's mellow voice. "Are you ready for our first date?"

Kelsey grabbed her apartment key out of the dish by the door and her wallet off the end table. Her cell phone was already tucked into her back pocket. Before they could leave, Jamie insisted on giving the cats two treats before putting them away in the cupboard. Then she reached for the doorknob but before she could get far Kelsey pulled her to a stop. "Hey?" When she turned with a questioning look on her face Kelsey stepped close again and ran a finger along her jaw line. "I really love you too. Sometimes it seems too good to be true. I wake every day like I'm still dreaming and I don't believe it's real until I hear your voice.

That's how much I love you."

Jamie was shocked by her normally more reserved girl-friend's words. She knew Kelsey loved her but when she put it in such a way it filled her with a deep and abiding awe. The smile that spread across Jamie's lips could have lit up an entire room. Instead it lit the heart of just one person.

After they exited it took Kelsey three tries to get the door to shut tight and locked. Her door frame was warped or something but no matter how many times she complained to the apartment management company, it never seemed to get fixed. "I know I say this all the time, but I'm seriously looking for another place at the end of the year. That's when my lease is up and I've had it with this shitty complex!" She sighed and looked into sympathetic brown eyes. "The dryer on my floor isn't even working anymore. I have to trudge down a flight of stairs like a peasant!"

Jamie snickered at Kelsey's dramatics but she understood her frustration because she herself had lived in a place very similar when she first moved to St. Seren. "You're more than welcome to do your laundry at my place." She left the invite open and truth-fully had been wanting to make it for a while. Even before they started dating simply because she craved spending time with Kelsey. "But for now, we have to get on with our first official date!" She was overjoyed to be going with the woman next to her and loved the fact that it was their very first date. She always believed that milestones should be acknowledged and celebrated.

Kelsey looked over her shoulder at Jamie as they made their way down the stairs. "You could argue that this isn't actually our first date. We've technically been going out and doing things together for months."

The other woman looked crestfallen as they made it to the bottom landing of the stairwell. "Oh, I guess you're right."

"Ah, but—" Kelsey paused until Jamie looked up at her. "This is our first date as a couple. It's just that much better that it's also with my best friend."

"That was incredibly cheesy." Both of them laughed and the blonde added to her statement. "But still true."

When they got outside, Kelsey abruptly pulled her date to a stop again. "I, uh, didn't get a chance to say this at the door but this—" She inserted her finger underneath the nearest suspender strap and ran it underneath the navy band, down the front of Jamie's chest. The blonde shuddered as Kelsey's hand brushed over her small breast and sensitive nipple. "This is really fucking hot. Especially the bow tie!" She removed that finger and Jamie was able to take a breath again.

"Oh yeah?" Jamie indicated that Kelsey should turn in a circle and the Irish-Latina obliged her. "Those jeans are a sin! But yeah, I'm totally digging this look on you. You're like cafeteria plan girlfriend."

Kelsey thought about her time in college and the unappetizing array of food at the cafeteria. "What?"

Seeing the dark look on her lover's face, Jamie rushed to explain. "I mean, if I could pick and choose all my favorite things in a woman, all those things that attract me the most, you have them."

"Ooh, so that makes me your dream girl then!" Jamie gave her a goofy grin and nodded and Kelsey giggled at her. "With the exception of one or two things, I'm gonna say ditto babe!"

Jamie walked around to the passenger side of Olivia and opened the door for her date, then went around and got in on her own side. She pushed the brake pedal and waited as Kelsey excitedly pressed the start button. "It never gets old for you, does it?"

Kelsey grinned at her. "Nope."

As they pulled into traffic Jamie brought up Kelsey's comment from minutes before. "So what were the one or two things?"

"Huh?"

She persisted. "You said that with the exception of one or two things, I'd be your dream girl."

"Oh!" Kelsey's look switched to that of understanding. "Before you, I'd always had a thing for girls with blue eyes. And I'm a big fan of dark hair. But don't worry, there are always exceptions to every rule and apparently you're one of them. I like your eyes and as you've said before, your hair is 'on fleek'." When Jamie glanced her way again Kelsey gave her a dimpled grin. "Honestly, I think you're perfect the way you are and I love your dark eyes."

Kelsey's words were not something that Jamie was used to hearing. Though it had been five years since her last relationship, she well remembered how terrible it was. Her previous girlfriend only ever told her what was wrong, or needed to be changed. But with Kelsey it was different. She legitimately seemed to like Jamie's quirky, oft-times, nerdy appearance. And she apparently really liked dark hair. The blonde gave a little secret smile and thought that maybe Richard may get his wish after all. She didn't tell Kelsey any of that. Instead she just nodded and smiled. "I'm glad you like me for me. I think that is one of the most important things for any relationship."

Since it was past happy hour but before a lot of downtown clubs really got going, Jamie found a lucky parking spot just down from Harvey's front entrance. Within a few minutes of exiting the car they were seated in a booth with high back faux leather red seats. Kelsey was practically giddy in her seat, staring around the walls at the graffiti style murals. Then her head whipped back and forth as she took in the arcade machines at opposite ends of the place. Some alternative band that neither of the women had heard of piped through the sound system in the restaurant/arcade. "This place is awesome! You have no idea how excited I am to finally come here!"

Jamie looked at her in shock. "You've never been here before?" Kelsey shook her head. "But this is like, one of the best places in town!"

Kelsey lightly drummed the table with both hands. "I know! That's why I wanted to come here." The waitress interrupted their laughter a few seconds later.

"Hey James! I haven't see you in a while." She glanced at Kelsey, then moved her gaze back to Jamie and subtly flirted. "What can I get you to drink, hot stuff?"

Jamie's face darkened and she reached across the table to interlace her fingers with Kelsey's. "Hi Christy. I don't think you've met my girlfriend Kelsey yet, have you?"

"Girlfriend?" Christy looked from Jamie, to Kelsey, then back down at their joined hands, and back to Kelsey.

Kelsey just peered up at her and winked. "Nice to meet you, Christy. Say, do you have Oberon on draft?"

The poor waitress was still in shock to hear that the perpetually single blonde woman was finally taken. She had spent one night with Jamie about a year previous and never forgot it. But no matter how much she flirted and texted, Jamie insisted they were better as just friends. Her gut burned with jealousy as she looked down at the curvy woman who had finally landed one of the hottest girls she'd ever been with. Before she could answer Kelsey's question, Jamie spoke up. "Yes they do, and I'll have the same, Christy."

The waitress turned and walked away, calling over her shoulder as she left. "Sure thing, James."

"Wow, awkward much?"

Jamie had the decency to blush and shrug her shoulders. "Sorry about that." When Kelsey gave her a curious look, she elaborated. "It was about a year ago, and only once. She got really clingy after that so I had to tell her that we could only be friends.

She was not happy that I didn't want to date."

Kelsey snorted. "She's clearly still not happy about that. What do you want to bet she doesn't remember my drink?"

"What? No way. She's a good waitress, Kels. That other stuff is old news."

Sure enough Christy returned a few minutes later and set a tall glass of beer with an orange slice on the rim in front of Jamie. "Here you go. Are you ready to order yet?"

Jamie looked over at her girlfriend to see if she was mad but Kelsey merely smirked back at her. She sighed. "Actually, Kelsey ordered an Oberon as well, before I did. So I'll just give her mine and if you can bring me one too that would be great. Thanks." Her words were clearly a dismissal and Christy turned away with an angry expression on her face.

"Told you so!" Kelsey pointed her finger toward Jamie's face and the blonde nipped at it with her teeth.

"Hush you! And if you're not propositioning me, put that thing away!"

Christy returned after that with another beer for Jamie and glared at them both with a sour look on her face. "What would you like to order?"

Kelsey cleared her throat and when Christy turned her way she met the disgruntled woman's gaze dead on. "Listen, are we going to have a problem here? Because no matter what sort of past you had with Jamie, right now we are two paying customers who tip well. Jamie and I are dating and we are very committed to each other. Now if that causes you distress, you are welcome to find another waitress to cover your table and receive your tip. Okay?"

Christy glanced around quickly and turned back to Kelsey with a contrite look on her face. She abruptly realized that she was letting something that happened over a year ago affect her job now. And she couldn't afford to lose her job. She took a deep breath and did something she hated. "I'm sorry. Kelsey, is it?" Kelsey nodded and smiled. "It won't happen again. Now what would you two like to order?"

"But she didn't even get to look at the menu!" Jamie was a little concerned when Kelsey confronted Christy but she was also a little flattered that their relationship meant so much to her.

"It's okay, James. I looked at the menu online so I already know what I want." She turned back to the waitress. "I'll have the stuffed jalapeno and pepper jack burger with a side of crack fries."

Jamie grinned at her. "Ooh, spicy!" Then she shook her head. "That one is definitely not for me! I'll have the Harvey Blue and crack fries please, Christy."

Christy's smile was a lot more honest than before Kelsey's little talk. "I'll get that right in for you ladies."

They didn't have any problems after that from the jealous waitress. They ate their stuffed burgers and laughed at the oddest things, as they had always done before becoming lovers. It was hours before they got their fill of food, beer, and games. Jamie looked on as Kelsey lost her final life on a classic standup console. Her beer already finished, she watched as Kelsey drained her own. "So what would you like to do now?"

Kelsey walked both of their glasses over to the nearby bar then came back. "I don't know. Is there anything you'd like to do? I only really know about the club and the pool hall."

"Have you been on the Riverwalk?"

Kelsey thought hard. "I think once when I came to visit Tam and Shell last spring. It's a cool walkway but a little drab in the springtime." She glanced at her cellphone and noted that it was after 10 p.m. "Is it even open right now?"

Jamie shrugged. "It's lit, that makes it open enough for me. Come on, let's go check it out!"

The Riverwalk wasn't far away but they passed a few other businesses and stores before they got there. One such store Jamie had been in numerous times and she pulled Kelsey to a stop. She pointed at the modest display of outfits in the window and wiggled her eyebrows up and down. "Want to go in there?"

All thoughts of scandalizing her girlfriend went out the window when Kelsey's eyes lit up. "Absolutely!" Jamie's jaw dropped open and Kelsey gently reached up to shut her gaping mouth, then deposited the quickest of kisses on her lips. "Come along, James, maybe I'll buy you something nice!" In total they spent nearly half an hour in the store, giggling over some of the more unrealistic items. Jamie ended up buying a pair of black leather wrist cuffs that looked like a cross between biker and kink. She was over by the storeroom door while one of the employees went to get a package from the back, so she couldn't see what Kelsey had purchased. Whatever it was must have been small since Kelsey wasn't carrying any bags after. Jamie just shoved her own purchase into her messenger bag because they didn't really go with her outfit that night.

The Riverwalk had an entrance that was just around the corner from Clara's Closet, the costume and sex toy shop. Kelsey gasped at her first sight of the water at night. The river itself was a dark and serpentine shape that cut through the city center. The entire area was well lit as they went down the stairs to the path below. They had to climb a small gate to get to the lower path but that was the only obstacle. Kelsey stared in amazement as they walked along the wood planking. "I've never been down here at night before. It's gorgeous!"

"They have every bridge lit up in the evening. During big national and international events they even change the colors. When the Supreme Court ruled on gay marriage there was a big celebration at the Blue Bridge and all the lights along the river had been changed to rainbow colors. Of course, they also changed them for the sadder events like the shootings in Paris and Orlando." She sighed. "I really do love this city and the community of acceptance we have here. St. Seren has a lot of heart and I'll never regret moving here."

Kelsey smiled at her. "Me, either."

They walked for a while until they eventually came to the end. The lights along the path had stopped about twenty feet previous so they found themselves in a shaded little nook next to a large tree. Jamie subtly maneuvered Kelsey so her back was against the tree and leaned in to whisper in her ear. "This is the best date I've ever been on."

She pulled back to see Kelsey's reaction but Kelsey was already in motion. She didn't need words to tell the blonde how she felt. Instead she pulled her into a deep kiss. They lost track of time as they made out against the rough bark of the tree. Kelsey nearly collapsed when Jamie insinuated a knee between her legs. The delicious pressure had her whimpering into Jamie's mouth. Finally she couldn't take it anymore and pulled away from the tantalizing lips in front of her. Mouth unclaimed, Jamie moved her lips down along Kelsey's jaw and onto her neck. Despite breaking off the kiss, Kelsey was still going a little bit insane because Jamie kept rhythmically pressing a muscled thigh between her legs. Her voice came out as a hiss. "Jaaaam-mmeesss!"

Jamie pulled her lips away from nibbling on Kelsey's earlobe. "Yes?"

Kelsey tried to speak like normal but the pressure continued to build. "Nghuh, y—you have t—to stop! God, baby, I'm so close!"

A wicked grin came over the blonde's face as she took in her girlfriend's parted lips and panting breath. "Oh, really? I thought you were a hard sell, Kels?"

Kelsey opened her eyes and made a face. "A—apparently I do—don't have that problem with you." Her hands had moved from Jamie's waist down to her hips. "Baby, we can't do this here."

"What's the matter? There's no one around. Haven't you ever wanted to be naughty?" Jamie watched Kelsey's eyes darken as she licked her lips, and she had her answer. While Kelsey continued to grind down against her leg, she managed to move her hand around to open the top button of Kelsey's jeans. Once the button was open it was nothing for Jamie to push her hand into the front of her girlfriend's pants. She moaned as she slid beneath Kelsey's underwear and her fingers were enveloped in wet heat. There was no way she could go inside at that angle and with such tight pants, but she could feel Kelsey's hard clit as she stroked along the sides of it with her fingers. They both moaned at the contact and Jamie could feel herself getting wet as well.

"James."

Jamie brought her lips close to Kelsey's again. "Shh, just let go and let me catch you, I'm right here, honey. Oh God, you're so close, aren't you?"

Kelsey whimpered. "Mmm hmm." She was barely noticing anything at that point but a few figures coming down the path about thirty feet away caught her eye. Jamie looked in the direction of her girlfriends gaze and rather than stop she sped up her ministrations. Kelsey's wide-eyed gaze turned back to her just as she stiffened with her impending orgasm. Jamie was an experienced lover and if there was one thing she knew for sure, that was when a woman was coming. Kelsey's mons and clit hardened further under Jamie's fingertips and that was how she knew to steal her girlfriend's scream with a kiss. The auburn haired woman bucked beneath her fingers but she remained silent with Jamie's help. The group of teenagers never even noticed them in the darkness by the tree and they passed the amorous couple to climb the blocks at the end of the path. Jamie slowed her fingers and eventually stopped all movement. Her forearm was killing her from the awkward position but it was well worth it to see the satisfied smile on Kelsey's face as she pulled away from her lips. "You are so bad, Schultz! What if those kids had seen us?"

Jamie shook her head and laughed, then stepped away so Kelsey could do up her button. Wobbly legs held them up as the two women attempted to straighten their cloths. "That is not what you said earlier this week. I'm pretty sure you called me very, very good!"

The other woman snickered. "So I did." Then she pointed at Jamie. "But don't think for a second you're not going to pay for that!"

"Oh, I'm already paying for it." Jamie grimaced. "It is going to be the most uncomfortable walk back to the car for me!"

Kelsey smirked. "I could just finish you off here, if you'd like?"

Jamie shook her head. "I think we've pushed our luck enough tonight."

Rather than try to convince her girlfriend, Kelsey merely nodded and focused on something at Jamie's shoulder. "Yes, we probably shouldn't stay down here." Then in a move that was faster than Jamie could really prepare for, Kelsey's hand came up and flicked something from the blonde's shoulder. Jamie thought it seemed large by the sound it made as Kelsey's finger connected with it.

Alarmed, Jamie glanced at her shoulder then back at Kelsey. "What was that?"

Kelsey looked up then grabbed her girlfriend's hand and moved them away from the tree. When they were safely back on the walkway, she spoke up. "You never mentioned there were big spiders along the river."

"What!" Jamie's screech and panicked dance had Kelsey in tears with laughter. Jamie was flailing around, frantically brushing at her clothes while reciting her usual mantra of fear and revulsion. "Oh my God, oh my God, oh my God!"

Kelsey did her best to still the laughter and quickly grabbed Jamie's hands. "Hey, hey! There's nothing on you now. You're safe!" She smirked. "I promise not to let the big bad spiders get you." She leered at her girlfriend and tightened her grip. "But I will make no such promise for myself! Can we go now? I believe I owe you some attention. Perhaps we can go park somewhere and break in Olivia?"

Jamie glanced from their joined hands to Kelsey's face and looked startled. "Oh. Um, Olivia's never, uh, been broken in like that before." She raised a pale eyebrow. "It's a little small inside, don't you think?"

Kelsey just grinned and pulled her back up onto the boardwalk. "Come along 'hot stuff,' I think we can make it work."

Fifteen minutes later they were back in Jamie's car and she turned to the woman in her passenger seat. "So do you want me to take you back to your apartment, or would you like to go to my place?"

"Nuh uh, not so fast! We're going to christen Olivia, remember?"

Jamie's lips parted but nothing came out at first. She had met a lot of women who, in varying degrees, all loved sex. But she had yet to meet anyone who seemed to fill all her needs as Kelsey did. She was her best friend, and she was fun and funny and spontaneous. She also loved sex and adventure. It was almost too good to be true to find so many perfect qualities in someone she loved and who loved her in return. "You were serious about that?"

Kelsey's dimple went away as her lips pulled into a frown. "We don't have to, James. I know not everyone is comfortable doing something so open and possibly awkward. I just thought it would be fun."

"No!" Kelsey startled and Jamie rushed to explain. "No, it sounds hot! I'm definitely game to break in Olivia. It's long overdue." She drove them to a secluded park that was close to Kelsey's apartment complex and parked near the trees. There was one streetlight shining down on a basketball court at the opposite end of the park, but that was the only illumination. It was perfect. She turned to her girlfriend, wondering about the logistics of her plan. "So, ah, how are we going to do this? We could maybe go outside to a picnic table."

Kelsey reached down and grabbed the lever to slide her seat back as far as it would go, then she leaned it back slightly and patted her lap. She gave Jamie a wicked look. "Or you could come over here and sit on my lap." On closer inspection, there was room on either side of Kelsey's legs for her own knees so she could hypothetically straddle her girlfriend's lap. However, they would be short of head room. Kelsey crooked her finger at her and motioned her closer. "James, you at least owe me a try."

Jamie smirked. "So I do." Through a lot of awkward maneuvering, she climbed across the center console and settled in above Kelsey. She only hit her head three times on the sunroof window.

"How's your head?"

"It's perfect." With Kelsey's seat leaned back, she had no problems with headroom once she leaned down and started kissing her. After making out for a good ten minutes, Jamie pulled back and groaned. "You have no idea how turned on I am right now but I don't see how this is going to work."

Kelsey unbuttoned the blonde's pants and pulled down her zipper. "Trust me."

"Kels, it's no good. My pants are too tight like this!" She pouted and stared down at Kelsey, extremely frustrated.

Her girlfriend smirked back at her and wiggled around so she could get a small item out of her own pants pocket, then reached into the other side and withdrew another item. "While you were in the back waiting on your cuffs, I had the front sales lady clean this off for me and put batteries in."

Jamie looked down curiously and saw a silver oval in Kelsey's left hand and a small box with a switch in the other hand. "Is that?"

"A remote control bullet? Why, yes it is! Care to try it out?" Jamie nodded excitedly and Kelsey handed her the bullet. "Put this down where you want it most." The blonde sat up a little to do as instructed. Once it was in place she smiled and gazed down at Kelsey expectantly. The woman on the bottom abruptly flicked the switch and Jamie threw her head back and connected solidly with the roof window again.

"Ow, shit, oh my God!" Jamie moaned and Kelsey quickly turned the vibrator off, then Jamie whined. "That was mean!"

Kelsey chuckled as her girlfriend ran a gamut of different reactions. "Sorry, James, I should probably turn it down, huh?"

Jamie leaned down and whispered in her girlfriend's ear. "To start at least."

Her ears were very sensitive and Kelsey shuddered to have Jamie's lips so near. When they started kissing again Jamie moved her hands up and found Kelsey's nipple rings through the fabric of her shirt and bra. As Kelsey got turned on more and more she started increasing the slide that controlled the bullet and Jamie ground down into her. Jamie pulled away for a second to moan loudly in the small car and Kelsey took that opportunity to increase the speed a little more. "You like that?" Jamie didn't say anything. She couldn't. She was wound too tight as her hips moved against Kelsey's abdomen and her hands pinched the nipples below her. Then all vibration stopped and she shuddered and looked down to see Kelsey grinning evilly.

Jamie whimpered a sad and pathetic sound. "No—" But before she could protest again, the sensation came back stronger than before. "Oh shit!" Kelsey's lips curled into a satisfied smile as she watched Jamie come apart above her. Just as the blonde went into the throws of orgasm, someone knocked on their window. Kelsey glanced to the right and saw a very stern-faced police officer looking in on them. She was dressed for patrol with the hat and the prerequisite flashlight in hand. With no small amount of panic at being caught, Kelsey's finger slipped the rest of the way up on the remote and sent Jamie into another round of intense orgasmic contractions. Jamie too had seen the cop and was dismayed to find that rather than winding down enough to function and talk their way out of the situation, she was instead losing her mind to pleasure that was very inappropriate to the situation. "Oh my God, fucking hell Kels!" As the orgasm waned, she weakly pawed at the crotch of her pants and Kelsey quickly shut off the device.

"I'm so sorry, are you okay, James?" She looked dismayed at her spent girlfriend and the tapping sounded again at the window. Kelsey twisted her head around and gave the cop an evil glare. "All right already, can you give us just a minute to be presentable?"

It was in that moment that Officer Jan Stevens realized that the perverts she thought she had caught in the park afterhours were none other than two women discussing their mutual love of Georgia O'Keeffe paintings. Her sour face disappeared and she grinned down through the window of the little blue car. "No problem, ladies. Take your time. But you should probably move along soon." Then she tipped her hat at them and said a few words as she walked away. "Have a *great* night!"

Jamie had collapsed onto Kelsey's chest so she was jostled as the woman below her started laughing hysterically. "Holy hell! That is absolutely a first for me!"

The blonde slowly lifted her head and looked down into the dimpled face of the woman who had stolen her heart. She only had three little words for her. "Best. Date. Ever."

Chapter Twenty

THE WOMEN ENDED up spending Friday night at Kelsey's apartment and Saturday night at Jamie's condo. On Jamie's urging, Kelsey even brought her laundry over to wash in Jamie's machine. It was a lot nicer than using the sketchy things at the complex. The view was much better too as they lounged around in boxers and tank tops half the day, watching bad movies and making out. But it was a sad parting on Sunday night when they separated again to complete their weekend routines. Even though they hadn't been officially dating very long Kelsey hated going home on Sunday nights. They had been spending a lot of time together for months, at least since they started meeting for coffee and cocoa every Wednesday. So while the relationship was new, it felt a lot older to both of them. Monday morning Jamie was excited to get in her car and head to work. Not because she had any burning desire to put in time on her current engineering projects but because she wanted to hear Kelsey's voice. It was always a rush to see who could beat the other to a morning greeting. That Monday morning Jamie won. "Good morning rainbow car, how did you sleep last night?"

Kelsey's laugher came over the speakers first. "Since you're asking about my car, she slept fine once I removed the key. Now if we're talking about me, I was lonely!"

Jamie smiled, delighted that Kelsey had admitted to missing her. "Aww, I'm sorry Kels. I would have been there to snuggle you but we both had to get stuff done last night."

"I'm pouting."

"You're adorable." And Jamie knew that her girlfriend was adorable. Perhaps the most adorable woman she'd ever known.

Kelsey was in her own car pouting just as promised. She loved that she could hear the affection in Jamie's voice, even over the terrible little speaker of her phone. She remembered her conversation with her friend Tam the night before and relayed the invite to her girlfriend. Just thinking the word made Kelsey smile. "Hey, I was chatting with Tam last night and they invited us both to their annual end of July barbecue."

"I'm pretty sure your friend Tam hates me."

Kelsey glanced at her phone and switched lanes to position herself for the approaching exit. She responded. "She doesn't hate you. Why would you say that?"

"She wasn't too fond of me at the surprise party last month."

"Was it only last month? That seems crazy, doesn't it? I feel like we've been dating so much longer. And Tam has been my friend for a long time, so she tends to be over-protective. She'll be fine though, I promise."

Jamie smiled in her own car as she easily slid back into the center lane. "Me too. All right, I'll trust you, Kels."

KELSEY PROVED RIGHT on the day of the barbecue. Tam did corner Jamie at one point in the afternoon, under the guise of taking the blonde a beer. She looked up at the androgynous engineer. "So, you and Kelsey huh? I gotta admit, I've heard plenty about you, Schultz."

Jamie looked down at her seriously and shook her head. "I'm sure you have. Everyone has a past. Say what you need to say, but get it all out now because no matter what you tell me I'm going to give you the same answer."

Tam narrowed her eyes at her. "And what answer is your answer? That it's none of my business?"

The blonde smiled and her face was transformed in an instant. There was nothing anyone could tell her that would tear her away from Kelsey. "I love her and I would give anything to stay in her life."

Kelsey's friend and old college roommate peered at her for a minute after that to gauge sincerity and eventually found what she searched for. Her stance relaxed and she held out her beer to clink bottles with Jamie. "Welcome to the family, Jamie."

THE FOLLOWING TUESDAY found Jamie and Kelsey chatting on their way home from work. "So did you find out why your class was cancelled last night?"

"Apparently our instructor and his assistant both came down with chicken pox."

Jamie raised an eyebrow as she logged a vehicle into the app that was stopped on the side of the road. "And neither one had gotten them before?"

"I guess not."

They continued talking with the app for a while until Jamie had to sign off in order to run errands. She texted Kelsey after dinner.

```
    Hey, since you're not sore, would you be interested
in going to a movie tonight?
```

```
    Jaaammmeeesss! I'm already in my sweatpants!
```

Jamie laughed and texted back.

```
    Would you like to come over to my place for a movie?
```

She waited a few seconds for Kelsey to send another text. When it came through the blonde cracked up laughing. It was a picture of Kelsey on the couch with not one, but two cats in her lap. The caption was what had her laughing hardest though.

```
    Apparently I couldn't move even if a fire swept
through the building because...cats.
```

Jamie debated on what to do then sent another text.

```
    How would you like me to come over to your place for
a movie?
```

```
    Bingo, we have a winner! PS - throw some popcorn in
your overnight bag because I'm all out. Love you, see
you soon!
```

There was no one around to see her shake her head in astonishment at the way she had just been played. "Well done, Kels, well done." She suspected that Kelsey's troublesome cats were also in on the scheme. But she also didn't waste any time packing an overnight bag and grabbing a box of microwave popcorn on her way out the door.

FRIDAY ON THE way home from work Jamie excitedly messaged the rainbow car when Kelsey logged into the app. "Hey, do you have any plans tomorrow night?"

"Hello to you too, nerd. And I might have to check my busy social calendar and let you know."

Jamie snickered. "Oh, you mean go home and ask Newman and Pierre if they mind skipping their Caturday night knitting class?"

"Ass! Did you just think of that yourself?"

"Yup! Seriously though, my coworker Bill had two extra tickets that he won through a raffle for the comedy show downtown.

He offered them to me and of course I said yes."

"And what if I had said I was busy?"

Jamie smiled and joked with the woman on the other end of her app. "Then I'd ask my other girlfriend to go with me." She expected Kelsey to call her an ass again, or make some other remark, but there was only silence on the other end, a silence that continued for a few minutes. Suddenly she remembered that Kelsey had also been cheated on in her previous relationship and that her trauma was a lot more recent comparatively. She hit her forehead with the palm of her hand. "I'm such an idiot!" She quickly swiped down on the screen. "Hey, you know I'm only joking, right?"

The voice that came back to her seemed forced. "Yeah, sure I do. You were just kidding."

Jamie couldn't leave it like that. She had to try again. "Kelsey?" She waited for a response.

"Yeah?" Kelsey's voice was flat.

"I have never loved anyone like I love you, not even Gayle. And I have never felt safer with anyone in my life, the way that I do when I'm with you. You've got me all the way, understand? I'm all in with us."

Kelsey was about fifteen minutes behind Jamie on the highway and her stomach had initially flipped a few times at the offhand comment about asking her other girlfriend. She didn't realize until that moment how much her previous relationship had colored the current one. Jamie's words after that nearly made her cry. They had spent many hours talking, many nights up late telling each other about their pasts. She knew that Jamie had always been loyal in previous relationships, as had Kelsey. And it was also Jamie's words that prompted a wave of affection to sweep through her. Kelsey sniffed and decided she needed to check her menstrual app to see if she was getting ready to start. She quickly reassured her girlfriend that she was not a psycho who was overly-sensitive about the smallest things. Even though she probably seemed that way just then. "I believe you, and I'm in all the way too. I'm sorry I got weird for a second." She smiled at Jamie's response a minute later.

"It's okay. I'm a nerd and I love weird so, you know, it's all good! Now about the tickets?"

Kelsey smiled at her sweet, if nerdy, lover and responded to the question. "I'd say it's a date, but only if you wear one of those bow tie combos you know I like so much. Just text me the details when you get home."

"Will do!"

THEIR DAYS PROGRESSED that way with lots of conversation and many mini-dates between them. One week later found them chatting on the way to work. It was Friday morning and Jamie was nothing but nerves. She had finalized her decision the previous night in a frantic texting session with her hairdresser. Truthfully she had been thinking about the change for a while but hadn't worked up the resolve to actually schedule the appointment. She was two weeks early for her regular cut and color but sometimes you just had to step outside your box and break the rules.

Because Jamie was nervous and distracted Kelsey beat her to the morning greeting. "Good morning, nerd. Are you ready for tonight? Do the drag kings pack underneath their outfits? I've always wanted to know what the bulge was."

Jamie started choking on her coffee as Kelsey's cheery voice came through her sound system with its very naughty question. She grabbed some napkins out of her door but luckily the coffee only spilled on her jacket. "Seriously woman, you just made me choke on my coffee again!"

"I told you when you met me that you should learn how to swallow better instead of spitting all the damn time!"

Jamie waited for an entire ten seconds, then she couldn't hold it in any longer. She responded with glee. "That's what she said!"

Kelsey's snort came back to her. "Ass! And you didn't answer my question."

"I guess you'll just have to wait until later to find out. Now you're still planning on staying at my place tonight, right?"

"Yes ma'am I am! I'm riding with Tam, Shell, and Jenn to the club. I'll put my overnight bag into Olivia. Burke is coming into town early and riding with you to the club two hours before the show starts, so he'll save us all a table near the stage." There was a few seconds pause after Kelsey's message finished, then her cute little whine came on again a minute later. "Why can't I just go early with you and Burke?"

Jamie smirked at the abundant curiosity that Kelsey had displayed on a nearly daily basis when it came to the drag show. Specifically, Jamie's outfit and routine for the drag show. She tried to ease some of the curiosity. "Because Burke will be running the lights for the stage. We've got everything all worked out. It's going to be fine. Trust me!" A response came back a few minutes later.

"So why are you so nervous then? I can hear it in your voice."

The blonde sighed as she signaled to get over out of the middle lane then answered her girlfriend. "Because I'm always nervous before performance. Because what if I forgot my words, or my moves, or even the entire song?" Before she could forget her news with another bout of show-oriented nervousness, she relayed information about her afternoon. "Hey, we're not going to be able to talk on the way home after work."

"What do you mean?"

She tapped the custom shifter underneath her fingertips then reached up to reply. "I'm getting out of work a few hours early so Richard can give me a last minute trim and style."

"Really James? It's only been a few weeks. Oh, and watch out for the dead skunk in the center lane."

Jamie laughed. "Did you find it with your tire?"

Kelsey's bold voice huffed back to her through the sound system. "No, I was in the far lane, thank you very much. Had I been in the center lane I would have nailed that sucker before I even knew it was there! See? I keep telling you that sometimes you have to break your 'rules of the road.'"

After a glance to see that there was indeed an object on the road listed just ahead, Jamie quickly changed lanes. She did not need Olivia smelling for the evening ahead. She responded once she was safely around the smeared and reeking hazard. "Ha, ha, my rules work very well for me, thank you!" She drove along for another minute before she thought of the other thing she needed to tell Kelsey. "And just as an FYI, I'll be pretty busy today since I'm leaving early but I'll text you whenever I can."

"Aww, you're pretty sweet when you want to be. Such a loving little nerd!"

Jamie thought about Kelsey's words and responded with nothing but the truth. "Only with you." They didn't say much more during the drive, which was probably good for Jamie's concentration. She was already focused on her commute, her current project at work, and the choices she'd made concerning the evening ahead. Jamie grinned, nervous but still resolute. She was definitely all in.

"ARE YOU SURE?" Richard stared at Jamie through the mirror from his place just behind the chair. "I mean, your hair looks great the way it is."

Jamie reached up and ran her hand through the blonde locks on top of her head. Then she met his sympathetic eyes. "I can't move on with my future if I'm still living up to past expectations."

He nodded. "Sweetie, I don't think I've ever heard you say truer words." He started fussing with the top. "I may have to tweak the style just a bit with such a dark shade, but it will look great! Let me just go mix the color. I'll be right back." A few minutes later he returned with a little cart that had the bowl of paste and various brushes on it. "It's been a long time but I think I remember what your original hair looked like." Ten minutes later he had her coated and moved off to the side to set. She texted Kelsey on her phone while she waited and Richard did a trim on a few other clients. She felt nervous butterflies all the way until he had her dried and styled and spun the chair around so she could see it in the mirror.

She couldn't speak for an entire minute. It had been a long time since she last saw herself with dark hair. At least ten years. She continued to stare at the foreign face in front of her and felt something break free inside her. "That's it." He looked at her curiously. "That's all that was left tying me to her. It's taken me five years but I think I'm finally back to just being me."

Richard smiled and rested his hand on her shoulder. "Honey, you've always been you. But she put a patina over your shine for the longest time. We just cleaned you off a bit." He jokingly brushed off her shoulder with his hand. "So what are you performing tonight? You know I'd totally be there if I could but I have tickets to see *Wicked* and I'm not giving those up for anything! Besides, you know some queen will want her face immortalized and will have a video of the entire show posted online. I'll watch that."

Jamie smirked into the mirror and ran a hand through the nearly black mop. "You think I could pull off Adam Lambert?"

A delighted smile came over his face. "Oh girl! I think you will bitch slap Adam and steal all his fans! Now I know we made the right decision. Your lady love isn't going to know what hit her tonight!"

She grinned back at him in the mirror, still nervous but more confident than she'd been in years. "I'm counting on it."

JENN ACTUALLY LIVED down the street from Tam and Shell so she just walked to their place. The three of them picked up Kelsey from her apartment. They arrived at quarter after six so they'd have time to order a pizza from the kitchen and eat before the show started. Kelsey didn't see her girlfriend anywhere but found Burke seated on a high box where the spotlight was located. "Hey handsome, have you seem Jamie?"

Burke broke out into a smile and swung down from the box like a monkey. "Kelsey! How have you been, beautiful?"

They hugged and Kelsey couldn't help flashing her dimpled smile. Not only had she gained an amazing girlfriend, but she had also made some great friends through that girlfriend. She had discovered over the months since she'd come to know Burke and Jenn that they were both very real and wonderful people. Even if they were making bets on the outcome of Kelsey and Jamie's relationship. "Things have been really great lately."

He gave her a knowing look. "Yeah?"

Kelsey blushed. "Yeah, she makes me smile so much, it's crazy!"

"Good for you, Kels! You two deserve each other because you're both good people and you're just too damn cute as a couple!" He gave her another one armed hug and laughed as she blushed even darker.

"Thanks, buddy." She looked around one more time. "So do you know where Jamie is?"

Burke smiled because he knew a secret that was going to shock everyone. "Yup. She's in the dressing room upstairs but no one can go up there unless they're performing tonight. So you're just going to have to wait to see your sweet Baboo."

Kelsey chucked him in the arm. "You're such an ass! Fine, I'll just go back to our table and eat pizza while I patiently wait for her to come down." She watched him for a beat longer but he wasn't giving anything away. After a few seconds of his infernal smirking she sighed and gave up before turning back to the table. She got there just in time to hear the bickering start.

"Y'all know I can't eat that, right?"

Tam looked at Jenn like she was crazy and Shell just shook her head. "What? It's just cheese, onion, and mushrooms! There is no meat at all on this pizza"

Jenn gave the short butch woman an irritated look. "How long have we been friends?"

"About six years, why?"

"And have you ever known me to eat cheese?"

Tam pointed at her triumphantly. "Yes! You eat cheese whenever we go to Brick Road for pizza!"

Jenn sighed and Shell gave her wife an eye roll. Kelsey put a hand on her long time friend's shoulder. "Tam Tam, you know that's vegan cheese, right? It's not regular cheese."

Tam turned to look up at her. "What do you mean it's not regular cheese? Cheese is cheese!"

"And what is cheese made of?"

The shorter woman thought for a minute. "Milk? And uh, yellow magic?"

Kelsey snickered and Shell finally stepped in at least figuratively since they were all seated but Kelsey. "Babe, you're right in that regular cheese is made from milk. But vegans don't believe in eating anything that comes from animals. So that means milk, eggs, cheese, yogurt, meat, and a lot more. Do you understand now?"

"Oh my God!" Tam whipped her head around to stare at Jenn with horror. "What the hell do you eat, woman?"

Jenn wiggled her eye brows in response. "Yes."

Tam wore her confused look well, but Kelsey had also tried it on. "Huh?" Shell started laughing before an explanation could be given so Jenn elaborated.

"Yes, I eat woman."

"Oh fecking hell!" Shell snickered to herself because Kelsey had started to pick up Jamie's favorite phrase. Unaware of the scrutiny, Kelsey continued her rant. "Seriously, you are all crazy!" Kelsey turned to Jenn specifically. "I already checked ahead of time and the bar has a small vegan menu. Just ask the server." She shrugged. "I mean, it's probably only twigs and berries but at least you'll have something."

Jenn stuck her tongue out. "Why are you guys always hating on me? So mean!"

Kelsey winked at her. "Come to the dark side, Jenn. We have bacon!" The black woman rolled her eyes and the other three started laughing at her so she flipped them off.

The three other women chorused together. "We love you, Jenn!" Then they all burst out laughing even harder.

Before long the leftovers of their meal were packaged up and the show started. They had one announcer for the night, Kitty Deville, who was a hilarious drag queen that regularly hosted bingo on Sunday afternoons. Kitty was actually the one who gave Jamie her drag name and always referred to her as "drag family", a brother. The show alternated drag kings and drag queens as they went, and she announced each performer before they came out. Of course there was plenty of color commentary.

The four women moved from their table to stand at the end of the dance floor once the show started. Everyone had fistfuls of dollar bills to tip the kings and queens that strutted their stuff to a variety of music. Most of it was faster paced with a lot of dancing, but once in a while someone came out as a classic crooner or ingénue. Kelsey was starting to get impatient, wondering when Jamie was going to go on, when Kitty introduced the next drag king in the lineup. "I'd like you all to give a big gay welcome to our next performer, Devin Deville!" Then she waved vaguely off toward the bar staff. "And you all might want to get a broom out here for cleanup because after this number some panties are gonna hit the floor!"

All Kelsey could see was a king sporting dark hair who was dressed in some sort of post-apocalyptic punk outfit. She sighed in disappointment. "Holy shit!" Kelsey whipped her head around and looked at Jenn curiously. The black woman's mouth was open and she pointed at the drag king who was waiting to go on. "Devin Deville is Jamie's drag name!"

Kelsey turned to look back at the drag king walking toward the center of the stage area. They had the lights down so it was impossible to make out his features, just the clothes. Her eyes worked from the ground up. Heavy black boots started the look. Black pants with zippers all around the legs had chains crisscrossing slim hips. A sleeveless leather jacket with more zippers was left open to the tight black t-shirt below. The king's hands were in fists, side by side straight down in front of him and Kelsey was drawn to the leather cuffs on Devin Deville's wrists. They were the cuffs that Jamie had just purchased on their first official date. Her head jerked up quickly, trying to see the features she had come to know and love, silently begging the lights to come up.

She didn't recognize the music when it started but as soon as the lyrics began she gasped. The lights came up and Jamie was in motion as soon as the first words to Adam Lambert's "If I Had You" came across the sound system. Besides the massively different color change from her normal look, Jamie's hair was altered slightly from the normal undercut to an undercut fade. The black hair was lifted and styled back to give her face a look that was nothing but fierce angles and shadow in the flashing lights. Kelsey's response slipped out unwittingly. "Fuck me." She didn't think it was loud enough to be heard over the music but Jenn laughed next to her. The smell of sandalwood invaded her senses as Jenn leaned closer to speak into her ear.

"She's singing to you. You might want to get some dollars out and step a little closer." Then the black woman gave Kelsey a little shove to her back. Kelsey was still in shock as she watched Jamie strut around the dance floor that had been roped in and turned into a makeshift stage. James thoroughly worked the crowd while lip-synching to the fast paced romantic ballad of sorts. The drag king Devin Deville was all motion and sex appeal as he made his way around the people lining the stage, graciously accepting dollars and offering hugs and handshakes. Occasionally he would dance back to the center, then continue around the opposite side. Devin Deville was amazing and Kelsey parted her lips with her attraction to the new side of Jamie that she'd never seen.

Jamie was nothing but nerves leading up to the performance but she felt good in her outfit and she had the words memorized completely. It wasn't her first time doing drag after all, so she knew all the right moves and how to work the crowd. It was a given that every single person who tipped her got a little personal attention in return. A hug, a kiss on the cheek or a hand shake, most of them had known her for years.

She smiled inwardly at the thought that most of the people in the crowd assumed she probably dyed her hair just for the show. But only one for certain knew the truth. She hadn't even told Burke that her natural color was nearly black. She scanned the crowd for Kelsey before her song, but it was too dark to see. And once the spotlight came on she really couldn't make out anyone until she was right in front of them. That was how she found herself staring into Kelsey's eyes during the quietest most intimate part of the song. Jamie drank in Kelsey's expression of love and lust. She reached up to caress a soft cheek as she mouthed the lyrics to her as if they meant everything, and maybe they did. Then she pulled away abruptly as the music picked up again.

Kelsey rolled her eyes as her girlfriend danced away with the music. Jamie had purposely teased her and would definitely pay later. Oh, how she would pay! When the song was over Jamie exited the same way she came in and a volunteer ran around collecting the money that had been dropped. All of it was going to the same place that night, but at least the drag kings and queens didn't have to scuttle around picking money off the floor after their number was done. Kelsey stepped back out of the crowd once Jamie disappeared. She was determined to find the sexy, dark-haired king who had stolen her heart. Her friends followed her back, all of them in shock for various reasons at Jamie's performance. Shell was the first to speak out of the four of them. "Fuck me! That was hot."

She was all matter-of-fact about it and Tam turned to protest the declaration. Then she stopped and shrugged her shoulders. "You know, she's right. I can't even deny it." She looked at Kelsey and smiled at her old college roommate. "And I can't deny that she only had eyes for you as she danced around just now. All those hot young girls and she couldn't take her eyes off my good friend. You were right about her, Kels."

"Of course she was right. Jamie is good people!" Jenn was all smiles with a little astonishment left over. "I still can't believe she dyed her hair for this one number though. Talk about bold!"

Kelsey smiled that secret little smile that brought out her dimple in high relief. "She didn't." All three women turned to her with incredulous looks as another dance number went on in the background. She laughed at their expressions. "I mean, she did dye it, but I believe only back to her natural color."

"What?" Jenn's voice was a mid-level screech. "How the hell didn't I know that?"

Kelsey arched an eyebrow at the only other woman of their immediate group who had also slept with Jamie. "How didn't you know that? I mean, it's not like the curtains match the carpet."

Jenn panicked, suddenly feeling awkward. "I, uh, I don't want to talk about that with you! She's your girlfriend!"

Kelsey shrugged. "What? Her past is the past. I'm not threatened by it. I know she loves me."

After a long sigh Jenn finally caved. "At the time we uh, were messing around, she was usually shaved."

"Ooh!" Tam made a face. "I tried that once but I scratched at my crotch for a week, like I had crabs."

Shell nodded. "It's true, she did. It was not a good look for her, either."

Tam spun her gaze around to her wife. "What do you mean it wasn't a good look?"

Kelsey giggled as Shell shrugged her shoulders at her wife. "You looked like a pug with its tongue hanging out, only all hairless and funny looking. Sideways."

Tam's face turned pink just as Jenn slapped a palm over her own mouth to avoid saying anything. Kelsey just turned away to laugh where her long-time friend couldn't see. That was when she locked eyes on Jamie who was making her way slowly down the stairs. Everything else fell away in that moment as they worked their way toward each other. Jamie's face alternated between hesitant and predatory. Kelsey had a feeling she knew why. She herself wore jeans that had practically been poured on, showing her ass to perfection. She had tall black boots that came up to her knees. But the most revealing part of the outfit was the leather vest she wore over top of a black lace bra. Most everyone else was still off by the dance floor so they met in the middle of the tables where it was pretty empty. Kelsey spoke first. "Hi."

Jamie lowered her eyes shyly, unsure of Kelsey's reaction to everything. It was a lot to throw at her girlfriend at once. The drag show, the outfit, and the extreme hair change. She was out on a limb, thrown into the past that Jamie had been buried so long ago. "Hi." She could feel the bass thump of the music through the soles of her boots but it was the gentle pressure on her hand that garnered the most attention. She looked up into a pair of beautiful green eyes done with only a hint of dark makeup.

"That was the hottest thing I've ever seen. You, the performance, those pants." She trailed off as she glanced down the front of her girlfriend, noting the distinct bulge at the crotch. Kelsey licked her lips and continued. "And your hair, sweet Jesus!"

"Do you like it?"

Kelsey brought both hands up to pet the sides of Jamie's hair where it was buzzed short. "Do I like it? No, I love it like my cats love tuna! Like Burke loves the gym!" Both women snorted at that and Kelsey continued. "I like it." She stepped a half step closer so they were about six inches apart. "I love it." She stepped closer yet and molded their bodies together from knees to breasts, bound though Jamie's were. She brought her lips near Jamie's as her hands snaked behind the newly darkened hair. Her breath was a caress and Jamie shuddered. "I need it."

Jamie closed that last little distance between them and moaned as their tongues met in the middle of the slow and sensuous kiss. When they were finally able to pull away Kelsey left her arms draped around Jamie's neck and Jamie couldn't resist leaning down for one last kiss to Kelsey's single dimple. She pulled back again and smiled. "I love that dimple."

Kelsey pouted. "Just that dimple?"

"Nope. I love the other two as well, the ones you have on each ass ch—" She didn't finish her sentence because the other woman quickly covered her mouth.

"So what made you change the hair? You didn't do it just because of what I said, did you?" Kelsey looked at her in concern. "I don't ever want you to think you need to change yourself to please me, James."

Jamie shook her head and smiled with all the honesty she had inside. "On the contrary, I decided to stop pleasing everyone but myself. This is the real Jamie." Then with a moment's hesitation she asked the question she absolutely needed an answer to. "Is this the Jamie you want? Is she good enough for you?"

"No." Jamie's face fell and she started to step back but Kelsey wouldn't let her. "No, this Jamie is good enough for anyone! I'm just lucky enough she chose me." Jamie looked close to tears and Kelsey knew how much her girlfriend didn't like to be emotional in front of people so she quickly changed the subject. "So are you going to tell me what the bulge is?"

Jamie leered at her. "I don't know. Have you been good tonight?"

"If by *good* you mean, have I been mentally peeling off your outfit with my teeth? Yeah, sure, I've been good. Excellent even!"

Laughter bubbled forth through Jamie's lips and she was reminded again of how much she absolutely loved how fun and playful her girlfriend was. She also loved how insightful the Irish-Latina could be. "Those naughty thoughts are going to have to wait because I'm stuck here until the end of the show. But you are more than welcome to sit on my lap if you like."

Kelsey groaned and hung her head then grabbed Jamie's hand and started pulling her toward their table. "Fine, deal! You're going to kill me but at least I'll die happy."

The show didn't go on much longer since Jamie was one of the last performers. When the evening was over, only four of them wanted to go to breakfast. Normally Jamie would have agreed to the idea but she only had one thought running through her mind. Well, two, but she wasn't sure how well one of them would be received. Kelsey also didn't want to go to breakfast so it was decided that Burke would just ride with Tam, Shell, and Jenn to a late night diner near Jenn's house. Hugs and smiles were exchanged and then both cars were on their way. As Jamie drove the six blocks to her condo Kelsey turned slightly in her seat to take in the dark hair and gorgeous jawline of the driver. "So are you going to tell me what the bulge is now? Because sitting in your lap was the most painful turn on I have ever experienced in a crowded place!"

Jamie smirked as she glanced at her girlfriend and signaled to turn into her condo's parking garage. "I have something to ask you first." She parked and shut the car down but didn't speak for a minute. She merely looked around Olivia's black leather interior then let her eyes rest on the custom shifter.

"James." The engineer's eyes startled upwards to meet Kelsey's. "What's the matter?"

"Nothing, nothing at all is wrong. That's what is so strange, Kels. Everything finally feels right!"

Kelsey looked at her as if she'd gone nuts. "You're very confusing."

Jamie shook her head and tried again. "You know we've only been dating officially for, like, a month. But it feels like a lot longer to me."

"I have a confession." Jamie looked up at her in surprise. "I kind of think of us as dating since spring. I know it's not correct, but that's just the way I feel. I think it's because we've spent so much time together, getting to know each other." She snorted. "If that were true though it would be some kind of record for how long two lesbians can date before they have sex for the first time."

Jamie laughed too and reached down to grab her spare set of keys from the cup holder. She had set them there when they got in the car to leave the bar. There was a carabineer clip that held the fob to the ring containing the key to the condo and a small RFID card chip that scanned them into the front of the building. She removed the fob and put it into her pocket then looked back at Kelsey with the keys in hand. "If we're all about setting records, then I should ask if you want to move in with me now that we've had a whole entire month together."

"What?" Kelsey's mouth dropped open in shock. When she saw Jamie's actions with the keys she just assumed that maybe her girlfriend was going to give her the spare set so she could get in and out easier. Never in a million years did she expect what actually came from Jamie's lips.

"Not right this second! I mean when your lease expires at the end of the year. You don't have to say yes right away, or you can say yes and then change your mind if yo—" Her rambling was cut off as Kelsey stole the words with a kiss.

When Kelsey pulled away she smiled at the sweetly flummoxed look on her girlfriend's face. "You didn't expect me to say yes, did you?"

Jamie sheepishly rubbed the back of her freshly shorn neck. "I, uh, I'm not sure?"

Kelsey cocked her head at Jamie's confused expression. "So why did you ask me now? As in right now, rather than waiting another month or two?"

"To quote a smart woman that I know intimately, 'if she's

that cute and amazing you better ask her before someone else does. What if she has plans?' I didn't want to take a chance that you made other plans."

The Irish-Latina was delighted that Jamie remembered exactly what she said, word for word. "I see. Well, as it so turns out, I do not have any plans and I would love to move in with you!"

Jamie was overjoyed but she tried to play it cool. "So, are you ready to live with a full-time nerd who's a baby when she's sick and an asshole when she's PMSing?"

Kelsey smirked at her. "Are you ready to live with someone who couldn't cook snot on a hot rock and has two cats, one of which is an asshole all the time?"

"Eww, Kels!" Jamie's face scrunched up in disgust. "That was a mental image I did not need! But yes I am. I can't wait actually!"

Kelsey abruptly reached over with both hands and gripped Jamie's shoulders excitedly. "So we'll plan on December for the move, yeah?" Jamie nodded happily. "You know what we need to do now?"

Jamie shook her head. "No, what?"

"Christen the condo!"

"But babe, we've already don—" Her words were cut off by a single finger.

Kelsey leered at her from the passenger seat. "Not in that outfit we haven't! Let's go, hot stuff!" They made record time up to the condo and Jamie even had Kelsey do the honors of getting them through both doors with her new keys. In no time flat Kelsey had Jamie pushed back onto the engineer's large bed and was grinding into the delicious bulge that had been taunting her all night. She shuddered and finally pulled away from Jamie's lips. "I can't take it anymore. I need to see what it is!" She quickly moved off Jamie to the side and looked at her girlfriend's heavy lidded gaze.

Jamie's lips were red and puffy from all the kissing they had done and Kelsey was half mad with desire herself. She reached for the button of Jamie's pants and when she saw no signs of protest, she undid it swiftly. Then Kelsey took reverse care with the zipper, slowly drawing the metal tab down, one click at a time. The shirt had come untucked long ago while Kelsey ran her hands all over Jamie's bare stomach. All that was left below the pants was a pair of men's briefs with a bulge inside the pouch. "What is this?" There was a definite twinkle in Jamie's eyes when Kelsey glanced up but she didn't let it deter her from the treasure hunt.

She reached beneath the underwear and withdrew something that looked like a balloon filled with sand, weird sand. She looked up at her girlfriend. "What the hell is it?"

Jamie smirked. "It's a balloon filled with kinetic sand so that it holds its shape."

"Oh." Kelsey looked disappointed then suddenly perked up again. She got a positively evil look on her face and tossed Jamie's sand bag on the night stand before getting off the bed.

"Kels?"

Kelsey crooked a finger at her from where she was standing next to the bed and Jamie rushed to obey. When they were standing face-to-face Kelsey bent and began sliding the tight pants down Jamie's legs. The boots had been discarded as soon as they came into the condo. Of course the underwear came down with the pants, leaving Jamie feeling strangely exposed. Kelsey straightened again and motioned back toward the bed. "I want you back on the bed. We're going to put those wrist cuffs to good use." Seeing nothing but good things ahead, Jamie quickly complied with Kelsey's order. The woman in charge opened the infamous toy drawer and removed two long lengths of silk rope. The first she looped through the metal rings in Jamie's wrist cuffs, then she attached each end to the posts at the head of the bed. She did the opposite to the prone woman's ankles. She looped the rope around the outside bed corners then tied each end to a foot, keeping Jamie spread wide open.

Jamie's breathing started to increase when Kelsey withdrew the butterfly toy from the drawer and slipped it on. Jamie had worn the vibrator before, but always underneath a harness so both women could potentially get off at the same time. Her lips parted when Kelsey withdrew the harness next. "Oh."

Kelsey looked at her after she had everything buckled into place. "There are only two rules tonight, no touching unless you ask first, and I get to do whatever I want. Is this okay?" Jamie licked her lips and nodded. Kelsey got up on the bed and sat back on her feet between Jamie's spread legs, the sex toy jutting out obscenely, the straps cutting into the soft skin of Kelsey's hips and upper thighs. "You have to say it aloud or it doesn't count. Is this what you want, James?"

Jamie smiled at her girlfriend. She was absolutely perfect. Her heart hammered in anticipation and wanting and she spoke with honesty straight from her heart. "I want it all."

Kelsey slowly leaned forward, careful not to touch anything but Jamie's lips with her own. Then she pulled back and looked into her lover's eyes. "I love you."

The woman on the bottom pulled at her bound wrists with frustration. "I love you too and I want to hold you but I can't." Kelsey laughed and Jamie blew out a breath. "You tease me like no one I've ever met before!"

Kelsey smirked. "Aren't you glad you broke your own rules and fell for me?"

Jamie stilled instantly and a tear came to her eye when she looked up at the woman who held her heart. "Absolutely."

"Really? But you're so adamant about your rules!" Jamie snarled playfully and bucked her hips. That jostled Kelsey enough that she fell down chest-to-chest with the woman below. When their lips were close enough Jamie quickly stole a kiss. Kelsey pulled back and wagged a finger at her. "That's cheating, James!"

Jamie smiled up at her. "As I've been told many times before, sometimes I have to break my rules. Clearly I need to keep hold of that woman that keeps giving me such good advice."

Kelsey smiled down at her. "Clearly that woman loves you very much."

"Kelsey?"

"Yes?" Kelsey looked at her curiously, noting the gleam in Jamie's eyes.

Jamie licked her lips. "I broke your first rule."

The woman on top wore a look of wicked pleasure as she turned on the butterfly vibrator she was wearing then slowly ran her hands up Jamie's nude legs. "So you did." Jamie shuddered and couldn't wait for December to come.

About the Author

Born and raised in Michigan, Kelly is a latecomer to the writing scene. As an introvert with self-taught extroversion, she has traveled to nearly every state in the US and draws from her experience with everything she writes. Over the years she has loved playing a variety of sports including volleyball, bowling, softball, and most recently, roller derby. But when bad knees became worse Kelly returned to the comfort of fan fiction to fill the void. Reading the amazing tales she found prompted her to try her hand at writing again. The ability to turn out an engaging tale was discovered and a bittersweet new love affair began.

Kelly works in the automotive industry coding in Visual basic and Excel. Her avid reading and writing provide a nice balance to the daily order of data, allowing her to juggle passion and responsibility. Her writing style is as varied as her reading taste and it shows as she tackles each new genre with glee. But beneath it all, no matter the subject or setting, Kelly carries a core belief that good should triumph. She's not afraid of pain or adversity, but loves a happy ending. She's been pouring words into novels since 2015 and probably won't run out of things to say any time soon.

OTHER YELLOW ROSE PUBLICATIONS

Brenda Adcock	Soiled Dove	978-1-935053-35-4
Brenda Adcock	The Sea Hawk	978-1-935053-10-1
Brenda Adcock	The Other Mrs. Champion	978-1-935053-46-0
Brenda Adcock	Picking Up the Pieces	978-1-61929-120-1
Brenda Adcock	The Game of Denial	978-1-61929-130-0
Brenda Adcock	In the Midnight Hour	978-1-61929-188-1
Brenda Adcock	Untouchable	978-1-61929-210-9
Brenda Adcock	The Heart of the Mountain	978-1-61929-330-4
Janet Albert	Twenty-four Days	978-1-935053-16-3
Janet Albert	A Table for Two	978-1-935053-27-9
Janet Albert	Casa Parisi	978-1-61929-016-7
K. Aten	The Fletcher	978-1-61929-356-4
K. Aten	Rules of the Road	978-1-61919-366-3
Georgia Beers	Thy Neighbor's Wife	1-932300-15-5
Georgia Beers	Turning the Page	978-1-932300-71-0
Lynnette Beers	Just Beyond the Shining River	978-1-61929-352-6
Carrie Carr	Destiny's Bridge	1-932300-11-2
Carrie Carr	Faith's Crossing	1-932300-12-0
Carrie Carr	Hope's Path	1-932300-40-6
Carrie Carr	Love's Journey	978-1-932300-65-9
Carrie Carr	Strength of the Heart	978-1-932300-81-9
Carrie Carr	The Way Things Should Be	978-1-932300-39-0
Carrie Carr	To Hold Forever	978-1-932300-21-5
Carrie Carr	Trust Our Tomorrows	978-1-61929-011-2
Carrie Carr	Piperton	978-1-935053-20-0
Carrie Carr	Something to Be Thankful For	1-932300-04-X
Carrie Carr	Diving Into the Turn	978-1-932300-54-3
Carrie Carr	Heart's Resolve	978-1-61929-051-8
Carrie Carr	Beyond Always	978-1-61929-160-7
Sharon G. Clark	A Majestic Affair	978-1-61929-177-5
Tonie Chacon	Struck! A Titanic Love Story	978-1-61929-226-0
Cooper and Novan	Madam President	978-1-61929-316-8
Cooper and Novan	First Lady	978-1-61929-318-2
Sky Croft	Amazonia	978-1-61929-067-9
Sky Croft	Amazonia: An Impossible Choice	978-1-61929-179-9
Sky Croft	Mountain Rescue: The Ascent	978-1-61929-099-0
Sky Croft	Mountain Rescue: On the Edge	978-1-61929-205-5
Cronin and Foster	Blue Collar Lesbian Erotica	978-1-935053-01-9
Cronin and Foster	Women in Uniform	978-1-935053-31-6
Cronin and Foster	Women in Sports	978-1-61929-278-9
Pat Cronin	Souls' Rescue	978-1-935053-30-9
Jane DiLucchio	A Change of Heart	978-1-61929-324-3
A. L. Duncan	The Gardener of Aria Manor	978-1-61929-159-1
A.L. Duncan	Secrets of Angels	978-1-61929-227-7
Verda Foster	The Gift	978-1-61929-029-7
Verda Foster	The Chosen	978-1-61929-027-3

Verda Foster	These Dreams	978-1-61929-025-9
Anna Furtado	The Heart's Desire	978-1-935053-81-1
Anna Furtado	The Heart's Strength	978-1-935053-82-8
Anna Furtado	The Heart's Longing	978-1-935053-83-5
Anna Furtado	Tremble and Burn	978-1-61929-354-0
Pauline George	Jess	978-1-61929-139-3
Pauline George	199 Steps To Love	978-1-61929-213-0
Pauline George	The Actress and the Scrapyard Girl	978-1-61929-336-6
Melissa Good	Eye of the Storm	1-932300-13-9
Melissa Good	Hurricane Watch	978-1-935053-00-2
Melissa Good	Moving Target	978-1-61929-150-8
Melissa Good	Red Sky At Morning	978-1-932300-80-2
Melissa Good	Storm Surge: Book One	978-1-935053-28-6
Melissa Good	Storm Surge: Book Two	978-1-935053-39-2
Melissa Good	Stormy Waters	978-1-61929-082-2
Melissa Good	Thicker Than Water	1-932300-24-4
Melissa Good	Terrors of the High Seas	1-932300-45-7
Melissa Good	Tropical Storm	978-1-932300-60-4
Melissa Good	Tropical Convergence	978-1-935053-18-7
Melissa Good	Winds of Change Book One	978-1-61929-194-2
Melissa Good	Winds of Change Book Two	978-1-61929-232-1
Melissa Good	Southern Stars	978-1-61929-348-9
Regina A. Hanel	Love Another Day	978-1-61929-033-4
Regina A. Hanel	WhiteDragon	978-1-61929-143-0
Regina A. Hanel	A Deeper Blue	978-1-61929-258-1
Jeanine Hoffman	Lights & Sirens	978-1-61929-115-7
Jeanine Hoffman	Strength in Numbers	978-1-61929-109-6
Jeanine Hoffman	Back Swing	978-1-61929-137-9
Jennifer Jackson	It's Elementary	978-1-61929-085-3
Jennifer Jackson	It's Elementary, Too	978-1-61929-217-8
Jennifer Jackson	Memory Hunters	978-1-61929-294-9
K. E. Lane	And, Playing the Role of Herself	978-1-932300-72-7
Kate McLachlan	Christmas Crush	978-1-61929-195-9
Lynne Norris	One Promise	978-1-932300-92-5
Lynne Norris	Sanctuary	978-1-61929-248-2
Lynne Norris	Second Chances (E)	978-1-61929-172-0
Lynne Norris	The Light of Day	978-1-61929-338-0
Paula Offutt	Butch Girls Can Fix Anything	978-1-932300-74-1
Surtees and Dunne	True Colours	978-1-61929-021-1
Surtees and Dunne	Many Roads to Travel	978-1-61929-022-8
Patty Schramm	Finding Gracie's Glory	978-1-61929-238-3

Be sure to check out our other imprints,
Blue Beacon Books, Mystic Books, Quest Books,
Silver Dragon Books, Troubadour Books, and Young Adult Books.

VISIT US ONLINE AT
www.regalcrest.biz

At the Regal Crest Website You'll Find

- The latest news about forthcoming titles and new releases

- Our complete backlist of romance, mystery, thriller and adventure titles

- Information about your favorite authors

- Media tearsheets to print and take with you when you shop

- Which books are also available as eBooks.

Regal Crest print titles are available from all progressive booksellers including numerous sources online. Our distributors are Bella Distribution and Ingram.